Walk Beside Me

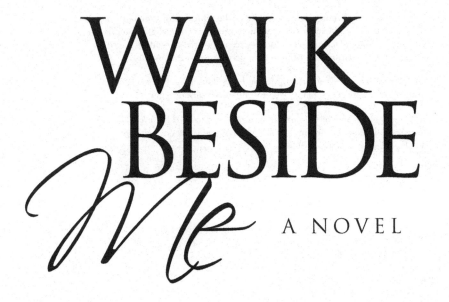

WALK BESIDE Me

A NOVEL

CHRISTINE HANDY

NEW YORK

NASHVILLE • MELBOURNE • VANCOUVER

Walk Beside Me

Published in New York, New York, by Morgan James Publishing. Morgan James is a trademark of Morgan James, LLC. www.MorganJamesPublishing.com

The Morgan James Speakers Group can bring authors to your live event. For more information or to book an event visit The Morgan James Speakers Group at www.TheMorganJamesSpeakersGroup.com.

ISBN 978-1-68350-161-9 paperback
ISBN 978-1-68350-163-3 eBook
ISBN 978-1-68350-162-6 hardcover
Library of Congress Control Number:
2016911798

Cover Design by:
Chris Treccani
www.3dogdesign.net

Interior Design by:
Chris Treccani
www.3dogdesign.net

In an effort to support local communities, raise awareness and funds, Morgan James Publishing donates a percentage of all book sales for the life of each book to Habitat for Humanity Peninsula and Greater Williamsburg.

Get involved today! Visit
www.MorganJamesBuilds.com

Table of Contents

Chapter 1

NOT ME

I t was a warm day in September when I decided to kill myself.

I stood in the parking lot outside the doctor's office. I had just seen the specialist, but I would have to wait four endless days for that fateful phone call. Why did they always do these sorts of life-altering tests before a weekend? I feared the worst.

In my left hand I held my car keys far too tightly, the sharp metal ridges digging deep grooves into my fingers. But I couldn't feel anything. In those first moments, all I felt was fear and disbelief. The anger would come soon enough.

"Willow," said Oliver, my husband. "Willow, listen to me. You're going to be all right."

I didn't hear him. I had started to scream.

I was literally screaming in broad daylight, leaning against our car, as if the car itself would support my weight. I felt sharp, guttural pain, as if something was tearing me apart from the inside. And now it was only going to get worse. The diagnosis wouldn't come for four days but I already knew it in the marrow of my bones: the worst was coming true.

I couldn't wrap my brain around having to undergo more suffering. I had spent the last three years in constant pain, *every single day.* Was I being punished? Was everything I had gone through not enough? I screamed and screamed and screamed some more, unable to grasp what was happening to me.

Not me, I cried. *Not me.*

"Stop screaming, Willow," said Oliver, gently taking the car keys out of my hand. "Let's get you home." He seemed a bit irritated. How could he be so cold? He must have seen that question in my eyes because he tried to hug me.

I ignored him and climbed into the passenger's seat.

I stared out the window the entire ride home, crying softly. Sunlight shone through the tall, stately trees of Bexley, the affluent suburb of Columbus where we lived. It was a beautiful crisp fall day. Kids were outside playing in jeans and T-shirts. The weather had not yet turned.

But inside the car, I had broken out into a cold sweat. I felt sick. It seemed cruelly unfair to see families outside, enjoying the pleasant weather, leading lives so happy and carefree when my own life had become a living nightmare. I looked down at my arm and let out a guttural whimper.

The tears kept flowing. All the emotional courage I had mustered over the last few years went up in flames and crumbled into ash. This couldn't happen to me—and yet, it was happening.

Hadn't I suffered enough? Hadn't my *family* suffered enough? My daughter Isabella and son Wiles, fourteen and eleven at the time, had suffered. So had my husband.

I looked at Oliver now, staring straight ahead, his hands gripping the steering wheel. He said nothing. I desperately needed comfort—a kind word, a reassuring touch—but he had none to give. He was fighting his own demons, tethered to a wife who had been in constant pain for the last three years. When he took his wedding vows, I'm sure he hadn't imagined "in sickness and in health" to be quite so literal.

And then, I had the thought. It came as a shining epiphany, hitting me like a bolt of lightning. *If I end my life*, I thought, *my husband and children won't have to suffer anymore.*

I loved Bella and Wiles more than life itself. I was their mother and I wanted to protect them, not cause them pain. Being a mother was all I'd ever really wanted to do, and I wanted to love them, not put fear in their tender souls. I wanted to be a good mom, not a woman needing constant care and help from others.

But I had failed miserably. And it was about to get so much worse.

I wanted to scream and yell and run and hide. The pain was excruciating, both physically and mentally. I didn't think I could bear it. Generally speaking I wasn't a "worst-case scenario" person, but then my whole life had become a worst-case scenario the last few years. I didn't have the diagnosis yet, but I knew what was coming, even then.

***

In four days, my worst fears were confirmed. I got the call early Monday morning. I was home alone when my phone rang. When I heard the doctor's voice, I knew what he was going to say.

I sat down on my bed and asked the doctor one question. "Am I going to die?"

He said something that was supposed to be vaguely comforting, not too hopeful but not too dire, but I didn't hear it. Everything had gone black.

That night I lay in bed, my cotton pillow hot beneath my head. Sleeping was impossible. I felt petrified, exhausted, and confused. I wanted to curl up into the fetal position and give myself comfort but I couldn't with the cast on my arm. *How many casts have I had on that arm?* I thought, and when I counted, the number was far too many. The realization only made me feel sicker. I wanted to press my warm body into my husband and hear him tell me he loved me. But he had been drawing further away from me these many months, getting increasingly unavailable. I felt like I was looking at him through the rearview mirror of a car: he got smaller and smaller, and eventually he would become so small that he might disappear completely.

I was only forty-one years old. I had gone from being a thriving wife and mother with an incredible passion and talent for yoga and other sports to a sick, frail woman. The "I can'ts" had replaced the "I cans" in every area of my life. I had not had a day without pain in almost three years, and I couldn't remember the last time I had been able to use my right arm.

I put on a tough face to the world, but emotionally I was dying inside. The days I wanted to quit were too many. I felt desperate to live to raise my children, but the suffering was endless—and that was all *before*. Now I had received the diagnosis that would change everything. It was too much. I knew my strength had run out.

I lay in bed that night, my husband turned away from me. He was coping in his own stoic way with my health issues, a way I couldn't understand. My children pushed me away out of fear. The love I had for Wiles and Bella was overpowering, but I was afraid I was no longer a blessing to their lives.

Still unable to sleep and racked by fear, I tiptoed into Wiles's bedroom. Oliver and I had told him the dreadful news earlier that night. Oliver wanted to wait but I couldn't stop crying; it was impossible for me to hide my trembling, sadness, and utter despair. The look in Wiles's eyes was one I'd never forget. He was terrified of losing me. Afraid that, after all the pain we had already gone through as a family, now his mother was going to die.

Wiles was sleeping fitfully, probably having nightmares about the bad news. I kissed him on the forehead and stroked his cheek. I could still feel the warmth of his newborn body in my arms when we brought him home from the hospital, how small and helpless he seemed. Now he was growing into a young man, but there was still a certain tenderness he carried with him. Wiles was a lot like me: he felt deeply for people. He was a child with great compassion; he always amazed me with his bleeding heart and enormous gestures for the poor and needy. But he was far too young to have to bear these kinds of burdens.

My daughter Isabella was at boarding school many states away. Our relationship had undergone its fair share of strain and tension. I loved Bella deeply, but the seventeen hundred miles between us was hard. The more she acted out, the more I thought, *It's my fault. I'm a horrible mother*. She was too much like me, in everything from personality to appearance, with her long legs and straight blond hair. The only physical difference was that her eyes were blue and mine were brown. Other than that, she was a mini-me.

It was the character traits that concerned me most. Bella desperately craved attention and wanted to start modeling, even though she was only fifteen. She was a beautiful girl, and I'd caved and let her do some commercial work around Columbus, but I really didn't want her to be exposed to the world I'd been exposed to as a model in my twenties—the drug use, the rampant partying, and the lack of self-worth. When you're a model, so much of your identity only goes skin deep. I didn't want that for Bella; I'd had enough of it myself. She reminded me so much of myself at that age: hot-tempered and entitled, absolutely determined to get her way. Frankly, I could *still* be a pain in the butt.

And now we had to give Bella the horrible news. We decided to keep the truth from her until Oliver could fly up to Andover and tell her in person: the news was too big and important for a phone call. Already I felt ill at the thought of Bella's reaction. I wanted to hold her tight and never let go. I wanted her to be home so that our family could be together again.

My fears were shadows clutching at my soul. I crawled back into bed, desolate, hopeless. Dark thoughts tugged at the corners of my mind. If I was going to die anyway, why not speed it along and save everyone the trouble?

A story popped into my head and suddenly I knew exactly how I'd do it. The previous week Oliver had read an article in the newspaper about a boy who had died using this exact approach. It was almost perfect, something that would look like an accident when it was anything but. No horrible aftermath, no mess for anyone to clean up. Quick and relatively painless, my suicide would end the suffering once and for all.

I watched Oliver's back rise and fall on his side of the bed, the easy unlabored rhythm of his breathing. I would wait until Bella came home from boarding school so I could say goodbye. And then I would end it.

It seemed like a rational decision. My friends and family had already spent far too much of their time and energy on my health issues over the last few years. I knew it was only going to get worse.

I knew it would be hard on them for a while. But a year after my death, my family would have mostly healed. My husband would be dating other people and my kids would no longer be worried about their mom dying every second of every day. My friends would remember me fondly, but they had their own lives, their own families to take care of. My parents and sisters would carry the sadness with them forever, but they would secretly be grateful I was no longer sapping their love and time.

I was resolved. In the morning I would start telling my friends and family goodbye. I didn't want to alarm them, but I also didn't want them to blame themselves when they learned Willow Adair was dead. I didn't want any of them feeling like it was their fault for not having said or done something to stop me.

I rolled over and shut my eyes, desperately trying to sleep. The tide of despair and confusion swelled to a crescendo in my head. *I'm making a rational decision*, I thought. *I'm better off dead.*

I'll do it in a few weeks. The pain will finally be over. The suffering will end.

I'll take my life.

***

October 1, 2012. That was the day my life changed forever. Things would never be the same after that. Everything—my family, my life, my values, myself—would be different.

But my story doesn't start in 2012. It starts seven years earlier when I almost bled out on the operating table during what was supposed to be a routine surgery.

In some ways, it feels like I haven't stopped bleeding since.

Chapter 2

STANDARD PROCEDURE

It was July 5, 2006, the day after Independence Day and the day before my colon surgery. I wasn't too worried about going into the operating room the following morning. I was scheduled for a colon resection—not exactly a routine surgery, but hopefully one that would cure the stomach troubles I'd been having for years with minimal effect on my routine. My doctor explained that my colon had gotten so long it had become twisted, which explained the terrible stomach pain. We needed to take care of it promptly, but there wasn't any particular reason for concern. My doctor assured me that the procedure was fairly simple: he'd go in, cut out maybe fifteen to sixteen inches of my colon, and stitch the whole thing back together. After six weeks of recovery, I'd be good as new. Which was a good thing, since I was mostly worried about getting it done quickly and well so that Oliver wouldn't have to miss his three-week vacation in Nantucket: something he looked forward to every year.

I'd been down to the doctor's office earlier that week to sign the pre-surgery paperwork. "We just need your signature on a few forms," he said, as I sat across from him in his immaculate office. "This is all standard procedure." His medical degrees were framed prominently on the wall behind him, illustrious and impressive, tinged in fine gold. Surely this man knew what he was doing.

I scanned the paperwork in front of me. *I should actually read these*, I thought. What was I even signing? I glanced down at the papers and started to pay more attention. *No more small talk*, I said to myself. *You have to focus.* Almost immediately one waiver jumped out at me: Would I accept blood if needed?

"What's this?" I said. "Why would I need to sign this one?"

"Oh, don't worry about that," my doctor said. "You're not going to need any blood. It's just a form we have everyone fill out. If you didn't sign it and something were to happen on the operating table, we wouldn't be able to give you blood."

My stomach knotted slightly. "But this is a standard procedure, right?"

"Absolutely. If there was any chance you were going to need blood, we would have had you donate your own blood prior to the surgery." He chuckled. "Better your own blood than someone else's, right?"

We laughed, but I felt slightly uneasy. Still, I signed the form.

***

I'd known Amelia King for several years—we were introduced by a mutual friend. We had children about the same age: my daughter Bella was seven and her daughter Ava was six. We were in the same supper club with three other couples. All four families lived within a few blocks, so twice a month we alternated houses to eat good food and get to know each other better.

That summer, we were supposed to be with Amelia and Quinn at their home in Taos for the Fourth of July holiday. We had stayed with them the previous summer and it worked. Their home was beautiful, and the summers there were spectacular. We played games with the kids at night, and lots of other Bexley families were there, including the Somervilles, who spent their summers in Vail. Gigi Somerville was another one of my closest friends, and she and her husband Ron were also part of the supper club.

We were planning on spending the 4th in Taos again—maybe even as the beginning of a new family tradition—and then the colon surgery was scheduled for July 5th. Suddenly I had to cancel the trip.

I called Amelia and told her I was stopping by. I walked over and we went to her back porch. It was the calmest spot in our neighborhood and such a peaceful place to talk. I sat with Amelia for a moment until my voice choked as I fought back tears.

"They scheduled my surgery, Amelia," I said, looking down. "I'm going into the hospital next week. We won't be able to go to Taos."

I couldn't hold back the tears: I started crying. I told Amelia everything; she was that kind of friend. She knew me intimately, seeing a side of me I didn't show to the rest of the world.

"I'm scared," I said. "I know it's a relatively normal surgery but I'm so scared."

"You have every right to be scared," Amelia said, rubbing my back. "I'm so sorry, Willow. Can I pray with you?"

Amelia was a great comfort that day; she sat beside me and prayed. She knew how bad I felt, since we had to cancel at the last minute and they wouldn't be able to invite another family in time. I kept apologizing.

"Willow, please don't worry about that." Amelia laid a gentle hand on my arm. Amelia had a really motherly instinct about her. I had never seen her raise her voice or get upset. "You have plenty on your mind already. I don't want you to spend another second worrying about us."

I tried to keep that in mind. Still, I was heartbroken that I wouldn't be able to go. And I was scared, scared to be alone in Columbus without Gigi and Amelia with the surgery looming.

***

The night before the surgery, I was frantically taking care of business around the house. I had a laundry basket pressed to my hip as I walked from room to room, putting away the kids' laundry and Oliver's. I knew I'd be in the hospital for a couple days, and then I wouldn't be doing much for six to eight weeks while I recovered from the surgery. I wanted to make sure the kids had everything they needed—that everything was in order.

I was standing in the laundry room, separating the whites from the colors, when the home phone rang.

I checked the caller ID. *Gigi Somerville.*

I felt relief course over me. *My dedicated friend calling me when I'm sure her house is totally chaotic.*

"Hi, Gigi," I said, picking up the phone. "How's Colorado?" Their home in Vail was a special place, a stately stone home that had been in the family for many years. After the death of her grandmother, Gigi and her husband Ron had bought the house, and it was truly Gigi's favorite place on earth. I often wondered how that felt to have a favorite place. We had flown to Colorado the prior summer after we stayed with the Kings in Taos and it was absolutely beautiful. I imagined where Gigi was in the house right at that moment: perhaps she was looking out the window at the snow-capped mountains or down on the crystal-clear spring that coursed through the property. *Boy*, I thought. *Do I wish I was there and not here right now!*

"Colorado is great," Gigi said. "We're having a wonderful time. Listen, Willow—I wanted to call because I know you have your surgery tomorrow. How are you feeling?"

I tucked the phone between my ear and collarbone while I folded a pair of Bella's skinny jeans. Multitasking: the single most important skill you learn when you're a mom.

"Fine," I said, trying to tamp down my fear. "The doctor doesn't think there's anything to worry about. It's standard procedure. I mean, you know how it is. It's always a little scary to be going on the operating table regardless."

"I don't blame you one bit for being scared," Gigi said. "I know you and I have talked about our faiths before, so I want to ask you: If something *were* to happen tomorrow—God forbid—do you know where you'd be going?"

It wasn't the first time Gigi and I had talked about God. I was blown away by the strength of her beliefs; Gigi had more faith than almost anyone I knew. Her faith was built on rock, and she lived by that faith. I felt like I was a part-time Christian.

Gigi took her knowledge and her faith and *used* it. She was wise beyond her years, and she was my teacher. Over the last few years of our friendship, she had talked to me a lot about grace: how we do nothing to earn God's love, He just gives it to us freely. Gigi CARED about teaching me. She had always invited me to Bible studies and encouraged my faith. Sometimes I didn't appreciate it as much as I should have. Hearing is easy, doing is harder.

"Can I pray with you?" Gigi asked. "I know with any surgery there are always risks, and I want to make sure you feel good about the fact that you are going to Heaven. Have you given your life to the Lord?"

I guess I felt like I had, being raised Catholic. But the God of my understanding was very different from Gigi's God of grace and mercy and forgiveness. Catholicism isn't the most grace-oriented belief system; to me it felt like guilt and shame. It took me years to finally learn that faith and fear couldn't exist at the same moment. I only knew fear. I was missing that force of faith.

"I don't know if your God is the God I know," I answered honestly, chuckling a little to myself, though maybe she heard me.

"Do you want to know Jesus, Willow? He died for our sins so that we might have eternal life."

I set the laundry down on the washing machine and gave Gigi my undivided attention. "I'd like that very much."

So Gigi walked me through what to say. That was the night she led me in prayer to receive Christ.

Her two young sons were in the room with her at the time. They were playing quietly on the floor, but they were also listening to the conversation unfold. Years later, they would say, "Mom, do you remember that time you prayed with Mrs. Adair on the phone?" It was something they always remembered: the day their mother led her friend to Christ.

***

Oliver and I got to the hospital bright and early the next morning. The surgery was scheduled for eight a.m. As we sat in the waiting room, I started to feel a little nervous, but I told myself these were normal pre-surgery jitters.

I went into the bathroom and prayed a bit. I even did a couple of yoga poses to calm myself down. I was learning how to self-soothe.

When they called my name, I was ready. The nurse led me back into the operating room, where my doctor greeted me warmly.

He wasn't the only friendly face in the room. Our next-door neighbor at the time was an anesthesiologist at the same hospital, and I had personally requested he be the one to perform the anesthesia for my surgery. "It would put my mind at ease knowing you're in that operating room," I'd told him.

He administered the anesthesia, and I drifted off, the drugs lulling me into dreamless sleep—this part I liked. I heard the low hum of the doctors and nurses speaking to one another, preparing for the surgery, just like any other day.

Standard procedure, I thought. *Nothing to worry about.*

Thank God our neighbor was in that room, because the surgery turned out to be anything but.

Chapter 3

WHO WILL PROTECT ME?

I woke up in a thick haze with blazing pain. *Where am I? What's going on?*
Above me was a blur of color, dark red and ominous. I had no idea what it was. I didn't have my contacts in, and waves of pain were crashing down on top of me. I felt frightened and disillusioned. Was the surgery over?

Something hard and cold was coming out of my neck.

Something didn't feel right about my stomach.

Something was very, very wrong.

I was shaking uncontrollably. I couldn't stop. I had no idea what was happening to me, but every breath I took, the pain seared through me like a dozen knives slicing me in too many places.

I was aware of movement in the room: a nurse. I tried to speak and felt gibberish spilling out of my mouth. The pain was indescribable. I reached up to touch my throat and realized that I had something round and plastic attached to my neck. *Oh my God,* I realized with horror. It was *in* my neck. And coiling out of it was a long, red line.

Slowly I began to piece together what had happened. The red blur above me was a blood bag, and the thing in my neck was a port. I wanted to cry but I didn't because any movement in my body caused the pain to intensify monstrously. *Stay still,* I thought, *Don't move, don't breathe. God, please help me.*

"Please," I said hoarsely, entreating the nurse. "It hurts. Please."

"Your blood pressure's too low," she snapped. "We can't give you any narcotics until it goes up."

My eyes filled with tears. "Can I at least have some ice?" My mouth was so dry.

She rolled her eyes. "I don't have time for this," she said, and stomped out of the room.

For the first time I felt sheer terror. The nurse had left me alone. I was hurting and scared to death, and I had no idea what was going on.

I reached down to feel my stomach, and that's when I realized: they had cut me open from hip to hip. Cut through all my muscles. My stomach was no longer smooth, soft skin; it was an ugly patchwork of stitches and staples where they had tried to sew me up.

As I would discover later that day, while the doctor was cutting *twenty-eight inches* out of my colon—a far cry from the fifteen or sixteen inches he'd expected—he had nicked a vein and the bleeding began. I had one blood transfusion during the surgery because I'd lost so much blood. When I woke up in the recovery room, I was having a second blood transfusion.

The doctor had originally agreed to perform laparoscopic surgery, also known as minimally invasive surgery. This is the modern surgical technique where the physician makes small incisions in the abdomen, a good ways away from where the actual operation is performed. Since I was still modeling at the time, I'd told the surgeon it was important that I didn't have my stomach cut wide open. I did lingerie and bathing suit ads and I couldn't afford the scars.

My doctor was doing the surgery laparoscopically and had no problem with my request. But doctors who play God never win. When he nicked a vein in one of my bones during surgery, he decided to play God. I didn't even know I *had* veins in my bones.

Thirty minutes into the surgery, I was bleeding. The doctor couldn't find where the blood was coming from, but it was pooling and pooling and harder to find the source. He was determined to stanch the flow, but time was running out and he couldn't do it; I was losing too much blood. Finally it got so bad that my neighbor barked at the surgeon, "Open her up and stop the bleeding!"

The surgeon was stubborn. "I'm not going to cut her open," he said. The subtext was clear: *I'm a great doctor. I can fix this.* It would be my first brush with the classic doctor's ego, but not my last.

My neighbor was scared I was going to bleed to death on the table. Finally the surgeon realized he'd have to open me up if he wanted to save my life. So he did. Instead of a quick, minimally invasive surgery, I was in the OR for several hours. Oliver and my sister were in the waiting room, wondering what the hell was going on. My name stayed on the "in surgery" board far longer than it should have, and because of the emergency nature of the situation, my family wasn't able to be in the recovery room when I woke up.

I woke up alone and frightened, unsure what was happening to me, why I had been cut open, why I was suffering from inexplicable pain—and no one would help me. No one was there to protect me. No one was there at all.

Why me? I found myself thinking. *What's going on here?* Especially because I had just given my life to the Lord. I had said those words with Gigi guiding me, so it felt like, "Why are you punishing me, God?" Gigi had taught me God was not a punishing God, but in that moment, it was hard to believe it.

The next day, my doctor came into my hospital room. He stood at the window for a long time, looking out on the rest of the hospital. He couldn't even look me in the eye.

I didn't know what to say. Was he going to apologize? Ask for my forgiveness over what had happened?

When he turned toward me, I saw the anguish in his eyes. He was a good man—arrogant, perhaps, but not malicious.

He sat down beside me on the hospital bed and took my hand.

"I'm so sorry," he said, over and over. "I'm so sorry. I'm so sorry."

I could see it in his eyes: he'd made a huge mistake. He should have opened me up immediately. On one hand, he was trying to do what he'd promised: keep the scars to a minimum. But I couldn't help but think his doctor's narcissism had flared up, too, clouding his judgment.

My eyes blurred with tears as I took in his apology. But I couldn't hold his gaze. It hurt too much. I pulled my hand away and looked in the opposite direction, staring out the hospital window. I believed his heartfelt apology, but it could only go so far. It couldn't undo the damage that had already been done.

***

I was supposed to be in the hospital for two days and ended up being there for ten. All my closest friends were still on their summer vacations—no one could come visit me.

I lay alone in the hospital bed for hours, often in too much pain to even watch TV, waiting for a visitor. Oliver was taking care of the kids. How could I expect him to be with me at the hospital? And yet of course I wanted that very much.

Once I begged him to bring Bella and Wiles to come visit me, and he did. My poor kids had to see their mom with a blood bag and a port coming out of her neck. *Am I truly this selfish?* I thought, seeing the horrified looks on their faces. *They shouldn't have to see me like this.* To see me in that condition—it was trauma for those young souls. Was I a selfish person to need them with me?

"You don't have to bring them again," I whispered to Oliver as he left, though as I said the words I felt like a part of me was dying inside.

I stared out the window for hours, wishing I could be anywhere else. Just as I was starting to get really depressed, I got a call from Amelia.

"I'm coming," she said. "I'm flying down to see you, okay?"

Oh my precious Amelia, flying from Taos to see me, to love on me and to help. I knew she had read my mind. I needed her.

"You don't have to do that," I said slowly, almost at a whisper. "I'm okay." But it was a lie. I was lying to her and to myself. I wanted to keep up this tough facade, but I was tepid in my telling her not to come. I was desperately hoping she could decipher the truth in what I was saying.

"Do you *not* want me to come, Willow?" she said.

Of course I wanted her to come. I was just trying to act strong, but not too strong. *Don't push her away, it's okay to say yes! COME! Hopefully she will see through me.* After all, she knew me so well.

"I'll be there tomorrow," Amelia said. "And don't for a second try and talk me out of it."

She flew back to Columbus the next night and stayed at the hospital with me. She actually left her wonderful home in Taos to spend a night with her scared and hurting friend. If I had not had ten thousand stitches at the time, I would have jumped out of that hospital bed and embraced her, but I didn't need to. The moment she walked through the door she came flying over to me and gently rocked me as I started to sob.

"You're here!" I whimpered like a sick puppy. "You came!" The tears wouldn't stop.

Amelia sat beside me on the hospital bed, rubbing my back and making me feel safe. "You're beautiful, Willow," she said. "You are beautiful and you are loved." She said it with such conviction, I believed her.

We talked for a while and I drifted off. But when I opened my eyes she was still there. "Up we go," she said, gently taking my arm. "Let's get a little blood flowing." Slowly and patiently, Amelia walked me around the hospital room to get me up and moving.

It was humbling how far I couldn't go. My feet moved like they belonged to someone else. I fought back tears, embarrassed to be so weak and needy. "Amelia, thank you for coming," I said softly, looking at her with such strong, fierce love.

She waved me off. "This is no big deal, Willow. This is just what it means to be a friend."

I smiled at her but something was roiling in my stomach. The short walk had made me extremely nauseated and I realized too late I was going to throw up. Amelia tried to get me to the bathroom but it was a mess. I was already vomiting, clutching my stitches and the port in my neck. *Please don't open up,* I said to my port, over and over. *Please stay in.* But the retching was relentless.

As soon as the vomiting stopped I lay on that cold hospital floor, helpless. And just as soon as I started to whimper in total exhaustion, I heard the slow, sweet sound of Amelia's voice.

She was singing to me. Singing a lullaby while she held my hair and rubbed my back. She wasn't disgusted or repulsed at all by me throwing up everywhere.

She was as gentle and patient as ever. In fact, in the midst of that, *she* was giving a gift to *me*: the gift of her beautiful voice in song.

After it was over, she cleaned up the vomit without saying a word. "Amelia, you don't have to do that," I whispered hoarsely. We were in a hospital, for goodness sake. They would come clean it. But it was just who she was. She didn't even call a nurse to help.

She had brought with her a pair of beautiful new pajamas to give me, so after she wiped me off, she got me out of the soiled hospital gown and into the pajamas instead. I started to feel like a girl again. *I have pretty pajamas*, I thought. *And my girl by my side.* She stayed with me all night, and every time I awoke, I looked over at Amelia and felt a comforting warmth spread over my body.

"I'm so sorry I have to go," Amelia said softly the next morning, kissing me on the forehead. I could tell it hurt her to see me hurting so much.

"Don't be silly," I said. "You've already done so much more than I could ever ask for. Go back to Quinn, go be with your kids. You're my angel today."

After she was gone, I would touch my silky soft pajamas and feel the strength of her love. Would I have flown back from a vacation for a friend like she did? I wasn't sure, but I was learning.

A few days later, my mom's voice was loud and vaguely distracted on speakerphone. At that point I still couldn't move much, but I had painkillers so at least I was able to talk.

"How are you feeling, Willow?"

"I'm better. I'm okay," I replied to my mother, even though I felt a long way from okay. I still had a port in my neck, and if my blood count didn't come up, another blood transfusion was on the table. I was so scared. But I was used to putting on a tough face for my mother. My family had always told me I was prone to exaggeration—that whatever I was going through, it really wasn't that bad. The underlying message was: *Stop complaining. Stop being desperate for attention.*

"I hope you're going to be back from the hospital by the time we get there," my mother said. "What's the point of us coming to Columbus if you're not?"

I've got to get myself up and out of here, I thought. *Or my parents are going to be pissed.* And the clock was ticking about our annual trip to Nantucket, too. Oliver had allotted three weeks for us to be on the island, and those weeks were growing nearer and nearer. That trip was the most important thing to my husband every summer. *I have to get better and not disappoint him. Get well and get home. Why am I being such a baby?*

It wasn't the first time my mom had seen me in the hospital. At twelve years old I developed an eating disorder that went on for years. I was anorexic and bulimic all throughout my teenage years, and by the time I was twenty-one, it had gotten bad enough that I knew I needed help. I came home after my junior year at Denison University and told my parents, "I can't control this anymore. I need to go to a hospital."

"No," my dad said. "You're not going to do that. We can do this outpatient. I want this under the radar."

As usual, my dad was concerned about the family reputation. Henry Davis was a prominent businessman and philanthropist, very well known and respected in the Chicago area. He didn't want word getting out that his daughter was psychologically "disturbed."

I turned to my mom and said, "Mom, please take me."

And she did.

I checked into a hospital and stayed for a month. And I got better. The doctors and nurses helped me realize what I was really doing: every time I binged and purged, I was trying to fill up the hole inside me. Something was missing—love, maybe, or affection, or security—and the eating disorder was just another way to try to fill it. I was insecure and trying to control how bad I felt by starving myself.

That day on the phone with my mom after my colon surgery, I could hear the edge in her voice. She had already been through "this" with me once, where "this" meant a daughter who was in the hospital. "Oh, the drama of the second born," I could just hear her say. I knew she wanted me to be out by the time she visited, well on my way to being her healthy and active daughter once again. Maybe I *was* dramatic. Maybe this was all my fault, too.

I ended up leaving the hospital too early, because I begged the doctor to release me so I could be home before my parents arrived. My dad stayed for a couple days, and my mom stayed for a full week. I tried to be strong and not complain. I didn't want Mom to think I was needy or—worse—just trying to get attention. But really I was in so much pain, all I wanted was for her to take care of me. *If someone—anyone—would just take care of me.*

But my mother wasn't there solely to take care of me. She came to Columbus to take care of Bella and Wiles. My kids were so little, and since I was laid up in bed, I couldn't do anything for them. Oliver had gone back to work the day after my surgery.

One day my mother took Wiles and Bella to the park. I had been feeling a strange, sharp pain in my leg for several days, like a pulled tendon but worse. I had suffered injuries from yoga and other sports before, but this felt different. More acute and severe.

I hadn't said anything to my mother because she had her hands full already. So did Oliver. But the day she took the kids to the park, a friend dropped by unexpectedly to see me. She took one look at me and immediately knew something was wrong.

"What is it, Willow? What's happened?"

"I'm hurting," I said, and tried to describe the sharp pain in my leg.

"Where's your mom?" she said. "Where's Oliver?"

"She's out with Bella and Wiles. Oliver's back at work."

"You have to call your doctor, Willow. In fact you know what? I'm going to call him for you. Where's his number?" *Crap, I don't know,* I thought.

"I'll find it Willow," she said, as I looked away in pain. She shuffled through the many papers in the kitchen and the numbers on the fridge until she found it. Then she touched my shoulder and called.

I described to my doctor the sensation I was experiencing in my leg. His voice crackled sharply through the speaker.

"Where's Oliver?" he said.

"He's at the office."

"Who else is there with you?"

"My friend just stopped by to check on me . . ."

"Call Oliver at work," he said, "and tell him to get home now. You should not be left unattended. This is not a joke. You should have stayed in the hospital," he ranted.

My doctor was furious. He had never met Oliver until the day of the surgery; all the prior appointments I had gone to alone. And there I was, just days after a surgery that had gone very wrong, and I was left alone. I made a mental note to try to be more honest and to care less about being needy. Wasn't it me who needed to ask them to stay? But I was too afraid to do that.

"I need to see you in my office," the doctor said. "Tell Oliver or your mom or your friend or *someone* to bring you in right now."

I went back to the hospital immediately and they found a blood clot in my leg. My doctor was furious. If the blood clot had remained undiagnosed, it could have killed me.

I was scared. I felt like I didn't have anybody looking out for me. I kept thinking, *Who will protect me?*

The "six to eight weeks" of recovery time stretched into a full year. I had no idea how long I would be suffering from the ramifications of that "standard procedure" gone horribly wrong.

That was when my fear of abandonment started. *I'm alone,* I thought. *I have to go it alone.*

It wasn't true, of course, but I didn't know that yet. My friends had begun to marshal their love and their resources—but in those first weeks after the colon surgery, I couldn't shake the feeling that I was irrevocably, inconceivably alone.

Chapter 4

MY GIRLS

K *nock knock knock.*

The sound of soft knuckles on the front door reverberated through the house, rousing me from a deep slumber. I jolted upright and as soon as I did, I felt searing pain in my stomach.

It was summer of 2007. Nearly a year after the colon surgery, I still regularly felt pain. It wasn't the same pain I'd felt immediately after surgery, when my body was still healing from being cut open from hip bone to hip bone; this was different. I felt nauseated most of the time. I tended to sleep fitfully, waking up at strange hours, sometimes having to climb out of bed at night and go into the bathroom to throw up. I'd crawl back into bed whimpering, and on more than one occasion, Oliver had rolled over and said, with undisguised annoyance, "Willow. Go back to sleep." I felt great guilt. *He has to get up for work in the morning,* I thought. *I should stop whimpering so he can sleep.*

Knock knock.

I lifted my head from the pillow, disoriented. It was a few minutes after ten a.m. Now I remembered: I had woken up earlier to take Wiles to a friend's house, then come home to eat some fruit and a bowl of yogurt. But shortly after eating I'd felt sick and run to the master bathroom to throw up. Terribly nauseated, I lay down in bed fully clothed in my skirt and tank top. If I could rest my eyes for just a few minutes, maybe I could regain my equilibrium. But I must have fallen asleep.

"Oliver?" I called out. "Can you get the door?"

Silence. Then I remembered: Oliver was away on business. He'd been gone for the last four days. Bella was off at summer camp and Wiles was playing with one of his good friends from school.

Knock.

I called out to the maid, but she, too, was nowhere to be found. I would have to deal with this myself. I was reminded how big our house was; my maid could never hear me. We had to use the intercom system to find anyone in the house. Sometimes I felt like this great big beautiful house I had picked out was turning on me. *Too much work,* I thought. It was also an unsettling metaphor for what was happening *inside* the house: we couldn't hear one another. I felt like my husband had stopped listening.

I raised myself onto my elbows, feeling my head swim. By force of habit I lightly touched the stitches on my stomach. They had mostly healed up but they were still white, ghastly things, surprisingly tender to the touch. My skin didn't feel like my skin anymore. It felt like a burlap sack, etched rough by scars. That was a bummer. Sometimes I'd look at myself in the bathroom mirror and start crying. I'd had two C-sections but this was nothing like a C-section scar. To think I had actually complained about that scar!

I should have appreciated what I had, I thought, before tugging my shirt down to cover the damage. I had a calculated body that had been ruthlessly worked out since I was fifteen years old. As close to perfection as I could get with my DNA. I was a model and worked to look like one—it didn't come naturally. And in one fell swoop, I was scarred.

Another wave of nausea hit me as I edged carefully down the long stairs. What was wrong with me? I was sick to my stomach all the time, particularly after eating something sweet. As if the physical effects of the surgery—and the shock of losing twenty-eight inches of my colon—weren't bad enough, now there was this unknown illness to contend with. It was disturbing. I played over and over in my mind all the different terrible scenarios it could be. *A tumor. Stomach cancer. Ugh, I'm my own worst enemy*, I thought. *Get out of your own head,* I said to myself.

I didn't know what was causing it. No one did. I'd been to see my doctor and two specialists, and no one could figure out why I was constantly throwing up.

At the front door I took a deep breath, mustered all my energy, and plastered a smile on my face. The summer sunshine hit me like a ton of bricks, and I shielded my eyes from the brightness. Standing on my front porch was my friend Grace holding a pot of hot soup.

"Hi, beautiful!" she said cheerfully.

The fact that *she* would call *me* beautiful was a huge compliment, considering Grace was one of the most beautiful women I had ever seen. She was a few years younger than me, married but no kids, and she was in the process of founding her own organic beauty product line. Grace was the perfect person for the job: she'd been a runner-up for Miss Ohio, and she was a recognized print and commercial model who was also a respected beauty expert nationwide. Grace was the sweetest girl in the world and we had gotten very close.

"Oh, honey," she said, the smile melting off her face. "You look like you don't feel well at all."

"I don't feel great," I admitted. It was getting harder and harder to act like everything was okay, even though I desperately didn't want my friends to know I was suffering. People had brought casseroles the first few months after the surgery, offering to take Bella and Wiles to and from school, but after a while most of the offers had stopped coming. People expected me to be up and running again, the same high-functioning mom and woman I had been before. The truth was, I expected the same of myself, and was frustrated at my lack of progress.

"I won't stay long," Grace said. She held out a pretty blue Le Creuset pot. "I just brought you some hot soup."

"You're too sweet. Come on in."

I ushered Grace inside and grabbed us each some water. We sat in the kitchen and she told me all about the new developments with Beauty Organics, what she was learning, and the products she was most excited about that would help women look and feel younger. I was grateful for the distraction, and I loved hearing Grace talk about something she felt so passionately about.

"About the soup," Grace said. "I tried to make sure it would be okay on your stomach. I know you said fruits and vegetables have been upsetting your digestion lately, so I wanted you to have something you could eat without getting sick."

"You remembered," I said. "Grace, you are so kind."

She reached out and squeezed my knee. "Don't let the adversary get in your head, Willow. You are STRONG!! One of these days, when you're feeling better, we'll go for a long walk and out to lunch, okay?"

I loved lunch dates with Grace. She was so wise and winsome. She was elegant and poised, and we had a lot in common from our modeling days. She made me feel better about myself. "You're so strong," she would always say, hammering the message into my head. She would never admit it, but she was somewhat a feminist, something I wasn't used to but was drawn to.

Suddenly I felt embarrassed by the way I looked. In the year since the surgery I had lost a good amount of weight since I couldn't keep anything down. I was weak and sickly. All the muscles I'd built from years of doing yoga—the smooth stomach, the toned arms—were withering away.

"That skirt is the cutest on you," Grace said, almost like she could read my mind. "Considering everything you've been through, I can't believe how chic and put together you look."

I smiled, grateful for the compliment. Grace wasn't one to flatter people; if she said something, she meant it. This was the woman whose motto was "Dress for yourself, not for others. You will be beautiful wearing what you feel beautiful in."

"Listen, I won't keep you," Grace said. "You must be exhausted. I just wanted to bring you a little something and let you know I was thinking of you."

"Thank you so much," I said, walking her to the door. "I really appreciate it." She hugged me and I tried not to grimace as she brushed against my stomach, which was still tender from the scars.

"Oh my gosh, I'm so sorry," Grace said. "I didn't mean to—"

"Not your fault. I'll be fine."

She blew me a kiss and sashayed out the door, her beautifully thick blond hair flowing softly behind her.

One she was gone, I fell onto the sofa, completely worn out. It was amazing how little it took to tire me. I still felt nauseated—that hadn't changed—and even though I was hungry, I was afraid to eat.

In the end hunger won out. I took a tiny spoonful of soup and swallowed it cautiously, waiting for the inevitable wave of nausea to hit. It didn't. Grace was true to her word: the soup didn't make me sick. A small miracle. Maybe I'd actually be able to eat a real meal that day.

Instinctively I looked at the little calendar I kept on my desk. *Oh no, I almost forgot!* I had lunch plans with Gigi, Amelia, and my neighbor Alice at noon. I looked at the blinking clock over the stove. It was a quarter past eleven. *Good. I still have time.*

I checked myself in the mirror, trying to make sure I looked presentable. It was hard to get excited about food, but I was always excited to see my friends. They were my support, my unwavering pillars of love and strength, pillars holding me up even when I felt low. As bad as things got, I knew I had my girls.

I dabbed on a little lipstick so I wouldn't look like a complete ghost and ran out the door.

***

"Your strength is shining through, Willow. I hope you know that. We all see it in you, even when you can't see it yourself."

It was Gigi speaking, but I looked around the table at the two other faces I knew and loved so well and everyone was nodding in agreement. To Gigi's right was Amelia, and to her left was Alice.

I'd lived across the street from Alice for quite a while. She was a few years older than the rest of us, and somehow that made her grounded and "grown up" in a way that was truly refreshing. When I was around Alice I had the feeling that everything would be okay. Her daughters were already preteens and she had a lot of wisdom to give me as I tried to parent my own. Her daughters were lovely and well mannered, just "good" kids.

Alice herself was down to earth and she had a huge heart for others. I knew I could call on her night or day and she would be there for me. Whether I needed a cup of sugar for something I was baking or a shoulder to cry on, Alice was always there.

The four of us were just finishing up our salads at the Columbus Country Club and were now debating that age-old question, the question that has plagued women since the dawn of time: Dessert or no dessert?

I lay my fork down gently. For now, my stomach wasn't bothering me. I was having a pleasant time with my friends and I truly hoped it would stay that way.

"You really are radiant, Willow," Amelia said. "I'm so glad you came out today. We've missed you at our lunches."

Alice nodded, folding her napkin and putting it neatly beside her plate. "There's not a day that passes that I'm not thinking of you. In fact, just this morning I was reading from Isaiah and I came across this absolutely beautiful verse I just had to share with you. Do you girls mind if I read it?"

"Not at all," I said, as she reached for the Bible in her purse. Amelia and Gigi smiled—the three of us had traded quite a few Bible verses over the years.

"It's from Isaiah 40:29–31," said Alice. "Gosh, I'm actually kind of nervous! I hardly ever read aloud." She took a deep breath and began. "'He giveth power to the faint; and to them that have no might he increaseth strength. Even the youths shall faint and be weary, and the young men shall utterly fall. But they that await upon the Lord shall renew their strength; they shall mount up with wings as eagles; they shall run, and not be weary; and they shall walk, and not faint.'"

My eyes were a little misty. "Thanks for sharing that. Those words are powerful."

"What a perfect verse for you," Gigi said. "Especially since we all know how much you love to walk!"

It was true: I was a huge walker, at least before the colon surgery, which had definitely thrown a kink into my daily routine. I loved the gentle movement of walking, how it allowed me to really take in the world around me. It was also the best exercise to do *with* someone. I could actually carry on a conversation with one of my friends.

"I love that," Amelia said. "'They shall walk, and not faint.' It's so lovely."

I had walked with Gigi, Amelia, and Alice dozens of times, and some of our most meaningful and poignant conversations had happened on those walks. I missed walking with them, and they knew it.

"You'll be up walking again in no time, Willow," Alice said. "I'm sure of it."

"And until then," Gigi said with a wink, "there's cheesecake."

We all laughed.

And then a server walked by with the dessert tray. It was absolutely beautiful, the crimson raspberry compote piled high on a creamy-white slice of cheesecake. It looked like a sweet dream.

Oh, wow, I thought. *Maybe I can risk it after all.*

"We'll have one slice for the table," Gigi told the server. "That way none of us go home feeling bad."

I'll just have a bite, I thought. *One bite of cheesecake never hurt anybody.*

I shouldn't have tempted fate. After that first bite, I immediately knew I'd made a mistake. I hardly had time to enjoy how good it tasted because the minute it hit my stomach, everything went wrong. "I'm so sorry," I said to my friends, who looked at me with concern. "Please excuse me." I pushed back my chair and rushed away from the table, determined to get to the ladies' restroom before it was too late.

Within seconds I was hunched over the toilet, retching uncontrollably. I regretted having the cheesecake. I regretted having the colon surgery to begin with. Tears were streaming down my face. My life was beginning to be marked by large patches of regret.

Alice knocked gently on the door. "Willow? Are you okay? We're worried about you."

"I'm okay," I rasped. "I'll be out in a minute. Just got a little sick."

But I couldn't stand up yet; I was still too queasy and too weak. I assured Alice I was all right and told her to please go back out to the table and wait for me. The last thing I wanted was to scare my friends or ruin their nice lunch date.

I lay my head on the cool toilet seat, mortified I had fallen so low. Was this really what it had come to? I couldn't even have a nice lunch with my friends without going into the bathroom to throw up? I had certainly done *that* song and dance when I was bulimic. I had no desire to do it again.

Five minutes later, I was still in the bathroom, my phone on the cold tile beside my feet, when my father called.

"Willow, there's a town car coming to pick you up tomorrow morning." That was my father, all right—he always cut right to the chase. "Can you be ready to go?"

"What?" I said blearily. "Go where?"

"The Cleveland Clinic. You're going to Cleveland."

Chapter 5

THE CLEVELAND CLINIC

It was late when I heard my husband come in the back door. I was restless, partly because I felt sick to my stomach, but also because I knew the town car was coming early to pick me up the next day. I didn't want to oversleep my alarm.

My dad had come to the rescue, as he so often did, getting me into the Cleveland Clinic. "Forget the doctors you've been dealing with," he said. My dad was a logical guy, and he reasoned that if the Columbus doctors couldn't help, then we would go straight to the experts. His little girl deserved nothing less.

Now my husband was back from his business trip a day earlier than expected. I was excited to see him. Even if it felt like he had been pulling away from me ever since the surgery, I loved him. I poured into him like a puppy looking for a pat on the belly.

"Willow?" Oliver's voice was soft. "You awake?"

He nudged the bedroom door open and golden light poured in from the hall. I couldn't see his face since he was backlit, but his voice was so comforting.

"I'm awake," I said. "Hi."

He came and sat down beside me on the bed: a rare moment of closeness. This is what I had been craving for months, but he was always at work or otherwise unavailable. *If we want to keep our lifestyle,* he'd say, *then someone in this family has to work.*

Oliver's hands were resting in his lap. He didn't touch me, but neither did he pull away when I laid my hand on his.

"How are you feeling?" he asked gently.

"I'm okay. Still nauseous when I eat. Dad's sending a car to take me to the Cleveland Clinic in the morning. Maybe they can figure out what's wrong."

"I'll go with you," Oliver said. It was just four little words but I felt like my heart was cracking open with gratitude.

"What about Wiles?" I whispered.

"He can spend the night with a friend for a few days. He'll be fine."

I felt like I might cry. My husband would go to Cleveland with me. It was all of two hours away, but the gesture meant everything. He loved me and cared enough about me that he wanted to be by my side.

A sliver of light pierced the darkness. Maybe I wasn't so alone after all.

***

The town car arrived right on time the following morning. The driver smiled. "Is this all your luggage?" he asked.

"That's it," Oliver said. "We won't be gone long."

The driver easily hefted our two suitcases into the trunk. We had each brought an overnight bag as we didn't expect to be in Cleveland long. Hopefully they'd run a few tests, diagnose what was wrong, and prescribe the right medication or treatment. Then we'd be on our merry way and I'd feel like myself again.

As so often happens—especially for me—things did not go as planned.

We had to go into the clinic for six days straight, and I had to do testing every day. Each morning we woke up early and went directly from the hotel to the clinic for a battery of tests. Oliver stayed with me. He moved things around at work so he could be there with me. But after those six days, I still wasn't finished: the doctors told me I would have to come back for two weeks. They needed to run more tests to figure out what was wrong.

While that news was extremely disappointing, I had to admit I had never received better treatment in my life. Everything at the Cleveland Clinic runs efficiently. The doctors are always punctual, and they schedule your tests every hour or two hours, on the dot. Doctors and patients show up on time and there is none of the "waiting around" that defines most hospitals and doctor's offices.

The other thing Oliver and I had learned over the last six days was that Cleveland was not a bad place to be. I'd never been particularly inspired to visit, but its location on Lake Eerie made it a lakeside gem. Whenever I felt up to it, Oliver and I would walk along the lake or through the city's many parks. I loved all the trees and the old-world feel of Cleveland. Everywhere we went, people were so polite, so warm and happy. From the hotel concierge to our servers at dinner, everyone was sweet, kind, and accommodating.

Our last night in Cleveland, after the doctors had told me I'd need to come back for two weeks of extensive testing, Oliver and I had a nice dinner at what had fast become our favorite Italian place. I was nibbling on a piece of garlic bread, scared that it—like everything else—would make me sick.

My husband took a sip of his wine. "I don't think I can take two weeks off work. I'm sorry, Willow. I know you'd like that. But look at how well we've been treated here. You are among the world's leading medical experts—you'll be just fine."

I nodded, trying to be chipper. I knew he was right: they were taking great care of me. But that didn't mean I wanted to spend two weeks in Cleveland alone without my family. And I knew he couldn't spend two weeks out of the office, not in light of the three weeks we were taking for our summer trip to Nantucket. Oliver worked hard and he only asked for that one trip. It was my fault I didn't like it there. It was not my favorite place, but it was his and I knew I should honor that and go. But why did it always feel so bad? Maybe because I wanted "our" place. I wanted a place we both chose.

Oliver seemed to read my mind. "Maybe your mom will come stay," he said. I didn't know how to tell him I didn't want my mother: I wanted my husband by my side.

I also wanted to be home in my own bed. The hotel staff couldn't have been nicer, but I was already tired of sleeping in a strange bed. I certainly wasn't looking forward to the prospect of doing it for two more weeks. Already I felt a strong pang of homesickness.

"I'll be home with Wiles so you don't have to worry about him," Oliver said. "Bella is still at camp. We'll all be fine for a few weeks. And you're in good hands here."

Tears welled up in my eyes and I looked away. *Keep it together, Willow,* I demanded of myself. *Keep it together.*

I wanted to beg him to stay. To throw my arms around his neck and plead with him to please not send me back alone. The Cleveland Clinic was only two hours from home! He could work here, if he had to, from remote. I didn't know anyone in Cleveland. I didn't like to be alone and I was scared, even more so now that they hadn't been able to quickly diagnose what was wrong. The doctors and nurses were great but I was just their patient, not someone they loved. Nobody wants to stay in a hospital alone.

"Okay," I said meekly, determined not to cry. I didn't want Oliver to think I was weak or needy. His life had to go on, and so did our children's. They could survive without me for a couple weeks. And I knew, surely, beneath all my fear and uncertainty, that I could survive without them, too.

Oliver's right, I thought. Already I had a warm place in my heart for Cleveland—they had treated me so very well. *After all,* I thought, *it's only two weeks. What could possibly go wrong in two weeks?*

Chapter 6

ALONE IN THE ER

It was a sultry summer day when I returned to the Cleveland Clinic, this time with two suitcases and no husband. I'd read online that Cleveland temperatures were usually a bit milder than the humid, muggy summers in Columbus, but of course I had arrived right in the middle of an unusual heat wave.

I could feel perspiration beading at the nape of my neck as I walked into the front door of the center. It wasn't just the heat, either. I was undeniably anxious. I was not looking forward to what lay ahead.

I did have one thing going for me. I wouldn't be *completely* alone at the Cleveland Clinic—at least not for the next week.

"Willow? Is that you?"

A familiar voice jolted me out of my thoughts. I felt hugely comforted to hear this voice far from home, here in Cleveland instead of where I normally heard it, back in Columbus.

"Cece!"

Cece Miller was rushing toward me in the foyer. She was a tiny woman, a few years younger than my mom, but she scooped me up in a big bear hug all the same. "It's so good to see you!" she cried. "I'm so glad this worked out."

"Me, too," I said. "You have no idea how glad I am to see you."

Cece had been to the Cleveland Clinic a few times before. She and her husband went there each summer for their annual doctor appointments. They liked the expertise of the doctors there and enjoyed making it an annual event. She'd once said to me, after we'd met years before, "You're different from anybody I've ever met." She liked my raw honesty and bubbly nature. "Those other women, they talk the talk," she told me. "But you, Willow: you walk the walk." She and I just clicked.

And now, here we were, away from home, here at the Clinic for very different reasons—but together. We hadn't planned it so that our trips would overlap, but because I had to extend my stay it worked out. Cece was only scheduled for the first week I was there, but I was glad for the company.

Cece's husband came up behind her and shook my hand. "Good to see you, Willow. Though of course I'm sorry you're here."

The Millers were wonderfully kind to me during our time at the Cleveland Clinic. They invited me out to dinner every night that week, adopting me as a kind of surrogate daughter. They told me funny stories and entertained me, keeping my mind off how sick I was and how alone I felt. We became even better friends that week, and I was undeniably grateful for that. I was becoming keenly aware of how important friendships were and how much I depended on them.

My mom came up to visit, just as Oliver had suggested, but she couldn't stay more than a day; she said she needed to get back for my dad. I took her to the private plane, waiting with her as she prepared to go back to their summer home in Wisconsin. I wanted to grab onto her and never let go. All I wanted was to say, "Please stay, Mom. Please stay." But I could tell she wanted to get back to her life, so I stayed quiet.

That night I went back to the hotel thinking about the next few weeks. Bella would be back from camp, and we would be off to Nantucket. Then school would start and the madness would begin. I was in the hotel room in total pity-party mode when I thought about my friends. They were sending emails, calls, and Scriptures. I started to read the Scriptures but was too entrenched in my own sorrow to focus on them.

The nature of my sickness was uncomfortable and sensitive. Every day I showed up at the Cleveland Clinic for a slate of tests. They did the standard blood tests and performed various cat scans. I drank barium so they could watch how it went through my digestive tract. Some days the tests required me to fast and other days I could eat. It was all so confusing.

I was starving those couple of weeks. *No rhythm to this dance,* I chanted in my brain. I started to get giggly, which was better than a breakdown. I was either walking around with my headset on looking for ways to escape, or constantly looking at the packet of "do this," "be here then," "don't eat," and "no liquids." *Yikes, can the Cleveland Clinic starve you?* I wondered.

I put my headset on and just walked to nowhere in particular. I didn't know this town but I was self-soothing. "Try to focus on the positive," I could hear my mom saying in my head. "Think of all the cancer patients you see, Willow."

She's right, I said to myself. *I'm not dying. And this is only a season of my life. Get a grip,* I repeated to myself as I kept walking around Cleveland. *Get a grip, Willow.*

One day they sent me to the allergy department, since they were trying to rule out various food allergies.

"We're going to put you under anesthesia, okay, Willow?" the doctor explained. "Nothing major. It's just so we can put a small tube down your throat and take a tiny piece of your stomach to biopsy it."

I felt myself grow cold. "I don't do well with anesthesia," I said, harkening back to the colon surgery. "Is there any way we can do it in a less invasive way?"

"Trust me: it's better like this," the doctor said. "You won't feel a thing."

Easy for him to say, I thought as I choked back tears. But for once the doctors actually had it right. I woke up afterward with nothing more serious than a sore throat and a little Band-Aid on my right arm.

"We tested you for celiac disease while we were in there," the doctor told me. "But those tests came back negative. You're not celiac."

"Okay," I said. On one hand I was grateful that I would still be able to eat gluten; on the other hand I was all the more frustrated that they couldn't figure out what was wrong with me. I stood up, got dressed, and went to the allergist.

The next step was to test me for a fructose allergy. I sat down with papers in hand, about to check the rest of the schedule, when they called my name.

Like most people, I *kind* of knew what fructose was. I knew the word, of course, but I didn't exactly know what foods had it and what foods didn't. They were interested in gauging my body's reaction since sugar seemed to aggravate my system the most. "Rule out" was their motto.

After the test was over, I was unplugged from the IV and I headed back to the hotel. *Another day of testing tomorrow,* I thought. *For now I'll rest. Hmmm, or maybe I can do a quick walk. That will cheer me up.*

I didn't walk or rest long. I started violently vomiting almost immediately after my walk. I was confused. I wasn't sure who to call or what to do. The Cleveland Clinic was literally 200 feet away but it was now night. Instead I called down to the receptionist at the hotel.

"Ummm, hi, it's Mrs. Adair." I paused to put my hand over my mouth, begging myself not to vomit. Once I regained composure, I blurted, "I think I need to go to the clinic!" I was still forcing myself not to throw up.

I stayed on the line while the receptionist put me on hold for a long moment. Then she came back. "Do you need a wheelchair, Mrs. Adair? Or can you walk down? We will drive you to the emergency room ourselves."

I felt immensely grateful but I didn't have time to express it. "I'll be right down," I said abruptly. I hung up and ran to the bathroom, emptying my stomach once more before heading down to the elevator.

I stayed in the ER for three days. My room was bitterly cold and sterile. The summer days in Cleveland were buttery warm outside my window, but I couldn't reach them. In contrast to the yellow light outside, the walls of my room were bright white and polished to a fine shine. Everything was impersonal. There were no flowers, no sympathy cards, no kind familiar faces.

Who will protect me? I asked, the same question that had haunted me after my surgery. My morphine drip kept me hazy much of the time, but I almost preferred that to being blindingly aware that I was in the emergency room by myself. When Cece Miller had been at the Cleveland Clinic, her husband had not left her side.

Once I called Oliver in the middle of the night. "I'm really sick," I said.

He sighed. "You're at the Cleveland Clinic. You couldn't be at a better spot."

Sure, I wanted to scream. *But they're the ones who made me sick! They injected me with high levels of fructose and I haven't been able to leave the ER for three days!*

At least then we had an answer: I was allergic to fructose. No wonder I couldn't digest fruit or yogurt or onions. Turns out certain parts of your colon do certain jobs, and the lower portion digests fructose. During the surgery when they took out the twenty-eight inches, they had removed the whole lower portion of my colon. That was why I could no longer digest fructose. I was learning a lot about human biology these last few years—and I didn't like it.

The most amazing thing was that I'd been going to doctors and nutritionists in Columbus for an entire year, feeling miserable, constantly sick—and none of them had guessed that it might be a food allergy. Not a one. They assumed something had gone wrong in the surgery, but didn't think to test for a particular allergen. Even my colon doctor at the Cleveland Clinic was shocked when he finally figured out what was going on. "This is rare, Willow," he said. "Exceedingly rare." I was a medical anomaly—and it wouldn't be the last time.

At least now I knew I was allergic to sugar. The tests at the Cleveland Clinic settled it once and for all. Anything with fruit sugar—anything that browns or caramelizes—would make me sick for the rest of my life.

***

A few days later I was back in Columbus, stifled by the muggy Ohio heat. Since I finally had a diagnosis, I took action. I overhauled my diet immediately, hired a nutritionist, and started to study fructose. It was so hard to figure out—it seemed like there was nothing to eat. I stopped eating the obvious stuff like chocolate, fruit, many vegetables, wine, and anything sweet. But I also learned that almost everything has fructose or sugar in it.

Still, I was on a mission to feel great. I had the fire in my belly. I wanted to get well. I had my answer and I would conquer this. I imagined I would make it all better. My life was going to be so much better now and I was taking charge. I stocked my diet full of the good kind of grains and fibers and proteins and of course my beloved pretzels. Phew—those were still on my okay list.

This new knowledge empowered me. Now that I knew what I could and couldn't eat, it got better. I no longer felt sick all the time. I had taken control of my own life once again, and bit by bit, I grew stronger.

My doctor had suggested I start walking after the colon surgery. I loved the idea—I was already a big walker. Especially since I'd had that blood clot, my doctor had described my right leg as having "sluggish" blood. So I walked. I was a good patient: I did what I was told. I was too young to die of a blood clot, so I walked and walked.

"Start slow," he said. "Maybe just walk around the block."

He had no idea what I was capable of.

That summer Gigi and I started making our walks more regular. We started to walk once a week, and we made a commitment to do so. She lived two blocks from me, so we'd walk down to the American Airlines center and back home, which took us about an hour and a half, sometimes longer. Gigi often told people, "Willow might be the one recovering from surgery, but *I'm* the one who has to keep up with *her*!" My strength was coming back to me in an exciting way. I felt stronger, healthier, more alive than I'd felt in quite some time.

Every Thursday, Gigi and I wound our way through our neighborhood of Bullitt Park, past all the beautiful grandiose homes with sumptuously manicured lawns. In Bullitt Park, looks were important. How your house looked, how your lawn looked, how your wife looked, how your kids looked: that was what mattered. There was a real emphasis on appearance—and I loved it. That was my comfort zone. After all, I was a model, and I had gone to Denison and dreamed about living in Bullitt Park. It was a perfect match. I didn't realize then that the sandcastle I was building was going to crumble.

Gigi and I walked through our sunny, bright, picture-perfect neighborhood. But in my own home, things were far from picture-perfect. In fact, they were ugly and only getting worse. The sand was starting to collapse.

Chapter 7

FALSE IDOLS

"Bella? Wiles? Breakfast!"

I waited for the telltale sound of young feet pounding down the stairs.

"Come on, kids! We're going to be late to school."

Wiles came bounding down the stairs and kissed me on the cheek. I smiled.

Bella was a somewhat different story.

God had blessed me with two beautiful, talented children, something I was grateful for every day. But my relationship with my daughter Bella was rapidly deteriorating. We'd been having some problems, but I kept thinking it would get better. Instead it had only gotten worse. Most teen girls rebelled against their parents, but Bella lied to me constantly and even tried to do me harm. I saw outrageous expenses on my credit card and called American Express to report a theft—and then went into Bella's room and saw all the shopping bags piled up on her bed. She'd stolen my credit card out of my wallet. And that wasn't even the half of it.

Things were tense and strained between us, sometimes even scary. But no matter how horrible she was to me, I was sure it was all my fault. *I'm a bad mom,* I thought, sure that if there was something wrong, I was somehow causing it.

On the outside, it probably looked like things had never been better. Bella and Wiles were both enrolled at The Wellington School, an elite private school in Columbus. On top of that, my husband was handsome and successful, and by most standards, we were living a life of wealth and ease. I was playing the part of the society wife and enjoying it immensely. If a high-society magazine was shooting important people, I wanted to be the first on their list.

For the most part, I liked being a part of the Bullitt Park community in Bexley. I hadn't intended to settle down in Columbus, or really anywhere in Ohio, but in Bexley I found a group of people who were a lot like me. I didn't like that Columbus was landlocked, didn't care for the muggy summers or the ugly, flat landscape. But I had to admit it was a great place to raise kids. Now that I had children, I was thrilled to be a Bexley mom. Though my kids were at a private school, the Bexley City School District was one of the best in the country—and for good reason. Our friends' children could walk or bike to school without fear of being harassed or kidnapped. How many mothers could say that with confidence in this crazy world?

I was also doing yoga every day. *I can't get through my day if I don't have my yoga*, I thought every morning. Why? Because I craved it like food or water. I played tennis on the Columbus Country Club team and worked out, but my love was my yoga. I was a healthy, fit, active mom and wife.

I was living and breathing it, this desire to be a perfect wife, perfect mother, perfect socialite, perfect yogi, perfect person. I was leading a plastic lifestyle, consumed by what I "should" look like to everyone else. But that wasn't foreign to me. I had always been a model and the external was my self-worth. My schedule was packed full of "important" charity events, the ones all the most "important" people attended. I kept all the pictures of myself from the newspaper. I was buying stuff because I could—clothes and jewelry and expensive gifts for my kids. I wanted to look flawless every time I left the house—or look flawless pretending to be messy—because what if someone saw me? And someone always did.

Now I look back on that time of my life as a period of false idols. Eventually I would lose my looks, and my perfect little family—every one of those idols would be lost to me and I'd be forced to change what I really cared about.

The truth was, I *did* like money. I grew up in an affluent neighborhood with parents who provided handsomely for my sisters and me. I knew the lifestyle I wanted to maintain. I was calculating and yet honest about my needs. For me, wealth equaled security. What I didn't realize was how money had become just as much a false idol as yoga, another sandcastle on which I was trying to build my foundation. Money, perfection, physical fitness—it was in the air I breathed. I was allowing the allure of these false idols to seep into my life and control me. It was like my drug.

Each year I would pledge to be better than the last. *I will be a better mother, a better wife, a better friend, volunteer more.* I was putting my faith in me and my ego. I was on the Willow crusade and feeling like I had control over my life and happiness. I was building my life around myself, not God.

Sometimes the pressure to be perfect was just too much, even for me. I needed an escape, somewhere I could go without having to worry about who I was wearing every single time I left the house. "That's why we have a house in Nantucket," Oliver reminded me. "So we can get away."

The home on Nantucket had belonged to his parents, and after his dad passed, Oliver inherited it with his brother and sister. Though he hadn't grown up there, he loved everything about it. But it was his personal heaven, not mine.

Nantucket is a lovely place, and the town on the island is beautiful. If the house had been in town, I would have been thrilled. But Oliver's house was out in the middle of the country. It took thirty minutes to get to civilization. If I wanted to go the grocery store, or take a yoga class, or go out for a nice dinner with my husband—it didn't matter. It was at least a thirty-minute drive.

We had access to a private beach, which should have been paradise, except for the fact that the beach was not easy to get to. It was a challenge and it felt more like a chore. Every time we went, it felt like gathering the family to go on a long car ride: "Kids, go to the bathroom." "Is the car all packed up?" We were only going a mile and a half down the road! But it was a trek. The car jerked and jostled down unpaved roads until we got to the ferryboat, where we would have to unload everything, which invariably caused a fight. "I'm carrying more than he is, Mom!" my kids would roar. "Why aren't you carrying the chairs?" Then we'd have to either take a paddleboat to the beach or walk through the pond while dodging hungry sharp crabs. By the time I got to the beach, I needed a vacation from the vacation.

The house itself sat on nine acres of land, an enormous property filled with beautiful trees. It could have been a spectacular place, and for people like Oliver, it was. But I didn't feel the same way. The house was old, and nothing had been changed or updated since it was built. It still had the original rugs, mattresses, and window shades. It even had the original plates and silverware! There was mold in the house, which caused more arguments: I wanted to get rid of it, and nobody else seemed to care. I wanted to hire a company to make sure there was no mold, but everyone told me to just shut up. *Am I crazy?* I thought. *Maybe there's no mold!* But I could see it, and I was constantly worried about Wiles's asthma flaring up. I didn't shower inside; I usually opted to shower outside with the bugs, even if it was raining, rather than lock myself into a grimy bathroom with mold and mildew caked onto the walls.

I finally hired a company to come out and test for mold, and I was right: the house was filled with it. Thankfully, we took care of it once and for all.

The whole house was hot, and there wasn't much circulation. There was no AC, so on any given night I was never sure whether I would be able to sleep in the heat. It created a lot of anxiety inside me; I didn't feel comfortable there. I wasn't one of those people who could just run with chaos. *It must be my fault*, I told myself. I tried to make the most of my time there, but most of the time I failed.

Years earlier, Oliver's dad had once asked me, "What would you do with this house, Willow? To make it better?" When I didn't answer, he said, "You'd bulldoze it, wouldn't you?" And I said, "Yes, I would." That's how I felt about the house. It was no secret—everyone knew it.

And yet, Nantucket was where our family took our annual summer vacation. For years I felt like I had absolutely no say in the matter. "Why can't we find a place together?" I said to Oliver. "Surely we can buy a home in a place we both love."

In 2008, Oliver finally agreed. "Okay," he said. "Let's start looking."

So we joined a resort club where we stayed in beautiful homes all over the world. We vacationed in a plethora of different places, and each time we scouted out potential opportunities. We were looking for a third home that was actually Oliver's *and* my decision. We stayed in Costa Rica, the Cayman Islands—all sorts of luscious, exotic locales.

Then we stayed in Miami, and we both fell in love.

Today Miami is one of the fastest growing cities in the country. It's ridiculously popular. But back in 2008, no one was going to Miami. We chose it because it was a little bit off the beaten track. Nobody from Columbus had any desire to vacation there. In fact, when I told my friends we'd bought a home on Miami Beach, they said, "Really? Why would you want to go to Miami?"

I was so proud of it. I felt like I'd picked it. It was my slice of paradise. Miami was cool, but it wasn't Taos cool. Everybody went to Taos. I wanted someplace that felt like my own.

Staying at the house in Nantucket never felt like a vacation to me. That's why buying the home in Miami felt like such a huge victory. It took twelve years out of Oliver's and my sixteen-year marriage to decide on a mutually agreed upon second home, but it was worth the wait. Every time I went, I got to know the city a little better. I bought maps and walked everywhere. I researched the history. I wanted to know everything I could because I knew I was putting down roots for my future. And when Oliver said he wanted to join the Country Club in Miami Beach, I was thrilled. "Absolutely!" I said. "Let's do it." Miami was *our* place.

***

"Bella!" I yelled at the top of my lungs. "We're going to be late for school! Please come eat your breakfast." My frustration was building. Why did she always have to push me to my absolute outer limits? It could never just be easy with her.

Chime. My phone went off on the kitchen counter. I knew that chime— it was Jules.

Jules was the first real friend I'd made in Miami, and I knew she was a friend I would have for life. She lived in our building, so before we officially met, I had seen her having lively conversations with our doorman. Jules was so kind and generous: she treated everyone equally. At some point I just had to know who this happy, grounded person was, so I introduced myself.

"I'm Willow," I said.

"Jules," she said, and her smile lit up the whole lobby.

By the end of that first conversation, I could tell how wise she was, how calm and at peace. I craved that for my own life. *Maybe if I spend time with Jules,* I thought, *that sense of peace will start to rub off.*

It was always so easy being with her. She really seemed to "get" me and understand where I was coming from.

"Bella! BELLA! I'm not going to call you again."

Wiles stared at me over his breakfast cereal, no doubt wondering what I would do. It was frustrating enough that Bella wouldn't show me any respect, but the fact that Wiles watched his older sister constantly disrespect me made it even worse.

I picked up my phone to read Jules's text. *I could really use some support right now,* I thought. And, as always, Jules seemed to have a sense for exactly what I needed to hear at exactly the right time. Sometimes it was downright uncanny.

"Hey mama," she said. "Just thinking of you and your sweet kids this morning. I am sending you over some extra strength and love. Xoxo."

My eyes filled with tears. I dashed out a quick response. "Thanks Jules! Having some trouble with one of the kids this morning. You know who."

Chime. Jules's reply was immediate. "Hang in there. Maybe your response and general attitude to her needs to be 'Bella, I love you very much. I know that you are so angry. I am so sad that you are hurting. Please know that I love you so much, and nothing u can say or do will change that.'"

I wiped the tears out of my eyes. She was so right, and I felt immensely grateful. "I'll try that!" I typed. "It's hard and I do a bad job. You are comforting to me! You always have been."

"Put some of that yoga training to work. You know—finding peace and being centered even when a train is going by the yoga studio."

I laughed. Jules was remarkable. She could turn my sadness into joy and gratitude, just like that.

Bella came slamming down the stairs. My darling daughter shot me a surly look before stomping into the kitchen, where she completely ignored the plate of food I'd made her. She snatched an apple out of the fruit bowl, took one bite, and set it down on the counter, leaving the rest of it for our housekeeper to clean up.

"Hey, Bella," Wiles said to his sister. She didn't respond.

"Did you do your English homework?" I asked. Still no response.

Oliver came into the kitchen. "Hey, sweetheart," he said to Bella.

"Hey, Dad."

Sometimes it felt like Oliver was the only one my daughter would listen to. He was certainly the only one Bella treated with any respect.

I asked Bella several questions about school and cheerleading practice, trying to engage with her. Still she didn't respond. I looked at Oliver, waiting for him to intervene or say something. If he would just say, *Show your mother some respect*, I knew things would be different.

But he didn't. He kissed Bella on the top of the head, ruffled Wiles's hair, and left for work.

"I love you, Bella," I said softly. "If you ever want to talk to me, you know I'm here to listen."

She rolled her eyes and gave me a look that chilled me to the core. Sometimes I got the feeling she wished I were dead.

"Make sure you've got your homework," I said, as I watched my kids trudge out the door.

I felt like my relationship with my daughter was falling apart. What I didn't know yet was that I was falling apart, too. Emotionally *and* physically. The worst was yet to come.

Chime. Jules's chime again. I felt a surge of hope as I checked my phone. "You are one strong little lady," she said. "Just picture yourself on that beach. Sun on your legs. Waves crashing."

I smiled and closed my eyes. For just a moment I could feel the sun warm and gentle on my legs, the waves crashing at my toes.

My whole life was about to come crashing down around me, but I didn't know that yet. Before my body betrayed me, I would have one last hurrah, one beautiful experience before black darkness.

But it wouldn't be in Miami. I would enjoy this last ray of sunshine in California at a secluded ashram tucked into the mountains where I would do hours and hours of hiking and yoga every day. And I would experience this reprieve with, of all people, my mother.

***

For my fortieth birthday my mom had offered to take me on a trip anywhere in the world. I surprised her by choosing an ashram in the foothills of Santa Monica, California, and she grudgingly obliged.

It was everything I'd ever dreamed of and more. We did an hour of yoga every morning, then had a very light breakfast before hiking seven to ten miles. After that we came back for a two-hour massage, did another hour of yoga, had a wholesome and simple dinner, some relaxed chats, and then went straight to bed. There were no electronics, no newspapers, no alcohol, no TV, and no caffeine—only water. We were in bed by eight o'clock each night and up by six the next morning.

It was one of the most wonderful weeks of my life. My wrist bothered me a touch, but I had learned to practice yoga in ways that didn't aggravate my injury as much, and obviously hiking was no trouble at all. My mom and I bonded; she wrote me the sweetest note at the end of our time there, a note I'll treasure forever. Everything else about that week was so perfect, I hardly noticed my arm.

That was the last week I would say that in my life. "No weapon will prosper against us," says the Lord. But that doesn't say weapons will not be formed.

I got back to Columbus on Saturday and had the arm surgery on Tuesday. The ashram was the calm before the storm. After that, everything went to hell.

Chapter 8

BLOOD CLOT #2

"You're going to be fine, Willow," my doctor told me. "You do realize that, right?"

"Sure," I said. "I mean, I guess so." We were seated in his office on October 11, 2011, the day before my arm surgery. His office wasn't like other doctor's offices I'd been in—he had all the cool toys, Apple products on his desk and shelves, big Bose speakers, even a rotating slideshow on his computer of him out on the lake and hiking with his family and friends. He was young and hip and healthy. *Kind of like me,* I thought.

"Look, you really seem freaked out about this," he went on. "But we're talking about a simple torn ligament. We'll do it right here in my office, outpatient. And we'll do the whole thing arthroscopic—I'll get in there, clean it up, and sew you back up." He grinned. "Trust me, this surgery is so easy I could do it in my sleep."

I felt my stomach tighten. The last time a medical professional had acted like a surgery would be no big deal, it hadn't turned out well.

He was young but boasted a very impressive pedigree: he'd been to all the right schools and interned with the best of the best. At the time I was a celebrity whore. I loved that stuff. I could feast on Stanford and Princeton grads for days.

"What sports do you play, Willow? You're clearly athletic."

"I am on the tennis team at Columbus Country Club," I said. "But yoga is really my first love. I do it every day. But then my wrist just started degenerating over time . . . and that's why I came to you."

He nodded. "You'll be doing yoga by Christmas," he said with a cocksure grin. "No sweat."

We did the surgery the next day and it went fine. I visited the doctor's office every couple of weeks to get new casts. I was doing my daily walks around Bullitt Park, showing off a different color cast every couple of weeks— cyan blue, hot pink, hunter green, lemon yellow. I actually thought I looked pretty cute when my favorite salesladies at the makeup counter would doll up my cast for me, put little stuff on it like baubles and glitter and CC stars.

This is okay, I thought. *This isn't half bad.*

Yoga before Christmas. I was counting down the days.

***

Chime.

My sweet Jules! I ran to my phone.

Sure enough, one new text flashed on the screen. "Hey kiddo. Sending u a big kiss. This time tomorrow you will be taking your walk. Sun on your face. Sand under your toes. Tiny chill in the air. Just keep your eye on the prize."

My heart soared. I was leaving for Miami that evening to meet my decorator for a few days. Jules was right: in twenty-four hours I would be walking down the beach in my favorite place in the world. Even if I had a cast on my arm and couldn't take a dip in the ocean, I was so excited to be going.

"Can't wait to see u," I texted back. "One more day!"

The following morning, I was exactly where I wanted to be: walking beside the Atlantic Ocean with Jules at my side. She had picked me up from the airport the night before—five weeks after my arm surgery I still had a hard time driving.

"Does it hurt?" she asked, pointing to my cast.

"A little. Not too bad."

"Can I see it?"

"Sure."

I held out my right arm. Immediately her eyes zeroed in on the tip of my index finger, which was black. "What's wrong with your finger?"

"Oh, nothing," I said, not wanting to be a bother. "I'm sure it's fine. Probably just my circulation is cut off from wearing the cast."

"That's kind of scary, Willow."

I shrugged. "I'm sure it'll go away." I wasn't actually sure, but I was good at pretending. I was tired of my medical issues, tired of seeing doctors and nurses and being a liability. I didn't want to be what everyone thought I was: a hypochondriac. Someone who was always exaggerating, running to the doctor every time a tiny little thing went wrong.

"No!" Jules said. One thing I really admired about Jules was that she was never afraid to speak her mind. "Sorry, Willow, but I can't accept that. There is something wrong here, and I'm going to figure out what." She reached for her phone. Before I knew what was happening, she had snapped a picture of my finger.

"What was that for?"

"I'm sending this to my cousin. She's an anesthesiologist. She'll know what's wrong."

She always had my back and took such good care of me. When I was with her, I felt safe.

Jules's phone buzzed two minutes later. "Let's see what she says," Jules said, and I peeked over her shoulder at her phone. Our jaws dropped in unison.

"That's a blood clot," the text said. "Get her to the hospital *now*."

Jules took me to Mount Sinai Medical Center in Miami immediately. Her doctor cousin was right: It was a blood clot.

They put me on blood thinners and kept me under close watch, the same drill as before. For the next few days in Miami, Jules hardly left my side. I felt like I hadn't been cared for that well in ages, and then it was time for me to go back to Columbus.

"I'll miss you," I said, giving her a long hug.

"You take care of yourself, mama. You are so loved."

My heart was heavy as I got situated on the plane. I hoped it wouldn't be long before I saw Jules again—or Miami, for that matter.

Chime.

Moments before take-off, I heard the warm familiar sound. I smiled to see Jules's name on my screen.

"This week you had it in the bag with elegance and grace," she said. "Hang in there. That's all you have to do. I love u girl. Xoxo."

I tucked my phone into my Birkin handbag and leaned back in my seat, feeling grateful and calm as the plane lifted off the tarmac. Jules's words trickled through my mind like a peaceful, soothing stream.

Hang in there. That's all you have to do.

Chapter 9

THE COLUMBUS ARTS BALL

December in Bullitt Park was my favorite time of year. The snowfalls were still fresh and white—they hadn't yet been sullied, the snow transformed into horrible brown slush. Everyone in the neighborhood took Christmas decorations very seriously. There was a sort of unofficial contest between homeowners to see who could put up the best light display. The mansions and estates on Bryden Road boasted lavish, fantastic masterpiece, and people came from miles away to drive down the street at night, cars moving at a snail's pace as everyone oohed and ahhed over the luminous tableaux outside their windows.

I'd always had a fascination with the month of December. Growing up in Chicago, the true bitterness of winter usually didn't start until January, so for the month of December, we were suspended in a kind of winter wonderland. Columbus winters were milder, though still dry and cold. In December the air was crisp and cool, nipping at my face and fingers as my kids and I bundled up in jackets and scarves, tugging snow boots onto our feet. The crowds in the shops at Tuttle Crossing were crazy, but there was still a festive and electric energy in the air.

In the midst of all this was the Columbus Arts Ball, my personal favorite charity event.

It really was the height of Columbus society, our very own Academy Awards: everyone was dripping with diamonds and elegance, some even donning masks and costumes for the occasion. Many of us women spent weeks choosing our gowns and at least a whole day getting ready. The Columbus Arts Ball was such a decadent event, and everyone looked forward to it, me most of all.

I was particularly excited because the doctor had taken my cast off five days before the ball. To my surprise and delight, my wrist and arm looked normal. I had two areas of stitches from the arthroscopic surgery but there was hardly any swelling. I was alive, happy, and felt great. I was on the road to recovery, eager to get back to my life as a mom and my yoga and my team tennis. Honestly, I was even excited about doing normal everyday chores. Laundry, cooking, cleaning, brushing my hair, putting in my contacts, putting on clothes, tying my shoes—it was amazing how hard it had been to do even the simplest things. I was ready to be back to my old self.

On the morning of the masquerade ball, December 3rd, I woke up in a lot of pain. I'd had post-surgical pain over the past two months, but this was different. The pain was intense. That week I had gone into the surgeon's office three times to do physical rehab—there was a gal in his office who was a physical therapist for all his patients. I didn't care much for her personality, but at least I was doing what I was supposed to. But maybe I'd done too much too soon?

"Oliver," I said at the breakfast table that morning. "My arm is *killing* me."

"Take it easy today," he said. "Just rest. Maybe next week you should only do rehab once or twice."

I nodded, convinced he was right. *It's my own fault,* I thought to myself. *That's so like me, doing too much at once and then suffering the consequences.*

I spent the day leisurely getting ready for the ball, but every time I touched my arm, I was paralyzed by fiery pain. My gown grazed my arm as I stepped into it and I almost vomited. Still, I managed to slip it on with my left arm, then eased my feet into my black Louboutins.

"Pretty," Oliver said when I came down the stairs. I always melted a little when he told me I was beautiful.

"You're not so bad yourself," I said. It was true: in his Armani tuxedo and bow tie, he looked very dashing.

He extended his arm, and when I took it, I gasped.

"What is it? What's the matter?"

"Nothing," I said quickly. "It's just, wow, my arm hurts." I looked down as I said it.

We arrived at the ball half an hour later and Oliver immediately found his friends from the club. I saw Gigi across the room and waved. She smiled and hurried toward me.

"Willow! You look radiant!" She hugged me and it was all I could do not to scream, that's how much my arm hurt.

I saw Alice and various other friends. Amelia looked particularly stunning in her Colts-blue Vera Wang gown. I was so happy to see them, but every time someone came up to say "hi!" and hug me, I winced in agony. After a while I didn't want anybody to be near me, which wasn't like me at all. The whole point of the Columbus Arts Ball was to be with my friends and revel in the beauty of the evening. Everyone looked crazy good, elegant, and glamorous. *It's like playing dress-up,* I realized. *For one night we women get to feel like princesses, and our husbands are the princes showing off their gorgeous arm candy.* Because I'd always felt like an ugly, picked-on kid, I drank up any and every opportunity to feel beautiful.

Later that night, when the band really got going, Amelia and I were dancing like teenagers. Our husbands were off in a corner somewhere, talking about something we didn't have much interest in, so we took to the dance floor ourselves.

"Did you have a good time tonight, Willow?" Amelia shouted over the band.

"I did," I said. "Though I wish my arm didn't hurt so badly."

"I'm sorry. It's almost over and you will be back to normal soon. Then you will be pain-free, my dear."

I sighed. *I hope so,* I thought, and said to Amelia, "For one night we all get to pretend to be Cinderella, and I am so happy."

Amelia smiled and twirled me out onto the dance floor. My gown fluttered around my ankles like a halo of rose petals. Then Amelia twirled me back in close—and accidentally knocked into my arm.

"OOOOHH," I moaned, unable to stop myself. It was loud enough that the people dancing close to us gave a start. The pain was horrific. It felt like I'd been stabbed. I almost threw up.

"Oh, Willow!" Amelia cried. "I'm so sorry. That hurt your arm!"

"No no no," I said through gritted teeth. "You didn't do anything. It's fine."

But it wasn't fine. I immediately knew there was something very wrong.

Chapter 10

THE PAIN MONSTER

I woke up the morning of Sunday December 4th to intense, agonizing pain. Not only was the pain excruciating; the swelling was horrific. I was shocked. My forearm was red and sore and had tripled in size. I could no longer see my wrist bone. My arm looked like my thigh.

I kept packing ice on it but the swelling wouldn't go down.

"Oliver," I said. "I'm scared. Look at my arm."

He touched it lightly and I shrieked in pain. "Sorry," he said. "It's really swollen."

"Whoa," Wiles said, peering over Oliver's shoulder. "Mom. That's intense. You should call the doctor."

I wasn't typically one to call a doctor on the weekend. In fact, until that day, I had never called a doctor after hours, not once. I wasn't a complainer, and I was afraid I'd be accused of being weak or a baby. But that Sunday I had no choice but to call my surgeon. There was something really wrong.

I thought of going to the ER, but a little voice inside me said *No, Willow. DON'T BE DRAMATIC. Just call your doctor.*

I called his cell and left a message, waiting anxiously by my phone. He called me back shortly thereafter. I explained the level of pain and swelling. "I think I have to go to the emergency room. There's something really wrong with my arm."

"There's nothing wrong with your arm, Willow. You don't need to go to the ER. Everything's fine." He asked very few questions, but one question he seemed to get stuck on was: "How much have you iced it?"

"For the last two hours," I said.

"You over-iced it," he said matter-of-factly, like that explained everything. "Take off the ice and I'll see you the next time you're in the office. When's your next appointment with the PT?"

"Wednesday," I said.

"Just come in on Wednesday and I'll take a look."

I hung up the phone feeling confused. I had never heard of "over-icing" as something that would exacerbate an injury. *How am I going to make it to Wednesday?* I thought. The pain was gruesome.

"He said I over-iced it," I told Oliver. "I've never heard of anything like that."

My husband shrugged. "He's probably seen it a dozen times before."

Oliver was right. The surgeon was the expert, not me. So I did what the surgeon told me to do—I'd always been a rule follower—and took off the ice. All I wanted was to crawl in bed and hide from the pain, but I couldn't do that. It was Caroline's birthday lunch.

Caroline was one of my closest friends and I certainly didn't want to let her down. We'd met many years earlier when we were on the same committee at a charity event. After that we became really good friends because we were backdoor neighbors. Caroline lived one street away. Her son had always looked up to my kids, and sometimes our families vacationed together. Ironically, the doctor who had operated on my arm had been Caroline's doctor, too.

"I'll be back in a couple hours," I told my husband and kids, trying not to grimace as I grabbed a sling for my arm and walked out the door.

Driving to Caroline's birthday party was the longest, most agonizing drive of my life—and it was only three miles away. She was having a big birthday lunch at Mitchell's Steakhouse downtown. There were probably thirty to forty of us there. I had been looking forward to it, but by the time I arrived, I had broken out in a cold sweat. It took every ounce of energy I had not to scream from the constant pain shooting up my arm.

Everyone at the lunch who knew about my surgery was perplexed that I showed up in a sling. "I thought you got your cast off last week?" said Caroline, eyebrow raised.

I squeezed out some kind of reply. The truth was I was barely there. I hardly remember that afternoon because of the pain. I hated to disappoint Caroline, but I left as quickly as I could because I needed to get home and crawl into bed.

I stayed in bed for the next two days. I didn't want to, but the pain was so bad I could hardly move. Every time I got out of bed the agony tore up my arm like a jagged blade. *Wednesday,* I chanted silently in my head, over and over. *Wednesday. If I can just make it to Wednesday.*

On Tuesday I was starting to lose my mind. "Oliver, you've got to call my doctor," I said. "I've got to go in. I can't get out of bed."

"You're going in tomorrow," he said. "You'll see him then. It's only one more day, Willow."

"I can't wait. I can't wait, Oliver! I've never felt pain like this in my life." I started to sob. The pressure inside my head was mounting. *Call the doctor, don't call the doctor* was going round and round in my head. I was going nuts.

"Willow . . . they're waiting for you to come in tomorrow."

"Please, Oliver! I can't even pick up the phone. Please call for me. You have to call." Monster tears streamed down my face.

He called. "Can we come in today?" he asked belligerently.

"Fine," they said. "Just bring her in."

I was so grateful as he walked me out to the car. I could no longer drive, and I silently thanked God that Oliver was home that day to take me. I held my arm the whole ride, trying not to yelp every time the car lurched or hit a bump in the road.

At the doctor's office, they ushered us back to see the physical therapist. She took one look at my arm and said, "You're doing too many exercises. Don't do them for three days and come back." She seemed kind of annoyed and made me very uncomfortable, even ashamed. Like I was putting her out by being there.

Outside the door I could hear the surgeon. I knew he was in the office.

"Do you think maybe the doctor could come in and take a look?" I said, hating how tiny my voice sounded. I even looked down as I asked.

"He's busy," the PT huffed. She always had an attitude. "I'm just going to put it in a splint for you, and then you're going to let it rest for a few days. Think you can do that?"

I knew the doctor was just outside the door. He was maddeningly, tantalizing close; I could hear him joking with the girl at the reception desk. When I'd spoken with him on Sunday, he made it sound like he would see me when I came in for PT. But he was obviously busy—too busy for me.

I gasped in pain as the PT started in with the splint, but I acted like I was okay. "The exercises you've been doing have caused inflammation," she said. "That's the problem."

"But," I stammered, "you told me to do the exercises." She had given me a handout the first day giving me reps of different exercises to do for my wrist.

"I know," she snapped. "But you're doing them too much. So just stop doing them."

She left a few minutes later. I could hear her in the hall outside, speaking to the doctor. But he never came in to see me or examine my wrist. He was oblivious to the pain I was in.

"C'mon, Willow," Oliver said, touching me gently on the back. "Let's go."

I walked out of the office like a dog with a leash around my neck. I kept looking back over my shoulder, but Oliver was leading me onward. It felt like I was being tugged away, a little puppy straining on her choke collar and wanting nothing more than to go back. I'd received my orders—*stop exercising your arm, leave the office, go home*—but I desperately wanted to stay and beg the doctor to help me. *Please. The pain is too much. Something's wrong.*

I couldn't believe the agony I was in. I was afraid of it, the intensity, and I couldn't wrap my brain around the fact that the doctor wouldn't even look at my arm. *Too much rehab? Too much icing?* That just didn't make sense to me.

I knew I was incredibly strong, and I kept thinking to myself, *There is no way people could handle this level of pain.* I felt in my heart of hearts that something was wrong, but I was filled with doubt. They were telling me it was "normal," and surely they knew better than I. The question that gnawed at me and scared me most of all was: *What if the doctor and the PT are wrong?*

As Oliver started the car, I turned to face him in the passenger seat, willing back the tears I could feel building behind my eyes. "Maybe I should get a second opinion," I said quietly, my voice wavering. I was opening myself up to him, begging him to take my side.

"Willow!" Oliver's tone was angry. "You see more doctors than anybody I know. If there was something wrong with your arm, they would know."

My cheeks burned hot with shame. My self-esteem was at an all-time low, and now my husband thought I was being histrionic. *I'm so ashamed. Oliver's right: I don't need a second opinion. I need to get my act together. Why am I going to see so many doctors? Am I making this into a bigger deal than it is? Am I making this up?*

Oliver drove me home where I immediately crawled back into bed. At that point I stopped eating and drinking anything, including water, because I didn't want to have to get up to go to the bathroom. If I got out of bed to pee, it would mean I'd have to move, and moving was excruciating. Even a gentle breeze across my arm was like a punch in the gut. I had to hold my arm to keep it from moving, and since the swelling was so out of control, it felt like I was holding a brick.

For days I lay in bed shaking. I was mad at my body for shaking, because even that hurt indescribably. Over the next few days, the pain grew into a savage monster with razor-sharp teeth. I had never felt or imagined anything like it. I was no longer icing my arm or doing physical therapy and that hadn't changed a thing. I wasn't sleeping, wasn't eating. The pain was getting worse, not better. I was weary and sleeping in the guest room. I didn't want to keep Oliver up at night.

Again Oliver drove me to my surgeon's office, and this time, the doctor saw me. But he wasn't happy about it. He was defensive and curt, even a little bit angry.

"The surgery went fine," he snapped. "Everything is fine. The torn ligament has been repaired."

"Don't you want to check it?" I wailed. Even him touching my arm was unbearable. Every time he did, the monster flared up and bit down harder with his viciously sharp teeth.

"It's *fine*," the doctor said again, this time with an edge.

He didn't take an x-ray or a blood test. Instead he leaned back in his chair and looked at me with pity, like I was a bored Bullitt Park housewife making all this up.

"Willow." He let out a long, exaggerated sigh. "I want to talk to you about something psychological I think may be manifesting here. It's a syndrome called CRPS."

Chapter 11

TEN OUT OF TEN

I blinked at my doctor. "What's CRPS? I've never heard of that before."

He frowned, tapping his fingertips against the desk. "Complex Regional Pain Syndrome. It doesn't happen very often, but I think we have a special case here. CRPS is a syndrome in which your brain is telling whatever part of your body that's inflamed that there is pain and trauma there, when in reality there isn't."

I was silent for a moment, trying to parse what he was saying. Was my doctor telling me I was inventing the searing pain I felt? That it was all a figment of my imagination? But how could he explain the swelling in my arm? For goodness' sake—it looked like my thigh.

Oliver was sitting beside me, stone still. I turned to look at him and he shrugged, as if to say, *I don't know. Maybe we should listen to the guy.*

"It's not your arm," the doctor continued. "Everything is fine in your arm. Your brain is where it's getting screwed up. Your brain is essentially sending messages to your arm telling you that you're in pain. There's a fundamental disconnect. CRPS is often the reason patients develop chronic pain after an injury, surgery, or heart attack. Their brain is telling them there is pain because there's been a trauma."

I opened my mouth to rebuff what he was saying, but no words came out. I looked down at my arm. The evidence appeared to be staring me in the face: it was still grotesquely swollen and pink. I could feel the pain pulsing out from my wrist at that very moment, almost like a sonar sending out wave after wave of unimaginable torment.

But at the same time I was consumed by indefatigable doubt. My doctor was smart and capable. He'd probably dealt with this exact situation a hundred times before. *What do I know about syndromes and surgeries?* I thought. *Maybe my brain is responsible for telling me I'm in unbearable pain. But oh wow, is it doing a good job.*

My doctor looked at me closely. "I'm not saying the pain isn't real, Willow. The sensation of pain is very real. The brain is very good at bossing the rest of the body around. If it tells you you are feeling pain, you will absolutely feel pain. So we have to get your brain to stop sending these erroneous messages." He reached for a notepad on his desk. "I'm going to refer you to the pain management doctor downstairs," he said, scribbling a name on a piece of paper. "I'll call her to let her know you'll be making an appointment. She'll give you some medication to control the pain and swelling, and to help you calm down."

I felt a flicker of anger flare up inside me. *Help me calm down? Like I'm some sort of crazy twitchy female manufacturing drama for the sake of drama?* I quickly snuffed it out. I was still the same good girl I had always been. I was ready to accept what the doctor said without question—his word was law. After all, what did I know? He was the one with all the experience and expertise. I wanted to be the "good patient," not the whiny "problem patient" my doctor clearly thought I was.

"Thanks," I said. "I'll make an appointment."

***

A week later I was sitting in the pain management doctor's office. She was absolutely stunning. She looked more like a model than a medical doctor. She was also frank and knowledgeable, and I liked her immediately.

She sat down with me, clipboard in hand, and started asking questions and jotting down my answers.

"How bad is the pain, Willow? On a scale of one to ten."

"Ten out of ten," I said.

She grimaced. "I'm sorry to hear that. Are you taking any pain medication right now?"

"Twenty-four hours a day. And it doesn't touch the pain. Not even a dent."

"Uh huh." She nodded, as if this confirmed something. "I concur with your doctor's diagnosis—this looks like classic CRPS. But your CRPS is pretty severe, so we need to a do a ganglion block to get the swelling and pain levels down."

"A ganglion block?"

"Don't worry. We do administer intravenous sedation, but you're only out for a short time. Then we inject the local anesthesia in the sympathetic nerve tissue of the neck. That helps block the messages your brain is sending down into your body."

My heart sank at the thought of yet another surgery.

Don't you want to take a blood test first? I thought. *Or do an x-ray?* The words were on the tip of my tongue but I bit my lip to keep myself from saying them. She had diagnosed me by sight and by how much pain I told them I was in, and surely that was enough.

The doctor thumbed through her calendar. "When can we schedule the surgery? The sooner the better. Once we've done the block we can get your pain level down from ten to something more manageable."

I sighed.

"We've got a big family vacation planned," I said.

"When do you leave?"

"We'll be in the Bahamas for a week leading up to Christmas Eve. We're actually hosting my sister and her kids, so I feel like I kind of need to go." I didn't feel like I could cancel on them, certainly not at the last minute.

"Uh huh. Well, it sounds like you're in an awful lot of pain to put this off."

"I can manage. I'll just suffer through it," I said, resolute. It didn't matter how much pain I was in: If my family didn't go, then my sister's family couldn't go. I wasn't going to ruin the holiday for anyone—even if it nearly killed me.

"How soon can you get me in after Christmas?" I asked.

"December 27th," she said.

"Done."

I felt vaguely relieved, though the prospect of two more weeks of near constant torture made me sick to my stomach.

The doctor scrawled a prescription on her pad, ripped it off, and handed it to me.

I nodded and thanked her for her time, then went back upstairs to see my surgeon. "Good," he said. "Great. So we've got a solution in the works, and the right meds to tide you over." He scrutinized me closely. "You are going to be traveling, Willow. And with CRPS, anything that touches your arm is going to make it more painful."

"So how do I protect it?" I asked.

"I'm going to put a cast on it."

"Okay," I said, naively, like a sheep to the slaughter.

It wasn't until much later, when I did my own research on CRPS, that I discovered the absolute *worst* thing you can do is to put anything constricting on the area the pain is emanating from, because the nerves in that part of your body just become more and more inflamed.

But at the time I didn't know anything about CRPS. The doctor had diagnosed me with a syndrome, and I took his word as gospel. *This doctor is from Stanford*, I thought. *I'm going to do what he's telling me to do.*

Years later, I would find out I probably never had CRPS. Everything that was going on with my arm was screaming, "Infection! Infection!" Of course, once the bones in my arm were destroyed, it was impossible to tell if CRPS had even been a contender, and now we'll never know the truth. What we *do* know is that, in light of the signs and symptoms I was exhibiting, CRPS should never have been high on the list of possible causes.

But my doctor had already settled on a diagnosis. No diagnostic studies were ordered or performed—no x-rays, no blood work. He refused to acknowledge what was staring him right in the face.

Chapter 12

SOMETHING'S WRONG

"What a gorgeous day," my sister said. It was our last day in the Bahamas and we were sunbathing on our private beach. She was sipping some fruity tropical drink with "sunset" in the name, and I was drinking white wine. The beverages matched our magnificent surroundings perfectly, since we'd spent the last week feasting our eyes, hearts, and souls on some of the most breathtaking white beaches and sunsets we had ever seen.

"This is paradise," my sister said. "Truly. Can you imagine if we were back in Lake Forest right now? Shivering in our winter coats and snow boots?"

I nodded, but I felt envy pour over me like the island sunshine, only it didn't feel warm, it felt cold and clammy. We were in one of the most ravishing places in the world, and I was utterly miserable. *Was I crazy to think I could suffer through this?* I thought. I was trying so hard to make everyone think I was okay so they didn't think I was being histrionic, but the pain was blinding.

"Don't you like your wine, Willow?" my sister asked.

"Mmm hmm," I said, blinking back tears. I wanted so much to enjoy this, but the week had passed in a blurry haze. Every step I took, every time anyone even brushed past me, tendrils of pain ripped through my arm, often enough to make me gasp aloud.

We flew back to Miami on Christmas Eve. On Christmas morning, my kids opened their presents. I sat on the sofa with my cast above my head in my robe, smiling as much as I could. By mid-afternoon, after the presents were put away, the wrapping paper was in the recycling bin, and the dishes were done, we were all on each other's nerves.

Maybe we're just all under a lot of pressure, I thought, as the anger and frustration in the house rose. Bella and Wiles were fighting, saying nasty things to each other with increasing hostility. *They're just playing,* I told myself. But as the day wore on, the screams escalated into physical altercations. I tried to intervene, to calm down their flaring tempers. But if I'd been hotheaded as a teenager, Bella was even more so. I heard them yelling in the kitchen, and when I ran up the two steps from the living room, I found Wiles in the corner, crying. He was rubbing a mark on his arm where his sister had pinched him hard enough to break the skin.

"Bella Adair!"

She scowled up at me. "What?"

"What do you say to your brother?"

"God, Mom! Why are you always on my case? You're always breathing down my neck. This family is a total joke. You want me to say I'm sorry? Well, I'm not! I'm not sorry. Wiles is an idiot. And so are you!"

She flew past me in a rage, and when I tried to catch her arm, she shoved me with such force that I stumbled down the two steps into the living room. I crashed against the wall and sank down onto the floor, pain searing up my arm. I gasped. I couldn't catch my breath, it hurt so much.

"Bella! BELLA!"

She didn't apologize. She stormed out of the house, her long blond hair whirling around her shoulders as she slammed the door behind her.

"Mom? Mom, are you okay?" My son's voice was wobbly and scared.

"I'm okay, Wiles," I said. "Mommy's going to need a few minutes, okay, sweetheart?"

I went into my bathroom and locked the door. I was shaking, trembling, crying. I stood in that bathroom, the sun reflecting off the mirror, the deep blue Atlantic Ocean undulating behind me. I stood and simply stared into the glass as the tears streamed down my cheeks. I took deep, steady breaths, looking into my own eyes as my eyes looked back at me. I was struck by how much my eyes look like a child's. They looked so young—not happy, more like a sleepy kid on Christmas morning after all the presents have been opened. They looked majestically sad.

I held my own gaze. Slowly, the tears stopped flowing. My mouth tightened as I continued to stare. It was amazing, watching the pity and sadness melt away, replaced by a newfound sense of empowerment.

I called American Airlines and on Christmas Day, I got on a plane and flew back to Columbus alone.

I'm going to take care of myself for once, I thought. *I spend all my time and energy taking care of other people, so this time I'm going to help myself by getting my arm taken care of. And fortunately, I've got a whole team of experts looking out for me.*

Unfortunately, they weren't so expert after all.

I texted Frenny as I took off and said, "I am on my way back to Columbus."

Frenny, short for Francesca, was a friend through the kids' school— her two daughters also attended Wellington, and her oldest, Lucia, was best friends with Bella. Her younger daughter, Daniela, was closer to Wiles's age. But Francesca and I were in vastly different social circles, and Frenny often felt out of place. She felt uncomfortable with my friends, so we had our own relationship outside of my friend group. From our very first conversation, I thought, "I really like this girl." She was the most selfless human being I'd ever met.

I was constantly reminding Francesca what a good person she was, how kind and generous, and how just because someone has money and things doesn't mean they're better or more important. Frenny loved me in a way that humbled and amazed me—she wanted to be by my side, to care for me and protect me.

And she knew enough of my family dynamics to know that I needed a lot of support at home.

My phone buzzed. It was a text from Frenny. "Breaks my heart. . . Can't imagine how scared you are. . . You're always in my prayers, sweetie. I'll be here when you get back. I love you." I could hear Frenny's voice in my head saying these words, her rich Peruvian accent turning them into a dulcet lullaby.

I put my phone back in my purse and wiped the uncried tears from my eyes. *I am strong. I can do this. I am worth more than what I've been settling for, and I will take care of myself.* In just a few hours, I would be home.

***

The first surgery was on December 27th as planned. The pain management doctor put a nerve block in my neck to stop the signal surging from my head to my arm. It's complicated surgery, because if they miss the spot in your neck—if they are even a millimeter off—you can be paralyzed for life. Because of the liability issues, I'd basically had to sign my life away. But it felt like I had no choice. They never said, "This is optional for you." For them it was just what you did for CRPS. Hindsight is 20/20, of course, and within a few months I'd understand the surgery had been a complete and total waste.

My husband and kids stayed in Miami for six more days, so I was by myself in our home, recovering from surgery. Most of my friends were out of town for Christmas but the few friends that were in Bexley came to help me. My friends were becoming a gigantic part of my life; I depended more and more on their nurturing presence.

But every day I awoke to a horrible truth: the surgery hadn't worked. The pain was as bad as it had ever been, if not worse. It felt like my arm had been cut open and flayed from the inside. Something was very wrong.

Frenny came over to stay with me. She held me while I wept, careful not to touch my arm. At one point I begged her to call my doctor and put him on speakerphone. "They can't do another surgery yet, Willow," he growled. "They can't do two ganglion blocks too close together. You'll have to wait a few days." We scheduled the second surgery for December 30th. By the time they did my second block, my husband and kids were home.

The second block took some of the swelling down, but not the pain. Even so, the doctors were high-fiving each other. "Nailed it! The block made the swelling go down. See, Willow? It *was* CRPS." It was almost like they were trying to convince me. And I was their guppy. I was so terribly willing to be convinced. And I didn't mention the pain.

I'm not a doctor, I reminded myself. *I've never heard of CRPS in my entire life. I've never had wrist surgery in my entire life, either.*

But hadn't my doctor promised me I'd be doing yoga by Christmas? And here we were, the week after Christmas, and I was nowhere close to doing yoga. I couldn't even pick up my mat.

What was going on?

After that second surgery, the beautiful pain management doctor came into my room. The surgery was outpatient, so I was slated to leave later that day. "What does your doctor want to do about your cast?" she asked me. "Does he want you to keep it on or take it off?"

"He told me to ask you that very question."

"What?" Her jaw dropped. What she said next was something I'd never forget. "He's your doctor. Why would I know anything about taking your cast off or not?"

Red flags were going up all around me, but I was too trusting to see and too afraid to ask.

***

On New Year's Eve, my phone rang. It was Cece Miller, my lovely friend, the one who had been at the Cleveland Clinic the same time I was.

"I'm about to have a dinner party for six couples," Cece said. "And I'm just down the street. Why don't you come over before the party? Put some sweats on, get out of bed, and get over here, because one of my best friends from high school is a wrist surgeon in Cleveland."

Cece knew I'd been struggling, that my plans for NYE mostly consisted of staying at home and lying motionless in bed so as not to disturb my arm. But she also knew the ganglion blocks hadn't done anything to diminish the pain, and that my doctor thought he'd "healed" me.

"Thank you, Cece," I said, immensely grateful she had called. "I'm going to try and get out of bed so I can come over. I really need somebody else to look at my arm."

Half an hour later we were in Cece's living room with the doctor, this sweet man from Cleveland. He was probably in his late sixties, and he was looking at my arm very intensely.

And I mean really *looking* at it. It was not like he glanced at it and went back to the party. I was touched by how gently he went about it, and by how thorough he was. Twenty minutes passed, then thirty. When he was done looking, he sketched out a drawing and wrote down a list of possible things it could be.

None of them were CRPS. "I know your doctor," he said. "He's certainly very reputable. I will email him when I get home tonight and suggest, in a respectful way, that this might not be as cut and dried as he thinks." He cleared his throat. "I certainly don't want to step on his toes. You're his patient, not mine. But I will tell him what I think in a polite and straightforward way."

He stroked his beard, contemplating what he was about to say. "I guess it's *possible* you could have CRPS with an infection. That's certainly one possibility. But he'll take an x-ray, he'll do a blood test." He was very nonchalant about it. "Don't worry, Willow. I'm sure he'll do the right thing."

I thanked the doctor profusely for his kind and gentle insight and left the party.

Two days later, on January 2nd, I got a call from my surgeon's assistant. She was snippy and said, in a very cold tone, "The doctor got an email from a surgeon in Cleveland on New Year's Day."

Uh oh, I thought. *I'm in trouble.* I immediately felt like I'd done something wrong. *I shouldn't have gone to see another doctor. I must have crossed some kind of patient-doctor line.*

I saw my doctor the next day. When I walked into his office, he was sitting behind his desk, arms crossed over his chest. I felt like I'd been sent to the principal's office.

"I got an email from one of my colleagues," he snapped. "Why did you go to see him?"

"I didn't go to see him." I was so nervous I was almost stuttering. "He's a friend of a friend, and we were at the same party." I backtracked, worried that if my doctor knew I'd been out socializing, he would think I'd been exaggerating about how much it hurt. "I wasn't there for the party," I said quickly. "I just went over there before the party and he took a look at my arm."

"There is nothing wrong with your arm, Willow," my doctor said, in a tone that brooked no objections. "Show it to me."

With hesitation, I extended my arm. He seemed so hostile I was afraid he would be rough, and the thought of the staggering pain I would feel if he jerked my arm was unendurable.

Instead he glowered and pointed to the wound on my wrist. "Why didn't you tell me this was open?"

"Well," I stammered, "it's *been* open."

Because they'd done the surgery arthroscopically, there were two surgical openings in my wrist. One of them had never closed. It was now January. Again, this should have been a huge red flag for the professionals treating me, but not really a red flag *for me*. I didn't know what to look for or what was normal. I assumed my doctor would be the one doing that.

"And you didn't think to tell me?" he boomed.

Once again I felt like I was being shamed. "But it's been open for a while," I repeated, my voice barely above a whisper. "I thought you'd seen it?" *I know he has*, I seethed in my head. He was lying and I was beginning to see it.

"This is unacceptable. We're going to cauterize it," he said gruffly. "It must be open from the cast rubbing against it."

What cast? I thought. *That cast has been off for a week.*

He burned the wound shut and sent me home. I was out of his hair, out of his office, and out of his way.

And I was in the worst pain of my life.

Chapter 13

OUT OF SIGHT, OUT OF MIND

"That's good, Willow. Just relax. Take it nice and easy. I'm going to send a jolt of electricity through your arm now, okay? You got this. Piece of cake." Stuart smiled at me as he connected my arm to the machine.

"It hurts," I said, my voice quavering. "Oh God, it hurts so bad."

"I know it does. But you're doing great. You know you're my star pupil?" He smiled again as the spike of electricity scissored through my arm. The pain was violent. Tears streamed down my face and I didn't try to stop them. I was grateful to Stuart for never judging me or telling me to "buck up." He was gentle and kind in an environment where most people were neither.

My doctor had sent me away. He no longer wanted me to do physical rehab in his office with his PT. He sent me down to a different physical therapist at Columbus Community Hospital, the public hospital, instead.

But my doctor wanted me out of his office. He didn't want to see the problem or deal with my "issues" anymore. *Out of sight, out of mind.* "I'm going to send you to a surgical rehab therapist at Columbus Community," he'd told me, before waving me out of his office. "His name is Stuart. He specializes in CRPS."

For three months, I went to see Stuart every single day, not on weekends. I couldn't drive. I mean, I *could,* but my casts were dangerous—there was always the chance they might get caught in the steering wheel. It wasn't safe for the other drivers on the road. So my friends would take me—Alice, Gigi, Amelia, Nicole, and Frenny. And when Oliver was in town and could take time off work, he would take me.

My friends were overwhelmingly devoted. They were never impatient or angry; they would sit beside me and wait, sometimes rubbing my back to console me.

My friends had a knack for giving me the most appropriate Bible verses when they knew I was running out of steam. Alice read Philippians 4:6: "Do not worry about anything, but pray and ask God for everything you need, always giving thanks."

But some days it truly felt like God had forsaken me. The pain was indescribable and unrelenting. I really didn't know what to do, how to function.

Stuart was the only thing I looked forward to during those visits—his jolly demeanor, his gentle touch. Because I saw him every day for three months, we became very close.

One day, while I was in the waiting room with Frenny, my phone rang. It was Wiles.

"Hi, honey. You okay?" Every time one of my kids called, I was gripped by fear that they were hurt, that something bad had happened.

"I'm fine, Mom. It's just, I'm still at school and . . . nobody's here."

I bolted up and wheeled around to look at the clock in the waiting room. Guilt shot through my heart like an arrow.

"What is it, Willow?" Frenny said, alarmed. "What's wrong?

It was after four p.m. Wiles was still waiting in the carpool line—all his friends had been picked up, shunted off to soccer practice and homework and warm, home-cooked meals around the family dinner table. I had completely forgotten to get him a ride.

"I'm so sorry, Wiles," I said. "Just go inside the athletic center and wait, okay? I'm going to call someone to get you right away." I was getting choked up but didn't want Wiles to hear it. I hung up quickly, then promptly burst into tears.

"Willow, sweetie, it's okay," Frenny said. "It happens."

"I feel awful," I said, thoroughly ashamed. "I've been so oblivious." My hands shook as I reached for my phone. I knew any number of my friends would pick Wiles up in a heartbeat—I was very fortunate that way. But it made my heart sick, the thought that Wiles might feel abandoned or neglected. I knew all too well what that felt like.

Back in physical therapy, Stuart encouraged me to keep at it. "We have to keep working," he said. "Don't get discouraged. The thing about CRPS is, your arm can freeze after six months. And we don't want that. So we have to work it really hard."

Stuart's touch was light and he was always as gentle as possible, but he still had to pull my arm in every which direction, which often made me cry out in pain. The electricity was only one part of treatment: he had to physically pull on my arm to make sure it wouldn't freeze.

"How's the cast?" he asked.

"It's awful," I answered honestly.

"I know it hurts, but it really is helping. I promise."

Every time I cranked the pressure knob on my cast, it cranked up the pain, too. The cast itself was quite a contraption—I had all sorts of accoutrements poking out of my arm, little metal knobs sprouting out of the holes from the original surgery. My friends, always trying to make me laugh and keep my spirits up, told me I looked like a Rube Goldberg machine. "A very cute one," Caroline added.

"Cute" was the last thing I felt. The ordeal had started to have deleterious effects on my physical appearance. With the stress and the pain and the constant doctors' appointments, there was no way I could cook, and I had started to shed pounds. I was very underweight—and not in a good, sexy, "look at those toothpick-skinny models" kind of way. I wasn't working out and I was way too thin. Worst of all: my hair was thinning. Every time I looked at myself in the mirror I felt red hot fear. My hair thinning felt like a bona fide trauma. I had always taken such pride in my hair—it was an identifying characteristic. My friends always commented on my blond tresses and my hair stylist, Liam, loved running his fingers through it. "You've got the most beautiful hair," he would tell me. Now it was thinning, and the notion of losing my hair was unthinkable.

After three months, the hole in my arm kept opening up. The surgical site had still not closed up—a clear sign of infection, though I didn't know that yet.

My doctor should have seen it during our checkups, but it was clear he couldn't be bothered by me anymore. He ushered me out of his office as quickly as possible every time. *Out of sight, out of mind.*

Unfortunately, my arm was only getting worse. And no one would listen. I was like Cassandra in the Greek myth, chanting so loud—screaming, even—but no one could hear me. No one even looked up.

Chapter 14

GAME OVER

I t had been four months since my surgery and the wound in my arm kept
opening. When a long piece of metal and plastic sprouted out of that opening
in my arm, I knew I had to call my doctor. Surely this was an ominous sign.

I took a picture of the metal piece that had emerged—small and silver—
and emailed it to my doctor. "This came out of my arm," I said.

He fired off an almost instantaneous reply. "How do I know that came
out of your arm? You could have just taken a picture of something else."

I couldn't believe it. Was he serious? Was he mocking me? Or did he
honestly think I would make something like that up?

Though my gut reaction was anger, it was quickly replaced by corrosive
and sweeping shame. *Oh my god,* I thought, reading his email over and over. *Is
he right? Am I making this up?*

It took me two weeks to tell Oliver what he had said, that's how ashamed
I felt. We were sitting across from each other at the kitchen table when I finally
read my husband the email. Wiles had gone upstairs to do his homework so it

was just the two of us. The silence was so vast and empty, it felt like it could swallow me whole.

Oliver let out a long, exasperated sigh. "You see a doctor almost every day, Willow. If there was something wrong, they would know something was wrong."

"I love Stuart," I said, "but he's not a doctor, Oliver. He's a physical therapist."

"But you go in every few weeks for a checkup with your doctor. He's an expert. He probably sent that email because he's frustrated that you don't trust his expertise."

"There's something wrong here, Oliver. The pain is horrific. I cry in rehab every day and my wrist isn't getting any better."

He held my gaze. "I don't know what to tell you. You're seeing one of the best surgeons in the city, if not the country. He could have used more tact in his email, sure. But the guy's perspicacious. He's no idiot."

I nodded. *Oliver's right. I'm making a big deal out of nothing. What do I know?*

I tried to keep Oliver's words in mind when I went in for my next checkup. But another piece of the metal and plastic had come out of my arm, and I felt a flicker of vindication when the doctor examined the wound and saw that, no, I hadn't Photoshopped a fake picture.

"This is anomalous, Willow," he said, that same tight edge in his voice. "Everything about your case seems to be anomalous." He shook his head. "We're going to burn the surgical site shut again."

I was demure and accommodating, determined to be the "star pupil" for my doctor, too. "Okay. If you think that's best."

"Of course I think it's best," he said, vainglorious as ever.

I couldn't tell the doctor what to do. I was just the patient. I wanted to trust him and heed his medical advice. And if he felt we needed to burn the surgical site shut again, that's what we would do.

I must be crazy, I thought. *It's all in my head.* I questioned my own integrity, furious at myself for not trusting the people who clearly knew more than I did. I believed everybody but myself.

***

In March of 2012, the pain was bad enough that I called Cece Miller. "Can I have the phone number of your doctor friend in Cleveland? I think I need to pay him a visit."

"Sure, honey. Whatever you need."

I was in Miami on Spring Break with Bella at the time. Oliver and Wiles had already gone back to Columbus, so it was just the two of us. Bella had a longer Spring Break and I was happy getting some more time in Miami. Miami made everything seem better, even the pain. I took Bella out for dinner that night and for once she didn't push the food around on her plate and claim she wasn't hungry. She ordered a big salad—as did I—but we also splurged and got a plate of Parmesan cheese fries. I was relieved. Having struggled with an eating disorder of my own, I worried Bella might also be anorexic. It made me happy to see her devour every bite.

I picked up a parmesan cheese fry in my left arm and nibbled on it, heartsick over what I was about to say.

"I've got to go back to Columbus, Bella," I said. "I can't take the discomfort in my arm anymore."

She said nothing but her eyes were wide. Bella didn't often let her fear show through—she liked to put up a tough front—but I could see it in her eyes. She was tired of it. I was her mom: I was supposed to be strong and competent and okay. But there was always something wrong with me.

"Okay," she said. "I understand."

I felt horrible. *I never had a mom who was sick*, I thought. *I can't imagine how hard it must be for my kids*. But I was immensely grateful for Bella's understanding.

I managed to schedule an appointment with the doctor in Cleveland, and we flew back to Columbus the next morning. Oliver drove me to the doctor's office that very afternoon.

"Good to see you again, Willow," the doctor said. "How're you doing? How's your wrist?"

"It hurts so bad. It's not better. Five months and it's still not better."

"Oh, well—looks like you don't have much movement. But you know, I'm sure your doctor did a good job. Let's just take an x-ray and have a look at it."

I went out and took the x-ray, then came back in and sat on the examination table. The doctor was in a genial mood—he made chit-chat with Oliver while we waited for the nurse to come back with the x-ray. A few minutes later, she rapped lightly on the door.

"Here's the x-ray," she said.

"Thanks."

The minute he looked at the x-ray, the jocular grin vanished from his face. The doctor turned a shade paler. I saw beads of sweat break out on his forehead as he started to pace around the room.

I was still sitting on the examination table, unable to see the x-ray for myself. I stared at Oliver as paralyzing fear crept up my spine. I tried to communicate with my eyes. *What's he looking at? What's wrong?*

"I have bad news," the doctor said. He cleared his throat again. "Did your doctor at any point in the last five months take an x-ray?"

"No. I don't think so."

"I need you to be absolutely sure about this, Willow. Did the doctor at any point take a blood test?"

"No. He didn't." I stammered. I was trying to remain calm.

The doctor looked me straight in the eye. "You did not have CRPS. I believe you have an infection. Your wrist is destroyed. You have no cartilage. Your bones have all broken and dropped into a pile, which partially fused your wrist. This is why you can't move it." He started to point to a mass on the x-ray.

I was speechless. I felt like I had been shredded, decimated, completely destroyed. I tried to catch Oliver's gaze but he wouldn't look at me.

The doctor sketched out two separate drawings on his notepad. "This is the worst-case scenario," he said, "and this is what we have right now. Probably your wrist will go somewhere in between what it is now and the worst-case scenario. But the worst-case scenario is a full wrist fusion."

"What does that mean?" Oliver asked. I still couldn't speak.

"Once we fully fuse your wrist, Willow, it will never be the same. There's no going back. You can never replace that part of your body. See, you have so many functions in your wrist, so much movement we take for granted. Once we fuse it, you won't have any movement at all. You won't be able to pronate or supinate, and you won't be able to move it from side to side. That's why we don't like to fuse people's arms, especially young, active patients like yourself."

The doctor took a deep breath. "That's why it's the worst-case scenario. Because once you do that, well—it's pretty much game over."

Chapter 15

TRAUMATIZED

The rest of the meeting with the doctor passed in an incomprehensible blur. He said many things, but I couldn't hear any of it. His dark words circled through my mind with the somber, deadly finality of a funeral hymn.

Your wrist is destroyed. You have no cartilage. Your bones are all broken.

I was in shock. For months I had been suffering from a horrible infection that was eating away at my healthy wrist. Discovering the truth felt like a kick to the gut. No—it was far worse than that. It was confirmation that I'd been right all along. I wasn't inventing my pain. I had never had CRPS. Every day for *months* I had been brought to my knees by a very real infection that had, bit by bit, obliterated my arm.

And what had my doctor done? Sat idly by and watched it all happen. He had prescribed ridiculous casts and a daily regimen of excruciating physical therapy for a condition that didn't exist. Meanwhile, each of his "solutions" was in fact breaking every single bone in my wrist, one by one. My arm was shattered, reduced to an elephant graveyard of completely wasted tissue. I couldn't even pick up a paper clip.

My doctor, I thought, the epiphany roiling in my mind. *My doctor did this to me.* But my anger was vague and tenuous, not yet fully formed. The stunned disbelief hadn't given way to rage. I was still too traumatized.

"We need to get the infection out. Willow? Willow, are you listening?"

The surgeon's voice jolted me out of my reverie. "I'm sorry. What did you say?"

"This is serious. I would like to do the surgery tomorrow. We need to get the infection out immediately."

"Uh, what?" I asked, dazed. "Tomorrow?"

"We'll do the surgery at two o'clock."

But it was parent weekend at Bella's school in three days. I was supposed to be on a plane to Andover to see my daughter. *What about Bella? What if I can't go to parent weekend? I've already missed so many . . .*

The question turned over and over in my mind, gnawing at my guilt and sense of obligation. *What about Bella?*

***

Oliver and Wiles came with me to the hospital the next day. My family crowded around my bedside before the nurses wheeled me into the operating room.

"Mom?" I looked at Wiles's face, so close to mine. His eyes were wide and shining with unmasked fear. "Is this the last surgery you're going to need?"

I held out my left hand, clasped my fingers around his. "Yes, Wiles. I hope so. I'm praying this will be the last one." But I knew it wouldn't. This was just to dig out the infection.

"It know it hurts so bad," he said, his lower lip trembling. "I just want it not to hurt anymore."

He was only eleven, far too young to see his mother in incessant pain. I hated that for him.

My new doctor, the surgeon from Cleveland, poked his head in the door. He greeted Oliver and introduced himself to Wiles before turning his full attention to me. "I want to brief you on what's going to happen next, Willow." He looked warily at Wiles. "You want to step outside, son? Or are you okay to hear this?"

Wiles nodded fiercely. "I want to stay with my mom."

"Okay then." The surgeon looked at me. "We're going to cut open your arm and dig out as much of the infection as we can. Now, mind you, this is not an outpatient surgery. You'll be in the hospital for a day or two, and you'll meet the infectious disease doctor, and then we're going to put a PICC line in your right arm."

The infectious disease doctor? I swallowed hard. "A PICC?"

"That's right. P-I-C-C: peripherally inserted central catheter. It's a form of intravenous access that we can use for a prolonged period of time. You won't be under anesthesia when we put in the PICC, but don't worry—it'll hardly hurt more than a pinch."

It was happening again: the words he was saying no longer seemed to be coming out of his mouth. They were dissociated, coming at me from all sides. I was terrified. *A PICC in my arm? No anesthesia?* I couldn't help it—I started sobbing. My poor son watched in horrified silence. He was trembling from head to toe.

The doctor cleared his throat. "Oliver? Maybe you want to be there with your wife when they put in the line."

"Yes. All right." Oliver nodded, looking from Wiles back to me back to Wiles again. He wasn't sure where he was needed most—with me, his scared wife, or with Wiles, his scared son. And then there was Bella's parent weekend looming on the horizon.

"Let's get you ready to go," the doctor said, waving the anesthesiologist in to administer the general anesthesia. I started to fade out of consciousness as the doctor made a good show of telling my son the surgery was no big deal.

"The anesthesia won't take but a minute," the doctor chuckled. "She won't even feel a . . ."

Blackness fell.

***

Infectious disease doctor. The name alone was frightening. I didn't even know they existed until I needed one.

When he came to see me at ten o'clock that night, the doctor explained to me that I had a bone infection called osteomyelitis, an infection that was very difficult to get rid of. The massive antibiotics were necessary, and there was no other way to get them into my body than to insert a PICC line. I was so frightened by the PICC line, I begged for oral antibiotics. He kind of laughed when I made my plea.

"Can't I just stay on them longer?" I begged. "*Please?*"

"Mrs. Adair, this infection is serious and dangerous. I am trying to save your arm." He cleared his voice and spoke very clearly. "I trust you'll let me do my job."

Case closed. I sat back and tried to digest the beginning of the end. *Oh my God*, was all I could think. *Oh My GOD.*

Chapter 16

THE PICC LINE

"Help me," I texted Oliver. "Help me, please."

Silence. No response.

I hadn't really expected one. For days I'd sent him texts like these, unabashed and pitiful cries for help. The subtext of every message was: *Help me. Find someone to help me.*

And there *was* someone, in a manner of speaking. After being in the hospital for two days after my latest surgery, I had a home healthcare nurse come to our house each day for thirty days. Every morning she hooked up the PICC line to the World War Three antibiotics. It took two to three hours for the intravenous drip to be completed. By the time it was done, I was exhausted. Some days I threw up my guts afterward. The antibiotics were strong.

"You okay, Mrs. Adair?" she said, smiling in her broken English. "You good?"

"Yes, thank you," I said. "I'm fine."

In reality I was scared to death.

Soon the nightmare will be over, I thought. *For all of us.* My poor husband and kids were forced to weather my tumultuous moods. I was often crabby and difficult, trying desperately to care for them and feed them, but my fuse was so short. I felt hopelessly limited in every area. I couldn't cut cheese or bread, couldn't chop vegetables. I couldn't carry a pot of water to boil pasta for dinner. I couldn't even open a water bottle.

Bella was in boarding school in Massachusetts and since I couldn't go see her, my husband was up there a good deal when he wasn't traveling for work. The PICC line and I were not friends. I couldn't get used to it or feel comfortable with this live wire dangling out of my arm and threaded to my heart. The thirty days stretched on for what seemed like an eternity.

The fear was horrific. It slipped over me like a shadow, a grim reaper flooding my heart with terror and worst-case scenarios. I was afraid of deep vein thrombosis and blood clots, both of which the doctor had informed me could be caused by PICC lines. I'd already had two run-ins with blood clots and I knew how deadly they could be. I was constantly afraid of death, paralyzed by the thought that I might not wake up in the morning, terrified I would never see my children's faces again.

Amelia called, her voice flowing over the speaker like soothing honey. "Do you want to go out for lunch, Willow? I'll take you somewhere nice. Anywhere you want to go."

"I can't," I said softly. "I'm so sorry." I had tried not to be around people since the surgery. I felt overstimulated around groups, loud noises, even TV shows—it all made me extremely uncomfortable. And I was terrified of being in close proximity to people in the event that someone accidentally knocked into my arm. Plus, I felt ashamed. I had relied on my friends for so many months. I wanted to just hide, crawl away, and disappear. *I'm asking them for too much*, I thought. *Be strong. And if you can't, then hide away.*

Still, my friends were persistent. They loved me too much to let me wither away alone in my house and sometimes I didn't have the strength to fight them. Once Caroline came over in the middle of the day and wouldn't leave until I agreed to go out to lunch with her.

"I'm taking you to Lindey's," she said, arms folded staunchly over her chest. "And there's nothing you can do about it."

"But, but I—"

"Nope," she said. "Put a nice shirt on and grab your bag, because lunch is not optional today. This is an intervention."

I couldn't conceal a smile. Beneath my shame I was deeply grateful. And Lindey's was our place—the dim lights, the beautiful presentation of food on every plate, the gentle piano music drifting in from the lobby, and our ever-attentive waiter in his sharp black apron. Even the lemon wheel in my water glass felt like a tiny touch of luxury I had sorely needed.

"See? Isn't this nice?" Caroline said. She started to reach across the table to give my hand a squeeze, then quickly caught herself.

A few days after my lunch with Caroline, Simi dropped by my house. The late morning sun drenched her fabulous blond hair as she stood on my front porch. I'd met Simi years before on Halloween, when Bella was two years old and I was expecting Wiles. Simi was out trick-or-treating in the neighborhood with her children who were both babies at the time. We lived a stone's throw away from one another and became instant friends.

This was one of the most magical things about living in the cozy neighborhood of Bullitt Park: I lived within easy walking distance of so many of my friends. I was literally surrounded by them. Alice lived across the street from me, one house down, and Simi lived next door to Alice. Behind me, through the alley, was Caroline, two houses down. Gigi lived three streets south but on my same block, and Amelia lived one block south of her. Grace was slightly farther afield—a three-minute drive—but I was still encircled by the women I held most dear. It was like a halo of love surrounding me, even in the dark days when I could not open myself up to receive it.

The thing I loved most about Simi was her honesty. She didn't play the games some women had a penchant for—she was frank and forthright and never sugar-coated anything. She was down-to-earth and real, and she let me be real, too. Every morning she would drop my favorite Starbucks drink off and send me a text.

But like all my friends, she was desperately trying to get me out of the house. And she, too, wouldn't take no for an answer when I tried to beg out of going to lunch.

"In the car you go, Willow," Simi said. "Trust me: this will be good for you."

She took me to G Michael's, a cute little Italian bistro, and asked me about the PICC line that flowed directly out of my heart, dripping down from my upper arm almost to my thigh. I was deeply ashamed of it. Whenever I left the house, I would wrap it around my arm and then put a "sleeve" on to hide it. The sleeve was a very long sock I'd cut for exactly that purpose.

"Oh my gosh," Simi said, when I peeled back the sleeve and showed the PICC line to her. "That must be so frightening."

"It's terrifying," I answered honestly.

"I can't believe how badly the docs butchered the surgery," Simi said, shaking her head. "It's truly unfathomable. It was supposed to be a routine procedure!"

She was speaking aloud the internal monologue that had been running through my head for months. "Exactly," I said. "That's exactly how I feel. I'm angry and hurt. I feel furious that the life I loved has been taken away from me."

"Thanks for being honest with me," she said.

"Thanks for bringing me here," I replied. "You're right: I needed to get out."

"Willow." She looked at me with great compassion "*This is what friends do.*" She was right, but I hadn't fully digested the message.

When my friend Nicole had her hysterectomy, it propelled me beyond my fear—and out of the house. Nicole was also in my circle or "halo" of friends—her house was two blocks south and one block west of mine. I was still afraid to be seen in such a pitiful state, but now one of my friends needed me. And when a friend needed me, I heeded the call.

Nicole was a newer friend. We had met at a birthday party where we were seated next to each other and just hit it off. Nicole was an easy friend, always up for anything. I wasn't so relaxed in life: I was someone who wasn't always up for anything, so Nicole fascinated me.

But now Nicole was trapped like I was. She was stuck at home recovering from her surgery, so I pulled on my sock sleeve and walked over to see her every day.

It was March in Bullitt Park and the flowers were blooming, the air fragrant and sweet. The days were balmy and not too warm, and I relished the simple joys of walking down the sidewalk, surrounded by charming homes. This was a neighborhood I loved. Gardens overflowed with newly planted tulips and pansies and begonias, the fecund smell of earth enriching the air I breathed.

Once I arrived at Nicole's, I rang the bell—with my left arm—and her mother answered, happy to usher me inside. Nicole's mom had come to stay with her for two weeks, so although she was suffering, at least she had her mom by her side. Nicole was very close to her family: her house was full of pictures of her children, her parents, her sister, and even her friends. On my way upstairs to her bedroom, I glanced at the dozens of framed photographs displayed on the shelves and the smooth lacquered surface of the Baby Grand piano. I could practically feel the love radiating off Nicole's family.

"Willow!" Nicole cried when I walked into her bedroom. She was propped up on pillows and her wan face brightened when she saw me. "You are too good to me. Fifth day in a row!"

"I'll be here every day, Nicole," I said. "I told you: you can't get rid of me."

"I'll never forget this, Willow. It's so awful to be stuck here, trapped in my own house."

"I know exactly what you mean."

I kissed her on the cheek before leaving. "I'll be back tomorrow," I said, and her sweet mom walked me to the door.

It was good for me to see Nicole. My daily walks helped me self-soothe. Even if I wasn't able to "work out" because I couldn't get my heart rate up with the PICC line, I could walk slowly around the neighborhood. But I was still ashamed of the IV. I would never have left my house if not for the "sock sleeve" I'd fashioned. I still wanted to hide the PICC line at all costs.

***

As I shuffled around the house, lonely and despondent, alienating myself from my friends, I constantly replayed the last six months. I couldn't fully wrap my brain around what had happened, the fact that I had been so grossly misdiagnosed. I was desperately trying to understand what had gone wrong, how the doctor's asinine "treatment" had essentially destroyed my arm.

He was supposed to help me. Isn't that the promise doctors make to their patients? "First do no harm." The trauma was uncoiling like a jagged ball of yarn. My mistrust of medical professions was ballooning inside me, tumorous and massive—but unfortunately I wasn't done with them yet.

Now, instead of seeing Stuart my PT every day, I had to go see the infectious disease doctor. I went from having *no* blood tests under the supervision of my surgeon to having *constant* blood tests—the infectious disease doctor was perpetually testing and retesting to see if the antibiotics were killing the infection in my arm.

I tried to take care of my kids, but the existential fear gripped me day and night. I was afraid I wasn't doing a very good job as a mom. And I hadn't been able to travel to see my precious daughter Bella.

One night Wiles tiptoed into the bedroom doorway, hesitating on the threshold. "Mom?" He coughed. "I'm kinda scared. Are you going to be okay?"

"Of course," I said, though I hardly believed myself.

"I just want this to be over. I don't want you to die."

"I'm not going to die, Wiles," I said, my voice shaky. "I'm going to be fine. This will all be over and everything will go back to normal."

But of course his words frightened me when I was already so scared.

The next night Alice spent the night. Alice had walked over and seen through my facade—I put on a brave face, but she knew I was afraid. When I told her what Wiles had said, she came back later with her jammies on, ready and willing not just to help me but to be around for Wiles. My friends were pushing through to me. Even though I was hiding, they were still breaking down my door.

During the times Oliver was home, I was unintentionally alienating my husband. When he *was* home, he had to take on all the duties, fulfilling the roles of both dad and mom. "I do more dishes than any other man on the planet," he told me one night, when things were particularly tense. That was like a hit in the stomach for me. I *wanted* to do the dishes. In fact I had never wanted to do dishes more. I was desperate to be able to do the dishes.

"I need your help," I said. "I'm sorry, I can't even put a dish away. I'm trying to be the homemaker but I have no use of my right arm."

I wanted to explain to him how overwhelming it was, the feeling of having this foreign object in my arm, more stitches. It was such a waste of pain, a waste of squandered happiness and of my family's suffering.

I didn't know how to take care of myself, but one thing I was learning was that I could not do it alone.

***

The waiting room was cold. Too cold. I tried to pull my sweater around my shoulders but I couldn't quite manage it—with my cast and the PICC line, it was just too complicated.

I was in my OB/GYN's office for my annual exam. I still couldn't drive and Oliver was up at Andover with Bella. Too embarrassed to reach out to one of my friends, I had called a taxi to take me to my appointment.

"Willow Adair?" A nurse appeared in the doorway holding a clipboard. "He's ready for you."

They always said this but it was rarely true. Sure enough, I walked into the exam room and sat on crinkly white paper where I continued to wait. It was at least twenty minutes before my OB/GYN came in, which gave me plenty of time to fret and worry and feel bad that I was sitting there alone.

The door opened and my OB/GYN walked in. He smiled warmly— by far the warmest thing in the room. "Hi, Willow. How we doing today?"

I liked my OB/GYN. He had always been kind to me, and I never got that "I don't have time for you" feeling from him that I'd felt with other doctors. "I'm okay," I said. I had taken off the sock sleeve, and now the doctor stared at the ugly PICC line snaking up my arm. "I've been better, I guess."

"Good Lord. How'd you even get here? Can you drive with that thing?"

I shook my head. "I took a taxi."

His jaw dropped. He was absolutely astonished. No one took a taxi in Bexley, Ohio, and this was before the age of Uber. "Willow," he said gravely, "I can honestly say you are the only one of my patients who has ever come to her annual exam in a taxi."

"Ha. Well." I didn't know whether to be proud or ashamed.

"I'll try to make it as quick and painless as possible. You clearly deserve a reprieve." He thumbed through my files and clucked his teeth. "Uh oh. Looks like you're due for your mammogram."

"Oh no no," I said, horrified at the thought of going through *that* rigmarole. "I don't need a mammogram. I've got the PICC line, I've still got the cast on my arm. Trust me: I've been to over three hundred days of doctors this year if you count my physical therapist." I laughed a small, bitter laugh. "I could never get cancer. Despite the absurdity of the last year, I'm the healthiest person ever. I eat well. I exercise—as much as I can with my arm. I work out every day, or at least I used to before this dumb cast. Please." I stared him in the eye. "Please let's put off the mammogram. Just a few months. I really don't think I can deal with one more test."

He looked at me for a long time. Finally he nodded. "Okay, Willow. If that's what you want."

It was March of 2012. If I hadn't had the PICC line . . . if I hadn't had the cast on my arm . . . my life might have turned out very different.

Chapter 17

A TORNADO AT EASTER

I t was two days before Easter and I hadn't done a thing to get ready.

My kids were too old for Easter egg hunts, but that didn't mean they were too old for the holiday itself. I liked to make the house bright and inviting, bathed in the soft pastel palette of pink and blue and white. The year before, when Wiles was ten and Bella was thirteen, we had dyed Easter eggs with a kit we bought at the grocery store. We had a great time together, laughing as we beautified our eggs with swirls and crayons and stickers. We even planned a vegetarian menu for Easter dinner: mushroom tarts, chilled pea soup, and a delectable carrot cake for dessert for the kids.

But this year there would be no decorations, no eggs, and no warm family meal around the dinner table. I hadn't gotten Bella or Wiles as much as a chocolate bunny. I couldn't go to the store, couldn't buy anything. I didn't even have the strength to dye an Easter egg, which just about broke my heart.

Ding. I heard my phone from the other room and my heart soared. Someone was emailing me. It felt like a lifeline, a message in a bottle to the deserted island that had become my sad existence.

I rose slowly out of my bed and hobbled toward the sound of salvation, careful not to pull the IV out of my arm. It felt like I had aged sixty years in just six months.

How can this be happening to me? I wailed inside my head. *And for what?* I thought. *For nothing. All a colossal, stupid waste.* I didn't have cancer, this wasn't brain surgery. Just a small torn ligament turned into a monumental problem. My stomach clenched in outrage every time I thought of those misguided months, all the lies I choked down that my surgeon had regurgitated over and over. *I have to get better. I have to have more motion in my wrist. I have to crank up this cast so that I can be a mom and wife, do yoga again, so I can write and drive and play tennis and write thank-you cards. My doctor knows what he's doing—I have to trust him.*

OMG, I thought, the wrath reaching fever pitch. *What has this stupid surgeon done to me. WHY?!!??*

I had almost reached my phone. Everything that had once been easy now seemed difficult, even the smallest task took four to five times longer than it once had.

I made my slow and deliberate way toward my phone, thinking once again how the house seemed unmanageable. *How will I ever be capable of taking care of my house, my family, myself?* I picked the phone up with my left hand. *One new email from Jules.* Sweet Jules, taking the time to write me from Miami, which seemed like a universe away from where I stood. I had emailed her in a cry for help the night before, and she had heard my plea.

I opened the email and started to scroll, savoring every word of her dear and thoughtful message.

"You are in a terrible situation right now. But you can't crumble! First of all, your kids are way too old to care about getting something for Easter, so cross that off your list. You can be a wonderful mother and wife by being calm, relaxed, and happy. So for the 1,000 times that you have done shavasana, go to that place and find it. When you are about to crack, get in your bed, calm down . . . and go to that super calm and relaxing place.

You are going to pull through this. You are a strong woman. Don't give into yourself. I am here for you, and so many others are, too. Now text all your

Bexley girls and see who can come over to your house to wash your hair, blow it dry, and give you a proper mani/pedi for Easter. Put something pretty on. Light a few candles and put on some good music. Smear on some lip gloss and find your inner goddess.

I love you.

Xo

Jules

I set the phone down and wept.

Jules had a way of always knowing exactly what I needed to hear and when I needed to hear it. And boy, did I need to hear everything she had said. I felt terribly estranged from my inner goddess, but Jules's message gave me hope that she was in there, somewhere. I just had to dig her out and brush off the dust.

I called Grace, who came over and painted my nails in pretty pastel colors. She washed my hair, dried it, and helped me put on a beautiful soft Easter dress that made me feel lithe and pretty. She even daubed cherry gloss on my lips.

"You are so beautiful," Grace told me. "You truly are."

I was grateful for her comforting presence, but I didn't feel so pretty. I missed my friends and I missed my life. Most of all I missed my freedom.

A simple wrist repair, I thought on Easter morning, as my kids shuffled reluctantly into the car to go to church. *That's what this was supposed to be. WTF.*

Our pastor read Philippians 3:10 during the morning sermon: ". . . that I may know him and the power of his resurrection, and may share his sufferings, becoming like him in his death." The pastor was well intentioned but his words chilled me to the core. *I* am *sharing in his sufferings,* I thought morbidly. *Will they ever cease?*

The tornado was swirling like mad inside my skull. *GO AWAY,* I wanted to scream. *I want to live and be free and happy!* The question cycled over and over in my head like a broken record. *How did this happen? How did this happen? How did this happen?*

I looked down the church pew at my children, so beautiful and young. *I have the best family, and yet they have to watch this nightmare unfold. My poor sweet kids, wondering, "Why is mommy always in pain?"* I hated that for them. It just wasn't right.

Maybe it's going to get better. Christ rose from the dead so that we too might walk in the newness of life.

I wanted nothing more than the newness of life. Something different, something better, something I didn't recognize.

Chapter 18

A VERY GOOD ACTRESS

L ate July in Nantucket: a sweltering 106 degrees and no AC.

I was in Oliver's Nantucket house, bored and restless. We'd been there for the past two weeks. I wanted nothing more than to wade into the ocean and think. But I couldn't get my bathing suit on. I was still getting over the trauma of the PICC line, even though it had been removed three months earlier. My arm was throbbing and the infernal heat did not help. Oliver and the kids were out doing something fun. They loved Nantucket in the summer. I had never liked it even when I *wasn't* in savage pain, and the condition of my wrist made it ten times worse.

In the meantime, I was talking to my friends, no longer confident that my doctors knew what was best for me—or that they'd prescribe the right course of action if they did. I had a friend in Nantucket who had a home near ours. Paula was peaceful and calm. She and I had become friends over the years, summer friends. "Why don't you come up to the Hospital for Special Surgery here in New York City while you're in Nantucket? It's the best orthopedic hospital in the world."

"I've never heard of it," I answered honestly. *I guess that's what Google is for,* I thought. So I looked it up and liked what I found. A patient had to be accepted into HSS—the doctors didn't take every case. *Might as well apply,* I reasoned. *Why not?*

So I sent my information to the wrist and arm department and waited for an opening.

***

On July 29th, Oliver, the kids, and I flew down to Florida to meet up with the rest of my family. It was an annual tradition for my sisters, parents, and me: every year we all convened in Palm Beach and brought our spouses and our children along. The landscape was pristine—white beaches dotted with sunbathers and picturesque sailboats bobbing just off the coast. There were three golf courses at Keller Island, an enclave in Palm Beach, which Oliver and my father loved. Even the architecture was ravishing, elegant Georgian town homes and a year-round climate that never deviated from perfection.

It was a wonderful place for families—full of fun, laughter, and healthy competition. The Keller Olympics was a family tradition started by my dad, his brother, and eight of their Chicago friends. Growing up we went to Palm Beach each summer, where I would spend hours on the beach with my cousin Ella, talking about our lives and dreams as we soaked up the sun's golden rays. Ella was like a sister to me—she knew me better than just about anyone in the world.

For many years the Keller Olympics was made up of just those ten families: my dad, Ella's dad, and the eight others. Back at the beginning, the heads of each family—the dads—were the captains. When the dads got older, their kids began to take over their respective teams.

The Olympics used to be every summer, back when my dad was still in charge, but around ten years ago we started doing it every other year. It was the one time each year I saw all my sisters. By then there were still only ten teams, but well over two hundred people. It was mostly Lake Forest families, but so many of the original ten had brought other families and friends that the whole event had become quite large.

It had also become significantly more structured than it was when I was a girl. The Olympics included all kinds of sports and events—softball, swimming, volleyball, tug-of-war, tennis, golf, bowling, even gin rummy— and the competition between the teams was fierce. At the end of the week, the winning team received a big golden trophy, and the victors would hold it high overhead, glistening in the noonday sun. And *everyone wanted that trophy.* They'd stop at nothing to get it.

The opening party was opulent but relaxed. That night we all gathered at one of the family homes to eat, drink, and form the teams. Once the teams were formed, a bus came and picked everybody up, and the whole group went to bowl at the same bowling alley we had gone to when I was nine years old. The memories were warm and sweet as I sat in the food court, watching my kids bowl from afar. *So much tradition. So much fondness here.* I was glad Bella and Wiles got to be a part of such a rich tradition. *This is all really cool,* I thought. *I wish I could bowl right there with them.*

The next four days were a whirlwind of activity. And drama. So much drama! The Keller Olympics were VERY competitive—like crazy competitive. Even though the dads no longer played on teams or acted as captains, they were always around helping and betting against the other dads in favor of their team colors. It amused me how dramatic our Olympics had become.

For me it was dramatic, too, but in very different ways. Because all the families were from Lake Forest, I knew them well. There were a lot of people my age I had gone to high school with or even dated. Now they were married with kids, of course, so that was water under the bridge. The point was: everyone knew everyone really well.

Maybe too well, I mused, as I forced myself to attend the endless cavalcade of events. I couldn't participate with my arm, but I couldn't *not* participate—I would have been the talk of the town, and not in a good way. I already felt like people were whispering about me behind my back. *What's with Willow's arm? She's still in that cast? Hasn't she been sick for years?* I hated that.

I was simply in too much agony to enjoy the Keller Olympics. But I was committed to making sure that not a soul knew how much I was struggling. I always wanted to make the people around me feel better, not worse. I didn't want them fussing over me, and I was determined to not sap their enjoyment in any way.

What am I even doing? I wondered. *Why am I putting up such a front?*

Every day I downplayed how bad I felt and how afraid I was. I presented myself a certain way to my family and to the world around me, "healthy happy Willow Adair with perfect gloss and polish," when inside my soul trembled and quaked.

If I share how I really feel, I thought, *it will make everyone around me uncomfortable. I won't do that to them.*

So I grinned and smiled, cheering on my family's team from afar. The final party was on Sunday night, and the same band played that had been playing for the last thirty years: The Landsharks. I tried to enjoy them, wanting to feel peaceful and at ease, and when the photographer came around to take our picture, I lit up like a firefly.

If anyone were to look at that photograph today, they'd see me beaming at the camera, the perfect picture of happiness and contentment.

I was a very good actress. No one had a clue.

Chapter 19

JUST THE TWO OF US

"Let's go to Miami," I said to my husband. "Just you and me."

We were sitting on our balcony at my parents' guest cottage, watching the waves curl and crash into the shore. My parents had left earlier that day for their main home in Palm Beach, and Bella and Wiles were off playing with their little cousins who thought the world of them. Far off in the distance, a firework blossomed over the ocean, exploding in the air like a burning rose.

"Please come with me," I begged Oliver. "Just for a couple days. So we can get away."

"Okay," he said. "Let's do it."

I was flabbergasted. I practically had to scoop my jaw up from the balcony floor. Oliver never wanted to go on a trip without the kids, and I'd risked a lot—my pride, my dignity—in asking. And there he was, agreeing with a simple, "Okay."

Okay, I thought. *Okay! Maybe I will finally get the one-on-one time with my husband that I crave so much.* I was hungry for it. Starved.

I was abuzz with excitement as we dropped Bella and Wiles off with my parents in Palm Beach the following morning. We drove the remaining hour and a half with our windows rolled down, the wind in our hair as we careened down I-95. Out the window sunlight bounced off the blue waves of the Atlantic. I felt honey warm inside. I looked at my husband in the driver's seat and thought how delicious he looked. *Finally! Some alone time.*

"Just the two of us," I said.

"Just the two of us," he echoed.

Why did I feel so guilty? I felt guilty about asking him, and inexplicably guilty when he said yes. I was nervous. *Why am I nervous to be alone with my husband?* The truth was that I didn't feel like I deserved it, almost as if I wasn't worthy of Oliver's undivided attention.

We got to our place in Miami on Sunday evening, just as the sun was setting.

Oliver and I dined at our favorite Italian place and enjoyed a pleasant night together. My love for my kids was fierce, but I also loved my husband, and I had missed his company. *I want to feel like a woman again around Oliver. I haven't felt like a woman in so long.*

I had always been the one to spice things up in our relationship. I was flirty and sexy, and sometimes I did sappy stuff, even a little bit racy. *It's my husband, right?* I thought. *I'm allowed.* So early Monday morning, I took a walk. I pulled on a tank top and shorts and went for a walk on the beach. In the soft morning light, the waves looked like a million silver fish gliding softly over the shore. Oh, how I loved the ocean.

I texted Oliver. "Come down to the beach in five minutes," I told him, "and bring a towel."

I could feel the brisk chill in the morning air as I saw him walking toward me. And there, standing tall with my toes sinking into the soft sand, once I was sure I had Oliver's full attention . . . I started to strip.

No clothes on. I'm bare and I'm there. I stood, completely naked and vulnerable, feeling the heat of my husband's gaze. Longing poured over me, over both of us. I felt reckless and daring and even a little bit titillated. *This is exciting. I haven't felt this excited in a long time.*

I threw my clothes onto the sand and jumped into the ocean, the inviting water swallowing me whole. My tanned skin disappeared beneath the deep blue sea and salt stung my deep brown eyes.

Yippee! I'm totally naked in the ocean. At 8:30 in the morning. In broad daylight. The naughtiness of it was delectable, flooding me with unrestrained glee.

I also felt more "in control" of my life than I had in months. I had arranged for Oliver and me to have this time, just the two of us, and I wanted to make it exciting and fun. At the moment I didn't care if I was the one making advances on my husband. I was used to it.

He loved it. For the first time in I don't know how long, Oliver had looked, really *looked* at me. I could feel his eyes raking over me before I jumped into the bracing water. He took his clothes off, too, and got in the ocean with me. I admired his broad back and muscular arms, the shape of the man I had loved for all these years.

We swam together for what seemed like hours, though it was probably no more than twenty minutes. It was crazy good. I felt connected to Oliver in a way I had sorely missed. When our muscles felt fatigued and our eyes were burning from the salt, we walked out of the ocean, buck-naked.

"WOO HOO!" yelled a couple of guys doing construction on the beachfront condos. "AY, MAMI! HOT STUFF!"

Hand in hand, Oliver and I walked back up to our place. He went into the bedroom to change, and I stood in the kitchen, my whole body alive and buzzing. All I'd ever really wanted was for Oliver and me have to special times like this. It was an increasingly rare occurrence, but I felt overwhelmed with gratitude that we had spent one delicious morning, just the two of us. I was happy. He was happy. We were happy to savor the sweetness of being together, with no distractions, swimming naked in the ocean, and buffered, at least for a brief moment in time, from the storms brewing all around.

Chapter 20

FUSION

I t's too hot. It's blistering. I can't breathe. Why do I live here again? Who can survive 102 degrees? This weather isn't made for human beings.

Oliver, the kids, and I were back in Columbus, and suddenly it was August 17th. I was scheduled to leave for New York to go to the Hospital for Special Surgery the next day.

That night I threw a single change of clothes into the smallest carry-on suitcase I could find. Outside I was calm, keeping my emotions under lock and key. Inside I was panicking. Oliver was away on business and I desperately wanted him to come with me.

"Gotta go to New York tomorrow," I texted my husband. "I really can't have someone else put needles in my arm, ya know?" I didn't tell Oliver how scared I was. I was still living in a shell, afraid to be honest about my fear and anger. It was easier to maintain the facade than be honest about my confusing snarl of emotions.

I got off the plane in New York and went straight to HSS. I was a couple of hours early but I hadn't eaten, so I got a salad and ate it in the waiting room.

They called me in around 4:30 p.m. and the doctor's assistant took an x-ray of my arm. *Hope,* I kept telling myself. *There has to be hope.*

A few minutes later, the doctor came in and introduced himself. As he spoke he started to sift through my files.

"I haven't gone through all of your records," he explained, "because sometimes we have people from out of town schedule appointments and then they just don't show up. But gosh—looks like you have 5,000 pages of records here on your arm." He let out a low whistle. "Let me just read through these real quick."

So I sat there, silently, while he thumbed through pages and pages of reports. I wondered what was going on in his brain, what he thought of this quiet, somber woman from out of town who had flown up to New York all by herself. *Had he seen this before?*

"Uh huh," he murmured, whistling from time to time. "Wow. Holy." Finally he looked up. "Susie, bring me the x-ray."

Susie placed it on the wall and switched on the light.

"Huh." The doctor stared at it for a long time. "Where did you say you were from, Mrs. Adair?"

"I live in Columbus."

"And how'd you get here?"

"I took American Airlines."

He did a double take. "By yourself?"

"Yeah."

"Did you bring a carry-on?"

I nodded. "Yes. Very small. But even that was difficult. It's over there."

He shook his head as he glanced over at my luggage. "I have never in my life seen an x-ray like this. And I have never in my life seen a person fly across the country by themselves with an arm like that." He looked at me with genuine compassion. "What the hell did those doctors do to you in Columbus?"

Immediately I started to cry. I couldn't help it—the months of frustration and anguish and helplessness came crumbling down around me as hot tears streamed down my cheeks. I was embarrassed that this unfamiliar doctor was witnessing me fall apart, but I had no choice. I had been locked inside a shell for so long, and in that moment, the shell cracked wide open.

The doctor sat patiently with me during my outburst of raw emotion. He handed me a tissue, called in his assistant, and pointed to the x-ray. "This is Mrs. Adair's arm. It needs to be fused to get her out of pain. I will cancel any day next week so we can schedule her surgery. This woman has suffered enough."

I felt immensely relieved. I blubbered my gratitude, completely unable to understand this act of generosity. I wasn't used to doctors being nice to me. I was used to them being cruel, narcissistic, condescending, and wrong. *Finally, somebody's going to help me. Finally, someone sees how bad this is.*

"Willow." He touched my back gently. "When can you come back?"

I wondered if Oliver would come to New York with me for the surgery. *You know what? I am so tired of worrying about if he has a meeting or if he'll be "inconvenienced" once again by my health issues.* In the past I would have immediately called my husband to make sure it was okay with his schedule, but not this time. I was going to schedule this surgery regardless of how it affected Oliver. I was going to come back to New York and take care of myself.

It was Friday afternoon. I stood up and wiped the tears from my face. "I'll fly back first thing on Monday morning."

And that's exactly what I did. I flew back to Columbus the following day and immersed myself in a flurry of activity. I got everything set up—the family Wiles would stay with for the week, who would help out with the house. Oliver cleared his work schedule so that he could go with me to New York. He understood that, while any kind of fusion is drastic, the very hardest fusion is the wrist, because it's so debilitating.

I felt immensely grateful and relieved. *Now we can be there for each other. Neither of us will have to be alone, no matter what scary health stuff we face.*

"The doctor has to get bone grafts from a cadaver to fill in my arm," I told my husband. "It's complicated. I'm terrified."

"I'll be with you," Oliver said. "You've been through a lot but it's coming to an end now, okay? The worst part is about to be over."

In some ways the worst part had only just begun.

Chapter 21

THE WAY IT WAS BEFORE

September was upon us, and hardly anything had changed. The surgery had been a success, but the recovery was still slow.

Outside my window the pansies were blooming. I saw my friends in their shiny black and gray SUVs, driving their children to and from school. The kids who walked by my window were outfitted in cute back-to-school plaids and rich autumnal colors.

Meanwhile, I sat inside my house, withering like the leaves on the beautiful pecan tree outside my door.

Ring. Ring. I recognized Poppy's ringtone, plucked my phone out of my bra, and answered.

"Hey, Poppy."

"Hey, Willow."

I'd known Poppy forever—at least that's how it often felt. We'd met in middle school and had gone to a Catholic all-girls high school together, where we became very good friends. Poppy still lived in Lake Forest with her husband and two kids.

"I've been thinking about you," Poppy said. "How's life in Ohio?"

I debated how honest to be with Poppy. I hated that every time we talked I sounded like an invalid, complaining about this or that ailment.

"You can tell me the truth," Poppy said. "You don't have to sugar-coat it."

"Yeah," I said. "It just sucks."

I could hear Poppy shifting in her seat to get more comfortable. I felt a pang of envy that I could never get comfortable, no matter how much I rearranged myself.

"How does it *feel,* Willow?" Poppy said, pulling me back. "I want to understand what you're going through physically."

"Stick a knife in your right wrist," I said, "and then put it behind your back for eleven months. That's how it feels."

"That sounds awful. Do you ever just wish things would go back to the way they were before?"

Oh my gosh, Poppy, I thought, tears springing to my eyes. *Every minute of every day.*

***

At least one of my friends called me every single day, usually several. It was always better when I was on the phone with them, or texting, or trying to type out an email one-handed. They helped me forget how frustrated I felt. But the moments between the calls stretched out long and empty. They were filled with all the things I could no longer do.

Thankfully my friends were incredible. Amelia showed up with dinner and helped me take hot baths. Gigi came by to sit and pray with me, and she also got me out of the house to walk, even if it was just down the street. Francesca brought Wiles home from school every day. Nicole cooked my family and me hot delicious food. Simi dropped off my morning coffee. Alice called to check on me and sent me such incredible texts. Caroline dropped by to see how I was doing and always got me out to lunch. Jules sent me comforting emails. Grace brought me flowers all the time. Ella sent me daily texts that made me laugh.

I couldn't stand asking and asking for their help. Eventually I caved and hired a woman to move in so she could do all the dishes that I was supposed to be doing. She helped me dress, zip my pants, bathe, make food, make the beds, iron the clothes, do the laundry, and answer the door. I felt like I was paying her to help my family and me survive. And all the while I was so ashamed that I had hired live-in help.

I wasn't one of those women who luxuriated in having someone else do everything for her. The real bummer was: I hated it. I couldn't stand that people had to take care of me. I wanted my life back. I felt like a prisoner in my own house. I wanted my freedom. I wanted to be happy. *When will life go back to the way it was before?*

"Mom?" I heard Wiles's voice in the foyer, then the front door swinging shut behind him. *He's home from school.*

"Hi, honey," I said, coming out to greet him. We did a half-body hug that we'd been perfecting ever since my arm was in the cast. *So basically since forever.*

"How was school?"

"It was okay." Wiles avoided looking at my arm like he always did. He toed the floor nervously with his sneaker. "That was really the last surgery, right? You mean it?"

Every few days he asked me again, and I would assure him that, yes, there would (hopefully) not be any more surgeries. *It can't get worse,* I kept telling myself in my head. *It can't possibly get worse.*

"Yes, Wiles," I said. "I'm okay." I needed to assure him that I was okay, even if I didn't always feel that way. He was too young to be filled with such fear.

At least Wiles loved the x-ray picture of my arm. Once all of my bones were broken, they had put in the bone grafts from the cadaver, and then inserted a long piece of metal with a bunch of little screws to keep the bone grafts in place. Wiles thought the metal was so cool. The x-ray made me look like a superhero, like Wolverine with his Adamantium claws.

"I'll take the metal," Wiles joked, "but I don't want your pain!"

***

The next afternoon, Wiles was at school and Bella was at home watching daytime soaps. She flew back to boarding school the very next day, and I wanted nothing more than to spend this last day with her. But I couldn't make her lunch, so I had one of my friends drop off Chik-fil-A. Not that she'd eat it anyway. Bella rarely did anything but pick at her food, which worried me more and more.

"Okay if I sit with you?" I asked.

She shrugged. "Sure."

Poor Bella, I thought. *With Oliver off at work and Wiles off at school, she's stuck with me. She can't really say no.*

Bella eyed me in her peripheral vision. "Why aren't you eating?"

"Why aren't *you* eating?" I retorted.

She gave me the silent treatment, and went back to her show. All Bella wanted to do was watch TV in peace. The reason I couldn't eat was because I would have to use my left arm, and I didn't want to drop my food in front of my daughter.

It's depressing to be around me, I thought, *sitting here in my bathrobe.* My heart felt like it might crack open and disintegrate. *How sad. This is a situation no mother should ever be in with her daughter.*

I felt like ripping the cast off and going to a yoga class and waking up from this horrible nightmare. *I want my arm back. I want my kids to not be so afraid that their mother is in horrible pain.* I hated that my kids couldn't even look at my arm. It wasn't fair that they had to see their mother like a gargoyle, her wrist destroyed, her arm shriveled into a grotesque shape in a hideous cast.

I want to do what I love, but now I can't. And I never will. How do I cope with that reality? How do I get over this?

Will my fingers ever work again?

***

"That's it, Willow. Good. Full range of motion. Just extend, then back. Extend, then back. You're doing a great job."

I was back at the hospital I dreaded: Columbus Community.

"I missed you," Stuart, my PT, said.

I liked Stuart, so I didn't tell him the truth, which was that I had hoped I'd never have to see his face again.

I'd been trapped in this too-bright room from last December to April, and now I was back. It was all very confusing to me. The reason therapy had hurt so much before was because of the undetected infection. Stuart had been trying to pull my wrist up and push it down to get supination, but of course now we knew the truth: every appointment and every fancy cast was breaking every bone in my wrist.

And now I was back on September 17th—with a fully fused wrist—working with Stuart, trying, suffering, fighting through the pain *again*, this time just to get my fingers to work.

"How you doing, Willow?" Stuart said. "You hanging in there?"

Ruined. My wrist is ruined.

"I'm trying," I said.

"I know you are. Chin up! You'll be better in no time."

It's what he'd said a million times before, but he'd been misguided. It wasn't his fault—we both had.

***

That night in bed, I woke with a start at three a.m. Oliver was sleeping peacefully beside me. I could tell I'd been grinding my teeth—my jaw was throbbing. My stomach was a mess and I was exhausted from lack of sleep.

There, in our bed, I started to cry.

"Willow? What is it?" Oliver was groggy, annoyed that my crying had woken him.

"Please, Oliver," I begged. "Please just rip my cast off. It hurts too much."

"Willow, come on. You know I can't do that."

My cries melted into sobs.

"I'm tired, too, you know," Oliver said wearily. "Can we please just go back to sleep and talk about it in the morning?"

My husband was exhausted. He was up early every morning to feed Wiles, get him to school, and then carry on a full day of work. But I knew he wasn't just fatigued from taking care of our kids—he was tired of dealing with my disability.

This is nuts, I thought, as I tried to will myself back to sleep to make Oliver happy. *This is awful. I want everything to go back to the way it was before that stupid surgery last October.*

Chapter 22

THE LUMP

"I'm going to take a shower," I said to my husband, around 10 on a Saturday night.

"Mm hmm." He nodded, hardly listening, engrossed in the bad movie we'd been watching at our crappy hotel.

"It won't be long." Not that it mattered. For all Oliver cared, I could spend the next two days in the shower and shrivel like a prune. At least that way he wouldn't have to deal with me and my litany of complaints.

I got up off the bed where we'd been lying, happy to leave the nasty duvet cover behind. *There's no nice hotels in Andover, Massachusetts,* I thought to myself, not for the first time.

It was the last weekend before October, and we were at Andover to visit Bella at boarding school.

Both Oliver and I had been looking forward to the trip. We had timed it so that the visit coincided with my six-week post-surgery checkup with my surgeon in New York City. On Monday I'd see my doctor, but that weekend, we were entirely devoted to Bella. I hadn't been able to visit my daughter since school started in early September, and I felt awful about it. Now both Oliver and I were there to make it up to her.

But Bella was unhappy. She couldn't accept that we were there to see her—she felt like our behavior over the last few months had proven quite definitively that we didn't care about her. So she didn't want to spend time with her parents. Maybe it was her way of punishing us. At night she'd go hang out with her friends, and I worried obsessively over how they spent their time. Once, when I confiscated Bella's phone after a particularly horrendous fight, I found pictures of her friends doing cocaine. I was terrified she was doing it, too. I also knew she had a way with boys—boys always liked her—and I was scared to death she was sexually active. I was afraid for her, afraid that the boys at Andover would use her up and spit her out. Boys that age only ever wanted one thing. Bella was smarter than that, even if she was too busy rebelling to realize it.

Every night, Oliver and I would go back to the crappy hotel and watch a movie on Pay-Per-View, while I fretted over Bella's social life. That night we rented *Date Night*. I needed to laugh, sorely needed a distraction, and I was hoping that movie was seriously funny.

"See you in a few minutes," I said to Oliver.

In the bathroom, I turned on the hot water faucet with my left hand. It had been almost a whole year since I could shower without fanfare. It had become yet another living loss—I usually had to have somebody help me shower if I actually wanted to get clean.

So there I was in the hotel bathroom, taking a shower—*kind of?* My hair was disgusting but I wasn't even going to attempt washing it. The steam was thick and white, coating the mirror and all the glass surfaces in the room. *This has not been the best day. But this feels nice. The hot water feels good.* That night, instead of letting the soap drizzle over my breasts, I decided to work it into my body because I just felt so gross.

As I was washing myself, I started to think about my mom's best friend who had died of breast cancer a few years earlier. *Oh, that's so horrible,* I thought. *My arm sucks but it ain't cancer!*

Suddenly my fingers stopped massaging. *What is that? It's something hard. Is that . . . a lump?*

I'd found a lump under my left nipple. *No. Impossible. That has to be something else. I'm too healthy.* But I couldn't deny it. It was a lump and it was big.

My heart stopped somewhere in my throat.

"Oliver?" I called out. "Oliver!"

I stepped quickly out of the shower and wrapped a thin white towel around me. I didn't want to wait for him to take his own sweet time.

He looked up at me from the hotel bed, surprised, as I towered over him. "Will you feel this?" I said, pointing to my left breast. "I think there's a lump."

Oliver was very calm. He felt my breast, massaging his fingers around the nipple with practiced detachment. More like a doctor than a husband. "Let's look it up online," he said, reaching for his computer. "It can't be anything, Willow."

His words sounded like they were coming from the bottom of a very deep well. *It can't be anything. It can't be anything.* I wanted so much to believe him.

I lay down on the bed next to him, my head resting on his chest as Oliver began to read through various articles on WebMD and other sites about breast cancer. The more he told me, the more hope ballooned in my chest. "See, I'm looking at info on breast cancer lumps," Oliver said patting my head, "and what you just showed me does not have the physical characteristics. The feel isn't typical. The size isn't typical." He felt it again to be sure. "It kind of moves around when I push on it. That's not breast cancer, according to the almighty Internet. And when is the Internet ever wrong?"

If my husband was trying to cheer me up, it wasn't working. *Oh my God,* said the scared little girl in my head. *This can't be happening. We've already been through so much.*

I was panicking, but I kept it to myself. I wasn't going to ruin yet another vacation for Oliver. So for the rest of the weekend, I let my panic fizzle beneath the surface while I painted on a beautiful wifely smile.

Inside, of course, the worry was eating me alive.

***

We drove from Andover to New York City on Sunday afternoon so we could spend the night and see my surgeon bright and early Monday morning—we had to fly back later that afternoon to be home for Wiles. During the two-hour drive, I checked my phone and saw that I'd just missed a call from one of my friends in Chicago. *Huh,* I thought. *That's strange.* She never called me on a Sunday.

"Hey, Oliver—I'm going to make a quick call, okay? I'm worried about a friend."

"Sure," he said. "Do what you need to do."

She picked up on the first ring.

"Oh, Willow. Thanks so much for calling. I'm home alone and I just need you to know what happened."

"Okay," I said. "Now I'm scared."

"They found cancer in my ovaries." Her voice cracked. "I didn't want to tell you because of everything you have going on with your arm. I had surgery on Tuesday, and they think they got it all out, but of course they won't know for sure . . ."

I started crying. *Oh my God. One of my best friends has ovarian cancer. And she didn't feel like she could tell me because of all* my *medical issues.*

Awareness was slowly creeping through me. *The lump. I found a lump in my breast.* But I said nothing. I didn't tell her that I found a lump because what she was going through needed to be about her. It wasn't about me. She needed to share, and I needed to be quiet and hold her up. So she talked and I listened for most of that two-hour drive.

We got to the hotel in New York and I slept fitfully. *Oh my God,* I kept thinking. *Oh my God. What next?*

But on Monday morning, my appointment with the surgeon was easy. Almost *too* easy. "Everything looks good," he said. "See you in another six weeks." This surgeon cared about me. He thought I was a rock star because of everything I had gone through. He was a kind and dependable man, unlike so many of the other doctors I'd dealt with over the last year. As we started to walk out of his office, the fright began to take over me. *It might not be over yet,* screamed a voice inside my head. *It might only have just begun.* I tried to crush the voice, begging for silence, for a reprieve, but I was obsessed with what could be.

We landed in Columbus later that night. Boy, was it a relief to see my son. I'd missed Wiles desperately and clung to him as soon as I saw him. I didn't sleep a wink Monday night. Tuesday morning after I got Wiles off to school, I fished the cell phone out of my bra where I'd been keeping it for easy access since my arm became unusable. The anxiety had reached fever pitch and I was going to silence it. Whether the lump was cancer or nothing at all, I needed to know the answer.

I called my OB/GYN. "I have a problem," I said, and told him about the lump.

"I'm going to call the breast specialist immediately," he said. "He'll get you in tomorrow."

I hung up feeling only slightly mollified. The horror closing in around me was complete. I thought I had just made it through the war—to hear my New York surgeon talk, I was a true survivor.

But as fear flowed through me, I realized I was moving toward a new fresh hell. The worst news of my life had yet to wrap its icy fingers around my ankles and pull me down, down, down into the murky depths.

Chapter 23

I'M GOING TO KILL MYSELF

"Willow Adair?"

I bolted up from the chair in the waiting room, grasping for Oliver's hand. We were in the breast specialist's office bright and early Wednesday morning.

I looked straight down and walked to her without saying a word.

"Come on back," she said.

I didn't look at Oliver. Of course I wanted him to come back with me for the mammogram but was too embarrassed to ask. He was taking care of some work stuff from his phone in the waiting room, and I didn't want him to think I was weak or needy. I'd already been "needy" for way too long.

The nurse held the door open and led me down a long, brightly lit hallway. She was young and chipper, and I felt angry at her energy, angry that this was just another normal day in the office for her while for me this could be the day that changed the rest of my life.

The nurse chatted idly while she looped the sensor around my left arm to check my pulse and blood pressure. "Everything sounds good," she chirped, as she stared at my right arm in its huge cast. "The doctor will be right in," she said, gathering her things and closing the door behind her, still gazing at my arm.

"Trust me," I felt like saying to her. "You don't want to know what happened to my *arm*. We'd be here all day."

I stared at the wall, trying to meditate, forcing myself through some breathing exercises I used to do in yoga. I didn't have to wait long.

"Willow!" boomed a voice as the door swung open. The breast specialist was even more cheerful than his nurse, it seemed, a jolly round man with a thick white beard and bright blue eyes.

"Thanks for seeing me on such short notice," I said. "I really appreciate it."

"Absolutely." The doctor got right down to business. "Now where's this lump that's causing you concern?"

I pulled up my shirt with some difficulty—I still had a full cast on my right arm, all the way up to my shoulder. *I hope this doctor has read my medical file,* I thought, *and knows to be gentle.*

The specialist began to massage around my left nipple. "Uh huh," he said to himself. "Interesting. Okay."

"What is it?" I said, unable to contain myself. "Is it cancer?"

"Well, now, I can't be sure—but no. I don't think so. It really feels like a cyst to me. See how it moves around?" I felt a bit like cattle, a strange man poking and squeezing and prodding me, talking about my body almost like I wasn't even there.

"So what does that mean?" I asked. "If it's a cyst it's not cancer, right?"

"Right," the doctor said. "It doesn't have the characteristics of a tumor necessarily. I feel 90 percent certain it's not cancer. But let's do a mammogram, just in case, and we'll see what it shows."

Phew. Maybe it's all going to be okay.

I felt a tremendous waterfall of relief tumble down over me as the doctor directed me to the nurse who would perform the mammogram. *90 percent. He said there's a 90 percent chance it's not cancer.* But the relief I felt stopped short of giving me complete peace of mind. I couldn't shake the nagging feeling that it wouldn't be this easy. *It's not a cyst,* whispered my own worst fears. *Not even close.*

When the doctor came back a few minutes later, I could tell from the look on his face that I had been eerily prescient—and not in a good way. This time the nurse was beside him, and now *she* was staring at the floor like I had been an hour before.

"You know what?" the doctor said, his face clouded. "I want you to come back tomorrow and do a needle biopsy."

I started to feel dizzy. I tried to focus my eyes on the nurse who was still staring at the ground. "Could you go get my husband? He's in the waiting room." She nodded and trotted out.

"There's still a chance it's nothing, Willow," said the doctor softly, though I could tell from his voice he was no longer convinced. "But from what I gather from the medical records on your arm, better to be safe than sorry." Like *that* was supposed to make me feel better.

Oliver knew something was wrong the moment he walked in. *I'm scared,* screamed the voice in my head. But I didn't have to say it. Oliver could see it in my eyes.

"This is Oliver," I said to the specialist. "My husband."

Oliver turned toward the doctor and asked quickly, "What did you find?"

"We're going to schedule a needle biopsy for tomorrow," the specialist said. "I want you here first thing in the morning. And Oliver?" He locked eyes on my husband. "Tomorrow I want you to be in here with your wife."

***

Bright and early Thursday morning, I was back in the specialist's office with Oliver by my side. The right side of my body was already uncomfortable, and now there was a nurse sticking a long, thick needle into my left breast.

This does not feel good. Ha. Now that's *an understatement. It freaking hurts.*

The nurse with the needle was the same one from the day before. As if her bubbly attitude weren't painful enough, she was *horrible* with a needle. She missed a couple of times, and I groaned in pain. I looked over at her and said, "Did you notice the cast on my arm? Can we try a little harder?"

I knew I sounded like an ass, but by that point, I was pissed. I often joked with my friends that I could fill a book with all the times nurses had missed the veins in my arms before a surgery. *What a depressing book* that *would be.*

After the biopsy was completed, I turned to the specialist and said, "Now what?"

"Unfortunately, all we can do now is wait."

I blanched. "Until when? Tomorrow?"

The doctor cocked his head to one side. "It's Thursday now, and I'm going to send this off to the lab right away. They might get back to me tomorrow—but we'll see. If not I'll call you on Monday with the results."

I could feel my eyes pop out of my head. "I might have to wait *four days?*"

"I'm sorry, Willow." He patted me lightly on the left shoulder, which sent waves of pain crashing down around my freshly wounded breast. "Let's hope it's good news."

***

Oliver was silent as we walked to the car. Inside my head it was anything but quiet. The fear and doubt and uncertainty and rage that had been boiling inside me for *years* was bubbling to the surface. I didn't think I could contain it any longer. I wasn't sure I wanted to.

"Willow," said Oliver, looking at me closely. Perhaps he could tell I was about to explode. "Willow, listen to me. You're going to be all right."

I didn't hear him. I had started to scream.

I was literally screaming in broad daylight, leaning against our car, as if the car itself would support my weight. I felt sharp, guttural pain, as if something was tearing me apart from the inside.

"Why is this happening to me? I'm a good person! I'm a good person! I'm a good person! This isn't karma—this is some kind of sick joke!" My screams got louder.

But there were other things I wasn't screaming, thoughts that were much darker whorling inside my head. *There is no God. There is no way that God loves me. You've got to be kidding me. If this turns out to be cancer—that's it. I'm going to end my life.*

Chapter 24

THE PHONE CALL

A ll day I stared at my phone, wanting nothing more than to call Amelia, and Gigi, and Caroline, and all the friends I loved so much who had shown me, over and over again, how much they loved me.

I can't call my friends, I thought miserably. *My God, my friends! They've already walked with me through my colon and my arm for big chunks out of the last six years. How could I possibly ask them for anything else? I'm not going to scare them. I'm not going to scare my family. And I don't even know if it's cancer! It's probably nothing. I'm going to keep it to myself.*

That's what I told myself, like a broken record: *It's probably nothing. The biopsy is going to come back fine and it's not going to be anything.*

But the fear was like a rabid monster, wrapping its fingers tighter and tighter around my heart. *I have to call my mom. I at least have to call my mom.* My fingers were like putty as I scrolled through "favorites" and pressed the icon of her smiling face.

"Hi, Willow," she said when she answered, her voice warm and calm. I knew what I was about to say would shatter that sense of calm, maybe forever.

"Mom?" I burst into tears.

"What is it, Willow? Are you okay? What's wrong?"

I managed to say what I needed to say, and my mom started crying, too.

"I'm coming down," she said. "I'll call Oliver with my flights. Hang on, precious—I am coming."

She hopped on a plane and got to Columbus that night.

***

We didn't get the news on Friday like we'd hoped. *That means it won't come until Monday,* I thought ruefully. There was nothing to do but wait.

"Better not to wait alone," my mom said, and I knew she was right.

At my mom's urging, I called a few of my friends. Gigi came to my house and prayed with me. She actually got down on her knees and prayed.

We talked about one of her favorite Bible verses that she always spoke to me about. "I feel like this is your lifelong Scripture, Willow," she said. "It applies to everything from your colon to your wrist—and whatever happens next after you hear back from that specialist. I think of you every time I read it. Isaiah 41:10. 'Do not fear, for I am with you. Do not be dismayed, for I am your God. I will uphold you with my righteous right hand.'"

"*That's* ironic," I said, as we both stared at my right hand concealed in its ever-present cast. "Do not fear, for I am with you," I murmured, the words echoing in my mind.

But I had a hard time digesting the truth behind those words. My faith had dissolved into one pressing question: *What is my life worth?* What I wanted to know was how God played a part in my life. I'd been to plenty of Bible studies, and no matter how many verses I committed to memory, I simply couldn't understand why God was letting this happen to me. *If God is with me, why did he allow me to suffer through one agonizing trial after another? And if he will uphold me with his righteous right hand, then how can I have breast cancer after everything I've already been through?*

I called Amelia, who I knew was in Indianapolis, and left her a message. I kept it positive and upbeat. "Hey, Melia, it's Willow. Give me a call when you've got a second—no big deal. I'm getting some tests back, so if you'd lift me up in prayer, that'd be great. Let's plan a catch-up date when you're back in town? Love you!"

When I hung up, I realized I'd given *no* indication that something was wrong. The words belied the truth—I was smiling and in high spirits, determined not to give Amelia any cause for concern. She probably thought the "tests" had to do with my arm, since I hadn't said a peep about breast cancer.

My mom tried to keep my mind off things. We watched movies together and took brief walks around the neighborhood. She helped me with the physical rehab on my arm, working with me to regain movement in my fingers. Wiles didn't know yet what was going on, so we all tried to pretend around him. I could tell he was thinking, *Why is Grammy here?* But he loved having her there—we all did—and she made sure no one in my family went hungry. The biggest comfort was knowing she was there for me.

But even with people around, I felt locked in the dungeon of my own warped mind. It was strange that I could be in a room with someone else and still feel so isolated. I wondered if my mom had any notion of the dark thoughts swirling through me. *If the diagnosis is positive, I'm going to end my life. My mom doesn't want to be here with her grown daughter, having to pick up the pieces. My husband doesn't want to deal with any more of my health issues. My children are sick to death of me being sick to death. If I have breast cancer, that's it. It's over. I have no energy left.*

When my mother flew back to Chicago on Sunday night, I slapped on a happy face, something I'd gotten terrifically good at over the years. She kissed me on both cheeks and gave me a long hug. When she stepped back, I saw her brush the tears out of her eyes before they had a chance to fall.

"You're going to be just fine, okay, Willow?"

"Thanks, Mom." I whimpered quietly.

"I love you. Don't you forget it."

She turned around, but I could still feel her sadness as she walked away. For years my mother had watched her best friend Virginia battle breast cancer. Ginny had two girls of her own, and my mom was always over at their house, caring not just for her friend, but for her two young daughters. When Virginia finally lost the fight after thirteen years, my mom was devastated. I knew she still missed Ginny every day.

As I watched my mother disappear into the horizon, the sun setting around her, I felt an impending sense of doom. I wasn't sure what I would do to myself if I got bad news the next day. Or rather, I *was* sure what I would do—but I didn't know if I had the nerve to go through with it. Was I really going to kill myself? Did I have the guts to end my suffering so that I could end my family's pain?

The truth was, even with Oliver sleeping by my side on Sunday night, I felt utterly alone. I felt like everybody else could go home. Everybody else could go to sleep. Nobody was worried that the next day they were going to find out they had cancer. Sure, they were all worried about me, but my mom could fly back to Chicago and get distracted and escape it. Oliver could watch TV and go to work and get distracted and escape it. I couldn't escape it. I had to go to bed with the *real* worry. Nothing could distract me from the fears screaming inside my head.

When I did sleep, it was a sleep ravaged by shadows and nightmares.

***

I woke up on Monday morning, tired and disoriented. I blinked at the morning sun slanting through the windows. *It's kinda late*, I realized. *I must not have slept much last night.* I reached for my robe and slipped it on gingerly over my cast.

"Oliver? Oliver?"

Blearily I stumbled into the hall, careful not to bump my arm, and then inched slowly down the stairs. The kitchen clock stared at me from over the oven. *Huh. It's after eight a.m. That means Oliver has already dropped Wiles off at school.* I couldn't for the life of me imagine where he was. Surely he hadn't gone to work or had a breakfast meeting. *Maybe he went out to get us a nice breakfast and is bringing it back to the house?* I was in no state to eat anything, but that would have been a sweet gesture.

"Oliver!"

I went into the garage and his car was gone. *He's definitely not here. Strange.*

I couldn't eat breakfast, so after a few minutes of wondering where Oliver was, I went back upstairs. I was in my bathroom, putzing around, waiting for my husband to come home when the phone rang.

Ring. Ring.

Oh no. A sickening certainty coiled in my gut. I knew who was calling—and Oliver was gone. I was all alone.

8:53 a.m. Monday October 1st. Is this the day my life changes forever?

Slowly, I stood and walked toward my ringing phone, my feet pounding one in front of the other like a death march.

Ring. Ring.

It wasn't Amelia's ring, or Julia's, or Gigi's, or Grace's. I had individual rings for every one of my girlfriends, usually a riff of music that made me think of them or encapsulated their personality in some way.

Ring. Ring.

No. This ringtone was none of those. It was sinister, echoing against the walls. I reached for my phone, my heart freezing when I saw the unfamiliar number.

"Hello?" I said shakily.

"Willow?"

I recognized the voice of the breast specialist himself—it wasn't a nurse. I knew instantly he wasn't calling with good news. He was barely speaking above a whisper.

"The results came back positive," he said. "You have breast cancer. I'm sorry, Willow."

The news came crashing down around me like an avalanche. I sank into the nearest chair, fighting for words, fighting to make sense of everything in my muddled, raging mind.

I could only find my way to ask one question.

"Am I going to die?"

"I want you and your husband to come to my office today," he said, sidestepping my question. "We'll discuss everything then. Can you and Oliver be here at five o'clock?"

"I don't know where Oliver is," I said faintly, amazed that my own voice was unrecognizable to me. "I'm not sure he can . . ."

"Oh, he can. And he will. I'll call him myself if I need to." The doctor cleared his throat. "I'll see you both at five."

I hung up in a daze. All I could do was stare straight ahead, groping in the dark for some kind of answer, something that would make sense.

Why me? Why me, God?

Bitterly I thought of Gigi's Bible verse. It seemed like a cruel slap in the face.

Foggy. Everything is foggy. I looked down to see my legs were moving. I was walking, moving, wandering around the house in a daze. *Am I holding my phone? Is that my phone in my hand?* I set it down, suddenly afraid. What horrible news would come out of it next? Then I picked it up and shakily called my husband.

"Hi, honey," he answered, as if nothing was wrong.

"Where are you?" I snapped back.

"I'm at work."

I was beyond astonished. He had gone into the office. Oliver had gone into work on the day he knew my doctor was going to call with the results. He was having "just another day at the office" when I got the worst phone call of my life. It made me want to vomit.

"I have cancer," I told him. "The doctor called and I have breast cancer."

I don't remember what he said next. I felt like my mind was detaching from my body. *I don't feel normal. Nothing feels normal about this. I am not okay.*

I didn't feel like my feelings were my own, more like I was watching someone else's. Nothing felt like it was mine—my fury, my heartbreak, my utter and complete despair. *I just got diagnosed with breast cancer at home alone. Oliver went into the office. My husband left me here alone to take that call.*

I clutched my stomach and fell to my knees, weeping. *I want to throw up. No, worse.*

I want to die.

Chapter 25

THE BLACK MARK OF CANCER

This can't be happening. It can't be real.

My sister Chloe flew to Columbus as soon as she heard the news. She arrived on Tuesday and stayed for three days. Chloe is the youngest of my three sisters, and she and I have always had a special bond. Ever since childhood we've been fiercely protective of each other. When she heard I had cancer, she dropped everything in Lake Forest, leaving her three young girls to come be with me.

At that point I was going to see a psychologist every single day. He was our family therapist, and we'd seen him for various issues over the years. I went to see him when I was coping with the pain in my arm, and he helped me work through the anger I felt toward my doctor. Once I got my cancer diagnosis, going to see him felt like life or death. Different friends would pick me up and take me to my therapist's office, where I would sit for fifty minutes and either sob or try to talk through what I was feeling. Usually some combination of the two.

"Chloe," I said on Wednesday morning, as we were the sitting in the kitchen, the TV humming softly in the background as we sipped our coffee and tried desperately to act like everything was normal. "Would you take me to my therapy appointment? I'm not sure what time it is today—I'm kind of foggy."

"Sure, Willow," she said. "Anything you need. I'll drive you."

Chloe and I didn't talk much on the drive over. We were both pretty depleted. We walked in and sat in the therapist's waiting area. She thumbed through a glossy magazine in the sitting area until my therapist called me in. No sooner had we sat down on his sofa than he said, "Do you want your sister to come in for the session today, Willow?"

I thought for a moment. "Yes," I said. "Sure. I'd like that." I could use all the support I could get.

He opened the door and said to my sister, "Chloe? Would you like to come in with Willow today?"

Chloe did *not* want to go into that room with me. I could tell she was uncomfortable. She'd never been to a therapist before, and she had mixed feelings about it. "Isn't it supposed to be confidential?" she asked him, raising an eyebrow. "I'm happy to just wait here in the lobby."

My therapist smiled. "It'll be good for you to come in, Chloe," he said. "If you want to."

I nodded. "I really want you to," I added.

Chloe stood up stiffly. "Okay then." I knew my sister well enough to know that she was thinking: *This is so weird.* But she was also willing to do whatever she needed to do if it meant it would help me.

Once we were both seated on the sofa, my therapist started telling Chloe how much I'd been struggling. When he told her I was talking about ending my life, she interrupted.

"I already know that," she said, starting to get angrier. She whirled around on me. "Are you serious about killing yourself, Willow?"

My eyes filled with tears. "I told you—I don't think I can make it."

She shook her head furiously. "You're strong. You can get through this."

"I think it would be easier on everybody if I weren't here."

My sister was spitting mad. I'd seen her get angry before, but this was like nothing I'd ever seen. And the thing about Chloe is, when she's mad, she lets you know it. "I'm so pissed at you!" she half shouted, half teared up. "You're so, so selfish. You think you're going to end your life and that we're all just going to sit around and be like, 'Oh, we feel much better now.' You think you're actually going to *help* us? That's the most ridiculous thing I've ever heard!"

She was full-on shouting now. I didn't even look up from the sofa—I just looked straight down.

"I'm not going to coddle you," she said. "I'm not going to say, 'Please don't kill yourself, Willow.' You are so selfish! And you have to stop being selfish. Stop thinking that way."

My therapist was watching calmly from his chair. He maintained his usual equanimity—he wasn't easily riled. He turned to me and said, "How do you feel about that, Willow?"

I didn't feel much of anything. There were tears dripping out of my eyes, but I still felt numb. "I don't know how I feel about that," I answered honestly.

"It's not just about you," Chloe said, a little more quietly. "If you kill yourself, how do you think the rest of us are going to feel? What do I say to my daughters about their aunt? What do I say to our mom?"

She was really getting choked up now, and strangely enough, it was easier to have my sister yell at me than to see her cry. "How can you possibly give up now? You have two beautiful kids, a loving husband, and a wonderful life outside your health. My God, look at all of your friends! Losing you would not make any of our lives easier. It would make them so much harder. You'd leave all of us here, thinking, 'How did we fail her? What should we have done differently?'"

She shook the tears out of her eyes. "You've got a full life ahead of you, Willow. You've got one awful year of treatments, and then you're going to be fine. Let's focus on the positive here."

Chloe was big on focusing on the positive. *Sure, I'll try to focus on the positive,* I thought, *the minute I find something positive in this whole mess.*

My head was spinning, but as we left my therapist's office, I thanked Chloe for what she had said. She looked at me sideways. "Promise me you won't kill yourself, Willow."

I stared at her. "I promise I won't kill myself. TODAY."

She rolled her eyes. "I want to know you won't kill yourself, period!"

But I couldn't promise that to Chloe, or to anyone. I clung to the idea of suicide like a sweet dream. It was so easy, so deceptively easy to be free of my pain, and to free my friends and family from the millstone around their neck.

Later that night, I sat alone in my bedroom while Chloe played a video game with Wiles downstairs. My phone rang. *Amelia.*

"Oh, Willow." Amelia's voice sounded hoarse. "I had no idea you meant tests for breast cancer . . . I knew you were going in for tests but I thought it was more arm stuff. On top of that I've been sick, I hardly have any voice so I haven't been talking on the phone . . ." She coughed.

"I'm so sorry you're sick," I said, and meant it.

"Are you kidding me? I'm sorry *you're* sick! This is just a silly cold." I heard her blow her nose. "I had to be at the game on Sunday and it just kills me I couldn't be there for you when you got the news."

"It's okay," I said. "My sister is here now."

"Oh, good. I'm glad Chloe's there."

"Me, too," I said.

"What happens next?" Amelia said. "Did you find an oncologist?"

"My dad got me in to the Cancer Treatment Center of America," I said. "Oliver and I leave for Phoenix on Friday. They're going to run more tests to see the variables of the diagnosis, staging, and stuff I don't really understand yet before we take the next step."

Amelia must have heard the despair in my voice. "You're going to make it through this. You are strong, you're so incredibly strong. This is just another blip in the beautiful story that is your life—and you have so many years left to live."

I wanted to believe her. Chloe, Amelia, all my friends—they said I would make it through this. But would I? And did I have the strength and the energy to fight?

I tried to act like a rational, thinking human being, but nothing felt rational. Fearful fragments whirled through my mind.

What's going to . . .

How will we . . .

What if I . . .

I couldn't answer any of the questions in my head. I couldn't even finish them. My brain felt like a hopeless muddle. I was confused and shaky. Nothing made sense.

My dad was a big believer in getting a second opinion, and after my horrible experience with the surgeon in Columbus, I agreed. It was a huge comfort, knowing he'd make sure I had the very best in doctors and surgeons. My dad took care of everything.

"Your father's got this under control," Oliver told me. "You're going to be all right, Willow."

"Mmm. Mm." When people spoke to me, it felt as if their words were traveling down a long, vicious wind tunnel, thoroughly distorted and stripped of any meaning by the time they got to me. I was physically there but shutting down completely emotionally. I was forcing my brain to be a "nothing," just a physical resemblance of a person, but with nothing inside.

The morning of the tests, CTCA sent a white limo to pick Oliver and me up at the hotel in Phoenix and drive us 20 miles to the medical center. As we waited for the limo, my knees felt like putty. I held onto Oliver because I was afraid if I didn't, I would collapse onto the concrete and my casted arm was throbbing after the flight.

Then the limo pulled into the valet and my heart plummeted. On the right side, in large black magnetic letters, were the words:

CANCER TREATMENT CENTER OF AMERICA.

The black mark of cancer.

I felt sick. I couldn't believe the sense of shame I felt, staring at that limo. Even the license plate, CTCA1, screamed "CANCER!" *It's real. It's all real. This isn't some horrible dream.* I felt desperate to be somewhere— anywhere but there. Tears were streaming down my cheeks. I wanted to vomit. I wanted to curl up into a ball and hide.

"Nooo," I moaned, but Oliver was already leading me toward the limo, and the valet was smiling, opening the door.

I felt hideous and sickly, like I was already half dead. I felt marked, branded as a "cancer patient" for all the world to see. I could see it on the valet's face. *That lady has cancer.* I could see it in the eyes of the young couple pulling up in their BMW. *That lady is going to die.*

I hated it more than anything. Even more than my arm. *It can't possibly get any worse.*

***

At the medical center, the doctors did a PET scan and various other tests to ascertain the size and severity of the tumor. It was definitely there—the doctor in Columbus hadn't been wrong. I had foolishly imagined that somehow, some way, they had gotten my biopsy mixed up. But it was true, and I had to face the horrible truth all over again: I had cancer.

We were able to schedule a lumpectomy for Monday, three days later. They were going to remove a discrete portion or "lump" of breast, and they were also going to cut into my armpit and remove three lymph nodes to make sure the cancer hadn't spread. It was technically two different procedures, all under the same anesthesia, meaning I'd have stitches in my armpit and in my breast. But I didn't care. I just wanted it out of my body, and as quickly as possible. *If the cancer has spread . . .*

I don't remember a single thing about the flight back to Columbus. Only that I was so very tired, and yet I couldn't sleep. Instead, I stared out the window of the plane, eyes glazed over, watching the lights blur across the glass as a light rain fell. *I'm fallen,* I thought, over and over. *I am completely fallen.* All I wanted was for it to end.

Chapter 26

"As Long as It's Not Cancer"

Oliver and I flew back to Phoenix on Sunday night and met my parents at the airport. "Oh, honey," my mother said, the moment she saw me. She started sobbing and I started sobbing, too. Neither of us could stop crying. Our husbands had to pull us apart and herd us toward the rental car before our tears puddled on the glossy terminal floor.

"I'm taking us all out for dinner," my dad said, and I was happy he was there.

On the car ride to the restaurant, my mother squeezed my left hand and wouldn't let go. "Are you sure you want to do a lumpectomy, Willow? Don't you want to get it all out at once?"

I knew why she was asking. Her friend Virginia had originally had a lumpectomy, so it was only natural my mom was concerned. She felt like if Ginny had had a mastectomy to begin with, her life might have been spared.

The problem was that we didn't have much of a choice. From what the doctors had already told me, most people diagnosed with breast cancer did chemo first to shrink the tumors. Then the doctors went in and did a lumpectomy (removing a discrete portion or "lump" of breast) or a mastectomy (removing all the breast tissue). But because I had bone grafts in my arm that were just six weeks old, going straight into chemo would have dissolved the grafts and destroyed my arm. Also, since I was coming off of six arm surgeries, a mastectomy would have been too much for my weak body. I was already so underweight and run down.

"We have to do something to get the cancer out," the doctors at CTCA had told me. "You might choose to get a mastectomy later, but it's best to get a lumpectomy right now. We'll get the cancer out and then let your arm heal."

I had explained all this to my mom, and she understood, but I could tell she was still worried sick.

"Have you told Bella?" she asked.

We still hadn't told Bella about my cancer. We'd told Wiles the night I'd gotten the diagnosis because I couldn't stop crying. I hated putting more fear and terror in his sensitive heart. "Please tell me you're not going to die," he'd said, as he clung to me before we left for Phoenix.

"I'll be home in just a few days," I said. "You don't have to worry."

It was harder with Bella. Wiles was still young enough that I could hold him in my arms—albeit awkwardly, with one arm out of commission—kiss him on the forehead and assure him things would be all right. Bella was more distant, both physically and emotionally, and our relationship had often been tumultuous. I knew she was already angry at how my health issues had affected her life.

Parents' weekend at Bella's boarding school in Massachusetts started in just four days. Of course I wouldn't be able to make the trip—I'd still be in Phoenix, recovering from the lumpectomy. I knew Bella would once again feel like she'd been abandoned in the wake of "Mom's many illnesses," which was why it was important that Oliver go without me.

The specter of parents' weekend hung over me like a dark raincloud. *I want so much to be there. How can I disappoint my daughter yet again? But there's just no way.*

"I'm not going to be able to go to parents' weekend," I mumbled to my mom, as my dad parked in front of the restaurant. "So Oliver's going to go alone. He'll tell Bella when he's in Andover. And maybe you can stay with Wiles and me?"

"Of course," she said quickly. "Of course I'll stay with you."

I sighed. "But we have to tell Bella why I'm not going to be there. We have to tell her *something*."

I called Bella that night from outside the restaurant. My parents and husband stood nearby, because I was afraid of my daughter's response. I wanted backup, and I didn't want to make that phone call alone.

"I'm so sorry, honey," I said. "I can't be there for parents' weekend. I have to have surgery."

There was a long silence on the other end of the line. "Is it your arm?" she said finally.

"No," I said softly, looking down at the pavement, waving my mom away. I knew if she stepped one foot closer I was going to start crying again.

"Colon?"

"No." I took a deep breath. "Your dad will explain it to you when he sees you on Thursday."

I heard Bella sigh with disgust. "What's new?"

Her words stung but I could understand where she was coming from. She was sick and tired of my endless surgeries. The whole prior spring I was not able to fly up to see her because I was having one arm surgery after another.

"You know what, Mom? I really don't care anymore. There's always something wrong with you—it's just another surgery. As long as it's not cancer, it's fine. Whatever."

She hung up on me.

Oh my God. I stared at the phone, tears welling in my eyes. *If only she knew.* My heart hurt, imagining the conversation she would have with Oliver in a few days when she would find out it *was* cancer. I hated knowing Bella would suffer, remembering the flippant comment she had made out of hurt and anger, when really, it turned out to be true.

That night I slept restlessly. I knew my mom was tossing and turning in her hotel bed, too, and there was some comfort in knowing how worried she was about me. The next morning all four of us were up early, and that same limo was back at the hotel, broadcasting my cancer to the entire universe.

It was early Monday morning, the sun barely up over the Phoenix skyline, but I knew my friends back in Bexley had already started praying. Amelia and Gigi had set up a prayer group to start at 6:30 the morning of my lumpectomy. As the limo wound through the dusty desert streets, my friends had already started praying, and by the time they rolled me in for surgery, they were still going strong.

Oliver sat in the waiting room, ensconced by my mom and dad, receiving one text after another from my prayer warriors back in Bexley. At that point Oliver was texting a few of my friends almost daily. The texts to me that rolled in that morning were incredible.

"Oh honey, we are praying for you."

"We're holding you up, Willow. So many people praying for you right now."

"Your strength is shining through and I hope you know that! You are radiant!"

"Yay!! Girl, you are almost done!!!

"We love you, Willow. God has not abandoned you. And neither have we."

Oliver texted Caroline and Amelia to let them know I was out of surgery, and word spread like wildfire. My prayer warriors were fierce—and they, too, were miracle workers. When I woke up from surgery, I was told my tumor was smaller than the measurements they had originally taken. The cancer wasn't in my lymph nodes, only in my breast. As I lay crying in my hospital bed, I got perhaps my first glimpse of the very real connection between prayer and healing.

When I'd first been diagnosed, I felt like God had forsaken me, that he wasn't there for me. In my darkest moments I questioned if there was a God at all. But when I found out the tumor was smaller than the doctors had thought, I felt a little ashamed that I had questioned God. *Maybe God* is *helping me,* I thought, *and he is going to heal me.*

***

It was Thursday afternoon, and I had just kissed Oliver goodbye. Now, as I stared at my mom, who was telling me some lively story to try and cheer me up, I swallowed the lump in my throat. I'd been in Phoenix for the last few days, recovering from the lumpectomy, and now my husband was on a plane to go see our daughter and tell her I had cancer. *I want to be there,* I thought. *I want that so much.* But I was living in a world that was far different than anything I'd ever wanted.

I was a sight to be seen. My left breast was stitched up, and I had a huge wound on my left underarm where they had taken the lymph nodes to test for cancer. I couldn't lift my left arm because of the stitches, and I couldn't use my right arm at all—I was still in a full cast up to my fingertips.

Now that neither side of my body was functional, I couldn't do much of anything. I couldn't feed myself, couldn't bathe myself, still couldn't drive a car. And I certainly couldn't attend classes and athletic events with Bella and do all the other fun things Oliver would be doing with our daughter over the next few days.

"It's all right, Willow," my mother cooed. "We'll go back to Bexley tomorrow and get you all situated. You'll get to see Wiles, and you'll be up walking around the neighborhood in no time. And you'll feel so much better in your own bed, surrounded by your own things, with your girlfriends nearby!"

Chapter 27

A Permanent Solution to a Temporary Problem

I was a weepy mess. I couldn't do anything, could hardly get off the sofa and walk into the other room. My friends called, one by one, but I didn't always have the strength to speak to them. There wasn't a single phone call where I wasn't sobbing. I felt desperate. The words that came out of my mouth were illogical, the thoughts forming in my head even more so.

I feel desperate to leave this earth. I feel desperate to just get through the day. I didn't feel much hope. The reality of my situation closed in around me and I felt suffocated by it, like all the air had been sucked out of the room.

When Caroline called, I started crying so hard she couldn't even understand what I was saying.

"Are you at home right now, Willow? Just answer yes or no."

I managed a garbled, "Yes."

"I'm coming over right now," she said. "Do not move a muscle."

Four minutes later, Caroline walked through my front door. She had literally left the minute she hung up her phone.

I sat sobbing on my front stairs. Caroline sat down beside me and just held me. We stayed like that on the stairs for a long time, me sobbing, Caroline stroking my back and just holding me close. When my chest finally stopped heaving and the sobs had melted into soft tears, she led me to my bedroom to lie down.

"What's going to happen to me, Caroline?" I moaned. "I don't think I can do this. I don't want to live anymore."

"You're going to be fine, Willow," she said soothingly. "You're going to be just fine. You're going to look back and your arm's going to be way worse than this cancer. We're going to get through this cancer, no problem. Your arm's going to be the much bigger deal."

But the black mark had obliterated my thoughts and feelings, and most of all, my hope. It had already seeped into my soul and made me believe there was no tomorrow. I wasn't going to be fine. No one was. The more people like Caroline had to care for me, the more I was a useless burden, a leech draining them dry. I wanted to cast off the black mark, but I could only figure out one way to do so.

The only way I'm going to be fine, I thought darkly, *is if I'm dead.*

But I wasn't going to kill myself without saying goodbye to my daughter. Bella was supposed to come home the weekend after parents' weekend, but she was in trouble at school once again. "No," the school administrators said. "Not this weekend." I argued with them, then begged, then pleaded, trying to get them to let Bella come home. They still said no.

So I stalled. *I won't end my life. Not yet. I'm waiting to see my daughter.*

The following weekend, I told the school administrators: "I need Bella home."

"Not this weekend, either," they said. "Bella stays with us."

I was set on suicide. It felt like the inevitable solution to my miserable life. But I wouldn't kill myself without seeing Bella first. And Bella kept being delayed, so I kept stalling.

I didn't know it then, but these delays would ultimately save my life. In reality, it wasn't me stalling—it was God. He wasn't allowing Bella to come home, and in so doing, He was buying me more time. My friends poured in to teach me my own self-worth, to sit with me, to remind me of everything that made my life worth living. They saved me from my loneliness and my despair.

Seeing Bella was the last thing keeping me from ending my life, but God didn't send her when I asked. He sent me something so much better. He sent me the precious gift of time—and He sent me His Angels to keep me alive. When my precious daughter finally did come home, I was ready to fight for my life.

***

As I contemplated how I would kill myself, my friends relentlessly came over to sit with me, watch me, feed me. And the texts, emails, and phone calls poured in from my nearest and dearest friends.

"You'll get through this, Willow. You're strong."

"After everything you've been through, you've GOT this."

"We love you, Willow."

I read and listened to each message in a haze of disbelief and doubt. Beneath every admission of love and hope, I felt like I could detect the *real* message, the subtext that had been left unsaid. *What, more bad news from Willow? How could one woman go through so many health crises? And she's so healthy! Is she a hypochondriac? Is she making it all up?*

Maybe I'm imagining things, I thought. *I'm being illogical.* But then, nothing was logical, nothing made sense. It was possible I was projecting outward what I was feeling inside, but one thing I felt certain of was that I had been a burden for far too long, and I would refuse to be one any longer.

They'd all be better off without me. I have to end my life.

It felt like I was listening to an opera only I could hear, every sad aria leading me further and further down the dark recesses of my mind. I had lost my way down a bleak, winding road. I could feel myself teetering over a precipice, and it was proving impossible to pull myself back from the edge.

Being in heaven is better than being on earth, I thought. *I know taking my own life is a sin—but surely God will still take me to heaven. He knows I can't go through any more.*

On Saturday morning my phone rang. *Amelia.* Hearing her ring always made my heart leap, but now I was just so sad. I didn't trust myself not to dissolve into sobs.

I swallowed the tears and answered. "Hey, Amelia, hi. Thanks for calling."

"Willow?" I heard genuine fear in her voice. She'd gotten several cryptic messages from me over the last week, hinting, in subtle and not-so-subtle ways, that I was thinking of ending my life.

"I hope you're home," Amelia said, "because I'm walking over there right now."

"Okay," I said numbly. "I'm here."

When Amelia appeared on my front porch a few minutes later, no sooner had I opened the door than the tears started flowing. She walked me over to the sofa, where I collapsed in her arms and wept. "I'm scared. I'm so scared."

Amelia sat on my sofa and just held me. She rubbed my back and rocked me back and forth. I felt like a baby—helpless, vulnerable, terrified.

"I don't think I can do this," I whispered into her neck. "I really don't."

"There's not a doubt in my mind that you can. And you will."

I pulled back and looked at her intently. I tried, unsuccessfully, to keep my voice steady. "I'm going to kill myself, Amelia. And I'm not telling you because I want you to stop me. I'm telling you because I want to protect you. I don't want you to feel like you had missed the warning signs."

She started to interrupt but I said, "Please, please, I have to say this now, I just have to. I'm not asking you to stop me. I'm telling you this so you feel no guilt after it's done. This isn't because you didn't try to help me—this is because it's what I have to do. Don't feel bad after I'm gone, thinking you could have done something for me. You couldn't. You can't."

I didn't know I was going to say all that. The words had tumbled out of me from some deep, secret place. I knew I had to tell my closest friends, though I worried people would think I was saying I was going to kill myself for attention. I wasn't. I meant every word.

"This isn't for attention," I said to Amelia. "This is something I have to do. Nobody can stop me." I gripped her hand. "You can't keep taking care of me, Melia. I won't allow it. I'm a burden on you. I'm a burden on everyone else."

"Willow, listen to me." Amelia reared back and looked at me for a long time. Her eyes were fierce, burning with something I didn't recognize. *Anger? Sadness? Love?* "Don't you for a second go down that path. I don't want to hear you say that, I really don't. You know I lost someone in my family to suicide, right?"

"Oh my God," I shook my head. "I had no idea."

"Well, I did. It was a really long time ago, but I still think about it. Suicide is the most selfish thing you can ever do. I truly believe that. You think you're saving other people from having to take care of you, but what you're actually doing is taking away their opportunity to walk by your side. You're taking away our gift of helping you survive this horrible disease. You're robbing them of the many blessings that come when we walk with one another through times of great suffering."

I tried to fully take in her words, so full of grace and wisdom. I wanted to absorb everything she was saying, but it was hard to see through my own dark veil of morbid thoughts. *I'm going to do this*, I thought, pushing out what Amelia had just said. *No matter what she says, she can't stop me from taking my own life.*

"You never know what tomorrow holds," Amelia said. "Life turns on a dime. Your circumstances can change so dramatically, so quickly. Suicide is a permanent solution to a temporary problem."

"But I've got breast cancer," I wailed. "That's not going to change. Even if I survive it, it's going to wreck my life . . . and my life already felt like it was ruined. And it's not just *my* life! It's my family's. Yours, too." I sobbed.

"I know your pain has been insufferable. I get that. And I can see how suicide would seem like a viable answer. It might seem like the easy way. But Willow." Amelia cupped my chin in the palm of her hand. "What appears to be the easy way is often not the best way."

"But I'm so miserable," I moaned. "And I'm making everyone around me miserable, too."

"That's not even remotely true. Do I look miserable to you?"

I craned my neck so I could look at my beautiful friend. She didn't look miserable at all. She looked calm and peaceful. Yes, she looked sad—her empathy poured out of her like warm honey—but she also looked gentle and full of lovingkindness.

"Can I tell you what this past Sunday was like for me, Willow?"

"Sure, of course."

"Well, you know October is breast cancer awareness month. And the NFL is really supportive of breast cancer—we raise money every year for breast cancer awareness."

I was keenly aware of that now.

Amelia's voice grew hoarse, and I knew what she was about to say was hard for her. "Last Sunday, the day you and Oliver went to Arizona for your lumpectomy was the day we handed out breast cancer awareness merchandise at the Colts game. This year we handed out little pink ribbons. And I had to be out there, in the stadium, smiling and helping them pass out pink ribbons to thousands of fans. Oh, Willow."

She hugged me tightly. "It was so emotional. Every single person I handed a ribbon to and talked to—each woman had your face. It had always been esoteric for me: raising awareness for breast cancer was great, but there wasn't a face or a name attached. You know there's been a lot of cancer in my husband's family, but breast cancer was not something I'd walked through with anybody. And then that night . . ."

Amelia's voice cracked. "It really hit home."

My friend wiped the tears from her eyes. "I don't know what this is like for you. I can only imagine how scared and sad you must feel, but I'm not in your shoes, so I don't know. But I can tell you that if you make the decision to take your own life, then you rob your kids of a future with you. You rob Oliver of a future with you. You rob *me* of a future with you. You rob us all of a lifetime together, both during your cancer and after you've survived it."

I was crying now, openly, not even trying to stop my tears from flowing. "Oh, Amelia," I kept saying, over and over. "Oh, Melia."

"I'm going to have a hard time forgiving you if you make that decision, because we have committed to walk through this with you, and we can do it together. All of us. But none of us can do it alone. And neither can you."

"I know," I gasped. "You're so right. About everything. I just . . . I'm so scared of being alone, Melia. I'm terrified. Because you want to know the truth?" I blurted out the truth through my sobs. "I think the real reason I want to kill myself is because I'm afraid of being abandoned. You've all done so much already—I'm afraid I can't ask any more. You've got your own lives and your own families. There's this ever-present voice in my head saying: *You are going to be left alone.*"

My chest heaved, squeezing the words out of me like a terrible confession. "I'm afraid no one will love me."

"Oh, Willow." Amelia smiled at me. She tipped my chin up so I could see the tears glistening in her eyes. "Do you have any inkling how much you are loved?

Chapter 28

CIRCLE OF ANGELS

I t was true: I was more loved than I knew.

I'd only been home a few days when people started to come over. Not distant friends, but my very best friends. They kept coming over to my house to check on me, or bring me coffee, or give me little gifts, or cry with me. *Gigi. Grace. Caroline. Alice. Amelia.* There was somebody there all the time. My mom tried her best to make sure I didn't get exhausted by the steady stream of visitors, but the truth was it was better when someone was around. At least then I wasn't alone with my dark thoughts.

"I'm so sorry," I said to them. "You don't have to be here."

"Willow," they said. "We know we don't have to be here. We *want* to be here."

I said to them, "I don't want other people to know, okay? So please keep it quiet."

I was humbled by shame. *The black mark of cancer. Suicidal thoughts. My broken body, my splintered life.* Up to then my life had always been picture-perfect—at least from the outside—and I hadn't made peace with the fact that it had been shattered. It was hard enough that everyone from the moms at Wiles's school to the construction guy working down the street saw me in my ridiculous full-arm cast. Now to have cancer, too?

I didn't want to deal with it. I didn't want anybody to know, at least no one who wasn't already in the inner circle.

On Sunday afternoon, I was sitting on the sofa, trying desperately to watch TV as a distraction, when my phone rang. It was Gigi.

"We just got home from church," she said. "Can I come by and bring you a book? It's one that's really meant a lot to me, and I think it will help you, too."

"Sure," I said. "I'd love that."

"I'm headed out for a walk in a bit. See you soon."

Later that morning, the doorbell rang. I shuffled to answer it and saw Gigi on my front porch. But she wasn't alone—a woman named Winnie stood beside her.

Winnie was a friend of a friend. I knew she was close to Gigi, but I didn't know her all that well myself—she and I didn't have each other's cell phone numbers, that sort of thing. But there she was, standing at my front door with Gigi. My heart sank.

Did Gigi tell her I have breast cancer? Of course she did. Now I was embarrassed. Humiliation clutched at my heart as I opened the door and plastered on a smile. The three of us exchanged brief hellos and pleasantries.

"So here's the book I promised," Gigi said, after she gave me a long hug. "I really think you're going to love it."

"Okay," I said stiffly, reaching for the book with my left hand.

I locked eyes with Gigi. We sort of looked *through* each other, one of those deep moments of understanding. She shook her head, like, *She doesn't know anything.* I looked back at Winnie, who seemed oblivious to the unspoken conversation Gigi and I were having in looks and glances. "I haven't said anything," Gigi said softly, but of course Winnie was standing right there.

I wheeled around on her. "I have breast cancer."

Immediately Winnie started to cry. Gigi's eyes fogged up, too, and she brushed away the tears with the back of her hand.

Oh my God. It hit me full force: *I can't believe I've been so selfish.* Not until that moment had I realized how selfish it was of me to ask my closest friends not to tell anybody. They were suffering, too. They needed to talk about it. And I wasn't allowing that.

It's been my rules, I realized. *I've been expecting everyone else to go along with my need for privacy.*

It was October 14th, thirteen days after my diagnosis. Something was shifting inside me. *From now on, when my friends come over, I want to tell them that if there are people in their lives they need to talk to about my cancer, it's okay.*

I still didn't want *everybody* to know. I didn't want all of Columbus society to be talking about my cancer. But the people who were close to us? The people we loved? I wanted my friends to be able to talk about my cancer with those people, because they needed to. It was a lot to process, and because I'd had such a hard time processing it myself, I forgot it would be hard on my friends, too.

Amelia put together an email list so that it was easy for my friends to send out updates, and also to arrange things like who would bring my family meals on which day, and who would come over just to say hi or sit with me for a while or take me to appointments.

"This is *your* list, Willow," Amelia told me. "I want you to know you have total veto power. If you don't want somebody on this list, just say so."

When people asked Amelia or Gigi to be put on the update list, they would come to me first and ask.

I appreciated being able to say yes or no. If it was someone I didn't know very well, I would say, "You know what? I don't really know that person" or "I've never really connected to that person. I guess I'd rather them not be on it." It was so personal—I wasn't trying to play favorites and pick this or that person, it was just such an intimate time.

One day Caroline was over visiting when her phone rang and I saw her reach for it in her bra. "Caroline," I said. "Don't tell me you are still keeping your phone in your bra."

Her eyes got wide. "I forgot. Gosh, how could I forget?"

"No doctor has told me that's why I got cancer," I said, "but if I were you, I'd be extra careful."

Caroline nodded fiercely. "Thanks for looking out for me. I won't do it again."

I was touched that my friends kept showing up, that they didn't seem like they were sick of me or my many ailments. In fact, quite the opposite: more and more women joined in on the fight to help me.

I felt buoyed by people's love and concern, but I also felt confused and overwhelmed, fuzzy over the many names being added to the email list, the various casseroles being dropped off at my house by some women I knew well and some women I didn't.

"We're your Angels, Willow," Gigi said one day. "How cool is that? You've got a whole host of heavenly Angels watching over you, but you've got your earthly Angels, too, and we won't leave."

Because my closest friends all lived within a few blocks of me, they quite literally formed a halo around me. *My circle of Angels, looking out for me.* I felt enwreathed by their affection, their attention, their tenderness and love.

She rubbed my back as she said it, and her touch was soothing.

"When do you start chemo?" she asked.

"Not yet," I groaned, dreading the mere thought of it. "You won't believe it, but: first I have to fly back to New York."

Chapter 29

TWENTY-EIGHT TREATMENTS

I was on a plane again, this time headed to New York City—and not to deal with my cancer. I was still dealing with my arm.

"Can I get you anything to drink?" the flight attendant asked.

"Just water," I said. "Thanks."

I sipped cool ice water from a plastic cup and resigned myself to my miserable reverie.

By now, most people would have started their chemotherapy. But not me. I was not on a level playing field with others who walked into breast cancer. My year of arm surgeries and bone grafts had turned me, a healthy woman, into someone who was sick and weak.

I can't believe things with my arm are still so bad that I can't treat my cancer, I thought.

When I went to see my surgeon, I expected the worst. But for once he had relatively good news.

"Your immune system is definitely compromised, Willow," he said. "No doubt about that. You've had one hell of a year. But you don't need to hold off on the chemo any longer."

"What about the bone grafts?" I asked. "Don't we risk undoing all the work we've done if I start chemo?"

He shook his head. "The grafts are grafted enough at this point for you to start."

"Okay. I guess that's good news." I swallowed hard. "When can I start chemo?"

He looked at me sternly. "Right away."

***

Oliver and I pulled up to the Arthur G. James Cancer Hospital at Ohio State University. The oncologist there had been highly recommended, and though I had my doubts, I was at least willing to meet him.

I left Oliver to park the car and went into the big square building, taking the elevator up to the fourth floor. My heart was pounding in my chest. Things were starting to become even more real. When I got to the waiting room, I went to check in at the counter and noticed a really cute girl who was standing in front of me. My heart clenched. *Oh my God. I know her.*

She was another mom from The Wellington School. There I was, standing behind her, wanting more than anything for her not to see me. *Don't turn around, don't turn around, don't turn around,* I chanted inside my head. Oliver was still parking the car, but I kept turning around, begging for him to get there. I didn't want anybody to know I had cancer other than the people who were close to me, and the people who were close to them. And it's not like I would be standing in that line for any other reason.

But what's she *doing here?* I wondered.

Then I remembered that she had had breast cancer a couple years back. *She's probably coming in for her checkup. I should ask her how she's doing.* But I was too scared and embarrassed. I didn't feel up to branching out of my own little bubble. To do so would mean acknowledging to the world that I had cancer, and I wasn't ready to do that yet.

Eventually she recognized me and we exchanged small talk, but all I really wanted to do was hide.

She left and I went to sit and wait. Pretty soon I would spend weeks and months, hours and hours sitting and waiting in that office. The oncologist was popular and a little overworked—there was always a line of people waiting to see him.

By then Oliver had come up to the fourth floor, and together we tucked ourselves into the far corner of the waiting room. I felt everyone's eyes on me. *The new girl.* Nervously I reached for Oliver's hand. "It's okay, Willow," he said, trying to calm me. "We're just here to interview the doctor, remember?"

I couldn't help but assess the other people in the room. *We all have cancer. All of us.* Everybody other than the Wellington mom was a good few years older than I was, so that was hard. The men and women in that waiting room were in their sixties and seventies. But there I was, barely past forty, sitting there in their midst.

Why me? Why is this happening? Why am I here? I'm forty-one years old. This is nuts. I was so mad. I'd spent most of the last few weeks feeling angry, and also scared to death, while at the same time plotting my exit. The most terrible thoughts paraded through my mind relentlessly. *I'm not going to be able to raise my kids. I'm not going to watch them get married. I'm not going to have grandchildren. My husband's going to marry somebody else. My kids are going to suffer their whole life because of my death.* It was horrible. The knowledge that I had a really aggressive form of cancer made it worse. And it was a fast-growing cancer, too.

I didn't have it in my lymph nodes, I thought. *That was a miracle. I mean, praise God. And thank God we are finally starting chemo so I can get the cancer out of my body once and for all.*

"Willow Adair?" A nurse poked her head through the door. "Come on back."

Oliver walked beside me into a small bright room where we sat waiting in silence. The longer we waited, the more I told myself I wasn't going to like this doctor.

After about fifteen minutes, the oncologist strode in breezily.

"Hi!" he said. "You must be Willow—I've heard about you. And that must be the ARM." He smiled.

I liked him immediately. He had done his homework.

"How're you feeling today, Willow? Because you look absolutely fantastic, other than that ghastly cast you've got working."

He was so upbeat and happy. He was also encouraging. As I filled him in on my arm and my version of the cancer diagnosis, he nodded and acted like it was no big deal. "You got this, girl," he said. "We'll get through this, and you're going to come out kicking on the other side, make no mistake."

I knew in that first five minutes that this was the doctor I'd been waiting for, someone positive who wasn't going to screw things up for me.

"I'll be right back, okay?" he said with a smile.

When he left the room, I turned to Oliver and said, "I think he's not going to make me do chemo."

"You think? That seems unlikely."

"I don't know. It kinda sounded that way, didn't it?"

But when the doctor came back in, he had written down my chemo regimen on a piece of paper and started to explain it to me.

"I want to see you here next week," the doctor said, "for treatment number one. October 31st, okay?"

"Halloween?" I said.

"That's right. But there's nothing scary about this. Goblins are much scarier," he joked. "And before that, you'll have to check into the hospital on the 30th to have them place the port in your chest. It's day surgery."

I could feel myself go white as a sheet. "What? A port, too?" I immediately flashed back to the PICC line they had put in my arm for my infection and, years before that, the port in my neck after the colon surgery. The thought of having another wire coming out of me made me nauseated.

"I'm afraid so," the doctor said. "We'll put in the port and then you'll start treatment. Now that the big doc in NYC says your bone grafts are healing, it's time to get serious and start chemo right away. We'll leave the port in for about a year."

My stomach dropped. *A year? Come on. You've got to be kidding me.* My brain was still fighting desperately to convince myself things weren't that bad. *Maybe it's minimal. Maybe he really just means a few chemo treatments, and then the worst part will be over.*

I looked down at the paper: *Twenty-eight chemo treatments. I must be wrong.*

Oh my God.

Chapter 30

HALLOWEEN

"It's not twenty-eight, Willow. It's sixteen chemo treatments." Oliver brandished the paper in my face. "It says right here, see? You're reading it wrong."

We were standing in our bedroom, the moonlight peeking through the blinds, and things were tense between us. I squinted at the paper for at least the tenth time that night. "I don't know how you're reading this differently than I am, but it clearly says twenty-eight."

Oliver exhaled in frustration. "Sometimes I really can't reason with you. Do you want everything to be the worst-case scenario? Are you trying to make this harder than it has to be?"

"No! Why on earth would I do that?"

"Beats me!"

Oliver and I stared at each other. We were at an impasse: he felt certain the doctor had outlined sixteen chemo treatments, and I counted twenty-eight. To be fair, it was kind of confusing. The paper did not exactly make it clear.

"Willow," Oliver said. His voice was lower and calmer now. "Neither of us wants you to have any more chemo than you absolutely have to. I understand that. I don't want you to suffer, and I know you don't want to suffer, either." He took a deep breath. "It seems pretty clear to me that he's saying you'll need sixteen treatments."

Sixteen was still an unthinkably high number. At CTCA, they'd told me I would probably need between six and nine. And I'd certainly done my research. Jules had connected me with three different women in Miami who'd all survived breast cancer, and none of them had had anywhere close to sixteen chemos. Sixteen was absurd, but then twenty-eight was even more so.

I laid the paper face down on my dresser. I didn't want to look at it anymore. "Okay, fine," I said, suddenly exhausted. "I believe you. It's sixteen."

Oliver was wrong, unfortunately. But for the first month of chemo, I chose to ignore the signs that it was really twenty-eight. It was simply too much to grasp, and it was better not to face it.

***

It was the week before Halloween. A friend had come over to put up Halloween decorations since I couldn't do anything myself, not with my arm in a cast and the stitches from the lumpectomy still healing up. We had two big boxes of decorations in the attic, filled to the brim with clay pumpkins and wall hangings of witches and goblins. Both my kids loved when we made the house seasonally festive, and in Bullitt Park, holiday decorations were very popular.

But that year, the skeletons dangling from doorways and hanging ominously from the eaves of our front porch suddenly took on a more sinister meaning. I was still thinking seriously about killing myself. Some days were better than others, but when I really got to thinking about the sixteen—or twenty-eight—chemo treatments that awaited me, it was easy to lose hope. *I could end it,* whispered a persistent little voice in my head. *I could end everything, right now.* I wasn't even conscious of it, but every time I walked past those decorations, I was staring death in the face.

It felt like I was doing that every day anyway. By that point I was having regular night terrors. The nightmares would close in on me just as I drifted off to sleep, so full of death and darkness that I would often wake up shaking in a full-body sweat. Death felt like it was never very far away. It was creeping in around me, and I felt most vulnerable when I was asleep.

Ring. My phone went off on the bathroom counter as I tried to brush my teeth. *Gigi.*

"Hey, Gigi, hi."

"Hey, Willow. Amelia and I were wondering if we could drop by for half an hour?"

"Sure. I'd love to see you."

"Eleven o'clock?"

"Sounds good."

I hung up the phone feeling vaguely curious. Gigi and Amelia had been over at the house plenty of times over the last few weeks, but rarely together. And I knew Gigi well enough to know when she had an agenda for something she wanted to get done. She definitely had that tone in her voice: this wasn't just a pleasure visit. Gigi was on a mission.

Wonder what this is about? I mused.

An hour later, Amelia and Gigi were sitting on the sofa, staring at me with tremendous love and concern. I felt lucky to have such dear friends. I knew Amelia and Gigi were always looking out for me. They had my back.

"The Lord put something on my heart, Willow," Gigi said, pulling her well-worn Bible out of her purse. "There's a Scripture in Deuteronomy I'd like to read to you."

I nodded. "Yes."

"Deuteronomy 30:19. 'This day I call the heavens and the earth as witnesses against you that I have set before you life and death, blessings and curses. Now choose life, so that you and your children may live.'"

Gently Gigi closed her Bible. "I know you've been struggling, Willow. You've talked about wanting to kill yourself, about wanting to relieve us of the burden of caring for you and relieving yourself of the pain you're about to experience. I know you're thinking a lot about death, and I hope you hear us when we tell you how much we love you, and how much God loves you, and how valuable your life is. Taking your life isn't just a mistake because it's a sin.

It's a mistake because it gets carried on through many generations. It affects your children and your children's children. Suicide is never the answer."

Gigi pointed to the string of skeletons hanging between the kitchen and the living room. "That's why we don't want anything having to do with death in your house."

I stared at the decorations. They'd seemed so innocuous in former years, but Gigi was right: they didn't seem so cute or fun anymore.

Amelia chimed in. "You know we all love Halloween, Willow. It's so fun. Our kids get to dress up and go trick-or-treating. Gigi has a party every year. But we also talk about not glorifying what's evil, and only glorifying what is good."

She gestured toward the large skeleton hanging on the front door. "I know you've been having night terrors. I'm worried that all the skulls are contributing subconsciously to your nightmares. You're having a hard time sleeping and then you get all these awful, frightening visions. The thing is, the stuff we look at while we're awake? It's also the stuff we see at night when we're sleeping."

"Wow," I said. "Oh my gosh. I never even thought of that." I hadn't drawn an explicit connection between the Halloween decorations and my night terrors, but it made perfect sense.

"The skeletons really do symbolize death," Amelia said. "And death is something we don't want to have anywhere in this house. We want everything in your house to be about life. Everything should be positive and uplifting. So we're going to remove anything that has the feel of darkness or death. We're going to do that for you. You don't have to lift a finger—I'm going to take you out to lunch, and Gigi is going to do a little spring cleaning. Only it's fall cleaning now."

I felt my eyes well up with tears. *My friends are so good to me. What did I do to deserve friends this amazing? They are not forsaking me. I will survive this,* I thought. *I will not be alone.*

"Thank you," I said. "Thank you both."

That day, Amelia took me to lunch and Gigi went through each room of my house and took out all the skeletons and witches and goblins. She combed 9,000 square feet and removed anything that had even a remote connotation of death or dying. Even our dog bowl had skulls and crossbones on it, so that went, too.

But not only did she take everything out—she replaced it. She brought in Halloween decorations that represented life in all its fullness. She decorated my house with things that were living, not things that were dead. Amelia and Gigi taught me never to speak about death in my house or around my kids, but to only speak life.

It was a really big day for me. When Melia brought me back to my house and I saw all the new decorations Gigi had put up, I broke down and cried. My home still looked festive, and Wiles would come home from school to a house that looked warm and cozy and full of holiday cheer. But instead of skulls and skeletons, my house was now full of love and life. And Bella was coming home from school, too; I knew she would love the new decorations. Oh, how I ached to see my daughter.

"Choose life, not death," Gigi said.

"And it's not just about Halloween," Amelia added. "Let's make this a choice. Let's get back that positive mindset that you are going to *live*."

I felt awareness flowing over me like buttery warm sunshine. *Huh,* I thought. *Maybe I* should *stick around. Maybe this suicide thing isn't such a great idea. Maybe God has bigger plans here, and I shouldn't be selfish in taking my life because that single act is going to have grave consequences for other people for many, many years.*

Slowly but surely, I was coming around. There was a subtle shift happening inside me, one I wasn't even fully aware of yet. Instead of fighting for the right to kill myself, I was beginning to fight for my life. *Maybe I don't want to die,* I thought. *Maybe I want to live.*

Chapter 31

FRIENDS AND FACE PAINT

"How do you feel, Willow? Are you scared?"

The crisp autumn sun poured through the cafe window, shimmering off Caroline's blonde hair. We were at lunch, she and I, with the specter of chemotherapy looming over me. I would have my first Red Devil, the most severe of all chemo cocktails, in just one week.

"I'm terrified," I said. "It doesn't even feel like it's my life."

Caroline sipped her iced tea. "I can only imagine."

"I've been talking to a lot of women who've had breast cancer," I said, "and they tell me the Red Devil is the absolute worst. I guess it's the strongest of all the drugs. They said once I've made it through the Red Devil, the rest of the treatments will feel like a walk in the park."

Caroline's face was awash in sympathy. "I'm just so sorry, Willow. I don't know why you of all people deserve this. You're such a good person. It just doesn't seem fair. I would take it for you, I really would."

I stared out the window. Two large oak trees framed the cafe, and their leaves were beginning to turn burgundy and rust. I poked at my omelet with a fork, but I didn't have much of an appetite.

Then I heard a familiar voice behind me. "Willow??"

I turned around in my chair, careful not to knock my arm, and saw Grace hurrying toward me with two shopping bags slung over her arm. I didn't even like shopping and I still felt nostalgic, remembering a time when I could throw a Marc Jacobs bag over my right arm without thinking twice about it.

I jumped up and hugged her.

"I'm so glad to see you," Grace said, kissing me on the cheek. "You know Emily, right?"

"Yeah, sure! Yes, I do." I smiled at Emily. She was more of an acquaintance than a friend. I knew she had four kids and a husband who commuted between Toronto and Columbus on a regular basis, which meant Emily had her hands full.

"Great to see you, Willow! You look gorgeous as ever. You're so pretty it hurts just to look at you." Emily was one of those women with a big personality—big voice, big smile, big heart.

Does she know? I wondered. Every time I had run into a casual acquaintance over the last few weeks, my heart was gripped with that very question. *Does she know I have cancer?* Since Emily was Grace's good friend, it was totally possible Grace had confided in her. But I also knew Grace was fiercely protective of my privacy, and she had told me that, unless I was okay with it, she wasn't going to talk about my cancer with anyone.

I looked into Emily's eyes. I was pretty sure she had no idea.

"You girls know Caroline, right?" I asked.

We all chatted for a few minutes about our kids and our Halloween plans, until Grace said, "We won't keep you. Just wanted to say hi, precious."

And with a swoosh of shopping bags, they were gone.

"Do they know?" Caroline asked. "About . . ."

"Grace does. I don't know about Emily. I just don't know her that well, you know?"

But later that night, as I sat in the living room watching TV with Wiles, my cell phone rang. It was a ring I didn't recognize, so I picked up immediately.

"Hello?"

"Hey, Willow? It's Emily."

"Oh, hi, Emily." I stepped out of the living room so as not to disturb Wiles.

"Listen, can we have breakfast someday soon?" Emily asked. "I feel like there's something up. There's something you're not telling me."

"No no no," I said, my heart thumping in my chest. "Everything's fine."

"Really? Because I got a weird vibe today, seeing you at the cafe. And I just feel like—I don't know. I feel like there's something going on."

"I'm fine, Emily. But I do appreciate you thinking of me. I've got to run now—my son needs me, and I need to call Bella before the night gets away from me."

I felt slightly guilty as I hung up. *But this is your choice, remember, Willow? You get to decide who you want to be on the inner circle. You don't want people involved whom you don't know intimately.*

I nestled back into the sofa beside Wiles and tried to quiet my mind as I dialed up Bella's cell phone, hoping she would pick up. But for the next few days, Emily kept calling. She really wanted to get breakfast, and I kept putting her off. It wasn't just that I didn't know her all that well—it was that I felt selfish. Every time I told someone I had breast cancer, I felt like I was taking from them, and that I didn't really deserve it. *I don't know Emily well enough to take her kindness, sympathy, and worry,* I thought.

But she was persistent. Three days before my chemo, I finally texted her and said, "Just ask Grace what's going on."

An hour later, she was standing on my doorstep, crying. As soon as I opened the door, I started crying, too.

"Oh my God, Willow," she said. "I want to be here. I want to be here for you and walk through this by your side." I was stunned. I still had a hard time trusting that people would show up.

From that moment forward, she never turned back. Emily was full force. She went from not even knowing I had cancer to being one of the Angels at the heart of our growing group.

A good thing, too, because I was about to need all the Angels I could get.

***

Amelia and I were sitting at 89 Fish & Grill, a cute seafood restaurant in downtown Columbus. She nibbled on a plantain chip as I stared down at my veggie wrap. It looked beautiful, and yet I couldn't imagine eating a single bite.

"I don't blame you for not being hungry," Amelia said gently, "but maybe you should try and eat something. You might not be able to eat anything over the next few days."

It was the day before my first chemo, and Amelia had offered to take me out to lunch. There were a billion thoughts and fears swarming inside me, but Melia was wise enough to know that, instead of talking endlessly about my worst fears, what I really needed was peace, quiet, and the comforting presence of a good friend.

Halloween was on the horizon, and a table away from us, a mom was eating fish and chips with her young daughter. Both of them had their faces painted—the little girl was a butterfly and her mom was a tiger.

"Look at that," Amelia said. "If that isn't the cutest thing I've ever seen."

An idea flickered in the corners of my mind. "I want to talk to that woman," I said. I stood up, walked over to the table, and introduced myself.

"I love your face," I said to the mom, and she smiled shyly. Amelia had followed me to the table and stood by my side, probably not sure what I was doing.

"Oh, thanks. It's for my daughter's Halloween party at school."

"Where'd you get it done?" I asked.

"Actually, my husband did it. He's an artist."

"Daddy paints pictures!" the little girl chirped, clearly proud of her dad.

I smiled at the girl before turning back to her mother. "Listen, this is kind of a strange request, but I go in for my first chemo treatment tomorrow." I swallowed. "Do you think your husband would paint my face?"

"Oh my God," the woman said, all traces of her smile disappearing. "Yes, of course he'd do that. I mean, let me ask him, but I'm sure he'd love to. You go in tomorrow, you said?"

"Tomorrow morning."

She was already reaching for her phone. "I'll text him right now."

Within seconds her phone beeped with his reply. "No problem," he said. "Tell her to come over first thing."

I felt a faint surge of hope as the woman scrawled her address on a napkin and handed it to me. The nightmare of what lay ahead was black and powerful in my mind, but a shimmer of hope shone amid the darkness.

At least if my face is painted, no one can see me. No one can see my face.

Chapter 32

A LIVING HELL

I sat quietly in the house of a stranger. *Almost* a stranger, anyway—it was the husband of the woman Amelia and I had seen the day before at the Fish & Grill.

"I'm sorry," he said, his hand trembling slightly. "Just give me a minute. I've never . . . no one's ever asked me to do this before." Amelia sat next to me and squeezed my hand. She didn't think this was the best idea, but she brought me here and supported my decision.

I couldn't look at Melia because I knew we both would have burst into tears. We just squeezed hands tightly. I was asking a lot of a perfect stranger, but I was starting to ask for what I needed, and that was empowering.

Usually the man painted cute tigers and butterflies on the faces of his wife and little girl. "For my daughter's last birthday party," he'd told me, "I did custom-tailored face paint for all the girls. Whatever they wanted. We had so many Princess Meridas, you would not believe."

I smiled.

The man took a deep breath. "But I can honestly say this is the first time I've been asked to paint someone's face before they start chemo," he said, his tone somber.

"Well, I really appreciate you doing this," I said softly. "Especially on such short notice."

Oliver was waiting at home. He'd taken the day off from work so he could go with me to my first chemo. When I told him I was getting my face painted, he nodded. He knew it wasn't for Halloween. It was because I didn't want anyone to see my face.

"I want a princess," I told the man, as he stood above me, his paintbrush poised, ready to work its magic. "A pretty princess with a crown." Amelia clutched me tighter.

I'm so afraid, I thought, as I closed my eyes and felt the brushstrokes soft against my face. He began to gently paint a swirl of sparkly pink on each cheek, but I kept my eyes shut tight. *At least now, no one will be able to see.*

***

Stay calm. Just breathe. Focus. Center yourself. It's all going to be all right.

I tried to focus on my breathing like I'd done in yoga, though yoga seemed like it was a million years ago. I was back on the fourth floor of the James Cancer Hospital at OSU, waiting in line to see my oncologist, and the line was five or six people deep. This was standard procedure as the doctor had explained it to me: each time before getting chemo, I would sign in with him upstairs, wait in line, and then go back to get my blood work done. Then we'd wait for the lab results to make sure my count was high enough to *get* chemo. Once he had cleared me for chemo, I'd go down to the third floor to wait, at which point I wasn't quite sure what would happen next or how, but I knew that was the chemo floor.

"Hi. Hello." I was finally at the counter. I signed in with the two girls there and paid my copay. Then I sat with Oliver for a few minutes, which seemed more like a few hours. People stared at my face paint. One older woman smiled and told me I looked beautiful. I thanked her but inside I was simmering. I didn't want to be waiting here, stuck with all these sick people. *I don't want people looking at me. The whole point of having my face painted is that no one can see me.* They did see my face, of course, but it wasn't *my* face, and somehow that made it better.

"Willow Adair?"

A nurse with a warm smile motioned me back. "I'm Shay Shay," she said. "Nice to meet you."

"I'm Willow," I muttered, and Oliver introduced himself, too.

"Love your face," Shay Shay said. "You go, girl."

This nurse was a beacon of light in the darkness. She took me to a small, quiet room and took a blood sample so they could run the labs downstairs. Shay Shay was good. I'd had my share of horrible nurses, but she got the needle cleanly into my vein on the first try and extracted the blood smoothly and efficiently. I turned to the left so I didn't have to watch. I always turned away.

"You're all done here," said Shay Shay. "I'm going to send this down to the lab."

Shay Shay led me down the hall that opened up onto a larger waiting room. She pointed to another counter. "Sign in there now and Tiffany, your oncologist's nurse, will come get you, okay? But fair warning: get ready for a wait." She gave my arm a gentle pat. "You're going to be just fine, honey."

Helplessly, I watched her go.

I stepped up to the counter and cleared my throat. "Hi, I'm Willow Adair?"

"Sign in right here," said the woman behind the counter. "And then make yourself comfortable."

Why can't Oliver sign me in so I can be more anonymous? I thought.

I looked around the second waiting area. The room was bigger than the lobby outside—there were TVs and a coffee machine. In the corner I spied a basket of hand-knit hats for people going through chemo. There were magazines stacked up on the chairs, and postings on the wall of cancer support groups.

I closed my eyes. *I don't want to be here. This is the last place on earth I want to be.*

"Let's sit down," Oliver said. "Since we're here for the long haul."

I followed him to an open chair, his words striking terror into my soul. *Here for the long haul.*

The waiting was horrible. Twenty minutes passed, then thirty, then forty minutes slid by on the overhead clock. Every time I looked at that clock I got madder. *You don't make people wait who are about to get chemo,* I seethed. After fifty minutes, I was livid. I knew I was being irrational; the lab work wasn't instantaneous. They had to run tests in my blood to make sure I could sustain chemo that day. But my irrational brain was in total control. *It's bad enough that I have to be here at all—now the doctor is going to make me sit in this waiting room like a caged beast?*

"You doing okay, Willow?" Oliver asked. He was sitting beside me with his legs crossed, ankle resting lightly on one knee.

"No," I rasped, though my voice was barely above a whisper. "I just want to get it over with. The longer I wait, the more worked up I get."

An hour and ten minutes. That's how long we waited. I was actually shaking, so angry at my doctor for making me spend that much time in a waiting room surrounded by crocheted hats and the people who needed them, imagining all the horrors that were to come.

"Willow Adair?"

A pretty brunette nurse in turquoise scrubs appeared before me. She smiled. "Sorry for the wait. I'm Tiffany. I'll take you back to see your doctor now."

Tiffany was another breath of fresh air. This was my doctor's nurse, and I knew this meant I would be seeing him soon. She installed Oliver and me in a smaller room, then took my blood pressure and my temperature. Tiffany had me stand on a scale so she could record my weight. "So far, so good," she said, smiling warmly. "Your doctor will be in in just a few minutes."

As soon as she was gone, the fury started to choke me again. *More waiting. I can't believe this.* I started pacing the tiny room, which made Oliver nervous.

"Can't you just sit, Willow? You're only getting yourself more riled up."

But I couldn't sit. I was a teeming ball of rage and hurt and terror, and I knew I'd have to sit for the next God-knows-how-many hours, waiting for the actual chemo. The last thing I wanted to do was sit. I wanted to call Bella and be home when Wiles got home from school. This waiting wasn't helping me reach my kids, and I wanted to cling to them, too.

Five minutes later, the doctor strolled through the door.

"Howdy, Willow," he said. "How ya doin' today, and how's that arm of yours?"

I blinked. *Did he actually just ask that?* The doctor's laid-back, cheerful attitude that had seemed so appealing now just added insult to injury. *I'm here for chemo. I've been waiting in your lobby for an hour and a half. How do YOU think I'm doing today?*

"To be honest?" I snapped. "I've had better days."

I was being a jerk. I couldn't help it. I felt rage boiling inside me, at everything and everyone.

"Uh huh," the doctor said. "I hear you. Sorry about the wait—the waiting room's a doozy today."

"That's one word for it." I clamped my mouth shut before I could say anything else.

I knew it wasn't the doctor's fault that all these people had cancer. It certainly wasn't his fault that *I* had cancer, though he was an easy target. *Every day he deals with people who are really sick,* I reminded myself. *He's probably used to people being jerks. He's certainly seen it before—but that's not who I want to be.*

The doctor had a small portable computer with him. I saw something yellow pop up on the screen. "Uh huh," he said. "Looks like your labs are ready. Let's have a look, shall we? We'll make sure everything checks out." He started scrolling, checking various numbers, nodding and *mm-hmm*-ing to himself.

This is torture, I thought. *Standing here like this, waiting to see if I can get chemo today. It's excruciating. Who on earth invented such an arcane system?*

My phone buzzed. It was a text from Alice—the perfect distraction. "Whenever you think of chemo," she said, "this is what you need to think: CHEMO. Christ Has Eliminated My Opponent."

I smiled, tears springing to my eyes. *Oh, Alice.* It was exactly what I needed to hear at that moment. *Christ Has Eliminated My Opponent.* On that very sad day, with my face painted up like a princess, I clung to those words like a life raft, the only thing to buffer me from the crashing waves.

The doctor snapped his computer shut. "Your blood work looks good. You're cleared for chemo, so we can start today as planned."

He looked at me and grinned. "I like your face, by the way. Perfect for Halloween."

"Thanks," I hissed, hating how vindictive I sounded. I wouldn't look at him—I was looking straight down at the floor. I felt sick to my stomach. To be honest, I wanted to claw the doctor's eyes out. *Why is he grinning at me like a fool? Why is everyone acting like this is okay? There is nothing okay about this. I am not okay!*

My doctor stared at me for an extra beat, as if he could sense something awry. "Willow," he said. "I know you're pissed. That's okay. Be pissed. Be pissed at me if you need to. I can take it. I've been doing this a long time."

"How can you be so laid back about this?" I asked hoarsely. I still wouldn't meet his gaze.

"Because this is nothing," he said. "Because you are going to outlive this thing. Look at me, Willow."

Slowly I raised my eyes to meet his. I didn't want to, but he was insistent. "I am going to chemo the crap out of you," he said. "And do you know why? You are so young and you are going to live the rest of your life. So I am going to put you through hell, and you're going to be awesome when you're done. You're not going to have a shred of cancer left anywhere in your body."

My eyes were welling over now, and I wasn't even trying to stop them. I could feel Oliver in his chair, shifting his weight. I was too afraid to look at him.

"But I am telling you right now, Willow," the doctor continued. "It's going to be a living hell. And you're going to be mad at me, and you're going to ask me, 'Why? Why are you doing this?' Your friends are going to be mad at me, your family's going to be mad at me. But I don't care. Honestly, I don't give a crap how mad everybody is. I'm going to keep giving you more chemo. And do you know why?"

I shook my head, tears streaming like hot ribbons down both cheeks, smearing the paint and turning my face into that of a sad, ruined princess.

"Because once we're done with your treatment, I never want to see you here again."

Chapter 33

THE RED DEVIL

The nurse I was assigned to on the third floor was a total nightmare. She was the polar opposite of the nurses I had met on the fourth floor. Whereas they had been warm and kind, compassionate and confident, this nurse was not only bad at her job—she was a jerk about it.

"Ms. Adair? I'm not going to call you again."

Wait, what? You didn't call me the first time. I was confused.

"You didn't—" I started to say.

"Ms. Adair, I really don't need any of your attitude today." The nurse slammed her hand down on the sign-in clipboard. "We need your insurance information."

She looked at me like I was ruining her whole day. *That's funny,* I thought to myself. *Because I'm pretty sure* you *are ruining* mine.

"I gave you my card when I came in," I snapped. I nodded toward another nurse. "She made a photocopy."

"I don't see it here."

"Well, you have it. Can I please sit down now?"

I was angry at this woman for ruffling my feathers, angry that she'd managed to make a bad day even worse. She glowered at me as I trudged back to my seat beside Oliver. *That nurse is so cold and mean. How am I ever going to make it through sixteen of these treatments?*

"Ms. Adair?" she called out a few minutes later from behind the counter. *She must have found my card.* I felt a faint glow of triumph. *I told her I'd already given it to them.* "We're ready for you now." She glanced impatiently at her watch. "We don't have all day."

My jaw dropped in utter amazement. I'd been waiting for an hour in the chemo room—even more waiting tacked onto the waiting I'd already done. And now she was trying to make it sound like it was *my* fault?

"I'm ready," I said sourly. "And I'm not the one holding things up." I hated that I was being mean to her, but she was asking for it. I was so unhappy to be there, and Oliver was standing right beside me, silent as usual, not intervening. I could tell he was profoundly uncomfortable, and maybe even embarrassed.

The nurse put her hand on her hip and cocked her head to one side. "Who painted your face? Because it's a wreck. I don't know if you've been crying or what."

This woman was downright cruel. *Of course I've been crying. I'm here for my very first chemo treatment. Who wouldn't be?*

I bit my lip, trying not to cry more as I followed the nurse down a long hallway, back to the chemo room. The last thing I wanted was for her to see me cry. She led me to a far corner and, grumbling the whole time, hooked up my port. Needless to say, she was a long way from gentle, and I wasn't sure what hurt more: my body or my pride.

"That's your section," she said gruffly, pointing with one long and terrifying curled purple fingernail. She jerked her head toward one of the nurses. "That's her section. When she gets a chair open, she'll come and get you. But don't you be expecting none of that special treatment in here. Down in the chemo room, everyone's the same."

With that she sauntered off, flipping her hair, as if she were trying to shuck off any memory of me.

I felt sick. I shrank even further into myself. I knew I probably looked ridiculous, the pink sparkly princess paint smeared on my face. There just wasn't anywhere else to hide.

"How long do you think we'll have to wait?" I asked Oliver.

"I really have no idea. Maybe you can read a magazine or something. Try and keep your mind off things." He brought me a big stack of glossy fashion magazines, but the last thing I wanted was to see beautiful, healthy women with long flowing hair. And with the cast on my arm, I wasn't really able to flip through magazines. *Oliver should know that.* Instead I tried to meditate. I couldn't believe I had to spend more time waiting. It took everything in me to just sit there and wait.

My phone buzzed. It was a text message from Frenny. "Just wanted to tell you I have you in my heart baby. I'm praying. I want you to be ok sweetie. I love you."

To my surprise, I saw a handful of other text messages I had somehow missed. *My phone must have been on silent.* Hungry for words of love and comfort, I scrolled through them.

Gigi: "I wanted to share a few verses with you, Willow. Maybe you can have it in mind during chemo today. It's Psalm 103:1–4. 'Praise the Lord, my soul; all my inmost being, praise His holy name. Praise the Lord, my soul, and forget not all His benefits—who forgives all your sins and heals all your diseases, who redeems your life from the pit and crowns you with love and compassion.'"

Jules: "Hey. You will push through. You will do great. You don't have a choice. Your brain will be so foggy that by the time you are thinking clearly, treatment will be over. So just move forward. Hang in there. That's all you have to do. Big kiss. Sending u a kiss and the sun. Keep us posted. Xoxo."

Amelia: "I know it's the Red Devil today, and I know it's going to be hard. So I want you to know that I love you, Willow, and I'm one of many. We, especially us Christians, are to serve. To be the hands and feet of Christ. We love you, so we love helping you. Remember that your Angels are lifting you up today."

My eyes fogged over. *I am beyond blessed to have my friends.*

"Hi, Willow." It was a small, petite nurse with red hair, her voice just as small as she was. "We're ready for you now."

She led me to an open chair in her section of the chemo room and got me situated. She fiddled with my port and picked up a sinister looking bag of red liquid. "The Red Devil today, huh?" she asked.

"Yes. It's my first treatment."

She shook her head. "Your doc is starting you out full force. This is the worst one. But it really does get better."

My throat felt parched like cotton. I'd done enough research on the Red Devil to know what I was in for. The breast cancer survivors I'd spoken to said it was hands down the worst of all the chemo treatments. The Googling I'd done didn't make it sound any less dire. The drug's official name was Adriamycin/Cytoxan (A/C), and its side effects were many—everything from mouth sores and low platelets to, of course, hair loss. This disgustingly potent chemo had even been linked to heart failure, which was all the more horrifying. I couldn't help but wonder: *Is the drug that's supposed to save me actually going to kill me?*

Because of the severity of the drug, I could only have four Red Devil treatments in my entire life. Meaning, if the cancer came back, Adriamycin/Cytoxan was no longer an option. But according to my doctor, that wasn't a concern. He was starting me out on the Red Devil because he was staunchly committed to kicking cancer to the curb.

As I stared at the red bag of drugs the nurse was hooking up to my port, I felt sick to my stomach. The potion was bright red, sickly looking. *No wonder they call it the Red Devil.*

"All hooked up," the nurse said. "Now just sit tight."

I turned my head away. I didn't want to look at the red crap shunting through my veins.

***

Eight hours.

If I'd thought I was waiting a long time before, that was nothing compared to the time I had to sit in that sad, terrifying room, the Red Devil spreading its nefariously toxic "cure" through my body. The redheaded nurse assured me that this was typical: since it was my very first chemo, they had to give me two hours of Benadryl in case I had an adverse reaction to the A/C.

Five hours of the Red Devil, two hours of Benadryl, and one hour of just fluids. *This is a nightmare. A nightmare I can't wake up from.*

By the end of those eight hours, I was woozy, less from the actual drug—it would take a couple days to go into full effect—and more from the fact that I'd been in the same seat for so many hours. Jules was right: my head was so foggy. Oliver had gone out and come back in a couple times, leaving once to grab lunch for us, though of course I wasn't hungry. Sometimes I saw him furiously typing away on his phone, probably taking care of business. *Oliver,* I thought, through the thick fog in my brain. *Oliver, look at me.* He didn't.

It was a full day. By the time Oliver held my hand, steadying me as we walked out of the building and back to our car, the sun was setting. The sky was awash in brilliant hues of pink, gold, and yellow, but I couldn't see it. Or if I could, it was just a blur, something beautiful that I couldn't fully take in because my own experience was awash in horror.

"What happens now?" I asked Oliver, scared. "What do we do now?"

"We go home. You rest and try to eat something. Remember to drink lots of fluids—that's what they said."

I watched as a family tottered out of the hospital and toward their car in the parking lot. The kids were wearing superhero costumes and the mom was dressed like a witch with a tall pointy hat.

"It's Halloween," I murmured. I'd almost forgotten. "I think I'm going to try and go to Gigi's party tonight."

Oliver blinked. "You're joking, right? Willow. Come on. You just had your first chemo treatment."

"I'm not joking." I grimaced. "Wiles will want to go, and I want to keep things as normal as possible." I also desperately wanted to see my friends.

Oliver just shook his head at me. I could tell he thought it was a bad idea, but neither of us wanted to argue.

I did go to Gigi's party, waiting every minute to feel sick. I didn't eat anything because I was so afraid I would have to run into the guest bathroom to vomit. But I didn't get sick that night.

The next few days? Those were another matter.

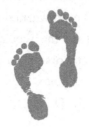

Chapter 34

MAKING ME SICK

The nausea meds were worthless. The doctor had prescribed anti-nausea pills for the side effects of the Red Devil, but they didn't do a thing.

I sat in my bathroom upstairs, hugging my knees. The tile was cool and smooth and sometimes I leaned down and laid my cheek against it. But closing my eyes only made the nausea worse. I could hear Wiles downstairs, chatting happily with Oliver. They were eating the dinner that one of my friends had brought. The thought of putting a single bite of food in my mouth turned my stomach.

It was Thursday, November 1st: the day after my first chemo treatment. Things weren't as horrible as they could be, but they weren't great. The nurse had warned me that I might experience bone pain from the drugs, and indeed I had—the pain oscillated from a low, dull throb to a sharp spike of pain deep in my bones. But to be honest, after everything I'd gone through with my arm? *Piece of cake.*

There were other side effects that were just plain weird. When I peed it came out bright red, though the last few times I'd used the bathroom it had faded to a neon orange, so dazzling it was hard to look at. I found it unnerving, seeing the fluid come out of my body the exact same color it had gone in.

My mouth was very sore and my gums were painfully sensitive. My throat was extremely scratchy. They'd warned me about this, too.

Still, looking ahead toward the weekend was like looking down the barrel of a gun. I knew it would get worse—probably much worse—and I wasn't looking forward to what was coming next.

I mentally replayed the "To Do" list I'd been handed by the nurse after leaving chemo:

> **Drink plenty of fluids.**
> **Your fingernails may break easily or turn black—that's normal.**
> **Don't be alarmed by the color of your urine.**
> **Foods may taste metallic, and the smell of the A/C may linger.**

It was true: everything had the worst smell. It was like I could still smell the drug on my skin, in my hair, even in the air I breathed. It felt like a ghost following me from room to room.

But the last item was the one that chilled me to the bone.

> **Some cancer patients make the decision to get their head shaved or their hair cut close to the scalp, rather than having to deal with patches of hair falling out. This is a very individual decision that only you can make.**

I was dreading that last one more than anything. I knew I wanted to get my hair cut before I lost all of it, but even that was a difficult decision. I loved my long, blond hair and took great pride in it. My friends always complimented it—it was kind of my signature thing—and my full head of hair had certainly served me well in my modeling career. For so long it had been an identifying attribute of my appearance, and in seventeen days—exactly seventeen days from that first chemo, my doctor had said—it would be gone.

My phone went off with Amelia's ringtone. *Music to my ears.*

"Hey, Melia. Hi."

"How are you holding up, sweetie?"

"I'm okay. I'm in the upstairs bathroom—Oliver and Wiles are downstairs eating."

"I hope you've been eating, too. I want to make sure you're getting nutrients. I know food doesn't sound good but we've got to make sure you have something in you."

"I tried to eat something this morning," I said. "But everything just tastes so bad. My stomach hurts. I still got down a few bites, though." I paused. "At least, I *think* I did." This was one of the scarier side effects of the A/C: short-term memory loss.

I rubbed my eyes. They vacillated between being very watery and very dry.

"Listen, Willow," Amelia said, shifting into full-on caretaker mode. "I've already sent an email out to all the girls about bringing food over. I'm guessing that meal tonight came from Caroline, right? Of course, we want to make sure Oliver and Wiles are fed, but we also want to make sure *you* are eating. So we're all going to pitch in to make sure you have a hot meal every day this week, okay?"

I nodded, even though I knew she couldn't see me. "You're the best," I said. "I apologize in advance if I don't have the appetite to eat all the delicious things you gals bring."

"As long as you promise to try."

"Okay. I can do that."

I could hear Amelia smiling. "And I'm going to come over right now and help you get some food down, okay?"

"Oh no no, you don't have to do that."

"It's okay," Amelia explained. "I want to come over and bring you something nice and plain and simple. The blander the better, I imagine. How does that sound?"

"It sounds great."

The truth was, the food part sounded terrible. But seeing Amelia was better than the most delicious meal imaginable. Being with her made me feel full and happy and loved.

"See you in a few minutes," she said.

After Amelia hung up, I mustered all the strength I had left to place a phone call. There was one thing I knew I had to take care of. As much as I was dreading it, I couldn't put it off any longer.

I hit a number on speed dial and a man's sweet voice answered. "Hey, beautiful."

It was Liam, the man who had been my hair stylist for years. "How you holding up?" he asked.

"I'm okay," I said. "I'm hanging in there, I guess. Listen, Liam: I know you 'mentioned you might be able to get me into your salon on a day when no one's there. Is that still an option?" I cleared my throat. "I'd love to do this low profile."

"I completely understand."

Thank God. I didn't want anybody else in the salon, for obvious reasons. I knew I needed to cut my hair—it would be too traumatic to have it come out in long chunks.

So Liam, doll that he was, had been kind enough to offer to cut my hair on a day the salon was closed. He knew I didn't want a lot of people to know I had cancer, and his clientele was chockfull of acquaintances, people from our neighborhood whom I vaguely knew but who weren't exactly friends. Liam also understood the inherent shame of lopping off my long blond hair, something that had given us both great pride and joy over the years.

"How 'bout Sunday?" he said. "If you can come in around one p.m., I'd be more than happy to give you a cute bob."

"Thank you so much."

"I have to be honest, Willow: not every woman can pull off a bob. But you? Darling, you're going to looks *fabulous.*"

I tried to let his words buoy me up, to fill me with hope for the future. But when I thought of losing my long, soft hair—the hair that gave me so much comfort—the hair that made me recognize myself when I looked into the mirror—it just broke my heart.

"Thanks for saying," I said. "I'll see you Sunday at one p.m."

I thought I was going in for a private haircut, just Liam and me. But unbeknownst to me, my friends and family were mobilizing. They would not abandon or neglect me. They would not let me bear the weight of this alone.

Chapter 35

HAIR SHOPPING

*K*nock knock knock.

It was Friday morning on a crisp November day. Wiles was off at school and Oliver was working. Bella was home from boarding school for the weekend, but she was off hanging out with some of her friends. I had no idea what they were doing, but I worried they were doing cocaine. Once I'd confronted her about it and she swore to me she'd only tried cocaine once. As much as I wanted to believe her, I was having a hard time. During my modeling days I had dabbled in cocaine and I knew all the signs. *She's too much like me,* I thought, for the thousandth time.

I sat uneasily on a chair in my kitchen, sipping a cup of tea, trying to quell my roiling stomach.

I wasn't entirely up for a visitor, but then I didn't love being alone, either. It was Nicole's day to bring food. I shuffled to the door, still in my bathrobe. *I already care so much less about how I look*, I thought. *That's probably a good thing, since I'm about to lose all my hair.*

"Hey, hi, Willow," Nicole said when I opened the door. She was holding a bright red saucepan wedged between the potholders she held in her hands. The red color made me nauseated. Now, whenever I saw the color red, I felt a hint of post-traumatic stress disorder. I saw the Red Devil *everywhere.*

Nicole barged through the door and headed for the kitchen. She had a way of barging into my house, something I loved about her.

"How you doin'?" she said. Nicole nodded toward the saucepan. "It's organic bone marrow soup. I made it without carrots and onions—I know anything with fructose is a no go. So I wanted to make you something warm and comforting, but that you could eat without getting sick. Oh, and I brought a bag of cooked bacon for Wiles. I know it's his favorite."

Nicole knew all my food allergies, but I was still impressed that she could make a soup without carrots and onions—no small feat. I lifted the pot and smelled the soup because I knew this would make Nicole happy.

"Delicious," I said, smiling up at her, even though in reality everything had a sour metallic odor.

"Listen," Nicole said. "What are your plans for the weekend?"

"Tomorrow my friend Poppy gets here from Chicago," I said, before adding softly: "I'm also getting my hair cut on Sunday."

"With Liam, right?"

"Yep. You're welcome to come. I'm told there's a few friends gathering."

"And what about today?" Nicole pressed. "You think you'll be able to leave the house today?"

"Yeah, I might be up for a short stint outside. I need to cheer up and get outside a bit."

"Okay, well. Tell me the truth if this doesn't sound good to you—and I mean that—but would you like to go out and look at some hair?"

"Okay," I said, looking down. "Let's give it a whirl." She was thrilled but I fought back tears.

I sat in the passenger seat of her SUV, Nicole chattering the whole time. "You know how I basically have no hair," she said. "I mean, my hair is so bad. It's so thin and I always wear these synthetic hair pieces to help it look better." She looked at me sideways. "I'm not sure you knew that about me."

I tried to focus my attention on Nicole's face, instead of feeling every bump in the road, every little lurch wreaking havoc on my stomach. "Yeah, I know."

"You would not *believe* all the hair I've bought. I have clip-in hair, clip-in ponytails that are really really good. I've gotten so good at it that people come from everywhere to ask me about where I get my hair. I've got it down to a fine art."

I nodded absently. It was painful, all this talk about hair, but Nicole was such a live wire. She was kindly offering me a distraction, and I sorely needed to get out of the house.

"I took the liberty of doing a little research," Nicole said. "I mean, I've never worn a full-on wig—just hair pieces—so this is kind of a different thing. But I went ahead and made an appointment, hoping you'd be interested."

"You did that for me?" I said.

"Of course I did!"

Thank God for Nicole. I feel like I'm just sitting around, waiting for my body to go haywire on me.

"We're going to a town about thirty minutes away," Nicole said. "There's a guy up there who's expecting us."

I felt suddenly self-conscious. I hadn't even told most of my acquaintances about my cancer, and now a man I'd never met was going to help me look for wigs? But when we arrived at his shop, he put me immediately at ease. He was kind and uplifting without being patronizing. I didn't want anyone feeling sorry for me—that was the worst.

"There are all sorts of different kinds of hair," he told me. "There are dozens of options. You get to pick and choose what works for you."

Nicole and I both tried on a ton of different hairpieces. I tried to push past my own heartbreak and the knowledge that, in a few more days, my own hair would be shorn, and that a couple weeks after that, it would be gone completely. Nicole kept looking at me, and I knew she wanted me to have fun. *This isn't exactly my idea of fun,* I wanted to explain to her. *I didn't choose to be in this situation.* But I was certainly grateful for Nicole's joyous spirit.

"And don't forget," said the man. "If you cut your hair, save it. That way you can have a custom-made wig with your real hair."

I found the idea unsettling. *But then, it's all pretty unsettling, isn't it?*

We left the shop with a bag full of hair, a bunch of different kinds and varieties. I got short wigs and long blond wigs—even a brunette wig, just for kicks. I also got two of the coolest hats, baseball caps with long blond hair coming out the bottom. We took the hats over to a monogram store and had Bella's initials stitched onto one of them, and Wiles's initials monogramed on the other. *I want to feel their presence everywhere I go*, I thought.

On the drive home Nicole said, "You're going to be the most fashionable cancer girl, ever."

"I don't want to be a cancer girl at all," I sighed.

"Well. I think you're very wise to have Liam cut your hair. At least that way you're not losing it all at once. Baby steps, right?"

"I guess so."

Nicole appraised me. "When does your friend Poppy get into town?"

"Tomorrow morning. On the early side."

"Uh huh." I could see the wheels turning in Nicole's brain, but I had no clue as to why. "Must be nice to have Bella home this weekend," she said.

"Yeah. I haven't seen enough of her—she's been out with friends. She did ask me when I was going to lose my hair. I think she's grossed out by the idea of her mom losing her hair. I can't say I blame her. It's a lot to digest."

"It's certainly no picnic. But you're doing great so far." Nicole pulled up in front of my house. "Come on, let's get you inside. You've got a big weekend."

"I do?" I said, not understanding.

She smiled. "Yes, you do."

Chapter 36

THE HAIRCUT PARTY

"**Y**ou ready, Willow?"

Poppy was standing in the doorway of my bedroom with her purse slung over her arm. She was tall and statuesque—she had the same body she had in high school. Poppy's bright blond hair, blue eyes, and perky smile always made me feel better. She had a bounce to her step and was always impeccably dressed. *I guess that's why she became an interior designer,* I thought. Other than Ella, Poppy was my oldest friend. We were like sisters.

"Almost," I said. "I can't quite get this shirt buttoned up . . ."

"Here. Let me help."

She tossed her purse on the bed and helped me with the buttons. I'd taken to wearing looser, simpler clothing because of my arm and now the port, but I was no slouch in the fashion department, and I wanted to at least look cute the day I cut my hair off. I had on a blue-and-white checkered button-down shirt, navy shorts, and brown suede boots with cute fringe.

"How do you feel?" Poppy asked. "Because you look great."

"I feel really grateful. I'm happy you're here."

I was touched when Poppy told me she wanted to spend a few days in Columbus with me. I knew she had her own family to take care of, so her presence meant a lot. Especially today of all days. She was a rock I had grown up with, and I was homesick for my roots and my hometown.

It was Sunday November 4th, the day I'd been dreading. It was time for my haircut.

"You girls ready?" Oliver hollered from downstairs. "Bella and Wiles are already in the car."

To my surprise, both Bella and Wiles had agreed to come with us to the salon. "We've got your back, Mom," Bella said, and even Wiles was ready to come. I felt grateful that my family and I were doing this as a unit. As awful as it was, at least I wasn't going through it alone.

"We're ready," I called back. Poppy and I walked out of the bedroom, down the stairs, and hopped into the car with my family. I sat in the front seat, face planted into my phone as I scrolled through all my iPhoto pictures. Nobody asked me any questions. They knew the dark sunglasses and my face buried in the photos was code that I was going to either scream or cry.

"Who all is coming?" Poppy asked. "You said a couple of your friends knew about it."

"It's really just you and maybe two others," I said. "My friends Nicole and Emily—I'm not sure you guys have met." I didn't look up.

Amelia was in Indianapolis at the game, so she couldn't come, and I really wasn't in charge of inviting people, so I didn't know who else was on the list.

But when we pulled up to the salon, I definitely sensed something was up. There were too many cars in the parking lot for a day the strip mall was purportedly closed. As we got out of the car, I felt like Poppy and Bella and Wiles were jittery with excitement, almost nervous. *What the hell is going on?* I put down my phone and started to emerge out of my protective shell as I stepped out of the car.

"What—" I asked hesitantly, then stopped short as I peered in the glass doors of the salon. *Are those . . . balloons?*

The doors swung open. "Surprise!" Nicole called out, as my friends swarmed out of the salon and came over to hug me.

The salon wasn't empty at all: it was full of Angels. Emily and Nicole were both there, Nicole in an adorable print dress—I could tell she'd dressed up for the occasion. With them was my other friend Millie, who looked fabulous in her Carolina Herrera dress and stylish Bottega Veneta clutch. As a contributing editor to *Vogue*, Millie always had the most gorgeous bags and clothes. Grace was there, too, and so was Frenny and her daughter Lucia.

"Come on in," Emily said, leading me into the salon. "Liam's waiting. Today's your day, okay? This is your party."

I nodded, truly overwhelmed with Poppy by my side.

The salon was alive with color and commotion. There were bright balloons tied to the salon chairs and a big silver bucket filled with ice and bottles of champagne, and soft drinks for the kids. Lucia and Bella ran off into the corner right away with their Diet Cokes to gossip about who knows what. A boombox was set up in the corner playing fun, upbeat music, a mix of all my favorite songs. *Someone put together a playlist for me. How sweet.* There was also a wonderful food spread with some of my favorite things. I got teary-eyed. *I can't believe my friends did all this for me.* I was truly in awe of their efforts. *Wow. Just . . . wow.*

They'd brought cameras, too. I also saw that Nicole had brought some new wigs for me to try on. She must have gone back to the hair store after we'd left. Nicole had also brought some bandannas and other fun accessories.

"We thought we might as well make it a day to remember," Nicole said.

"Oh my gosh." I'd thought I was just going to get my hair cut, but my friends wanted to make it special—a happy celebration instead of a sad event. With tears in my eyes, I turned and looked at Wiles. He was grinning.

"Did you know about this?" I asked.

He nodded. "Yep," said Wiles. "We weren't supposed to tell."

Poppy was beaming. "I was in on it, too. Your friends planned all of this. They love you so much. Honestly, Willow? Your friends are amazing." She couldn't believe how they'd pulled out all the stops.

My Angels crowded in around me, saying hi to Oliver and joking with Wiles, who ate up all the attention. Liam, my stylist, hugged me for a long time.

"You know what I love about you?" he whispered in my ear. "You can get dressed up and look like you just stepped off the cover of *Vogue* when you need to. But you can also fly in here in a pair of flip-flops and sweats and be the realest friend I've ever had." His voice caught. "I know this is a hard day, but I'm glad I get to share it with you."

If Liam was getting choked up, there was no way I was going to be able to hold it together. I took a deep breath and tried to lighten the situation. Liam took the hint. "Let's get you shampooed," he said, escorting me to the chair.

"Girl, where's that smile?" Millie called out. "This is a party, remember? We're here to celebrate. I'm bringing you a glass of wine!" Millie moved easily among the group, cheering people up as she always did with her peppiness and motherly spirit.

"And wait! Before you get it all wet . . ." Nicole pulled out her camera. "Picture time! Let's do some before-and-after shots."

I struck a pose, playing to the camera like I'd done for so many years. I turned on my megawatt smile, even though I felt a million miles from happy.

But Nicole was right: it definitely made it better to pretend like this was a celebration. It was good to see my kids' smiling faces, to see my Angels munching on cheese and crackers and pouring each other glasses of champagne. My heart felt very heavy, but knowing that I was surrounded by people who loved me—that made it seem bearable.

But it still hurt like hell. As I lay back in the chair, Liam's fingers gently massaging the shampoo into my scalp, tears streamed down my face. They rolled sideways out of my eyes, pooling in my ears, and still I tried to smile through it.

Liam was having a hard time, too. I could tell he was trying to hide his tears as he washed my long hair for the last time.

After he was done, he laid a brown towel over my shoulders and led me to his chair. To my surprise, he pulled out a makeup brush and some eye pencils.

"This is a full-on makeover," Liam said. "You're getting the full treatment today, Willow. We're going to make you look fabulous."

Millie and Nicole snapped a billion photographs as Liam filled in my lips and layered my eye shadow. They kept telling me how pretty I looked, and I soaked it up, needing desperately to believe it. I saw Millie on her phone and

I knew she was posting the pictures. Her mega personality and her mega social media empire were surely buzzing. Millie was a devoted friend, and I knew whatever she was posting, as sentimental as it was, would make me happy when I saw and read the comments later.

Then came the moment we'd all been waiting for—the moment I was dreading. I felt a knot in my stomach as Liam pulled his shiny silver scissors out of a drawer. "Ready?" he asked.

I didn't answer. I just looked down into my lap and grabbed my phone.

He started to cut.

The girls brought me a plate of veggies and a flute of champagne but I declined. I couldn't drink the champagne, and I wasn't hungry. "This is going to be great," they said. "You already look fantastic."

Liam and I exchanged a look in his mirror. Our eyes said everything. *This is hard. So hard.* It was difficult for both of us to hold onto our emotions, and in some ways it was even harder with a whole roomful of people watching and telling me how great I looked. I felt so exposed.

I broke eye contact with Liam and glanced down again at the floor, afraid I would melt down.

But the floor was a dangerous place to look. I watched as long strands of healthy, lustrous blond hair cascaded down around me, making a halo at the foot of the chair. I'd never seen Liam move so quickly to sweep it up. He knew how painful this was for me.

"Don't forget what the wig guy said, Willow," Nicole reminded me. "Keep your hair so you can make a wig out of it." She scooped up my long locks from Liam's dust pan and stuffed them into a Ziplock bag she'd brought for that purpose. I felt my stomach lurch and closed my eyes so I wouldn't have to look.

Comforting words flowed through my mind. *You are not alone. You're loved, and you haven't been abandoned.* I opened my eyes and forced myself to take in the room. Bella and Lucia had Wiles in the shampoo chair and were washing his hair. I loved that. My friends were chatting happily—Nicole was taking a picture of Frenny holding my long ponytail. Oliver looked slightly uncomfortable in this roomful of women—he was sitting stoically in the zebra-print chair in the corner—but at least he was there. He smiled at me from across the room.

Emily waltzed by, shaking her hips to the music and goofing around. "Orange juice," she said, boogie-ing past me. "Champagne of the stars." I couldn't help it: I laughed.

"Okay," Liam said. "All done. What do you think?"

He swiveled the chair around and I blinked at myself in the mirror. I hadn't had my hair short in—I couldn't remember how long. *Maybe never?* Liam had done a beautiful job, cutting it into a textured layered bob. He gave me the hand mirror and I held it up as he swiveled the chair back around. It was a little shorter in the back and swung down to my collarbone in the front.

I never wanted short hair, but I have to admit: I don't look half bad.

The girls were delighted. "You look absolutely beautiful, precious," Frenny said.

"Oh my God," Millie crowed. "Your hair looks so cute short!"

"It really does," Emily said. "When you grow your hair out after chemo, grow it out to this haircut. It's really sexy. Picture time! Come on—you kids get in it, too."

Bella and Wiles crowded in, Wiles's hair still wet from his shampoo. I inhaled the sweet scent, indescribably happy to have them with me. Together we smiled for the camera. My kids knew how to crank up their smiles, too, especially Bella. If being photogenic was a genetic trait, she'd definitely inherited it.

"Now let's do a silly one," Emily said. "Bella and Wiles, you two put on the wigs."

Wiles groaned. "Do we have to?"

"Do it for your mom!"

Bella loved it—she chose the prettiest wig and pranced up and down the salon, checking herself out in the mirrors like she was on a catwalk. *My daughter*, I thought. *I worry she really is too much like me.* After a while, Wiles decided his sister was having so much fun that he wanted a wig, too. Even Oliver played along, to my surprise. We all posed for Emily, and it turned out to be one of my favorite pictures ever: me in the middle with Oliver and Bella and Wiles making funny faces in long, blond wigs.

Gratitude swelled up inside me. *My friends are a lamp in the darkness. I'm going to be all right.*

On a day that might have been one of the worst days of my life up to that point, I was no longer thinking of killing myself. I was thinking how lucky I was to be alive, and to have such phenomenal friends.

Chapter 37

AN ISLAND TO SWIM TO

"How you feeling, sweetie? Look at you—you are skinny as a wishbone!"

My mom hugged and hugged me at the Miami airport. I thought she'd never let go—and I wasn't sure I wanted her to. Since my cancer diagnosis, I felt like my mom had never showered me with so much love and affection. I was thirsty for it, and I happily gulped it down.

"I haven't been eating much," I admitted. "Nothing tastes very good."

"Well. We'll have to do something about that. Considering it's Thanksgiving and all. And you love the Club's food."

My mom grabbed my roller bag, which I'd been pulling along awkwardly behind me with my left arm. "When does Bella's plane get in?"

"Couple hours," I said.

"Perfect. I'll get her after I get you settled. You and me—we've got a lot to catch up on. Let me get you home and get you something to eat."

When I made a face, she held up her hands in mock surrender. "You don't have to eat a lot. Just eat *something*."

194

It was the week before Thanksgiving, and my whole family was headed to my parents' house in Palm Beach for the holiday. I'd had my second chemo treatment one day before getting on the plane in Columbus, and I felt like crap. I wasn't eating and I was nauseous and weak. I also felt like my heart was palpitating more than usual. *I don't know, maybe it's psychosomatic. Since I know the Red Devil can cause heart failure, maybe I'm just imagining things.*

Bella was flying down from Boston, and my mom, daughter, and I had plans to spend one night at my home in Miami before the three of us headed to Palm Beach. The next day Oliver and Wiles would fly in from Columbus, and my sister Chloe would come with her husband and three girls from Lake Forest, and we'd all enjoy a week together over Thanksgiving break.

"I've really been looking forward to this, Willow," my mom said as we walked through the airport parking lot. "You are so blessed to have such great friends—those girls in Bexley have been taking great care of you. But I've been saying to Henry, 'I can't wait for Thanksgiving so *I* can take care of my daughter!'"

Something inside me loosened and relaxed. I was looking forward to my mom taking care of me, too. Having her walk beside me through this ordeal made it feel a little less scary.

"Your hair looks adorable, by the way," she said. "Poppy and some of your other friends sent me the pictures but it's even cuter in person."

"Today is fifteen days since my first chemo treatment, Mom," I said. "My doctor said it will start falling out at seventeen days. Like clockwork."

My mom pressed her lips together. This was hard on her, too. I knew she was remembering how she had held Virginia, her dear friend, as Ginny sobbed over losing her hair.

"Then I'm very glad," my mom said, "that we're going to be with you when it happens."

"Me, too," I said quietly.

My mom had her car since she had just driven down from Palm Beach, so I laid back in her big black comfy Mercedes and filled her in on the amazing things my friends were doing back in Bexley. "Amelia sent an email out, Mom. It was crazy—she asked our friends to each pick one day of the week to come to watch over me, and I'm not kidding: within an hour I had a lineup of babysitters."

I went on and on about who was coming which days of the week. Alice had volunteered to be my Monday Angel, Grace would be my Tuesday Angel, and Amelia had claimed Wednesdays. Nicole would cover Thursdays, Caroline had called dibs on Fridays, and Frenny would take over on Saturdays when she wasn't at work. Nicole said she could take Sundays, too, so she actually had two days. Amelia had even set up floaters to fill in in case one of the weekly girls was sick or unable to come.

After a while, I got too tired to talk, and I could tell my mom just wanted me to let her take over. She probably already knew about the schedule Amelia had set up, but she was sweet to listen to me. I had come to love bragging on my friends. What they were doing was nothing short of remarkable, and I wanted the world to know. My friends had kept my mom in the loop. They all loved Nanette Davis—Alice texted my mom daily and of course she got all the email updates as well from Amelia.

My mom got me home and into my bed. She opened the shades so I could see the ocean, and once she made sure I was all situated, she went to pick up Bella at the airport. I must have fallen asleep, but when I woke up, Bella was standing in my room with a smile on her face, hoping to say hi. I looked up and started to cry.

Most of the year my precious daughter was so far away at boarding school, and I missed her so much. I slowly sat up and we hugged. For once she didn't push me away or act "too cool" to hug her mother. Bella let her defenses down, and as I held her, I could feel her crying, too. I could see out of the corner of my eye that my mom was standing at my bedroom door watching, holding back her own tears. I was so happy to be with them. I just cried and cried.

***

"Mom! MOM!"

Wiles was on the second floor of my parents' house in Palm Beach, standing at the top of the stairwell. I was downstairs on the first floor. My hair was coming out in my hands. It had been coming out all morning. I fought like crazy, trying to hold onto myself, my emotions. It felt like a losing battle.

Oh, God. Dear God, please help me. My hair. My beautiful hair.

"MOM!!!"

I looked up at him, blinking back tears. "What is it, Wiles?"

"Mom, you're not gonna believe this. You have a cross on your head."

I didn't understand. "What do you mean?"

"Hold on a sec, I'm going to show you." He pulled his cell phone out of his back pocket and snapped a picture before I could object. Then he ran down the stairs, skipping two and sometimes three steps, which almost gave me a heart attack. *If the Red Devil doesn't stop my heart, my kids will . . .*

"Look," Wiles said once he made it to the landing. He showed me his phone. "It's a cross."

I stared at the screen in disbelief. Wiles was right. My hair was falling out in the shape of a cross. The patches were not random: the white of my scalp shone through in a perfect cross. *Amazing.* I was shaking. It was powerful. I hugged my son close. *All these signs I can't ignore—maybe God is with me.*

"Can you send me that picture?" I said.

"Sure. Of course."

I texted the picture to Gigi and Amelia and a few of my other Angels. Their responses were powerful. "God has his hand on you, Willow," Gigi said. "Even on this incredibly difficult day."

Her words felt like a balm. My hair had been all over my bed when I woke up that morning. It was coming out in sections. It didn't hurt, but it was surreal, being able to grab large clumps of my hair and pull it out with no resistance.

My sister Chloe didn't want her girls to see it. She hadn't told them I had cancer—she didn't want to scare them. They were six, four, and one year old, so very young. We agreed to keep it hush-hush, and my mom cleaned up all the hair before my little nieces could see. She did a lot of laundry that week.

"Are you okay, sweetie?" my mom said. "You want to lie down?"

"I just want it to be over," I moaned. Cross or not: it was still excruciating to see my own hair in my hands. At the same time, I knew how lucky I was. I had my husband and my kids, my parents, my sister, and her family, all by my side. We were in this together, and I wasn't alone. That meant the world to me.

"Come on," my mom said, taking me gently by the hand. "I think it's time we see about getting you a new hairdo."

She smiled through her tears as we walked together into the bedroom. As soon as she closed the door behind her, I fell into her arms and cried.

***

"Why are you wearing that bandanna?" said my six-year-old niece. "And that hair. It's not your hair, is it? It looks fake."

We were at the Thanksgiving dinner table, us and another family who were my parents' Palm Beach friends. An awkward silence fell over the whole group. Chloe looked at her daughter sharply. "We do not speak to Aunt Willow that way! Certainly not at the dinner table. It's very impolite."

No one quite knew what to say. The girls were very curious about what was going on—they were smart and perceptive and could tell something was up, but no one would answer their questions with candor.

"Great weather we're having," my mom's friend said. She'd battled breast cancer herself and was very understanding about how hard this was for me. "Just a beautiful time of year to be in Florida, don't you think? The sand and the sun. Better than being buried under a blizzard in Lake Forest!"

"So much better," my mother echoed, shooting me an encouraging smile across the giant turkey.

The Thanksgiving dinner spread was indeed beautiful, like something out of a Norman Rockwell painting. The turkey was cooked to perfection, flanked by homemade dressing and cranberries and a whole array of mouthwatering pies. My mom had made me a plate of spinach, though I wasn't really eating anything. I tried to get down a few spoonfuls, but it took a good deal of effort. At that point it was even hard to swallow.

My niece's words cut to the core, though I knew she didn't mean any harm. But it was the first time I started to wear my wigs, and it was awkward. It was hard figuring out how to use them. I didn't have any of my girlfriends there to help me put them on. My mom and sister had both tried to lend a helping hand, but they didn't know how to make them work, either.

The conversation turned to football for a little bit, but after a while there was another lull. I felt the heat of someone's gaze. I turned to see my *other* niece, Chloe's four-year-old daughter, staring at me.

"Why did you cut your hair all off, Aunt Willow?" she said.

I took a deep breath. "I just want to make it really short for a while. Kind of fun, right? I've always had long hair, so I thought I'd try something new."

"But you look like a boy," my niece said bluntly. "Why do you want to look like a boy?"

Chloe scolded her daughter, but it wasn't really my niece's fault. "Excuse me," I said, pushing back my chair and standing up from the table before tears starting falling into my spinach.

I went and locked myself in the bedroom, and a few minutes later, I heard Chloe tapping lightly on the door. "I'm sorry, Willow. I'm really sorry."

"It's okay. I don't blame her." I opened the door a crack. "I'm just glad we're all here together."

"Me, too," Chloe said, putting her arms around me. "You're being really brave. It's not the best situation, but we're making the best of it. I love you and you're going to get through this, okay?"

The next few days unfolded in welcome distractions. My kids adored Chloe's daughters, and the girls thought the world of their cousins, who were practically grownups in their eyes. My mom loved taking care of me—we went for short walks on the beach, as long as I could manage without feeling sick. I prayed a lot. My mom insisted on taking me out to lunch at the Club, on the rare occasion I could actually stomach it.

I wasn't actively throwing up: it was more like I lived under a constant haze of nausea. It was the worst in the mornings—almost like morning sickness, except of course I had cancer, not a baby inside me. Then it would ebb and flow the rest of the day. I spent a lot of time in the bathroom. When Wiles went to play golf and Bella went with her friends to go out and tan, my mom and Chloe and I would sit and relax by the pool. I soaked up the buttery Florida sun and felt grateful to be alive, grateful to be surrounded by my family.

I took a lot of baths that week, because the chemo had started to give me horrible hemorrhoids. I would sit in a nice warm bath and talk to one of my girlfriends on the phone. Jules and I talked a lot. And I talked to my cousin Ella, too. Ella and I communicated in some way every day, either texting or talking to each other on the phone. Now that Poppy and I were back in regular touch, I'd talk to her from the bath, too.

When our time in Florida came to an end, I felt a sad, heavy despair moving in, like a cluster of dark clouds on the horizon. It had been nourishing to my soul to be surrounded by my family—just being together was hugely healing. Soon I would be headed back to Columbus where more chemo awaited. The mere thought made me sick.

But there was one tiny thing to look forward to: Oliver and the kids and I were driving back to Miami to spend the last weekend of vacation together, just the four of us. I savored the time with them, even as the depressing months that lay ahead grew nearer and nearer in the gloomy landscape of my mind.

***

Bella was having the time of her life, and I felt like I was dying.

"Never ever ever gettin' back together!" Bella screamed the lyrics of her favorite Taylor Swift song along with the crowd. We were at a concert, packed in with other teen girls and plenty of moms at the American Airlines Arena in Miami. I'd splurged and gotten us excellent seats—we were so close we could see the sequins on Taylor's dress.

Bella gave me a side hug, her face shining with joy. She absolutely loved Taylor Swift. "This is great, Mom. This is so awesome!"

"I'm so glad you're having a good time." I clutched at my stomach, which felt like it was turning inside out. "I'll be right back, okay?"

"Cool."

I staggered through the crowds and to the bathroom, crept inside a stall, sat on the toilet, and sobbed.

It was my last snippet of one-on-one time with Bella before the holiday was over and she went back to boarding school. Oliver and Wiles had flown back to Columbus earlier that day so that Wiles could be at school Monday morning. Bella didn't have to be at school until Tuesday, so I'd promised to take her to see Taylor Swift.

But I was so sick. The side effects of the A/C had kicked in full force, and I felt like I might pass out at any moment. As I sat beside my daughter in the blistering heat, the world swam in front of my eyes.

I don't know how I'm going to do this, I thought. And on its heels: *I don't want Bella to know how much I'm struggling.*

I staggered out of the bathroom twenty minutes later. By the time I got back to Bella, my eyes were dry and my face was no longer red and puffy. I smiled at my daughter, who was having a terrific time. She hadn't even noticed how long I'd been gone. She was busy belting out the words to every single Taylor Swift song.

"Thanks for taking me, Mom," she said. "This is the best!"

"Of course, honey."

Despite how sick I felt, it ended up being a good memory for Bella and me. She often felt neglected up at boarding school, but for that one day, I got to lavish her with all my love and attention. She needed it and so did I.

When I put Bella on a plane to Boston the next morning, my heart had never felt so heavy. A few hours later, I'd be on a plane to Columbus. I thought I would be coming back to Miami for the whole month of February, but it was not to be. I would be so sick from chemo in the coming months that I'd be lucky to get out of the house, let alone the state.

That was the last time I was in Miami until May 1st. On some deep cellular level, I knew it. I had to physically force myself to get on that plane. I knew I was going back to chemo. I knew I was going back to the horrors of cancer—and I wasn't sure what I had left to look forward to.

But as I waited in line to board my plane, a memory flitted over my consciousness that brought me great relief. When we were in Palm Beach with my family for Thanksgiving, Chloe and her husband had gone out for a "date night," just the two of them. So the rest of us put Bella and Wiles in charge of the girls and my dad took my mom, Oliver, and me out to dinner.

That night, my dad had said to me, "Just get through chemo, Willow, and when you're done, I'll take you anywhere in the world you want to go."

I looked at him for a long time. "Are you serious? Don't just make these promises, Dad."

"Cross my heart and hope to die," he said. "I'll take you anywhere in the world."

As the flight attendant welcomed me onto the plane, that was the thought I clung to. *Anywhere in the world. Anywhere in the world you want to go.*

My dad had given me an island to swim to. Even as the waves crashed and the sharks swam furiously around me, I envisioned that island. I held onto the life raft of my family and friends—and I swam like hell.

Chapter 38

AVALANCHE OF LOVE

Oh my God, I am so tired.

It was only four on a Monday afternoon when I crawled into bed, but I just couldn't stand up a second longer. Alice had come over that morning, my lovely Monday Angel, and for hours she sat with me, asked me what I needed, and even ran a few errands to help me out. Then she dropped me off at a charity luncheon I wanted to attend, but the lunch completely wore me out. *Maybe I shouldn't have gone. Maybe it was too much.* But I also knew I needed to get out of the house before I drove myself crazy.

It was December 10th. The date was seared into my brain because I was dreading the next day. *Wednesday December 11th: Chemo treatment #3 at 11 a.m.* The details scrolled miserably through my aching head. *11 on the 11th. 11 on the 11th.* I desperately needed a distraction.

Zzzz. A text from Jules popped up on my phone, just in the nick of time. "Tomorrow is the day! Thinking of you. With you in spirit. Tackle it. Big kiss. You are my hero!!!"

I held the phone to my chest, as if Jules's love could actually flow out of the screen and into my heart. Then I thought better of it. *Maybe keeping my phone close to my breast is not such a good idea.*

I had been continuously amazed by the outpouring of love from my friends and family. They just kept showing up. Every day I was buried under an avalanche of love.

I heard the doorbell ring. *Shoot. I just got into bed . . .*

"I got it, Mom!" I heard Wiles yell. *Oh, thank God.*

A few minutes later, Wiles came into my room holding a gigantic bouquet of flowers in a beautiful blue vase. "A lady just dropped these by," he said, setting them carefully on my dresser, along with a greeting card in a bright yellow envelope. "Gosh, Mom. You do get a lot of flowers. Can I keep one in my room?"

"Sure," I said. "There's a vase in the kitchen cabinet."

I inched the card out of the yellow envelope. The flowers were from Winnie, the woman who had been with Gigi the day Gigi dropped the book by, and who had cried real tears when I told her I had cancer. She had also been at the luncheon—in fact, she was one of the hosts—and I recognized the flowers immediately. They had been sitting up front during the lunch, and I had told Winnie how beautiful they were. *Aww. She saw me admiring them and remembered.*

I propped myself up on some pillows and Wiles helped me open the card. "You have many friends praying, Willow!" Winnie said. "Yesterday in mass I called on all the saints to intercede on your behalf. Prayer is soo powerful!!! 2 Corinthians 12:9: 'And He said unto me, My grace is sufficient for thee: for My strength is made perfect in weakness. Most gladly therefore will I rather glory in My infirmities, that the power of Christ may rest upon Me.'"

That's really sweet of her. Though I hadn't known Winnie all that well before my cancer, she had really stepped up to the plate, sending me texts and even forwarding me emails from another friend of hers who was battling cancer—*a lot more courageously and positively than I am,* I often thought. And to think I had tried so hard to keep the truth from Winnie and other friends I wasn't that close to. Her outpouring of love made me realize that maybe I didn't gain anything by hiding what I was going through.

"Can you hand me my iPad, Wiles?"

"Sure." He brought it to me and kissed me on the cheek before heading back downstairs to his video game.

Painstakingly, using only my left arm, I tapped out an email to Winnie. "What a treat to receive the beautiful flowers. I saw them at the lunch today and wished I had an arm to bring them home, so you read my mind. I have been so hesitant to tell people about my cancer but now that I have seen your reaction, your love, your lifting me up in your prayers, your emails, it's encouraging me to think about telling others. I mean, wowowwwww. If you can have such an incredible effect on me by showing such love and devotion, maybe I am missing out by keeping it a secret. You have blindsided me with the love u have shown, so thank u thank u. I am truly touched."

I started to set the iPad down but then decided to add a post-script: "P.S. Pardon the typos, I am limited with my cast."

Winnie's reply buzzed in my inbox only a few minutes later. "Willow, do not worry for one second about typos!! I have such compassion for what you are going through! I am glad you got out today and enjoyed the luncheon. And I am so glad you are feeling open to the idea of telling more people. We are all a part of the body of Christ. On a similar note: Gigi and I are cooking up a little surprise for you, and I think you're really going to love it! We'll drop by tomorrow morning before chemo if that's okay."

"Sure ok," I wrote back quickly, my fingers heavy on the keypad. *Wonder what the surprise is?*

But I was suddenly so tired, the words started to move around on the screen. I set the iPad on the bed stand, and no sooner had my cheek hit the pillow than I was fast asleep.

***

I woke up in a groggy haze the following morning. *Where am I? What day is today?* I looked at the familiar shape of Oliver asleep beside me. Then I remembered: *Chemo.* My whole body jerked, writhing at the very thought. It almost felt like I'd been whipped. *Calm down, Willow. You have to calm yourself down.*

I checked the clock: 6:45 a.m. I had a little over four hours. *Mental note to self: schedule chemo earlier in the day.* It was so horrible to have it hanging over me all day—it was best to get the first appointment.

The knowledge that chemo was looming felt like the Grim Reaper had slugged me in the stomach. *Good morning, Willow.*

Ha, yeah. "Good" morning. Nice to see you, too.

I tried to think of other things I was looking forward to that were happening later in the week, but that backfired. *Oh no! I'm going to miss Grace's baby shower.*

Grace's baby girl was precious, and I wanted more than anything to be at her shower. I groped for my iPad and wrote her an email. "I am not expecting to be out of bed by Saturday but if for some reason I am, I really want to stop by. I need things to look forward to. I will play it by ear. Want to see u and your baby girl and celebrate u both! Love u."

I tried to go back to sleep but lay in bed for a while, staring at the ceiling. I must have dozed off because suddenly I heard my iPad beep and woke with a start. I checked the alarm. *8:30 a.m.* I rolled over and saw the indentation in the mattress where Oliver had been sleeping. He was gone.

I reached for my iPad. I had one new *non*-junk email, and it was from Grace.

"You sweetheart! Don't you dare think about coming!! You will have just had treatment and you should not be going anywhere four days after! Your resting is the best celebration. I just want you well! xoxoxo."

I fought back tears. Grace was so gracious, and I wanted so much to be there for her, the way she'd always been there for me.

Slowly, with a heavy heart, I began to get dressed. I had already learned to dress comfortably for chemo; there was just no point in trying to get dolled up, since mostly I sat around waiting anyway. The most important thing was to be comfortable. So I threw on some comfy pants and a T-shirt. Amelia was taking me to chemo today since Oliver had to work.

I made it downstairs and poured myself a glass of tea. Iced green tea was fast becoming another "island to swim to" for me. Gigi and Simi would often bring me an iced tea as a treat—it was becoming an obsession, one of the few little luxuries I had left.

I was sipping my tea when the doorbell rang. I vaguely remembered something about Winnie and Gigi coming over. *Wonder if that's who it is?*

Sure enough, Winnie and Gigi were standing on my front porch. Winnie was holding a box in her hands and she was very excited. "Can we come in?" she said. "We've got something for you."

"Yeah, sure, come on in." I was so curious. What was in that box?

Once we were inside, Gigi set the box on the dining room table. "You know you've got an army of Angels praying for you, Willow," she said.

She opened the box and pulled out a bracelet. It was rubbery and stretchy, kind of like the "Livestrong" ones everyone used to wear. But instead of yellow, this one was white. And in big, bold, pink font, the bracelet said: **WILLOW'S ANGELS.** And on the other side: **LUKE 12:6–7.**

"'Are not five sparrows sold for two pennies?'" Gigi said, quoting the Bible verse from memory. "'Yet not one of them is forgotten by God. Indeed, the very hairs of your head are all numbered. Don't be afraid; you are worth more than many sparrows.'" She looked at me. "God knows each and every sparrow, Willow, and you are worth far more to Him than that."

"We wanted the bracelet to symbolize the power of prayer and friendship," Winnie said brightly. "A bracelet all your Angels can wear and look down at and remember that Scripture."

"Oh, wow. Wow. I don't even know what to say." I welled up.

"You don't have to say anything," Winnie said.

"We know you haven't wanted a lot of people to know," Gigi said. "But I also know that, every time you open yourself up and tell people what you're going through, you reap the rewards. So, if it's all right with you, we'd be proud to wear these bracelets. I know your other Angels will be proud as well. And we hope you'll wear one, too, so that you'll always have a reminder that we are your prayer warriors, and we'll never give up on you."

I was overcome with emotion. "I need to sit down," I stammered. I looked up at my friends. "I go to chemo today. And I'm going to wear one of these bracelets."

"So are we," Winnie said, reaching into the box and stretching a bracelet over her wrist.

"Every time you feel alone or scared," Gigi added, "just give your bracelet a tug. You know the movie *It's a Wonderful Life* with Jimmy Stewart?"

"Uh huh." I nodded. It was a classic and an old family favorite.

"You know how the angel Clarence says, 'Every time a bell rings, an angel gets its wings'?" Gigi smiled. "Every time you pluck on that bracelet, remember that there's another prayer going up from us to God."

Chapter 39

AN ARMY OF ANGELS

Two hours after Winnie and Gigi stopped by, I sat in the chemo room with Amelia beside me. Amelia was technically my Wednesday Angel, but she'd convinced Nicole to give up her Tuesday spot so that she could take me to chemo. "You have two days," she reminded Nicole. "I really want to do this for Willow." So Nicole had said yes, and there Amelia and I sat together. I had bracelets on both arms, and Melia was wearing a bracelet, too.

A nurse began walking toward me. I felt my stomach clench. At least it was the nurse I liked.

"Willow? I've got a chair open." I tugged on my bracelet to give me strength, and the nurse's eyes fell to my wrist. "Love your bracelet! Looking sharp."

"Thanks. It's new."

"Your friends are the greatest. You're lucky to have them—not everybody who comes in here has friends like yours." She smiled at Amelia, then looked back at me. "Right this way."

I made my way to the chair and took deep, steady breaths. Already it was starting to feel like a normal part of my routine, as much as I hated it. But I still looked away when she hooked up my port to the Red Devil bag. After that first treatment, I *never* looked at the Red Devil again. Not once.

Instead I just stared into Amelia's eyes. It was powerful: I really felt her strength. I did this for all of my chemo treatments: I would simply stare into the eyes of the Angel who had come with me. I would draw on their strength when I felt like I didn't have any left, and they would hold me up.

Zzzz.

"You've got a new text message," Amelia said, handing me my phone. It was from Alice, reminding me that "CHEMO = Christ Has Eliminated My Opponent. Every treatment gets you closer to forever healing, Willow! Just remember that each time you walk out of that room, you are one step closer to kicking cancer's B-U-T-T."

Zzzz. My phone beeped, this time with an email. I saw Grace's name and my eyes clouded over. "Grace's baby shower is this weekend," I murmured to Amelia. "I want so much to be there . . ."

"Shh, honey. I know. I know you do."

I let my eyes graze over Grace's message. There was a picture attached of her holding her beautiful, beaming daughter. They were both so pretty it hurt just to look at them.

"You can do this!!!!" her email said. "We will be praying for you during your treatment. You are not alone!! I love you and am so glad you feel the buoying up power of true love and friendship! You can do this!!!! Xoxo G."

The messages started pouring in. *Emily. Ella. Poppy. Caroline. Frenny. Nicole.* They loved me. They were thinking about me. They knew I needed them to help me get through this. I was strong. They kept telling me I was amazing, and even when I felt so unlovable, they told me I was loved.

I flipped through one message after another, savoring every picture and note and smiley face. Gigi and Winnie worked fast, because there were several photographs of my Angels rocking their new and fabulous bracelets. It helped me deal with my sense of unworthiness to see my dearest friends wearing them. Those bracelets provided exactly the comfort I needed. Winnie and Gigi's timing was impeccable. *I'll never forget what they've done for me. Never ever.*

I felt Amelia beside me. She was smiling, her bracelet proudly gracing her lovely wrist. "The Red Devil will not triumph over you, Willow," she said. "And the *real* Devil won't either. God loves you. Your Angels love you. We are storming the gates of heaven for you, today and always."

I nestled back in the chair and shut my eyes. This was horrible, no doubt about it. Chemo was never going to be fun. But I was starting to think that maybe, just maybe, my friends *didn't* think I was a burden. They were going to keep showing up. I was truly humbled—their faith in the Lord was inspiring. They were truly Angels, and I was in awe of their loyalty.

I have the best team on my side. No way will this beat me. I have the will of these women, their prayers, their love, their tremendous faith. It is awe-inspiring. I am truly blessed.

I realized, for the first time, that I no longer wanted to die. I had so much to live for. I wanted to *fight* for *me*. I wanted to storm the gates of heaven alongside my family and friends. I wanted to survive this thing. I wasn't just going through the motions anymore. I was fighting.

I dozed in and out, trying to focus on anything besides the toxic chemicals flowing through me. I knew their job was to scorch out the cancer cells, but I also knew they would take a lot of the good cells along the way. *It's just crazy—the cure can be even worse than the disease. It just doesn't make any sense!*

When I came to, Amelia was tapping away on her phone, her brow furrowed in concentration. "Wha r'you doing, Meia?" I noticed I was slurring my words from the chemo drugs.

"Nothing," she said coyly. "Don't you worry your pretty head about it." She clicked a few more buttons, then slipped her phone into her bag.

Ding. I had one new email.

"Did you just send me an email?" I said.

A mischievous smile played at the corner of Amelia's mouth as she handed me my phone. As suspected, I saw one new email in my inbox.

From: Amelia King
Subject: Current update for Angels' Chemo Schedule
Date: December 21, 2012 1:09:08 PM CST

To: Everyone

Sweet friends,

Here is a more current update of chemo schedule for Willow. If you are available, please let Willow know. I am in the room with her now and she's so brave and so strong! Please send your prayers.

Much love and Merry Christmas.

xoxox- Amelia

December 20 Nanette and Henry Davis—Willow's parents in town
December 27 Francesca
January 3 Gigi
January 10 Caroline
January 17 Nicole
January 24 Emily
January 31 Grace and Caroline
February 7 (Willow's birthday) Oliver
February 14 (Valentine's Day) Caroline

"But wait," I said. "I don't understand. You asked people to sign up . . . but all the spots are already filled!" I scrolled through the email. "There are people coming every single time."

Amelia's eyes were glistening, too. "I sent out an email with your chemo schedule so that people could fill in the blanks. Do you know how long it took for it to fill up, Willow?"

I shook my head.

"Three minutes. In three minutes it was completely full."

"Whoa. Oh my gosh." My eyes brimmed with tears.

She showed me the emails that had poured in. Different friends had volunteered for different tasks, and not even just friends in Columbus—Poppy and Ella also rallied to the cause.

"You are so loved," Amelia said, the resounding refrain she had been whispering in my ear for months and years. *Why is that message so hard for me to fully absorb?*

I was truly overwhelmed. *My friends just keep showing up. Even when I don't expect it, even when I haven't asked them to.* It was outrageous, the way they kept loving me. They told me they were doing this because it was where God wanted them to be right now—He didn't necessarily want them to be in a Bible study or serving in another way. I *was* their service. They were doing it for God, not to get praise or accolades. That was so foreign to me. For them it wasn't a contest—it wasn't about "So-and-so did *that* for Willow." They were doing this because God had laid it on their hearts. My own heart was filled to overflowing.

"How do you feel, Willow?" Amelia asked.

Grateful. Humbled. Loved.

"Like I'm going to throw up," I said, and we actually laughed a little. It felt good to laugh.

My Angels were here to stay. And so was I.

Chapter 40

OLIVER, BELLA, + WILES

"Mom? Hellooo? Anybody home?"

Wiles was back from school. I lifted my head from the pillow, heartened to hear his voice. *Thank goodness Frenny is willing to bring him home every day. She's such an angel.*

"Wiles!" I croaked. "Wiles!" But he couldn't hear me; my voice was too weak.

I was lying in bed after chemo, in my usual haze after the Red Devil. *But my son is home!* cried a voice in my head. *I have to be a good mom and get up to greet him!* Determined, I mustered all my strength and stumbled over to the intercom. "Wiles, hey, hi," I said into the speaker. "I'm in my bedroom— come on up."

Seconds later I heard his feet pounding on the stairs.

"Hey, Mom!" he said, flinging the doors of my room open. He perched on the edge of my bed. "How was chemo?"

"It was okay." I braved a smile. "How was school?"

"Fine. I thought about you a lot."

I smiled. *My sweet boy.* "Look what I got. Remember the lady who sent the flowers? She and Mrs. Somerville made me these bracelets with a Bible verse on them. Aren't they cute? They're for all my Angels to wear."

Something in my son's face changed. He went from happy and open to hurt and closed off. "There aren't any for me?"

"Oh, sure! You can take some to school if you want. We've got a whole box."

"But they're for your Angels. You said."

He feels excluded, I realized.

"Come here," I said, patting the bed beside me. "Do you know what verse is on those bracelets? Luke 12:6–7. It's the verse about God knowing and loving each and every sparrow, and we are worth far more than sparrows to Him." I did my best to rub his back with my left hand, but it was awkward.

"Do you know how much I love you?" I said. "God loves each of his sparrows, and I love you and Bella so much. You are precious to me."

Wiles and I chatted about his day at school. Ten minutes later, when he left to go start on his homework, I had an idea.

It had never really occurred to me that my kids and husband might feel left out by the overwhelming presence of the Angels. My girls were around me all the time, doing everything I could possibly want and ten times more. They were literally filling every need, sometimes before I even knew I had one.

But I'd gotten the sense from a couple things Oliver had said that he was starting to feel extraneous. And I certainly didn't want my kids to feel like they'd been replaced, or like they weren't on my team of Angels. They were the reason I got up in the morning. Their faces kept me going even in the darkest of times.

I reached for my iPad. *I'm going to get them a surprise,* I thought. *One that will make it crystal clear that my kids and husband are fighting this with me. They're my Angels, too.*

It was difficult to use my iPad with my left hand, but I stumbled jerkily through it as I got online. I began looking for a website where I could custom-order bracelets like the ones Winnie and Gigi had made me. There were a million designs and colors to choose from. I fought a wave of nausea as the images blurred together on the screen. *Not pink. I'm so sick of pink. Blue, maybe? Yeah, blue will be nice.*

I ultimately decided on a bright white bracelet with navy blue font. The message this time read: **WILLOW'S ANGELS** on one side and **OLIVER, BELLA, + WILES** on the other, with a small blue cross. I ordered a whole set.

Good, I thought in the moments before I drifted off to sleep. *They'll come next week before school is out, and Wiles can have as many as he'd like.*

I never wanted either of my kids to feel neglected. They were a huge part of me. There were days I didn't think I'd still be alive if not for them. *I want them to know they're loved.* It was hard to show them from my bed, but I tried. My friends had poured out their love on me, and I did my best to pour out my love on my family. But it was hard to pour myself out to anyone.

My head was flooded with love for my children as I fell into a fitful sleep.

***

"Wiles, you've hardly touched your broccoli," I said. Oliver, Wiles, and I were sitting at the dining room table. It took everything in me to stay upright in my chair.

"Neither have you," my son retorted.

"That's a little different," I said, though he did have a point. Just the smell of food made me nauseous: eating it seemed downright impossible.

"We need to talk about Christmas," Oliver said.

I looked away. I knew what he meant. We'd all been planning a trip to Taos over Christmas, but obviously, in the midst of the Red Devil, I couldn't just hop on a plane and fly to New Mexico.

I watched my son valiantly spear a head of broccoli and choke it down. He was trying to make me happy.

"I don't want to ruin your Christmas," I said softly. "I don't want the family to have to change our plans because of me. And Bella has been looking forward to seeing all her friends in Taos she sees each year." I didn't want to disappoint my daughter anymore.

Oliver nodded but was silent. Wiles looked up sharply.

"You mean you're not coming to Taos, Mom?"

I sighed. "It's not up to me, sweetie. The doctor says it's not good for me to be out in public, especially on a plane where there's a lot of recycled air. My immune system is really weak, and the last thing I need is to catch a cold from somebody on an airplane. And I don't have many days off between chemo."

My heart plummeted at the thought. I loved skiing, especially with my family. But it was out of the question this year.

Wiles's face dropped. He poked around in his mashed potatoes. "I don't want to go without you," he said quietly.

"I don't want to go without you, either," Oliver said.

"I'll be there next year," I said, painting a smile on my face. "Yep. Next year we'll all go together. You guys go and have fun this year. Make a memory and then come home and tell me all about it. Send me pictures."

My own words felt like a betrayal. *Why am I pushing them to go?* Deep down I wanted Oliver to just tell me, "No. We're here to stay."

But that didn't happen. And worse: I was the one enabling it. I kept insisting to Oliver, "Just go. I don't want to ruin the kids' Christmas." *I can tough it alone*, I told myself over and over. *I can do this. I've got this. I don't want to keep putting my kids out.*

The dark, unseemly truth was that I didn't feel worthy. *I don't want everyone to change their Christmas plans because of me. I'm not worth that.* Looking back now, of course, I see things differently. It was a huge mistake, both on Oliver's part and my own. The kids needed to see that their father was going to be there for their mother at Christmas. God forbid my kids might have to stay home from Taos for the holidays. But it was my fault, not theirs—it was the attitude of entitlement I had perpetuated in my kids their entire lives.

A morose Wiles asked if he could be excused, and Oliver nodded.

"You'll have a great time," I murmured, imagining my family up in Taos skiing the slopes while I sat alone at Christmas, wrapped in a comforting warm sweater and sipping a hot herbal tea, scared and sick.

"It's going to be a very Merry Christmas," I echoed, when in reality merriment was the furthest thing from my mind.

Chapter 41

MY DAD, MY CHAMPION

"**M**om! There's a package for you!"

Wiles ran gleefully into the living room, holding a big box. My heart did a little happy dance. The package had arrived the afternoon before, but I'd put it in Wiles's room so he'd see it when he woke up. I knew exactly what was inside, and Wiles was going to love it.

"Open it," I said, smiling.

"But it's got your name on it . . ."

"Maybe so, but what's inside is for you!"

Wiles ripped into the box eagerly, while the rest of us looked on.

My mom, dad, and I were sitting in the living room together. They'd flown into Columbus the day before—they'd be accompanying me to my fourth chemo treatment that morning, the last of the Red Devil. *Thank God this part is almost over.* I was holding onto hope that my breast cancer survivor friends were right: that the next round of chemo was not as horrific as the Red Devil. I knew the drugs had a cumulative effect, and they had told me it would get worse before it got better. But the next round of drugs had less intense symptoms, so even though I might be sicker, the mouth sores would get better—that sort of thing.

"What's in the package, Willow?" my mom said, eyeing Wiles as he eagerly tipped the box on its edge and started shaking it.

"You'll see," I said.

Suddenly one hundred white bracelets with **WILLOW'S ANGELS** and **OLIVER, BELLA, + WILES** in navy blue ink rolled onto the carpet. Wiles's whole face lit up.

"We got our own bracelets!" he hollered.

"Yep," I replied. "We're a team. Now you get to wear as many as you want."

"Seriously?"

"Sure," I said as I smiled.

"Today's the last day before Christmas vacation," Wiles said, his voice vibrating with excitement. "I'm going to wear them all!"

I laughed. "Well, don't wear them ALL. You have to leave some for your sister and Dad! And I want one, too."

Wiles grinned impishly. "Okay. I'll leave them a couple, but Bella will want the pink ones anyway 'cause she's a GIRL, Mom!" He tore through his morning routine like a happy tornado, and my mom, bless her heart, made sure he ate breakfast and had everything he needed for the day.

Beep beep. Frenny's car horn sounded outside. When Wiles came to hug me, I saw he had close to forty bracelets on both arms. He had on so many bracelets, he looked like he was in battle armor with sheaths around his forearms, all the way up to his elbows!

"I'm going to give them out to all of my friends!" Wiles shouted jubilantly.

My heart was awash in pride and tenderness.

I kissed him goodbye and walked him outside, watching as he climbed into Francesca's car. He gave Daniela a high five as he tugged the seatbelt tightly around him.

"Love you, sweetie!" Frenny called out to me, before Wiles closed the door. I gave a little wave as they drove off.

I felt my mom standing behind me in the foyer. "I'm glad you got the early chemo appointment today," she said, patting me gently on the back. I saw she was wearing two bracelets: the original white-and-pink one and one of the new white-and-blue ones.

"I am, too," I said. "I'm finally learning how to take care of myself. Better to get it done and over with."

"The worst part is almost over," my mom said. "That's something to celebrate."

If only that were true.

***

I was on the fourth floor at the James Cancer Hospital, having Shay Shay take my blood to see if I would be approved for chemo #4. It wasn't certain that I would be—after the third chemo treatment, my health had taken a turn for the worse. My immune system was suffering terribly. I was weaker than I'd ever been, throwing up after almost every meal. Since I couldn't really keep food down, I lost all desire to eat it. I'd lost over ten pounds in the last month— and as my mom would be the first to tell me, I didn't have that much to lose.

At least I had my team of Angels with me. This time the room was full of family as we waited for the doctor to come in with the results. Oliver stood by the door, silent and stoic as usual, and my mom and dad waited anxiously in two chairs. Of course, I was looking down at my phone. So many friends were texting me scriptures and words of fierce encouragement. I responded to some, and then I went back to flipping through my pictures.

By this point my friends had started sending me lots and lots of pictures of themselves leading their lives. I was accruing thousands of pictures in my iPhone library, and I had become dependent on them. There were pictures of my friends sitting around the dinner table with their families, all their kids wearing my bracelets. My friends sent me pictures of birthday parties and events they were attending. When it was Ella's birthday, she sent me a picture of her and eight of her friends, everyone smiling and giving me a thumbs up.

I craved getting these pictures. I loved looking at them again and again. Anytime I was waiting on my doctor or waiting to get chemo, anytime

I felt scared—which was often—I would just flip through my pictures. It had definitely become a coping mechanism for me. It became my comfort, my way of looking to my friends for love and support.

My dad had his arms folded over his chest. When I'd told him Oliver and the kids were going to Taos without me, he was not happy. I'd insisted that this was what I wanted—that I didn't want to ruin Christmas for anyone—but my parents were none too thrilled with the idea of me spending the holidays alone.

My dad, however, saw a shining opportunity and an upside to this sad situation: I would come spend the holidays with them in Lake Forest.

"Dad," I'd reminded him. "I can't go anywhere. My immune system isn't strong enough to travel. I've been in and out of the hospital for two weeks." *Maybe I'm just telling my dad this so that if my doctor says no, I won't be so disappointed.*

But my dad was not the type to be told no, and I needed that. When he set his heart on something, he got what he wanted. Earlier that morning, he had pulled me aside and told me, "I am not going to let you be home at Christmas by yourself. I want you to be in Lake Forest with us. And I am going to make sure your doctor tells me what I want to hear."

"But Dad," I'd stammered. "I told you! I'm not supposed to fly. You know that. It's dangerous."

"I'm going to make sure it's not dangerous," he said. "And your doctor is going to agree with me. You'll see."

There's Dad, playing my champion again. I couldn't help but snicker. He'd always been like this: stubborn as a mule, and hell-bent on getting his way. It was something my mom loved about him, even if it also drove her crazy at times.

So there we were, waiting in a tiny, stuffy room, when my doctor walked in. Little did he know the trap had already been set. He didn't stand a chance.

"Your blood looks good, Willow," he said, after introducing himself to my parents. "You're cleared for chemo today."

I opened my mouth to thank him but my dad had already jumped in. "I don't know if you know this, Doc," he said, "but my daughter's going to be by herself for Christmas."

My doctor raised an eyebrow. "Is she now?" Oliver looked away.

"Now, her friend Amelia," my dad went on, "whom you may have met, has invited her over for Christmas dinner. But I want my daughter to be with us in Lake Forest. I don't want her home by herself on Christmas Day. So. Let's you and me figure this out. How can we make this happen?"

My doctor stroked his chin. "You tell me. Give me details. What do you have in mind?"

My dad puffed up his chest like a proud peacock. He'd obviously thought this through. "I'll buy her a first-class ticket," he said. "She'll be in 1A on the way out and 1A on the way in. She'll wear a mask and she'll pre-board. I'll take her luggage with us so she doesn't even have to bring a bag. She'll be there December 24th through December 26th, and back in time for her chemo appointment on December 27th. This is what I want to do. And I need you to allow it."

My doctor knew when he was beat. I could tell. My heart was racing. "Okay," he said. "I'll give her a shot of Neulasta—it'll give her immune system a boost after today's chemo." He turned to me. "I don't like to give that shot very often, because your body can become immune to it. But under the circumstances, I'll give it to you so that you're safer traveling. Your blood count is very low, so I definitely want you to wear a mask. And you'll need to come in tomorrow to get fluids. But if you sit in 1A and pre-board, I'll allow it."

"Suits me just fine," my dad said, as he stood up and shook the doctor's hand.

"Thank you," I mumbled to my doctor. Honestly I had mixed feelings. Of course I thought my dad was the sweetest for going to bat for me. But the thought of not being with my husband and kids for Christmas was weird and unsettling. I wasn't sure quite how to feel, even if it was my own doing by sending the kids away.

Oliver left after my doctor okayed chemo. "You're in good hands," he said, nodding to my parents. "I'll see you at home tonight. And we'll open presents this weekend, okay? Before the kids and I fly out."

"Yes, okay," I said. "That's a good idea." But my heart was heavier than a ton of bricks, watching Oliver stay in the elevator as my parents and I got off on the third floor.

My mom was nervous. She tried to hide it but I could tell. "You sign in here?" she said, pointing to the counters.

"Don't worry. I know exactly what to do." I led my dad and mom through the whole routine, and within the hour, I was sitting in a chair, looking everywhere but at the Red Devil as the drugs flowed bitterly through my veins. *Last time. No more horrible red chemicals. It gets easier after this.*

My mom sat bravely beside me, telling me stories, trying to make me laugh, doing anything and everything in her power to distract me, even fielding my texts. After a while we lapsed into silence. I knew both my parents hated that I was suffering—it was written all over their faces, and on that day I just felt weepy.

"This part is almost over, Willow," my mom kept saying. "It gets better. It got better for Ginny."

I smiled grimly to mask my fear. *And then Ginny died,* I thought to myself. My mother realized her faux pas at the exact same moment: her face got three shades paler.

"I knew what you meant, Mom," I said quickly. "Please don't worry." Even from the chemo chair, I was still taking care of everybody else.

"I love you, sweetie," she said. "You're going to make it through this. And now you'll get to spend Christmas with us. Won't that be nice?"

I nodded. "Yes. Very nice."

Chapter 42

GOD'S WORD IN EVERY ROOM

When my parents drove me back to the house after chemo, I could hardly stand up. My knees were like Jell-O, my whole world awash in nauseating hues and smells. My dad parked in the driveway and my mom quickly jumped out of the passenger's seat to walk around and open my door for me.

"Henry," my mom said. "Henry, we need you, too."

She offered me her arm as my dad came around the other side. Even though I was frail and skinny, it took both of them to lift me up since I couldn't support my own weight. As I clumsily put my feet on the ground, I leaned on both of them. *Hard.*

My legs felt like they might buckle out from underneath me at any second. My mom was so tiny and petite, but my dad was broad-chested: together the two of them were miraculously strong. They hefted me forward and I hobbled up the sidewalk, leaning heavily on them. *How ironic*, I thought.

I feel like I'm leaning on my friends and family literally and figuratively. How could I possibly survive this without them?

"Careful, sweetheart," my dad said. "Go easy. No need to rush." Tears started streaming down my face as they carried me to the house. This was usually the time I started to weep. All the chemo drugs were churning around inside me, and as hard as I tried to fight my way through chemo with dignity, by the time I got home I was always a mess.

I feel like death warmed over. I don't know if I can make it into the house. Every step was a struggle. *Where is Oliver?*

My mom gently took my keys and opened the door of the house. *Thank God the kids aren't here to see me like this,* I thought, as my parents walked me inside and I crumbled onto the sofa in a heap of misery. I knew right now Wiles would be having a great last day at school, eating snacks and putting up decorations and having his end-of-year holiday party. Bella was on her flight back from Boston—we still had a little time before she arrived.

I wish I could be at Wiles's holiday party, I thought sadly. *I've missed so many special moments in my kids' lives over the last few years. Both kids—but especially Bella.* It still haunted me that I had missed Bella's parent weekends. It wasn't fair to her. It wasn't fair either of my kids had a sick mom.

"Willow?" My mother's voice had a question mark in it. "What's all of this? These weren't here when we left this morning."

"What are you . . . what do you mean?"

I lifted my head effortlessly, trying to see where she was pointing. Little squares of yellow color flitted across my vision. *What the heck? What are those?* In my clouded sight, they looked like little canaries or tiny sunflowers stuck all over the house.

"Can you see them?" my mom asked. "Here. I'll bring you one."

She plucked one of the yellow things off the TV and brought it to me. Once she was holding it in front of my face, I saw it was a Post-it note.

"What is that?" I said, confused. "I didn't put that there."

"Looks like your friends have been busy bees while we were out."

I lifted myself up so that I was sitting on the sofa. Then, slowly, rubbing the fog from my eyes, I looked around the living room. There were Post-it notes on the walls, on the TV, even affixed to the photographs displayed on the shelves. I forced my tired eyes to focus on the Post-it note my mom had handed me. *Deuteronomy 31:6.* "Be strong and courageous. Do not fear or be in dread of them, for it is the Lord your God who goes with you. He will not leave you or forsake you."

Who did this? I wondered. *What does it all mean?* I craned my neck and saw my dad squinting at a Post-it note tacked to the stove. "Matthew 11:28," he read, in his deep, booming voice. "'Come to me, all who labor and are heavy laden, and I will give you rest.'"

I felt that old familiar lump rising in my throat. "They're all Bible verses," I said, the realization slowly dawning. "Someone came and put Scripture up in my house." *I guess that's one way to "TP" someone's house.*

"Someone came into your house?" My mom arched an eyebrow.

"The Angels come and leave me nice things sometimes, Mom. Little treats and surprises. Wait, what day of the week is it?"

"It's Thursday," my mom said.

"That's Nicole's day. But this doesn't seem like something she would do. Bible verses aren't so much her thing."

"Well, I certainly have no idea," my mom said. "Pardon me for a second, I'm going to go powder my nose." She ambled down the hallway but I heard her cry out a moment later. "They're in here, too! On the bathroom mirror. The towel rack . . . even the soap dish has one!"

Now I was really curious. Who was this secret Angel who had peppered my home with God's holy word? When my mom finished up in the bathroom, I begged her to take me around the rest of the house.

My mom scrutinized me, her arms akimbo. "You sure you're up for that? I think you need to rest."

"Please," I begged. "I really want to see them."

Reluctantly, my mom offered me her arm again, and slowly, painstakingly, she walked me from room to room.

The secret Angel had put Scriptures on Post-it notes in every room of my house. On the cabinets, in the bathrooms, in my husband's closet, in my kids' rooms—everywhere. They lined every hallway and every room, affixed to mirrors, clocks, pictures, even the thermostat. There were probably close to 250 Post-it notes that this Angel had bought, a Scripture typed onto each one. She had put them up in every room of my house, choosing just the right spot for each Post-it treasure. Everywhere I turned, I saw God's words. His truth would uplift and strengthen me, giving me the courage to fight.

"Oh, wow," I kept saying. "Wow. Wow." It was a big moment for me.

When I got to the last room, there was a note from Emily. "Hope you enjoy the Scriptures, Willow," it said. "Love you."

Ah, my sweet secret Angel. I broke down and cried.

Chapter 43

FROM CHICAGO TO TAOS: A MILLION MILES

"Willow? Are you in there?" My mom rapped softly on the bathroom door. "Everything okay, sweetie? Are you sick?"

"I'm fine. I'm okay," I replied, my voice muffled. "I'll be out in a sec."

My face was hot and sticky as I sat hunched over on the toilet. For once I wasn't throwing up. I was sobbing.

It was Christmas Day, and I was in Lake Forest with my parents. I'd opened a few gifts, but really it was more my parents opening their gifts under the giant Christmas tree. Oliver and the kids and I had opened our gifts a few days before in Bexley. We'd sat around the tree, opening our presents, trying to dispel the solemn gloom of knowing we would not be spending Christmas Day together. Unbeknownst to me, Bella had made me a special gift—one Oliver told her to save for last. So I was cleaning up all the gifts when Oliver said,

"Willow, you have one more gift." He nodded to Bella, and Bella pulled out a Hermès shopping bag from where it had been hiding behind a chair.

"Oh, wow, Bella!" I cried. "You went to my favorite store."

She gave me a funny little smile as I reached into the bag—and pulled out a beautiful cross on a gold chain.

I started sobbing as Bella told me the story. After Oliver told her I had cancer, she'd been distraught, and she'd struggled to pay attention in her classes the next day. She was sitting in art class while her teacher taught a segment on jewelry making, and Bella couldn't do anything but stare straight ahead. The teacher took her aside privately after class. "Everything all right, Bella?"

Bella had responded that, no, actually, it wasn't, and she really couldn't see the point of making jewelry when her mom had cancer.

"Why don't you make something for your mom?" this woman said. "I'll help you work on it. We can cast it in gold. Is there a shape or symbol that's special to her?"

Bella nodded. "A cross."

So Bella started working with her art teacher after class, casting a beautiful gold cross. She'd put a lot of time and effort into it—more than two months—and then she collaborated with Oliver, who bought me a Cartier gold chain to hang it on.

I was crying by the time the story was over. "Mom, Mom, it's okay," Bella said as I sobbed over her gift. "You don't have to cry."

"I know, honey. This is wonderful. What an amazing gift."

I couldn't get over the irony, that my immediate thought when I saw the Hermès bag was, "She went to my favorite store!" I knew Bella liked designer clothes as much as I did. But if there had been a Hermès scarf inside, it would have meant *nothing*. I was still wrapped up in labels and superficial things, when in reality anything from Hermès would have paled in comparison to the gift she gave me. The cross my daughter made was my ultimate gift.

But now, on Christmas Day, my beloved Bella was off skiing in Taos with Wiles and Oliver. I was grateful to be in my childhood home in Lake Forest, and I was immensely grateful to my parents for flying me up, but the whole thing was painful. *I miss my kids. I want to be with my husband. I feel homesick for my family. Not my family of origin—my married family.*

"I've got some nice roasted vegetables out here," my mom said, "if you're hungry."

I wasn't hungry. Most of the stuff around the house I couldn't eat anyway, all the Christmas cookies and pies and butterscotch candies my mom had in crystal bowls around the house. The vegetables would have been okay if the chemo didn't make me want to vomit up every morsel of food I touched. Basically all I had to do was *look* at food to throw it up. I had become particularly fond of Cheetos by this point in the chemo process. They had a strong enough flavor that I could taste them, and my friends were constantly dropping off bags of them at my front door. They emailed my mom to make sure she had Cheetos for me at Christmas, which she did.

"I'll leave you in peace," she said, and the sound of her footsteps retreated down the hall.

I tried to stop crying but my emaciated body was racked with sobs. I didn't want my parents to know how unhappy I was. They had been so kind and generous to bring me home to Lake Forest for Christmas. The only problem was: This was no longer my home.

I reached for my phone and called my cousin Ella. She answered on the first ring.

"Hey, Willow. Hi. How you holding up?"

I blubbered a reply that would have been indecipherable to just about anyone else, but Ella knew me better than I knew myself. "I'm glad I'm not alone," I wailed, "but I miss Oliver and the kids. It's so weird, Ella! The whole thing is so weird."

"That's one word for it," Ella said sardonically. "It's totally screwed up, Willow. The whole thing is screwed up." My cousin wasn't one to mince words.

She was dumbfounded Oliver had taken the kids to Taos. "That's not what families do," she told me. "Families support each other. Families stick together."

Ella wasn't the only one who felt that way. Many of my friends were really pissed off about the whole thing. "But I insisted they go," I tried to explain. "I don't want anyone to change their life because I have cancer," I retorted. Most of my Angels would just press their lips together and sigh in disapproval, though some of them had a choice word or two on the matter.

I heard my mom change the music in the living room to old-fashioned Christmas carols. "My parents are *so* happy I'm here," I whispered into the phone. "It absolutely made their Christmas! They had all their friends over, and our extended family, and Mom and Dad are just so proud to have me here. They're so happy I can't bear to tell them I'm so sad."

"That's okay—you don't have to," Ella said. "That's what bathrooms are for. Crying and calling me."

A tiny smile broke through my tears. "Did I tell you the firemen came over last night?"

"What? No!"

"Oh, my poor Dad. We went over to our cousin Betsy's annual Christmas Eve dinner and when we got back, Dad tried to light a fire. It's snowing like crazy here—a big snowstorm blew in today."

"I saw it on the news. It's crazy."

"Yeah, so my dad tried to build a fire to warm us up, and he forgot to open the chute in the fireplace! The smoke alarm went off and ten minutes later the firemen had come over to the house."

"Oh my God! Uncle Henry must have been so embarrassed . . ."

I chuckled slightly, remembering the look on my dad's face. "He was embarrassed, all right. And there I was, in my cute little wig and baseball cap, with all these handsome young firemen parading through."

"That doesn't sound like a bad Christmas present," Ella joked.

"Ha. Well. Of course my mom told the firemen I was going through chemo, and they were all so sweet, encouraging me, telling me I looked great. My mom took pictures of all of us together! Talk about embarrassing. I wish she didn't tell everyone I have cancer!"

"Aww. That sounds like a Christmas Eve to remember. I bet your kids wish they were there—they might have gotten to ride in the firetruck!"

I laughed. "Yeah, maybe when they were three, Ella."

But then I got very quiet. "Yeah. I wish they were here, too." I sighed and dried my eyes on one of the festive Christmas hand towels my mom had in the bathroom. "I better go. I think Mom is making her special pumpkin pie and she wants me to help."

"You can't eat that! So don't go! Just rest."

"Nope. She loves taking care of me, Ella, and I want to be around her."

We shared a silent moment of understanding. Ella and I were good at that. We hung up and I pulled myself together.

I walked out into the hall and joined the others in the kitchen. "There she is!" my mom cried, her whole face brightening as she ran over and hugged me. I knew how happy it made her that I was there. I wished it weren't such a sad day for me. I loved the attention she was pouring on me, and I was getting sad thinking about not seeing her for a while after I left Chicago. They would be heading to Palm Beach for the season and I sure as heck wasn't heading to Miami anytime soon.

"Still going to help me with this pie?" she said.

"Mmm hmm. Let's do it." I slowly sauntered over.

Chapter 44

"KEEP ME POSTED"

American Airlines, Flight AA480: DELAYED.

I stood in the departures terminal at Chicago O'Hare International Airport on December 26th, the day after Christmas, my face mask clamped over my mouth and my eyes scanning a long list of flight updates on the departures board.

DELAYED.
CANCELLED.
CANCELLED.
DELAYED.
CANCELLED.

Yikes. I'm not going to make it back to Columbus, am I?

I looked at the ticket I was clutching in my left hand. I was holding it so hard it was crimped in the places where my fingers touched. *Seat 1A.* My dad had made good on his promise: I was in 1A coming in to Chicago and I would be in 1A flying out.

If I can get out of Chicago, that is.

A massive snowstorm had whipped through the city, leaving behind several feet of snow and grounding a number of flights. There was a good chance I would have to stay in Chicago for another night.

Oh no. This is not good. I've got chemo tomorrow morning . . .

It wasn't that I was looking forward to chemo—far from it. But the sooner I got through my treatments, the sooner it would be over.

I called Francesca, lifting the mask down below my chin so I could speak audibly into my phone. "Hey, hi, Frenny? It looks like my flight is delayed . . ."

"Are you ok, sweetie?" Her thick accent always gave her voice a rich, dulcet tone. "Are you alone in the airport?"

My parents had dropped me off at the terminal, then driven to the private airport so they could fly to Palm Beach with my sister and her family. I wouldn't have minded going back to my parents' home—but my parents were no longer there.

"Yes," I said to Frenny, "but I'm hoping they'll start boarding soon. They haven't cancelled the flight yet. There's still hope."

I looked out the wide glass window. The whole airport was bathed in soft white snow. The snow reflected the moonlight and the various flashing lights of airplanes, baggage carts, and other equipment. *It's almost pretty*, I thought. *At least it would be, if it didn't mean I was stuck.*

"I'll be here when you land, sweetie," Frenny said. "No matter how late. Don't you worry. I love you."

"Love you, too."

I popped my mask back into place, turned around, and walked back to my gate, avoiding everyone else in the terminal.

I knew my mask attracted attention. People giggled and whispered and stared. I felt the scrutiny of their gaze, the sting of their judgment, and, perhaps worst of all: their pity.

"Calling all passengers for American Flight 480." A woman's voice crackled over the loudspeaker. "Good news, folks: We're still going to Columbus. We'll begin pre-boarding now."

Oh, thank God, I thought. *What a relief.*

It was a strange cocktail of feelings: to actually feel *relieved* that I was heading back to Bexley where an empty house and chemotherapy awaited me. But then, none of my feelings had made a lot of sense ever since I'd been diagnosed with cancer. My friends who had survived breast cancer told me this was perfectly normal—probably even a good sign.

Home sweet home, I thought, as I moved slowly toward the jetway. *Home without my husband, my kids. Who knew the word "home" could inspire such conflicted feelings?*

***

Francesca stood at the bottom of the stairs. "Willow? You ready, sweetie?"

No sooner had I appeared at the top of the landing than Frenny was rushing up the steps. She took my purse out of my hand. "Let me help you with that! You don't need to worry about a thing." I leaned on her as together we walked down the stairs.

Frenny was the textbook definition of selfless. She had come to pick me up at the airport the night before—even though my flight was many hours delayed, meaning she was out late the day after Christmas. But she swore she didn't mind. She left her kids with her husband and spent the night in my guest room so that I didn't have to be in the house alone.

"Are you warm enough, sweetie? Why don't you take my sweater." She wrapped her soft sweater around my shoulders. "I've already warmed up the car."

Francesca was a special friend. Most of the other Angels lived in my neighborhood, and in many ways Frenny felt ostracized. She was afraid she was constantly being judged for not having the right clothes, or wealth, or status. She felt like the black sheep of the group. But like I always reminded her, "You are precious to me. And you've been a huge help. You are one of my Angels because I want you to be, and you are worthy."

"That's the only thing that matters," she said. She was fiercely loyal to me, and no matter what happened, I never doubted I could count on Frenny.

If I was able to get chemo, I'd send out a group text to my main Angels saying, "I'm all hooked up, I'm good to go, I'm getting settled into my chair"—that kind of thing.

Chemo passed comfortably enough, as "comfortably" as it could ever be. Frenny stayed with me and read me stories from a book she loved. I didn't notice any immediate difference from the Taxol instead of the A/C they used in the Red Devil, but I knew it wouldn't be immediate. When I accidentally peeked over at the bag, I was relieved to no longer see that deathly red color.

Frenny took me home and helped me upstairs, where I fell immediately into bed. "How do you feel?" she asked. "Is it better? Less sick this time?"

"Maybe a little less sick." The truth was, it was hard to tell. I had grown accustomed to an ever-present cloud of nausea hanging over me at all times, and it was difficult to tell if it was better or worse.

Frenny had to leave, but it was Thursday, Nicole's day. *Thank God for Nicole, my Thursday Angel.* She came to sit with me, telling me one funny story after another as I drifted in and out of consciousness. Nicole left that evening to go have dinner with her family, but not until Frenny came back to relieve her.

That night, I tossed and turned in bed, tortured by nightmares. I dreamed that Wiles had fallen down the mountain and broken his leg. I wasn't there to wrap my arms around him, to bring him to safety. I was thousands of miles away, and still his screams reached me.

"Mom!" he cried out to me in my dream. "Mom! My leg! MY LEG!"

I awoke with a start to a sharp, throbbing pain in my right leg. *Oh no. Is that what I think it is?*

By that point I'd had enough blood clots to know a sharp pain in my leg should not be ignored. I reached for it and gingerly massaged it with my fingers. It definitely felt swollen. *What am I going to do?* I was too sick to drive anywhere. Oliver and the kids were gone.

Call one of your Angels, said a voice in my head. *They'll come pick you up in a heartbeat and take you to the hospital.*

No way. I can't do that. I checked the clock: three in the morning. I was gripped by the same irrational fear: *Don't wake Frenny up. Don't overtax your Angels. They're already over-extended. They've already done so much. If you keep asking for more, they're going to stop coming. It's not worth disturbing anyone. You don't want to make anyone change their plans, remember?*

By some small miracle, I fell back asleep. I woke up the next morning when Frenny came in to kiss me on the forehead and say goodbye. She had to be at work at seven a.m.

I heard her walk out the door and my heart seized. My leg was still throbbing, even worse than last night. *What am I going to do?*

I flashed back to something Nicole had said the previous day. "Call me anytime you need me, Willow. I mean that. *Anytime.*" Many of my Angels were out of town for the holidays, including Caroline, who had volunteered to be my Friday Angel but was up in Vail with her family. Nicole, on the other hand, was in Bexley, and she had offered to help me. Finally I gave in and called her.

"I'm coming right over," she said. "But I have to tell you—I woke up with some kind of bug this morning. I think I got it from my kids. So I just want you to know I'm sick, and I'm not sure I *should* come over . . . but I want to be there if you need me."

My heart sank. "Oh no," I said. "I can't get sick. You can't come over, Nicole—I'm so sorry. I'll have to call somebody else." I felt crushed as I hung up the phone.

I sank back onto the pillows, feeling impotent and exhausted. The thought that had first bubbled up during my colon surgery six years earlier washed back up to the surface. *Who will protect me? I feel so terribly alone.*

As I was putting my phone back on my bedside table, my eye snagged on one of Emily's yellow Post-it notes. *Emily.* Why hadn't I thought of her before? As if on cue, my phone rang. I looked at the caller ID. *Emily.*

"Were your ears burning?" I said, by way of hello.

"Nicole called me," she said, "and I'm coming right over! I'm not sick—I'm healthy as a horse. So don't move a muscle. Oh, unless you should be moving to keep the blood flowing around a potential clot?"

My heart swelled with gratitude. Emily dropped everything and came over immediately. I was not forsaken. I was not alone.

I called Oliver from the passenger's seat of Emily's car. He didn't answer. "I'm on my way to the hospital," I said on his voicemail. "Please call me back."

No answer.

"Maybe he's out on the slopes," Emily said encouragingly. "I'm sure he'll call right back as soon as he gets your message. He knows you had chemo yesterday—he must be checking his phone!"

He wasn't. I called and called, and he didn't answer.

By the time we were waiting in the emergency room, he still hadn't returned my call. Desperate, I texted him. "I'm in the ER with Emily. I think I have a blood clot in my leg."

A few minutes later, my phone buzzed with one new text message. *That couldn't possibly be Oliver,* I thought. *He would pick up the phone and call!*

But it was, in fact, a text message from my husband. "Okay," he said. "Just keep me posted. We're out on the slopes."

And then he went off to ski with my kids.

At the time I was in such a haze of hurt and fear, I didn't realize how angry I was. I showed Emily the message, and it was only when I looked at her face that I saw my own feelings reflected in her eyes. She was so furious she was shaking.

"You're in the hospital," she said, spitting out each word like a tack, "with a potential blood clot . . . and they went *skiing*??"

All I could do was nod.

The ER doctor called me in soon after and did a Doppler ultrasound on my leg. I was lucky—this time there was no clot. But I was terribly dehydrated from the chemo, so weak I couldn't stand up without someone helping me. So the doctor gave me fluids. I was in the hospital for several hours, and Emily stayed with me the whole time, making me laugh. When it was all over and I was cleared to leave, she drove me home.

"I'm sorry about Oliver," she said, after she had tucked me into bed to get some much-needed rest.

"Yeah. Thank you. Thanks for saying."

Later that day, as I tossed and turned in fitful half-sleep, my phone rang. It was Oliver. I swallowed down my blistering anger and answered.

"I couldn't get a hold of you," I said. "I kept calling and calling. What was going on?"

"Reception is sketchy on the mountain," he said. "I couldn't hear my phone."

I felt the rage boiling inside me, but I was scared of it, too, scared of how Oliver would react if I told him how I was really feeling. Instead I mustered every shred of strength and willpower I had left and said, my words coiled tight: "Well. I hope you all had fun."

My husband knew I was in the hospital. He knew I might have a blood clot, and he took the kids off skiing. He couldn't be bothered to come down off the mountain, go to the lodge, and pick up the phone.

"Keep me posted." I felt like someone had kicked me in the gut and kept on kicking. I couldn't help but read into it, to invent my own subtext to the message. "Keep me posted, in case you're about to die."

He's always unavailable. My heart felt like it was cracking open in my chest.

I thought about something Frenny had said, about how she didn't feel Oliver had been there for me during my chemo as much as he should have. She told me he had once taken her aside and said, "You know, Francesca, Willow is a grown woman. She's forty-two years old. She's an adult, and I've never seen so many women caring for or babying her in my life."

Frenny said she was actually shaking, she was so angry. "Oliver, you're a man," she told him. "You're the husband. But we women have a special connection. We know what we need and we can hold each other's hand when we're suffering. I know I baby Willow all the time, but I do that because I think she needs it. She's sick. She's going through chemotherapy, and she's scared. So I am going to be right by her side."

When Frenny told me that story, she said, "I think he was jealous. Maybe he feels threatened with all your Angels here all the time."

"Maybe," I said. Before that it had never really occurred to me that Oliver might be jealous that all my friends were constantly around. *Maybe he feels like there's no space for him because my friends are filling the space instead.* But Oliver was busy. He was traveling and working every day. He couldn't be at every chemo, and he couldn't be home every day. So there *were* gaps to fill.

There were so many moments on this journey that stay with me to this day, so many horrors and fears and heartbreaks, but I will never, ever forget that.

***

Francesca spent the night again but I didn't even hear her come and go. I slept intermittently, yet still wasn't cognizant of life continuing on around me. When I finally woke and shook the cobwebs from my brain, I looked at my phone and saw it was just after seven a.m. *The kids come home today,* was my first thought. I was positively giddy about getting to see them.

A string of text messages from Frenny awaited me. "I love you baby. Today is going to be a better day. I'm praying. Please have breakfast ok? Maybe a little oatmeal? I'll check on u later. I wish I was there to take care of u . . ."

"Thank u," I texted back. "Just woke up. I don't even remember u being there, isn't that weird! I'm so glad u came."

"I love u!!!! You have no idea, sweetie. I'm praying with all my heart."

I tried to stomach some oatmeal, for Frenny's sake, but I just couldn't keep it down. It didn't matter—I had something to look forward to. In just a few short hours, my family would be back home. I was going to do my best to forgive Oliver for what had happened—it just wasn't worth holding a grudge. If I expressed my anger, then things would be tense and unpleasant, and all I wanted was to enjoy being with him and Bella and Wiles.

Zzz. Zzz. I glanced at my phone. "Kisses to you!" said a text from Grace.

"Kiss u back, Grace!" I texted. "You would have been in awe of Emily yesterday. We are so lucky we all have each other. So lucky! I wanted to have a fit and she kept me laughing! Xo."

"I am always in awe of her!" Grace said. "An angel. You both are! Xo."

Emily really had been amazing. Thursday's chemo was rough and had hit me hard—I'd had so many treatments close together, which was probably why my white blood count was so low. And then the scare with the blood clot very nearly sent me over the edge. But she'd made everything better. She made it okay.

I looked anxiously at the clock. *Only five more hours!* I was dying to go meet my family at the airport, though I knew it was out of the question. I had to stay put so I could stay clear of germs. Going to Lake Forest had been worth it, but it had also cost me in terms of my immune system, which was weaker than ever.

I was touched and overwhelmed by what Emily had done for me. And not just Emily—*all* my Angels. *How blessed am I to have friends like that?* I thought. Friends who, if I called them at the last minute for a 911 call, would drop everything and show up on my doorstep. "It's not us," Emily had said with great fervor when I thanked her profusely on the car ride home. "It's the Lord, Willow. It's the Lord who is giving us the time to be there for you, and the passion for helping you heal. He's put it on all our hearts."

I felt like my Angels were teaching me about a selfless faith. They were showing me the fundamentals of how to live out a Christian life instead of just reading about it. For years I'd seen and heard people who called themselves Christians talk the talk. But my Angels were walking the walk.

On impulse, I composed an email to Emily.

"I am exhausted physically and emotionally, and last night I ditched my phone. But when I turned off my light, ALL I could think about is you. I wish I could shout from the rooftops who u are because the whole world would want to meet u. I am so lucky, beyond any scope I could have ever imagined, that you are on my team and I am on yours. We will always be connected, and we will fight for each other always. In sickness and in health."

I swept away the tears that were rolling freely down my cheeks. "I love you, Emily. Thank you."

I wasn't the only one crying—Emily responded with an emoticon of a crying smiling face. Tears of happiness, I knew.

"Oh, Willow," she said. "You think we're giving to you, but really, YOU are giving so much to US!"

I smiled. Then I glanced at the clock. *Four hours to go. Four hours till I see my family.*

I settled in for a long Saturday, until the moment my kids came barreling through the door and I bundled them up in my arms and my love.

Chapter 45

TURNED AWAY

No. It can't be.

I was standing in Bella's bedroom at 6:30 a.m. She was still asleep—she hardly ever got up before noon when she was home from school—and I'd come in to get her laundry. That's when I saw it: the bag of white powder peeking out from under a notebook on her desk.

So my worst fears are true. She was doing cocaine.

"Isabella Adair."

She mumbled, still half asleep.

"Get up, Bella."

"Whaaat?" She sat up, groggy, rubbing her eyes. "What is your deal, Mom? I was sleeping."

"Isabella." I locked eyes on hers and didn't look away. "I found the coke."

That woke her up. Her eyes widened. "I don't know what you're—" She saw me holding the baggie. Then she shifted uneasily on the bed. "It's not mine."

"Don't lie to me."

She wouldn't look me in the face.

"Do you have any idea how worried I am about you, Bella? Do you have any idea the sort of trouble you could get into?"

"Whatever. I'm not addicted."

"I don't care if you're addicted. I've seen what this stuff can do. I was a model—I saw my fair share of coke. And it destroys you. It eats up your life."

"You don't know what it's like, Mom! Things are different today. If you don't play along . . ."

"Then what? You won't be cool? Boys won't think you're sexy? You'll lose friends because you'll stop being the life of the party?" My voice was calm and level. From the tears building in her eyes, I knew I'd hit the mark.

I took a deep breath and responded with compassion, "I know you think you've got it all figured out. I thought that, too, when I was your age. I thank God there were people in my life who loved me enough to take care of me, even when I wasn't doing such a good job myself. I *still* have people in my life who love me that much—my Angels love me even when I don't love myself."

My own eyes filled with tears. *She really is so much like me. She can't see her own beauty, her own worth.* "I love you, Bella. I love you and I will fight for you until the end. I'm going to call a drug counselor when I get back from chemo. You and your father and I will be going to see him before you fly back to Massachusetts."

She was angry, I could tell. She batted the tears out of her eyes. "I don't need a counselor!"

"Need one or not, you're going to see one. And then, as a family, we'll figure out how to proceed."

I walked out of Bella's room, shaking. My heart was racing, but somewhere deep down, I felt strangely calm. *I can't believe how well I just handled that. Jules would be so proud.*

My head was swimming. I checked my phone. Chemo in a little over an hour, so I knew I should probably be resting. But I felt strange and uneasy in my body after my exchange with my daughter. *I need to go on a walk. It'll help clear my head.*

All things considered, I felt like a pretty kickass mom as I grabbed my facemask and made my way out the front door.

***

"Willow Adair! What on earth are you doing outside?!!"

Gigi had busted me. I was on the sidewalk in front of my house, having just completed a very easy, very slow walk around the block. She had rolled her car window down so she could scold me.

I pointed to the mask over my mouth, then said sheepishly, "I had to get out of the house!"

"What would your doctor say about that?"

"I'm going stir crazy, Gigi! I'm not going to get sick—that's what the mask is for."

She parked her car at the curb and stepped out, folding her arms over her chest. Gigi had very strong, toned arms. "Well, you know *I* won't tell. I just don't want you to get any sicker! You look like a summer breeze could knock you over. Come on—let's get you inside so we can get ready for chemo."

Gigi held out an iced tea for me, and I noticed sweat from the cold drink beading on the outside of the plastic cup. A sip of iced tea sounded so refreshing, but even the most delicious things tasted foul in my mouth on account of all the chemo drugs. And the mouth sores were horrific—they were under my tongue, on the sides of my mouth, on the top of my tongue. It was torture. Even when I was hungry, it was still hard to eat; I was blistering all over my mouth.

"Just grab my chemo bag," I said to Gigi. "And we can go."

"No problem." Gigi took charge, sweeping inside to pick up my chemo bag. I was too weak to carry anything on my own, partly because of the chemo and partly because of my right arm. So my Angels would never let me carry my own bag.

"You got everything you need in here?" Gigi asked.

"Yep. I think so."

Inside the chemo bag were tissues, socks for when it got cold in the room, a bottle of water, a couple of magazines, a stress ball for me to squeeze, Chapstick for dry lips, and some pretzels. During most of the chemos, they wanted me to chew as the drugs were going in so that they didn't get in my teeth. It didn't have to be food—it could be ice or something else, but I'd found pretzels to be the most effective. At least they didn't make me want to throw up.

The doctors and nurses also had me put my hands and feet in ice. They didn't do this for the Red Devil, but for the Herceptin and Taxol, my oncology team had me plunge my hands and feet into two buckets of ice so that the chemo couldn't get to them. They did this to minimize the risk of neuropathy, or permanent nerve damage.

I smiled bravely at Gigi. *8 a.m. on Thursday January 3rd.* I had a date with destiny—if "destiny" meant my doctor and the chemo ward. *See, I haven't lost my sense of humor.*

"I'm glad you feel like walking," Gigi said, helping me into her car and making sure I was comfortable in the front seat. "I turned the seat heater on for you. I would have brought you breakfast but I figured you wouldn't be up for it."

I nodded. "You figured right."

As she drove, I told her about what had happened with Bella, and we prayed about it. Or rather, she prayed aloud and I listened. I loved listening to Gigi pray. She talked to God like he was her friend, a very close friend she could confide in. I was a lot shyer about praying out loud.

After Gigi prayed for Bella, I prayed my heart out that I'd be able to do chemo. When I'd been to the hospital the week before because of the blood clot scare, they told me my white blood count was 1,200 and that was getting too low for chemo. *It has to be better today,* I told myself. *I've stayed home all week. I haven't gone anywhere. Okay, fine—a couple times I've walked around the block, like this morning. But I always wear my mask. And I haven't been around anyone who's sick—I made sure of it.*

But there was another reason I desperately needed to do chemo that day: we had a trip planned for Wiles's birthday in eight days. Oliver and I had promised our son we'd take him to New York City. *I know I'm not supposed to go anywhere,* I rationalized, *but getting our family out of the house and taking a fun trip together is something we all need.*

In two days Bella would leave for boarding school, which was never an easy day for me, especially not now after I'd found the coke. We would talk to the drug counselor and see what he suggested. Hopefully he would lead us in the right direction. In the meantime, I knew Wiles was craving some quality time with my husband and me, and as much as I hated to admit it, Bella being gone meant Oliver and I could take Wiles to New York without worrying about her being surly and ruining Wiles's birthday.

Please, God. Don't take this away from Wiles, I thought, as Gigi drove me to the James Cancer Hospital. *I have to go on that trip. We all need this— Oliver, Wiles, and me.* Every day was a battle trying to create some sense of normalcy in our house in the midst of chemo.

And yet here I was, practically begging to get chemo that day. *How quickly things change,* I thought darkly. Because let me tell you: it was really uncomfortable. For hours I was plugged into a port with the drugs going through my veins, and then I had my fingers and my feet in ice the whole time. It literally felt like torture. *And this is what I want?*

While I sat in the front seat, worrying and fretting and feeling generally afraid, Gigi filled me in on what was going on with her husband and her kids. I was grateful for the distraction. She talked about the women in her Bible Study, and how she and Winnie had been studying Romans 12:4–9. "It's such a perfect verse for your Angels, Willow. We're all serving in different ways, using our gifts to show you God's love by showering you with *our* love. Is it okay if I share the passage with you?"

"Sure, okay."

Gigi recited the Scripture smoothly, her voice like deep, calming music in my ears. "'For just as each of us has one body with many members, and these members do not all have the same function, so in Christ we, though many, form one body, and each member belongs to all the others. We have different gifts, according to the grace given to each of us. If your gift is prophesying, then prophesy in accordance with your faith; if it is serving, then serve; if it is teaching, then teach; if it is to encourage, then give encouragement; if it is giving, then give generously; if it is to lead, do it diligently; if it is to show mercy, do it cheerfully.'"

Gigi smiled at me. "Love must be sincere. Hate what is evil; cling to what is good.'"

I smiled back. "Thanks for sharing that, Gigi. That was beautiful."

"Isn't it? Reading the Scripture always makes me realize God's word is the most beautiful poem ever written. 'Hate what is evil; cling to what is good.' I just love that." She reached over and squeezed my leg affectionately. "We're going to cling to what is good today, okay? Even in the midst of chemo. Because I'll tell you what's good: getting your chemo treatments out of the way so that you're on the road to feeling better!"

But God had other plans.

***

Shay Shay was working on the fourth floor and happy to see me, like always. Her smile was a beacon of light amid a dark, turbulent storm. I introduced her to my friend, since this was the first time Gigi had taken me to chemo. Shay Shay clucked like a proud mother hen.

"Girl, you are so lucky. You wouldn't believe all the patients I have who come in here all by their lonesome! They don't have amazing friends like you do. I hope you know how blessed you are."

"Blessed is exactly the right word for it, Shay Shay."

She patted my arm. "Well, let's hope for good news today. You look awfully pale and I know you've been stuck at home. You must be bored to tears. But I hope the doctor okays you for chemo so that you're one step closer to kicking cancer in the butt!"

She led Gigi and me back to the doctor's waiting room, where I started to scroll through the pictures on my phone. It seemed like the doctor was taking longer than usual, leaving plenty of time for me to get nervous. I tried to keep looking at the pictures but my heart was thumping wildly in my chest. *Something has to be wrong. What's taking so long? Do my counts not look good? Why won't he just—*

The door swung open. "Willow?" my doctor said.

I knew immediately, by the tone of his voice, that it wasn't good news. My heart plummeted down to the hard tile floor and shattered like a million pieces.

"Your blood count's at 600, Willow," my doctor said sternly. "That's a critical alert."

"No no," I said softly. "No, that can't be. I've stayed inside. I mean I've been on a few walks, but mostly I've been resting . . ."

"You can't do chemo today. No ifs ands or buts."

I started to whimper, tears pricking my eyes. I stared at Gigi, who looked at me with great tenderness and compassion. "I have to do chemo this week," I mumbled. "Next weekend we want to take our son to New York."

"I can't let you do that, Willow. You got to go to Chicago. But now I'm putting you on strict house arrest. No walks. No going anywhere."

"Even if I wear my mask?"

"Absolutely not. I want to impress upon you the seriousness of this: if your levels go any lower, to 500 or below, then we will hospitalize you in full quarantine."

I swallowed hard. *In Bubble Boy fashion, he means.*

He said a few more things, and I asked some questions to clarify, and then he was ushering us out of his office and back into the waiting room. I tried to stanch my tears as Gigi walked beside me to the elevators.

"It's okay, Willow," she said soothingly. "God must not have wanted you to have chemo today. This is all a part of his master plan, even if we can't guess or understand it."

"It's just so demoralizing," I said, trying to keep from breaking down and weeping. I never wanted to cry in front of a bunch of strangers. "It's not like I *want* chemo. Who would want chemo? But I want to take Wiles to New York, Gigi. I can't let him down. I've disappointed him so many times all these months and years I've been sick or injured."

"New York isn't out of the question. There's still hope." She rubbed my back. "We try to read God's plan and interpret it, but we're so tiny. His plan is way too big for us."

She smiled encouragingly at me. "I don't know what the silver lining of this cloud is, but God does. You may have been turned away today, but there is something in store for you, I just know it."

I nodded, wanting to believe her. It was hard to see the silver lining in any of this.

But Gigi was right, as usual. The silver lining was quite tangible this time, and it was literally delicious. *Food.*

Chapter 46

WILES'S BIRTHDAY

I sat at the kitchen table, ravenously hungry for the first time in months.

"Geez, Mom," Wiles said, highly amused as I plowed through a leafy green salad full of mushrooms and squash and all the things I liked. "I've never seen you eat so much!"

"Food has never tasted so good," I said, as I attacked my food with genuine zeal.

It all made perfect sense when I thought about it: part of the blood count plummeting had been due to poor nutrition. It was hard to eat on chemo—everybody knew that—and I'd hardly eaten anything over the last month, no more than a few crumbs here and there to keep myself going. *No wonder my blood count was so low. I haven't had anything of nutritional value in my body!*

Because I hadn't had chemo the day before, there were no chemicals inside of me, leaving me with a great appetite. I felt hungry. Hungry for the first time in months. *I forgot what it felt like to be hungry!* I thought. Even Oliver enjoyed watching me eat.

I couldn't believe it. *This is amazing. The nausea is gone. The chemical taste that has been in my mouth since October 30th is minimal. WOW.*

Wiles chuckled. "Slow down, Mom! You're going to eat us out of house and home."

"It just tastes so good!" I said. "I can't even describe how good it tastes."

My friends rallied to the cause. When I sent out an email that I had an appetite again, no fewer than five Angels showed up on my doorstep with different homemade goodies or my favorite dishes from restaurants in Bexley. Nicole made her bone marrow soup, and Grace brought fresh vegetables. Caroline brought me a smoothie and Amelia and Gigi brought me my favorite salads and iced teas from around town. And there were more Cheetos at my doorstep.

It wasn't all puppies and roses, of course. I had gone in that morning for the echocardiogram to monitor my heart but wouldn't have the results for a few days. On Tuesday I would meet with my doctor to discuss the critical white blood count and my options going forward. *I can't be that low each week. I know it. There has to be a way to keep my count up.* My doctor told me it really needed to be between 2,000 and 3,000. No more of this measly 600.

But the truth was, I felt good. As Wiles grinned at me over his tacos and I tore into my salad with gusto, I felt better than I'd felt in ages.

"You sure do seem like you're feeling better," my son said. "I hope this means we still get to go to New York for my birthday!"

The funny thing was, for once in my life, I had faith. I had faith that somehow, someway, we'd make it to New York. I knew the reality of my situation didn't look good, but I utterly refused to let that take away my hope.

Not this time. I have faith. There has to be a way. It's Wiles's birthday—he wants this so much.

My son smiled up at me. I couldn't let him down. Not again.

***

By Tuesday afternoon, I no longer felt quite so cheerful. I was in my bedroom, preparing to leave the house for my doctor's appointment and labs—my first time leaving the house after ten days of house arrest. My zest for eating wasn't quite as strong as it had been. I'd had a couple glorious days where food tasted good, but then the mouth sores flared up again, and my hemorrhoids were acting up worse than ever. It had also been an extremely stressful morning—my live-in had up and quit out of nowhere.

"Ready, Willow?" Oliver called from the hallway.

"Just a minute!" I was frenetically typing a thank-you email to my Angels with my left hand. They had all been so kind and generous, and I was truly saddened and sorry I was unable to write a personalized thank-you note to each one. *Someday my arm will allow me to write legibly and without pain. Because my friends deserve thousands of thank yous, and I wish I could send them all.*

"We don't want to be late," Oliver said.

"I know, I'm coming."

As I detailed how each and every Angel had specifically helped me, and as I relayed how it was giving me strength, I was overcome by emotion. I was sobbing, tears streaming down my face. "Willow!" Oliver called, poking his head in the door, but as soon as he saw me, he softened. "Are you okay?"

"I'm fine," I said, brushing the tears away. "I'm ready now. I just needed to say thanks to all my Angels."

I typed one final thing in closing: "SORRY NOT SO CHIRPY. -WILLOW."

Oliver looked over my shoulder. "Do you really think any of your friends expect you to be chirpy?"

I thought about it. "No. I guess not."

"Come on. Let's go see what the doctor has to say."

***

My doctor wasn't as ornery as I had feared.

"Let's discuss what we can do to keep you out of the hospital, Willow. I think we both want that."

"Yes, we do." I straightened in my chair.

"Well, you've got to eat more, for starters," he said. "That's number one."

"I've been doing that this week," I assured him. "Eating more. A lot more. And I've been at home for the last ten days. No cheating this time. I've done everything you told me."

"Good. That's good. The results from your echocardiogram were normal, by the way. Your heart is doing just fine."

I breathed a sigh of relief. *Thank God.*

"I'm going to go out on a limb and say you'll be able to get chemo on Thursday," my doctor said. "As long as you keep your blood count up for the next two days."

Oh, thank God. Thank God. Hopefully I'll be doing chemo on Thursday!

I took a deep breath. "I want to discuss something with you, Doctor."

"Shoot," he said.

"If I do chemo on Thursday, I'm hoping you'll okay me to travel on Friday with my husband and son."

He arched an eyebrow. "To where?"

"New York. It's Wiles's birthday and we've already booked our flights." *Okay, Dad's not here this time,* I said to myself. *It's all on you, Willow. You have to be strong. You have to tell him what you want.*

I pulled myself to my full height. "I'll take all the precautions. I'll stay in the hotel while Oliver and Wiles go explore the city. I'll wear my mask. I'll sit in first class. And I'll be back for chemo next week."

My doctor's brow was furrowed. He opened his mouth, then clamped it shut. What he did next truly surprised me. He shrugged.

"Okay," he said. "Have it your way."

I felt like cheering. I'd get to be with Wiles on his birthday. I didn't have to disappoint my son. *These small victories are worth everything.*

My phone buzzed with a text from Grace. My Tuesday Angel was checking in. "Hey, I know you're at the doctor's—just wanted to let you know, I'll be at your house waiting when you get back! And I brought treats. XO."

I smiled. I was already composing the next email to my Angels. I found it to be so narcissistic to email my precious friends about myself, but they kept asking me to send out an update, so I'd promised not to let them down.

"MY JOURNEY IS DRAMATIC, FILLED WITH YUCK, STRESS, AND DAILY HURDLES. UNFORTUNATELY, MY JOURNEY IS FAR FROM A CONCLUSION.

BUT THE PRAYERS THAT COME FROM YOU ALL EVERY DAY ARE BEYOND WHAT I THOUGHT PEOPLE ACTUALLY WOULD DO, EVER. IT'S AMAZING. . . AND THOSE PRAYERS MUST BE WORKING, BECAUSE ON FRIDAY, WILES AND OLIVER AND I ARE GOING TO NEW YORK."

Chapter 47

NEW YORK CITY

I peered out at the hustle and bustle of New York City from our hotel window. The city was beautiful, draped in twinkling lights from head to toe. People were yelling in languages I couldn't possibly understand and the honk of taxis was ever present. *Ah, New York.*

I was half lying down, half sitting up in bed—not exactly the way I would have chosen to see the city, but it was what it was. Even if I couldn't go out and do all the touristy stuff with the boys, I was glad that Oliver and Wiles were out on the town, living it up and enjoying every minute.

The hotel door swung open and Wiles charged in, talking ninety miles an hour.

"It was so cool, Mom! You should've seen it. We rode the subway to the Knicks game, and they won! They won! And then we went up to the top of the Empire State Building and it was AMAZING. Did you know that if you drop a penny from the Empire State Building it takes on so much mass from gravity that it can kill someone? Don't worry, we didn't do it."

He was breathless, on cloud nine from his adventures. It made me happy to see him happy. "Tonight Dad's taking me to a Broadway play," he said. "You sure you don't want to come? You could just sit in the audience. You wouldn't have to do anything."

"Oh, honey." I smiled. "I wish I could. It's just, there will be way too many people in the audience. If any of them are sick, it could be very bad for me. The mask is not 100 percent foolproof. We just can't risk compromising my immune system."

Wiles looked crestfallen. "Okay, I know. It was dumb of me to ask. I understand."

"But we do have a little something for you," Oliver said. He looked at me and winked.

"What do you mean?" Wiles asked.

I knew what was coming. I'd helped arrange it, even though I couldn't go get it myself. But I'd called around to the best bakeries in the city, and I'd had them deliver a beautiful, scrumptious birthday cake to our room.

I walked over to the refrigerator. It was a big cake and my dominant arm was still out of commission. "Oliver, can you—"

"Yeah, of course." He opened the fridge and pulled out the absolutely gorgeous cake.

It really was gorgeous. It was a double-decker cookie cake, with six little balls of icing on the perimeter and a huge ball of icing with "12" in the middle. In blue icing the message read, "HAPPY BIRTHDAY WILES."

"Wow!" Wiles said, clapping his hands together in glee. "This is amazing!"

"There's ice cream, too," I said, reaching into the freezer.

"Best. Birthday. EVER." Wiles grinned. "I don't ever want to go home!"

"Unfortunately you've got to, buddy," Oliver said. "Tomorrow you go with your mom to see her arm surgeon, make sure everything's up to snuff. Then you two head back to Columbus."

Oliver was heading in a different direction—he'd be meeting Bella at Cate School, a boarding school in the foothills of Santa Barbara where Bella would interview for the next academic year.

I missed Bella already. Our family never quite felt complete without her; Bella's absence left a gaping hole. She had sent me a picture of her and the other cheerleaders at the game on Friday night. *I'm so sad I can't be there to see her cheer. It breaks my heart.* But what I absolutely loved about the picture she sent was that she had on pink socks and a pink arm bracelet. *Nike's breast cancer gear.*

The funniest thing was: she had bought it *before* I had breast cancer, during football season at Andover! She bought all that gear when I went to see her in September, the week before I was diagnosed. On some uncanny level, it's almost like she *knew.*

"Will Mom wear her mask at the airport?" Wiles asked.

"Yes," Oliver replied. I'd taken to wearing it with my big movie-star sunglasses over the top, and the mask went all the way up over the bridge of my nose, so you really couldn't see any of my face. It was seriously hard to breath with that thing on.

"You look like a bank robber," Oliver said, "not a cancer patient." We both laughed. It was good to laugh.

"This is the best birthday, Mom and Dad," Wiles said. "Seriously."

In the midst of everything else, at least we had this.

I sent out an update to my Angels that night, including pictures of Bella cheering at the basketball game, Wiles with his cake, and me with my facemask looking like a bank robber. The responses flew in quickly, the way they always did. I needed that reinforcement and support.

From Alice: "I LOVE the update and LOVE the pictures! Sounds like the trip has been a success! A great recharging in a different city with lots of different sights and sounds! Something about being away in a new bed and different surroundings that just feels good!! I've been walking Cooper by your house and miss that you're not home but LOVING knowing you're off on an adventure!! Now get a good check-up with the arm doc and get back here safe and sound!! XOXO"

From Grace: "Hooray! So glad you had a wonderful time and are healthy!! Please be so careful on the flight home! Love and miss you! Adored all pics and especially love the God's answers to prayers. SO true!! You are an angel! Love you xo"

And from Amelia: "So glad it was a good trip! See you in a couple days. Wednesday is MY day and I will be there! Others are welcome, but I get a little territorial with my Wednesdays. JK. Love you, Amelia."

I laughed at Amelia's message. All of my Angles got a little territorial about their days with me, and I appreciated their loyalty and compassion.

A few days later, Amelia sent out an email to our team of Angels asking for some extra coverage since my live-in help had quit. It reminded me of the Scripture passage, "Let us not become weary in doing good, for at the proper time we will reap a harvest if we do not give up." Galatians 6:9.

Oh, Amelia. If only she knew. I felt like every day I was the one who reaped a harvest—the gentle lovingkindness of my beautiful, wonderful, Angelic friends.

Chapter 48

HOUSE ARREST FOR TWO

January 24, 2013. My email to the Angels began with:

"I WAS ABLE TO HAVE CHEMO TODAY!!"

Never, not in a million years, did I think I'd be typing those words. Life sure was funny sometimes. Now getting chemo was a GOOD thing, the thing I wanted. Every day I could get chemo was one more chemo out of the way.

"I ACTUALLY HAD A PRIVATE ROOM TODAY WITH MY OWN TV, SO NO FOOD NETWORK! :)"

Anyone who knew Amelia would know what I was referring to, especially my friends who had taken me to chemo before. Amelia had engaged in several, er, *discussions* with one of the nurses on duty in the chemo ward who insisted on keeping the Food Network on the big TVs. It confounded Amelia that a room full of people who felt sick and horrible—me included—were forced to watch salmon being grilled and beef being roasted and various other foods being chopped and diced and seared and served. These were cancer patients in the midst of chemo, people who were constantly nauseated, people who could not eat.

"Any channel would be better than the Food Network," Amelia had hissed to the nurse, who stared back at her with angry, cold eyes. Melia joked that the nurses knew when she was coming to chemo: they probably whispered behind her back, "There's that crotchety lady who's going to ask us to turn off the Food Network again." Of course, it made Amelia livid. "They just have it on for themselves!" she huffed. "Don't they have any respect for their patients?"

I turned my attention back to writing the email. Despite the fact that I'd been approved for chemo, not everything was sunny. I had a slight fever, even though my blood levels were up. And Wiles was home with a concussion until Monday.

My sweet Wiles! This was his first concussion, and I was very worried about him. I tiptoed into his room, where he was watching his fish tank and holding a cool compress against his head. "Wiles, honey? Why don't we go downstairs and build a fire in the fireplace?" I would have said, "Watch a movie," but the doctor had forbidden any and all screens.

He nodded, more quiet than usual. "Okay." *My poor son.*

My mom had come out for this chemo, and Emily came, too. Mom had just left for the airport, so now I was back home, trying to take care of Wiles as best I could. Now *he* was the one on house arrest.

My friends had buzzed in to help, of course, with Nicole getting Wiles's meds from Tom Thumb. Amelia had come over that morning to give me a great pep talk.

"THANK U ALL FOR THE ENCOURAGEMENT," I typed to my Angels. "AND FOR HELPING TAKE CARE OF MY SON. THANK YOU FOR TAKING THE WAR SO SERIOUSLY. THE BATTLE CONTINUES."

My oncologist did have one problem with me when I went in that morning: my weight. "If you don't gain weight by Monday, the next time you get weighed," he told me, "then we'll have to consider the possibility of a feeding tube."

Not going to happen, I told myself. *I will force-feed myself before I allow more tubes in my body.* When I told Amelia, she nodded in agreement. "I'm not going to let that happen, either. If we need to, we'll pack rocks in the bag with your wig, and we'll tuck them up under your baseball cap before you step onto that scale!" I didn't think she was really serious, but I knew she would've done something.

I also knew my doctor was right: my weight had dropped significantly in the last two weeks, and it was already pretty low. So I decided to start seeing a medical nutritionist. Alice had agreed to take me.

I still had one piece of good news to dole out to my Angels:

"CHEMO WAS CHANGED TO THE DAY *AFTER* MY BIRTHDAY, SO I WILL BE DOING IT NOW FRIDAY, FEBRUARY 8th, NOT THURSDAY FEBRUARY 7th. YIPPPEEEE!!"

Thank God for small favors. The thought of sitting in a chair in the chemo ward on my forty-second birthday was just too depressing. My doctor had been gracious enough to offer me a stay of execution—I was free and clear on my birthday, as long as I came back the next day for treatment.

"Sure, of course," I said. "I'll be there. Believe me, doctor: I want this to be over a whole lot more than you do!"

***

January 31, 2013. Another successful day, if "successful" meant toxic chemicals were shunted through my veins.

I lounged on the sofa in my living room, typing out an email to the Angels. They kept asking for these weekly updates, so I kept sending them. It gave me comfort to know that people *wanted* to hear, that I wasn't just talking to an empty room.

"I WAS ABLE TO HAVE CHEMO TODAY. MY LEVELS WERE HIGH ENOUGH FOR CHEMO BUT BONE MARROW WENT DOWN. SO I NEED TO WORK ON GETTING THAT UP FOR NEXT WEEK. BACK TO BONE MARROW SOUP, NICOLE!"

My chemo symptoms over the last week had been particularly hard. There was never any way to tell which treatments would hit the worst. I felt really sick, and even though I was not technically on house arrest anymore, I didn't go anywhere because I just felt too rotten. I was scared. That morning I had asked my oncologist why the last chemo was so hard and why I was sick for six straight days. When I gave him my list of symptoms, he said I'd probably caught a small bug.

"Nothing to worry about," he said. "That means it will be easier this time."

"I AM AFFIRMING THAT *WILL* HAPPEN," I wrote to my Angels. "IT WILL BE EASIER THIS TIME. IF I SAY IT WON'T, THEN IT WON'T. BUT IF I SAY IT WILL, IT WILL! THAT'S MY NEW ATTITUDE. WELL, I'M TRYING, ANYWAY. . . HEE HEE."

And of course, there was that silver lining Gigi had talked about: I was off house arrest!! I could leave the building, so to speak. YIPPPPPEEEEEEEE. Which meant, in one more week, I might actually be able to go out and celebrate my birthday!

I was trying hard to fight off the disappointment that had consumed me. I was originally told chemo would end February 1st, and that the port would be out by my birthday. Needless to say, that hadn't happened. I kept thinking about it, of course, but I refused to suffocate myself with disappointment.

"BUT I AM HUMAN," I typed. "WITH HUMAN EMOTIONS. AND WHEN I LOOK IN THE MIRROR, I DON'T LIKE WHAT I SEE. THE PORT, THE LACK OF HAIR—IT DOESN'T SUIT ME! I LOVE WHAT'S INSIDE OF ME NOW MORE THAN EVER, BUT I AM CHALLENGED BY MY PORTRAIT."

This was something I was learning: to love my own inner worth, even when I hated how I looked on the outside. It was a very new perspective for me.

I dragged myself upstairs to check on Wiles. He still had a concussion—what we had thought was a minor one surprised us by the impact. *Poor Wiles: he does not need any more stress.* My son had seen what my "house arrest" felt like. But he was only allowed part-time school, no homework, no reading, no screens, no TV, no video, no sports or running around. Ironically, I was more stressed than he was, as I tried to imagine all the work he'd have to catch up on!

I sat down beside my son. "Pretty sucky, isn't it?"

"Yeah. Totally. I guess now I understand what you mean when you say you feel like a caged animal in your own house."

I nodded. "Want to play a board game?"

He brightened. "Sure!"

The blessing in Wiles's concussion was this: we were going back to basics, since these were the only activities we could do. We were playing board games and listening to books on tape and music. At night we would sit in front of the fire and talk, and we had stopped arguing about watching sports at dinnertime. Now Wiles was home right after school instead of being gone until 7:30.

"Scrabble or Apples to Apples?" I asked.

"Apples!"

"Good choice."

I reveled in this time with my son. Suddenly someone was home with me, and chemo wasn't as lonely as it had been before.

But I felt more than a pang of guilt about my daughter. Oliver was out of town, because he had flown to Andover for Bella's parent weekend. *This is the third parent weekend I will have missed. In fact, since Bella left for boarding school I have not made a single one.* Her first parent weekend was when I was in the hospital with the infection in my arm. The second one was when I was with my parents in Arizona for the lumpectomy. And now this was the third one, and I was too sick and weak to fly because of chemo. It was heartbreaking for me AND for her.

"Frenny's coming over in a bit," I said to Wiles, trying to think about something more positive. "She was wondering if you'd want to help her bake cookies."

"Yeah, sure!" This was something I loved about Wiles: he was game for anything. Some twelve-year-old boys might have said, "Nah, that's girly." But he loved baking.

An hour later, he and Frenny were happily dusted in flour with her daughter Daniela, all three of them clanging and banging pots downstairs. I took the opportunity to jot down another quick update to my Angels.

"LADIES, YOU KEEP SHOWING UP. I WANT TO REACH THROUGH THIS SCREEN AND HUG EACH AND EVERY ONE OF YOU SO SO BADLY. I WOULD NOT BE HERE WITHOUT YOU. GRACE AND CAROLINE, THANK YOU FOR TAKING ME TO CHEMO TODAY. YOU ALL ARE A GOOD TEAM. SO MANY MORE TO THANK BUT I AM SO WEAK AND SLEEPY.

I NEED TO GET UP IN THE MORNING AND ORDER SOME VALENTINE'S GOODIES ONLINE BEFORE TOMORROW TO MAKE SURE THEY GET SHIPPED TO BELLA, SO GOODNIGHT ALL. OUR TIME TOGETHER IS WAY MORE FUN THAN SHOPPING AND TALKING ABOUT SILLY MEANINGLESS STUFF. OUR CONVERSATIONS ARE INTIMATE AND REAL. THAT IS A BLESSING.

OUR TEAM IS A FORCE TO BE RECKONED WITH. WE HAVE WON THE BATTLE, ALL THIS TOUGH CHEMO STUFF RIGHT NOW IS JUST THE INSURANCE.

WE ARE SO STRONG TOGETHER.

LOVE,

WILLOW."

My head was filled with visions of Angels as I fell into a restless, fitful sleep.

Chapter 49

WALK WITH ME

I t was a bad morning.

I was sick. Very sick. Maybe sicker than I'd ever been. But worse: I felt like the last ounce of hope had drained out of me.

Sometimes I felt like the chemo drugs pummeling my system didn't just scorch the cancer cells—they scorched my faith, my hope, my reason to live.

My friends and family had been amazing. When I said I wouldn't be alive without my Angels, I really meant that. But some days, all the love and kindness in the world couldn't change the fact that every breath I took hurt, every smell made me run to the bathroom and vomit, and every part of my body ached and burned and looked ugly. Just imagining my reflection in the mirror made me sick. Looking at it was even worse.

Zzz. Zzz. Miserably I glanced down at my phone. It was a text from Emily. "I'm bringing you an egg sandwich for breakfast," she said. "You have to eat, Willow."

No no, I thought. *I can't see anyone. I'm a mess.*

And I truly was. I had on no makeup—the little mascara I'd tried to put on had smeared down my face on account of all my weeping. I was still in my pajamas and robe. I was cold, so I had the fire on, but I felt like I couldn't move. I just couldn't deal with anyone. I couldn't deal with the world. It had gotten so bad in my head that I had crawled under my kitchen table to hide.

That's where I was when Emily barreled through the door a few minutes later. I was lying on the floor under the table, crying. I had a blanket over me but even then I was shivering.

Emily was on the phone; I could hear her talking to her decorator. She was talking about paint samples. "Lucy!" she called in an over-blown Ricky Ricardo accent. "Lucy, I'm home!"

But her jovial demeanor melted the instant she came around the table and saw me. "I've got to call you back," she said to her decorator. *Click.*

"Oh Willow. Oh honey."

I was curled up in a ball, utterly distraught. "Look at me," I said. "Look at what a mess I am."

I knew Emily's knees were bad, but she crawled right under the table with me. "Oh my gosh," she said. "Honey, I can't fit under here! We can't all be super skinny models with great climbing abilities like you!"

She wrapped her arms around me and I just cried and cried. And then, wonder of wonders, she made me laugh. Emily was so good at that—I'd be crying one minute and cracking up hysterically the next. Together we went from laughter to tears, and then from tears right back into laughter.

"Isn't this just like us?" Emily said. "One second we're crying, one second we're about to pee our pants laughing!" She got serious. "Willow, what time is it? It's Wednesday, isn't it?"

I dried my face on the sleeve of my robe. "Yeah, why?"

"Because Wednesday is Amelia's day! I have to get out of here before Amelia comes! Aaaahhhh!"

I laughed so hard my stomach hurt. "She does get pretty protective, doesn't she? I'm happy to have both of you. I feel so awful, Emily. Days like today—I just don't know if I can go on. I don't even want to kill myself anymore. I just literally don't know if I can survive this."

Emily lifted my chin so that I was looking right at her. Her eyes were just as red-rimmed as mine. "Who are you?"

I blinked. "What do you mean?"

"I mean, what's your name?"

"Willow Adair."

"Say it. I want you to say your name."

Emily was a mother of four, and sometimes that mother bear came out. She was a fighter—and she was going to make me a fighter, too.

"I'm Willow Adair," I said quietly.

"Say it louder."

"I'm Willow Adair!"

"I've always known how strong you are," she said. "You've always been tough. But I've never seen you as tough as you are right now. Yes, you're lying under the table. Yes, you're in your robe. I don't care about that stuff. You are fighting a war, Willow. And you are winning."

After a while, Emily pulled away and looked at me. "You have a satellite dish, right?"

"Yep."

"Would it be okay if we put on some Christian music? My favorite channel is called The Spirit. They play the most beautiful, uplifting songs—they always make me feel better. I'd love to share that with you."

I nodded. "Okay, yeah, sure."

We helped each other out from our spot under the table, a perfect metaphor for everything else. *I have to remember that. I feel like my Angels are only helping me, but they constantly remind me that we are helping each other.* Emily fiddled with the satellite and we sat together on the sofa, listening as praise songs flooded the house. I felt a calm drift over me that I hadn't felt in a long, long time. *Emily is filling my house with God,* I realized. *She has invited Him into this house.*

"I call this steak and potatoes of the soul," she said. "These songs. Oh! Listen! This one is one of my favorites." She started to tear up. "It's called 'Walk With Me.' The lyrics are so incredibly deep and strong. Just listen."

So we both leaned back onto the butter-soft sofa, and we listened.

"Author of the world walk with me,
Ruler of the earth walk with me,
Calmer of the storm walk with me,
Healer of my heart walk with me."

"Do you hear that?" Emily whispered. "Do you understand what that is?"

I nodded, too moved to speak.

For years my house had been tumultuous. There was fighting and discord, neglect and disappointment. But as I sat there, one of my dear Angels by my side, I truly felt my house—and my heart—become more peaceful. I could feel the energy changing around me—and within me, too.

This is the greatest gift, I thought, reaching out to squeeze Emily's hand.

My Angels had begun to teach me. They were teaching me what it meant to breathe in life and not breathe out fear and death. They were showing me how to set an example for my family, my kids. They weren't preaching to me—they were showing me what it meant to have real faith, not the kind where you go to church on Sundays once in a while and maybe show up at a Bible study. My Angels were showing me how to live out my faith.

"How can I ever say thank you?" I murmured. "What do I do?"

"Just love me," Emily said. "That's all. Just please love me."

"I do."

Emily was shining a light on my path, showing me how my faith could bring more peace to my children. Instead of showing them how scared I was, I would be able to show them I was going to be okay. And when my kids saw that I was faithful to God and trusted in his goodness, the fear in their hearts would be replaced with faith.

"Thank you, Emily," I whispered, as the notes of the music rolled over me, sweet and soothing as a summer wind, even in the dead of winter. "You've done so much more than I could ever have imagined. All of you Angels have taught me and continue to teach me. I love you so much."

"Oh, honey," Emily said, in that frank, no-nonsense tone I loved her for. "Don't you think for a second you're going to get rid of us. We've only just begun!"

Chapter 50

MY BIRTHDAY WEEK

"Everyone! Can I have everyone's attention, please?" Cece Miller tapped her fork against her water glass. "I want to say something. I promise I won't take long, because after all, there's cake."

My friends giggled appreciatively and lay their sterling Christofle silverware down as Cece stood at the end of the table, smiling warmly at me. "We're all here today because we love Willow Adair, and we know how special she is. She loves each one of you so much—that's why you're here. We have walked with her through her colon, and her many arm surgeries, and now, breast cancer. And she has been just as graceful and lovely and generous as ever.

"This is a horrible disease and it is quite a battle. But if you're sitting here today, then you know Willow well enough to know that—pardon my French—she is going to kick cancer's butt."

My eyes were already fogging up, and the luncheon had only just begun. My mom reached over and squeezed my left hand. I noticed her eyes were teary, too. "Oh, sweetie," she said. "We don't even need water pitchers at this luncheon—we're going to have nothing but waterworks all day!"

It was Tuesday February 5th, two days before my birthday, and Cece was hosting an intimate lunch for me at her house. She had invited a handful of my friends and their moms. Caroline and Gigi were both there with their moms, and Alice and Amelia were there.

My mom had flown into town just for the occasion. "This is just so nice," my mom kept saying. And it really was.

"Who's ready for cake?" Cece cried.

I expected the waitstaff to come out with a sheet cake or pound cake, something for everyone that they would slice up and serve. But suddenly, they were all parading out of the kitchen *with an individual cake for each of us*. It was amazing! I actually got butterflies.

They set my own cake in front of me. It was perfect, an adorably cute vanilla cake with white icing swirls, and a halo of violet icing at the bottom. On top were two exuberant flowers and a long, thin pink candle. Even if I couldn't eat sugar, it was the thought that counted.

A member of the waitstaff lit the candle, and my friends sang the Happy Birthday song to me. They laughed and clapped and cheered as I blew out the candle. It was so beautiful, and I was so grateful to have them there and to be alive.

"Thank you, Cece," I said, getting up to hug her as my friends feasted on cake. "This is the nicest luncheon anybody's ever given me."

She beamed. "You deserve it, sweetie. It's your birthday!"

"It's not her birthday until Thursday," my mom chimed in. "And her dad is coming in tomorrow to take her out to dinner. She's going to get to celebrate all week!" My mom smiled, happy to know I was so loved.

***

Wednesday, February 6th. I sat next to my dad at the beautiful banquet at the Pearl Restaurant, Tavern & Oyster Room, one of my favorite restaurants in Columbus. Al was a friend of mine, and his restaurant was my dad's kind of place—fancy atmosphere, nice steaks, expensive wines, and the perfect ambience.

Oliver sat across from me as I tried to conjure up an appetite. My dad looked at me with genuine concern.

"You okay, Willow?"

"I'm okay," I lied.

The truth was, my stomach was pretty queasy, and all over my body felt weak. The thing about chemo was that it made my body ache in strange, inexplicable ways, and I just felt so darn *tired* all the time. Sometimes it took great effort just to pick up a fork.

But I was so happy my dad was there. He had flown down to Columbus just to take me out to dinner. I was touched by the gesture. My parents were continuing to shock me with their enormous support.

"Your mother said the luncheon yesterday was great," Dad said.

"It was outrageously beautiful. Did you know it was the first time Mom got to meet Cece? They're about the same age."

"I think Nanette made a new friend. But you know your mother—she could make friends everywhere from the executive suite to the cattle barn." He chuckled. "She's got the gift of gab."

"This is really nice, Dad," I said, forcing myself to swallow a forkful of mashed potatoes. "I'm so grateful you came down to see me."

"It's my girl's birthday tomorrow," he said. "If that's not a good excuse for a trip to Columbus, I don't know what is." He reached over and hugged me.

I choked up a little, hearing him call me "my girl."

The three of us had a nice dinner together, enjoying each other's company. I had gotten all dressed up in one of my favorite Carolina Herrera black dresses, and I was wearing the long blonde wig I loved. My dad talked about my sisters and their kids, and I appreciated getting to hear what was going on in everyone's lives. Cancer could be so insular—it often felt like I couldn't see anything outside my own bubble of pain and misery, and to know that life went on for other people? To hear news of their birthdays and kids' birthdays? It was hugely comforting. *If their lives are going on, maybe mine will, too.*

"I love you, Daddy," I said. "Hey, Oliver—do you think maybe you could take a picture of the two of us?"

I still have the picture we took that night. If you didn't know I had cancer, you might not even know it's a wig. My collarbones are severely pronounced from all the weight loss, but I am glowing, just being there with my dad. He is wearing his navy blue dinner jacket and a bright white shirt, his ever-present handkerchief tucked into his breast pocket. He's got his glasses on, and he's leaning into me, happy to have me by his side.

***

Thursday February 7th. My phone rang at eight a.m. *Amelia's ring tone.*

"Happy birthday!" she sang the moment I picked up. My heart flipped with excitement. I had always loved my birthday.

"Oh my gosh," I said, smiling. "You're the first person to officially wish me Happy Birthday! Well, Oliver kissed me before he left this morning with Wiles and left the most stunning arrangement of roses on the kitchen island. And Wiles made me breakfast in bed before school. It was so cute." I yawned. "Did I tell you my dad came in last night to take me to dinner?"

"He's the sweetest." Amelia cleared her throat. "Listen, I know it's not my day—but I'm going to take you out to lunch today, okay? I cleared it with Nicole and she's totally fine with it."

My heart sank. *Amelia is so sweet. But I really don't want to go out today.* I was tired from being out with my dad and just generally felt like crap from the chemo drugs. *I can always be honest with Amelia,* I thought. *It's something I appreciate about her. So she'll understand.*

"I don't really feel like going out, Melia."

There was silence on the other end of the line. "Don't be silly, Willow. Of course I'm going to take you out. It's your birthday!"

"I just don't want to go anywhere," I said. "I'm exhausted. Why don't you just bring food to my house?"

"No no no," she insisted. "Look, let's just go to the Club, okay? It's across the street and it's your birthday, we have to do something special. So throw something nice on, because we're going to sit in the fancy room at the Club."

I sighed. "Okay, fine. You win." *Whatever. I can certainly muster enough energy for lunch with Amelia.* I threw on a blue jacket and the wig of the day and tried to make myself presentable.

I had no idea what was waiting for me at Columbus Country Club.

***

"SURPRISE!!!!!"

I was floored. With Amelia by my side, I walked into the "fancy room at the Club" to find it filled with my friends. There must have been thirty women smiling back at me—not just my Angels, but also some of the moms from Wellington.

"Did you know?" Amelia asked, grinning. "Did you guess?"

"I—I had no idea," I stammered.

"This was all Oliver's idea," she said. "He planned the whole thing!"

I listened in awe as she told me that Oliver had organized this surprise birthday party for me and my Angels. I was overwhelmed. Sometimes I felt like he was jealous or resentful of my friends, of how much time they spent with me, and how they were always hanging around the house. But he had done something nice for us. He had given us a day and a lunch to be with one another and celebrate my birthday.

"Come on in!" Grace said. "We've been sneaking around behind your back for days. You really had no idea?"

"No idea," I repeated.

The truth was, I *had* thought it was kind of weird that, as my birthday approached, my friends weren't giving me the kind of attention they normally would. *I guess they're just busy*, I thought, but I was a little bit suspicious. Still, I never would have guessed Oliver was secretly planning a whole lunch and taking care of all the details.

"Hi, birthday girl," Gigi said, as she came up to hug me. "Remember the book I gave you years ago? Look on the table! Now everyone gets one as a party favor."

She gestured toward the place settings. Everyone had their own copy of *Jesus Calling: Enjoying Peace in His Presence*, a book that had meant a great deal to me.

"Caroline bought them for everyone," Gigi said. "Isn't that wonderful?"

"And look what I brought!" Emily cried. "Here's one for you." She thrust a bejeweled ring over my finger that had a big pink flower on it. I saw that everyone was wearing them. *This is so unbelievably sweet.*

The table was bright and festive, bedecked with cheerful orange and yellow flowers. I sat down and Amelia sat down beside me. The servers began to bring out our lunch. While the food was good, the real treat was feasting on the company of my friends.

Toward the end of lunch, Oliver came up to CCC. He looked very handsome in his crisp blue button-down, and he shyly said hi to my friends. He wasn't the sort to bask in the attention.

"Happy birthday, Willow," he said, giving me a chaste kiss on the forehead.

It is *happy. So very happy.* In that glittering moment, I felt incredibly, wonderfully loved.

Chapter 51

VALENTINE'S DAY

Valentine's Day arrived and Caroline showed up bright and early at my house to accompany me. I should have known, as Caroline drove me to the James Cancer Hospital that morning, that something wasn't right. Caroline had clucked and clucked when she saw me, telling me how frail I looked. "Too skinny," she kept saying. "You look like a concentration camp survivor. You look like hell."

I look like hell AND feel like hell. Caroline was right. The week after my birthday had been a particularly bad one. I didn't know why. I was terrified my doctor wouldn't let me do chemo, and that seemed like the worst possible fate.

"Hey, girl," said Shay Shay as she led me to the now-familiar and always-dreaded room. "You look like you're not doing so hot."

"I just want to be able to get chemo today," I said. "Please please, dear God, let me get chemo."

She took my blood quietly. Something about her silence was unnerving. "I'm praying for you," she said. She nodded toward Caroline. "I'm sure your friend is praying, too. I figure you can use all the prayers you can get."

But all the prayer in the world wasn't enough that day. My doctor came in the room with that same grim expression, and I could hear the words before he said them. My eyes filled with tears. I looked at Caroline and her eyes were misty, too.

"You can't do chemo," my doctor say. "I'm putting you back under house arrest. We'll try again in a few days."

Happy Valentine's Day, I thought darkly, as my tears fell.

Caroline was on the move. I saw her immediately reach for her phone and I knew she was texting Oliver. The two of them were in regular touch about my cancer and my care, as were a lot of my other friends.

Caroline was still huffing and puffing five minutes later when we walked back out to the parking lot, me leaning on her as she supported my weight. "That doctor thinks he's just going to send you home?" she said. "Well. We'll just see about that. You may not be able to get chemo today, but we are going to make today special, you hear me?. It's Valentine's Day."

"What are we going to do?" I asked, as she started driving.

"We are going out for lunch."

"But, the doctor said house arrest . . ."

"Oh, you'll be on house arrest. I have no doubt you'll get *plenty* of time cooped up in your house over the next few days. But right now let's be Thelma and Louise and break the rules and go to Lindey's for lunch. It's our place. Then I'll take you home and you can stay in that room all day long. But before that happens, I'm going to take you out to lunch."

Caroline was on a tear, and when she was determined, there was no stopping her. "You've got your mask with you, right?"

"Yes," I said. It was in my chemo bag.

"Good. Because we're going to do this safely—but we are going to do it, so help me God. I don't care what they say."

I smiled. *Thank God for Caroline.* I wasn't scared about getting sick, because I knew Caroline would take good care of me. And she was right: sometimes breaking the rules was more important than sticking to them. In the midst of this nightmare, sometimes what I really needed was not the strict regimen prescribed by the doctor, but the feeling that I still had the power to live my life the way I wanted to.

***

"This is really nice, Oliver. Thanks for taking me out."

It was the day after I was put back on house arrest, but I needed to get out, and we were doing our own Valentine's Day at the Club. The management had set up a table for us behind the bar area so we could have a quiet, secluded, danger-free dinner.

"Excuse me for just a moment, Oliver," I said, laying my napkin in my lap. I hoped I was going to the restroom just to use the restroom. *I really really hope I don't throw up.* And I needed to adjust my wig.

I was at the sink, throwing a spritz of cool water on my face, when someone said, "Willow? Is that you?"

I wheeled around and, to my surprise, my friend Morgan was staring back at me.

Morgan and I had met in our early twenties. We were with the same modeling agency in Columbus, and we'd first become friends on set during a catalog shoot. Whenever we worked together, we acted like sisters, but I hadn't seen Morgan in over ten years. She looked as flawlessly beautiful as ever.

She hugged me. "Look at you!" Morgan said. "I love that cool braid! Oh my gosh, it's gorgeous. How'd you do that? Who did that braid?"

My stomach flipped. "You know this isn't mine."

Morgan looked at me blankly. "What do you mean?"

"Morgan, I have cancer. This is a wig."

She later explained to me that, in that moment, her heart fell to the floor. "It seemed like you were at the end of your rope," she said, "but you were still smiling. You were still the girl I knew."

"Oh, Willow." She held her hand over her heart. "Sounds like we are long overdue for a catch-up!"

We must've stayed in the bathroom for at least ten minutes, talking and reconnecting. Then we went back to our husbands and continued our own special Valentine's Day. But I felt heartened by seeing Morgan. I had a feeling we were going to rekindle our friendship—and, as weird as it was, it was my cancer that would bring us back into each other's orbits. Of course, she had triplets who were two and a half, so she looked like she was at the end of her rope, too!

Chapter 52

WE ARE WINNING

"Hi Angels,

"LET'S START WITH . . . CONTINUED HOUSE ARREST AND NO CHEMO LAST THURSDAY."

My letter to my Angels was starting on a glum note. *I can't really help it,* I thought. *This is the reality of my current situation.* I checked the time on my phone. Oliver would be bringing Bella home from the airport in a little while—our daughter was coming home for six weeks. I was excited to see her, though worried about her, too.

I've got half an hour. Plenty of time for an update. I took a sip of green tea and kept writing my Angels, filling them in on the details of my chemo and its aftermath. I leaned back in the chair, contemplating everything I'd just written and the sad state of my current existence. *Even if I lived in the Peninsula Hotel Beverly Hills, I think I would at this point want to jump ship from all this house arrest. The concept of a caged animal has all new meaning for me. I don't like it.*

I'd also received even more discouraging news. It seemed my mastectomy would be right after chemo. Somehow I'd thought I would have

278

more time in between. And then my final arm surgery was scheduled after that. *No rest for the weary,* I thought. *Literally.*

I closed my eyes and tried to pray. *I am not in control.* My friends had taught me to have faith in my doctors and in the Lord, and to focus on the good and the positive. Wiles's concussion was healing. Thank the Lord. He was happier and more active. Bella would be taking me to chemo in the morning. *She's never been in Columbus and able to go with me before.* That was good news. It would be good for her to see what chemo was really like, and it would be good for me to have her there.

And Oliver, poor Oliver. Oliver was a rock for all of us, juggling a mountain of responsibilities. I turned back to my computer and the email I was composing and continued, "PRAY FOR OLIVER, PLEASE," I entreated my Angels. "HE NEEDS SOME STRENGTH.

SOUNDS LIKE A LOT OF COMPLAINING. . . SORRY, ANGELS. I HAVE GOOD DAYS AND BAD. BUT I DO FEEL JOY.

I WANT TO RAISE MY KIDS AND BE OLIVER'S WIFE TILL WE ARE VERY OLD AND VERY GRAY. SOOOOO WE FIGHT. ALL OF US, WE FIGHT.

THANK YOU FOR THE ENDLESS MEALS, PRAYERS, VISITS, TEXTS, EMAILS, RANDOM ACTS OF KINDNESS, FOR CARRYING ME AND BATHING ME AND WALKING WITH ME AND TAKING ME TO MY APPOINTMENTS AND FOR OUR LONG TALKS AND LONG WALKS. THANK YOU FOR YOUR DEVOTION TO THE DAYS IN WHICH YOU COMMIT TO SIT BY MY SIDE. THANK YOU FOR THE TRIPS TO CVS, WHOLE FOODS, TOM THUMB, DENOS, ETC.

THANK YOU FOR THE CONSTANT LOVE AND ENCOURAGEMENT.

THANKS FOR THE VALENTINES.

WE ARE A REMARKABLE TEAM. I HAVE NEVER BEEN WITNESS TO ANYTHING LIKE OUR TEAM'S STRENGTH. WE ARE WINNING.

I LOVE YOU.

WILLOW."

***

God heard our prayers, because the next day, on February 18th, I was able to get chemo.

Bella took me. She was wide-eyed and unusually quiet. I think she was taking it all in. It took a long time—even longer than normal—because there were big doctor disputes over whether I should get it or not. My ANC level was .9. *Yikes.*

"It's too low," my doctor growled. "But we're overruling that. We're afraid if we wait any longer in between chemos, the cancer may have a chance to grow back."

Fear squeezed my heart. I looked over at Bella, wanting to reassure her, but her eyes wouldn't meet mine. *She's scared, too,* I thought.

"Don't worry, Willow," my doctor assured me. "We won't let that happen. We've weighed our options and I'm making the final call: we're going to give you chemo today."

I was scared, so scared. But I was glad to have one more chemo down. *Only four more after this. Four more. Then on to the next step.*

"What can I do, Mom?" Bella said, as the two of us went down to the third floor. "How can I help?" She was juggling all three of my chemo bags.

"I'll show you when we get inside," I said. "And Bella?"

"Yeah, Mom?"

"I'm really glad you're here. Thanks for coming."

Bella was a trooper. She fed me pretzels and did what I instructed her to do, keeping the buckets filled with fresh ice for my hands and feet. She watched the whole thing happen, watched the Taxol and the Herceptin drip through the IV and into my port. I could tell she was both fascinated and horrified. But I could also tell she was proud of me, especially when all the nurses came over and hugged me. She saw a lot of love being showered down on me at chemo. She saw that people loved and respected her mom.

Oliver picked us up afterward, and Bella had to hold me up to get me into the car. She was silent the whole ride home. I think seeing me that weak scared her.

Alice was waiting at my house—my Monday Angel—and I heard Bella talking to her as Oliver helped me upstairs.

"I didn't realize how hard it was," my daughter said. "I can't believe how weak chemo made her. I had to hold her up getting her to the car."

She understands it better now, I thought, as I fell back into bed.

"Thank you, Oliver," I said, as my husband nodded and closed the bedroom door behind him.

I had just enough energy to email my Angels with a report. I didn't want to let them down because they'd been texting me, and they needed to know I was okay. There were too many to text back, so I wanted to do it as a group.

"I GOT CHEMO TODAY. THAT'S THE GOOD NEWS. THERE'S SOME SCARY STUFF GOING ON WITH MY BLOOD LEVELS, BUT I AM TOO SLEEPY TO PUT ON PAPER. I'LL GIVE YOU THE DIRTY SCOOP LATER. IT'S TOO DEPRESSING FOR YOUR SWEET EARS TO HEAR, AND MY TIRED FINGERS TO TYPE.

BUT WE ARE FIGHTERS, LADIES. WE KEEP FIGHTING THIS HORRIBLE DISEASE. AND THERE ARE ONLY 4 MORE CHEMOS OF THIS ROUND. I TELL MYSELF THAT BEFORE I DRIFT OFF TO SLEEP. *4 MORE. 4 MORE.* INSTEAD OF COUNTING SHEEP, I COUNT CHEMOS.

I LOVE YOU ALL. BEST GET SOME REST NOW.

THANK YOU FOR GIVING ME SOMETHING TO FIGHT FOR."

Only four more, I thought, the words like a chant in my head, like a promise. *God, I hope that's true.*

Chapter 53

ALL I WANT TO DO IS GIVE BACK

E*ight pounds. Eight pounds! YIPPEEEEE!*
    I stood on the scale in my bathroom, blinking at the number, wondering if it was real. *I've gained eight pounds! This is great news!*
    I had to laugh at myself. In all my years as a model, I never once felt triumph when I gained weight. Fifteen years earlier, if I had gotten on a scale and seen that I'd gained eight pounds over a two-week period, I wouldn't have cheered. I definitely would have cried. Then I would have gotten a call from my agent, saying, "Um, Willow? We need to talk. This weight gain isn't going to cut it."
    How quickly things change.
    I walked back out to my bedroom, perched on the edge of my bed, and tapped out an email update to my Angels to share the good news and to thank them, as always, for their unending support.
    I leaned back on my bed, pausing to rest my eyes for a moment. I did feel better than usual, and the eight pounds probably had a lot to do with it.

But I was still worn out—physically, emotionally, and everything in between. I felt proud but weary. To be honest, sometimes I felt like Superwoman, the fiercest fighter in the world. I also felt like a broken child wanting the touch of someone's—anyone's—hand.

The knowledge that I only had three more chemo treatments to go was amazing. It should have been 100 percent joyous—but then, life rarely worked out the way it "should." I would be meeting with all the breast surgeons later that week, and I was terrified of the next step. *A mastectomy. Oh God. What if even that doesn't work? What if they don't get out all the cancer? What then?*

I knew I had access to some of the best surgeons in the world, but after what had happened with my arm, I knew that might not be enough.

The prior Sunday evening, I had been so dehydrated that I could hardly stand. I was talking to Oliver in the kitchen when I suddenly got dizzy and had to grip the counter as I started to go down.

"Willow?" Oliver said. He leapt forward and caught me under the arms. "Willow, what's happening? Are you all right?"

"I think I'm dehydrated," I said, as he helped me over to the sofa.

"Do we need to go to the hospital?"

"I think, maybe, yes," I said, my voice wavering.

We didn't want to leave the kids alone, so I called Frenny. I hated calling her at night, but she had told me to call her anytime. Sure enough, she answered right away.

"I'll be right there, sweetie," she said. "Fifteen minutes."

When she arrived, she hugged me as if she never wanted to let go.

If things were tense between Oliver and Francesca, they certainly didn't show it: he thanked her for staying with the kids, and then he took me straight to the ER. We spent three hours at the hospital—one of our shorter trips, funnily enough—and once I got some fluids in my body, they sent me home.

But when we got back, Bella was waiting up. She and Frenny were sitting in the living room and the TV was off. Bella looked up at me solemnly.

"Wiles was really scared, Mom. He didn't want to go to sleep."

My eyes filled with tears. *It breaks my heart how sad and scared my kids must feel, at such tender young ages.*

"I'm so sorry, Bella," was all I could say. "I guess we're all scared."

March 19th, I repeated to myself. *March 19th.* That was the date of my last chemo, I hoped. *What a glorious day that should be.* I imagined walking out of the James Cancer Hospital building with the sun shining on my face, my eyes staring toward the heavens. I imagined walking out with such pride in myself. *It will be a celebration. March 19th, here we come.*

I sent out a brief email update, then drifted off to sleep, tossing and turning, and ultimately waking the next morning to the chime of my phone. *Thirteen new emails. My goodness, my Angels have been busy bees.*

I saw all of the usual names, including my Miami Angels, who were mostly in touch by email. One email was from Sara. I hadn't seen Sara in months since I hadn't been to Miami in a while. She had a frank, funny, quintessentially Midwestern take on life. She was one of my four closest friends in Miami, Jules being one of the others. My Miami Angels were warriors as well—Sara, Jules, Sophia, and Evelyn, who was a two-time survivor of breast cancer herself, sent me packages and texts and daily inspirational emails. Evelyn had given me so many helpful tips and provided such generous guidance since I was diagnosed. She ran a nonprofit called Brave and Beautiful that supported women on their journey through cancer treatment, so she really knew how to help me.

Sara's email was sweet and funny and supportive.

"Good morning girlfriend. I'm sooo happy things went better this week. Keep eating! 8 lbs wow wow congrats.

I wish I could eat all I want. . . I just love food!!!

So. . . With the end in sight, do you have plans for a Florida trip before the surgeries? We don't head back to Wisconsin till about mid to late May. . . I might make a short trip back for Mother's Day weekend but not sure about that.
. .

Keep strong, dear. Eat some pasta or mashed potatoes for me. . .

Have a good weekend.

Xoxo Sara."

I sighed. I truly wished a trip to Miami was in the cards, but I just didn't know if I'd be able to pull it off over the next month. I looked down at my arms. *I'm so pale! I'm positively pasty. How I would love to soak up some sun and boost my feelings with a nice healthy dose of Vitamin D.* Miami offered a special kind of solace for me—something about being right by the ocean was hugely calming to my body and soul.

Then I noticed a new email in my inbox from my old friend Morgan.

I'd added Morgan to my update list after seeing her at the Club on Valentine's Day. And here was her email, characteristically fun-loving and light and supportive—all the traits I loved about her.

"Maybe we should schedule a spray tan!" she said. "Can you get those? I haven't since last summer but God knows I need one!!! Sooooo PROUD of you!!!"

I smiled. *Did she read my mind? I was just thinking how pale I look!* The thought of getting a spray tan during chemo was almost funny, if it hadn't been so sad.

I stretched—as much as I could with my arm—and then heard a peal of thunder cracking across the sky. I walked to my window and peeked out the curtains. The Ohio sky was deep purple, giant storm clouds darkening on the horizon. *Ooooh, a thunderstorm!*

February was one of the rainiest months in Columbus, and I kind of loved the thunderstorms. There was something magical about them, the way they lit up the sky, the way the color of the air changed, melting from clear into a yellowish gray. When it was cold it was less fun, but since I spent so much time under house arrest, I wasn't actually outside all that much.

I watched the first drops of rain pelt against my windowpanes. The raindrops were big, and as the glass begin to smear before my eyes, I had the most brilliant idea.

I feel okay this morning. Better than I've felt in a while—and at the very least okay enough to get out of the house and surprise my friends. They've done so much for me. It's about time I do something nice for them!

***

I was giddy with excitement. I loved giving gifts. It gave me so much pleasure to shower my friends and family with personalized, unique presents. The look of sheer delight on someone's face when they opened a package was an incredible feeling. And, in the midst of my chemo, I felt I had done so little for my dear friends.

I checked the forecast. It was supposed to rain all week. *Excellent.*

As I got online and started making purchases, I was over the moon. *I'm going to get my Angels the nicest little gifts. And it's going to be absolutely perfect.*

I had tried to give gifts the way I normally did over the last few months, but I was obviously facing a lot of challenges. I had to buy almost everything online. After an Angel took me to chemo, I would order her a little set of monogrammed linens and have them delivered to her house the following week. And I always brought the nurses in the chemo ward something, whether it was a gift bag of makeup or chocolates or other little treats.

For the holidays, I dropped presents off on my Angels' front porches a couple of weeks before Christmas. My friends were in absolute awe. When I got to Emily's house, her jaw dropped so low I thought I might have to scrape it off the floor.

"Willow Adair! You're incredible. How are you out of bed? I haven't even pulled *myself* together for Christmas—and here you are!"

But that's just who I was. Even in the midst of chemo, it was important to me that my friends knew I was thinking about them and how much I cared. I still hadn't done nearly enough—not in comparison with all my Angels had done for me. I knew no amount of linens or gifts would ever pay back this enormous debt.

After Christmas, I had received so many lovely gifts, but of course I couldn't write thank-you notes on account of my arm. One of my great joys was sending handwritten notes on beautiful stationery—I so preferred that to saying thank you by email or text—and it just tortured me that I couldn't write notes.

I called Emily one day and said, "Listen. I completely understand if things are crazy and you can't do this, but . . . could you maybe come over and write some thank-you notes for me?"

Emily snorted. "Um, in *my* handwriting? I don't even know if I'd spell all the words right!"

"That's okay," I said. "You're just being modest. And I'll help you with spelling if you want."

She paused. "I have the messiest handwriting in the world. Are you sure?"

"It doesn't matter! I really don't care about your handwriting. I just want you to be my scribe."

"Okay," she said. "I'll come over."

Emily loved my bespoke stationery, which was cream-colored cotton paper and had a customized design I had chosen. "Ooooh," she said when she ran her fingers across it. "This is really nice."

She sat down at my desk and picked up a ballpoint pen. "What do you want me to say?"

I spoke each thank-you note out loud, and Emily transcribed them for me. She was constantly chiding herself, saying, "Oh crap, I think I just messed up the D!" And I would say, "It's okay, Emily. I don't care. You're doing great."

"I guess even if I misspell something," she said, "they'll just blame it on chemo or your arm. They'll say, 'Chemo spelling' or 'Fused arm!'"

We laughed about that one.

Now, as I tapped my way through an online order, I was downright giddy. I ordered expedited delivery so the goodies would arrive the following day. I was about to have something unique and personal to give my friends that was even more tangible than a thank-you note.

And that wasn't all. Each umbrella was going to come with a message. Since I couldn't write myself, I ordered a little scroll for each of my friends. The scroll had a poem on it.

Even on rainy days you show up. I love you, sweet Angel. We have God on our side. Willow.

The umbrellas and poems arrived the next day. The umbrellas were gorgeous. I had ordered them from one of my favorite stores in Miami. They were bright and flowery and purple—I had been avoiding all pink since my diagnosis—and seemed wonderfully cheery amid a dull rainy day. I could picture each of my Angels with one of these umbrellas, a spot of color in an otherwise dreary landscape. *They brighten up my life,* I reasoned. *Why shouldn't I brighten up theirs?*

I went down to my wrapping paper collection, which I hadn't touched in ages, and struggled to tie a big bow around each umbrella. It was absurdly difficult to tie a bow with one arm, but somehow, I managed. Then I tucked the scrolls under the bows.

By the time I had each gift ready to go, I was spent, but my heart was soaring. My chest swelled with love and pride. *Finally. I can do something—even a little something—for them.*

So I got in my car and drove around Bullitt Park, dropping off the umbrellas to my Angels.

When I got home that day, I felt utterly triumphant. I knew that, when each Angel walked out of their house, or came home after picking their kids up from school, or went out to get their mail that day, they would walk out into the pouring rain—and find a little umbrella with a poem from me.

I got a million texts and phone calls that afternoon, a new one rolling in each time an Angel discovered her gift.

"Oh, Willow," Grace said. "What a simple, elegant way to say thank you."

"You're so creative, girlfriend! This is too neat," Emily said.

"Girl, you better get back into bed!" said Amelia. "Or I'll come over and put you there myself. And now I've got an umbrella to keep me safe and dry while I do it!"

I was exhausted, but it was totally worth it. As I gratefully collapsed into bed that evening, I felt just a tiny bit better that I was able to give my friends a small token of my gratitude. *On rainy days and sunshine days. They love me. And I love them. I am so very blessed.*

Chapter 54

MY TWO A.M. ANGEL

I awoke with a jolt, drenched in sweat, shivering.

The rain was still coming down. It had been raining solidly for the last five days. The yards in Bullitt Park were all very green, but the chill had settled into my bones. I felt cold to my very core.

I hadn't had a night terror in some time, but that night, it was a doozy.

I reached out for Oliver but he wasn't there. *Business trip. I'd almost forgotten.* I started to whimper but caught myself. *You're a grown woman, Willow.* I could hear Oliver's voice in my head. *You don't need someone with you all the time. You can handle this.*

But the nightmare had been horrible, the kind that lingers with you even after you wake up. I had seen myself lying very still on a bed of pink silk. Around me were dozens and dozens of red roses. And then I saw Oliver sitting in a church pew, Isabella and Wiles sitting beside him. Bella's eyes were rimmed red, and Wiles was sobbing. Oliver was trying to comfort them.

Only then did I realize they were at my funeral.

Now I sat in bed, trembling. Wiles was asleep in his room down the hall but I didn't want to wake him. I knew my own fear would scare him, and that wasn't fair. But I also knew I couldn't get back to sleep. *I hate being alone. Especially when I'm terrified.*

The fear quickly mushroomed into panic. My breaths were coming short and ragged, and I couldn't calm myself, no matter what I did. I tried praying. I tried doing chair yoga in my bed. But every time I closed my eyes I saw the same image: me in a casket, surrounded by roses, with my children crying over my pale, lifeless body. It was awful.

The lightning lit up the sky and I felt like shrieking in terror. Of course, I couldn't do that—poor Wiles would come running from his bedroom. But the thunder gave me a creeping sensation that my whole world was cracking wide open. *It's already cracked open*, I thought. *I'm not a "grown woman" who has everything under control. Nothing is under my control. I'm helpless and sick and maybe even dying.*

My hands were quivering as I reached for my phone.

I wasn't sure who to call. I knew any number of my Angels would drive over in a heartbeat, but it was the middle of the night and I didn't want to bother them—especially not the ones with young children.

What about Alice? said a tiny voice in my head.

Since Alice was my across-the-street neighbor, she wouldn't have to drive anywhere. And she'd begged me to let her know if I needed anything, anything at all. Her daughters no longer lived at home—one was grown, and one was still in college. So I wouldn't have to worry about waking up any sleeping two-year-olds.

I texted her. "Are you awake?"

Her response came so quickly that I actually thought it was a little weird. *She must sleep with her phone under her pillow.*

"Oh my gosh," she said. "Is everything OK?"

We went back and forth by text for a few minutes, and then she said, "I'll be right there."

Alice was on my doorstep four minutes later, still in her pajamas, a robe wrapped around her thin shoulders. She was holding the umbrella I had bought her, and the rain was dripping off it in long, heavy streams.

"Willow," she said. "You poor thing."

"I'm so sorry to wake you. It's just . . . Oliver is gone, and I . . . I didn't know what else to do." I was sobbing.

"Shh shh. Don't worry about that. You want to know the funny thing? You didn't wake me."

"But it's two a.m.!"

"I know." Alice shivered. "Let's go inside so we don't both catch our death of cold. I'll make us some herbal tea, and while it brews I'll tell you a story."

"Okay," I said, comforted by Alice's calm, steady voice. She had such a maternal way about her. She loved to mother me, and I always felt safe around her.

Alice knew her way around my kitchen, so she put chamomile tea bags into two cups and set the water to boil. Then she turned to me and gave me the most odd, curious look.

"What is it?" I asked.

She shook her head. "Nothing. It's just—God sure does work in mysterious ways."

"What do you mean?"

"I woke up at two a.m. tonight, Willow. I couldn't for the life of me figure out why. I haven't woken up at that hour in years, not since the girls were little. I'm usually in bed by eleven and I sleep like a log."

"What woke you up?"

"I don't know. But I felt wide awake, so I checked my phone. That was unusual, too—even if I do wake up at night, I never check my phone because I know I won't be able to go back to sleep once I've looked at the screen. And I never put it next to my bed, either, but last night I put it on the bedside table. And then I saw your message." She smiled. "It literally arrived as I was staring at my phone."

"Oh, wow. Wow."

"I think I know who woke me up, Willow." Alice's eyes got a little teary. "It was God."

I broke down and cried. Alice rubbed my back, saying kind things to me and praying. The tea kettle whistled a minute later and she poured us two cups of tea.

"God woke me up, Willow. God knew that you needed me, and God was there. I know you don't want to be alone," she said. "But you're not alone. You'll never be alone. You have God. He's walking through this with you. You have your faith. And you also have your Angels. You've christened us your Angels, and that's exactly what we are. We're God's hands and feet. Any time you need one of your Angels, one of us will come running."

My sobs lessened as I let her words flow over me. "God can't be here physically to do everything," Alice said, "but we can. Through us God gives us His words and love and comfort. We love you because God loved us first."

Slowly, gently, Alice took me upstairs, then ran back down and brought our chamomile teas up, too. I still felt shaky. "Would you stay the night with me, Alice?"

"Sure. Of course."

"Would you sleep here in this room?" I said plaintively. "Do you mind?"

"Of course not. Look—I'm already in my pajamas! I'm all ready to go. And I told Chuck I might be staying over." Chuck was Alice's husband and a cancer survivor himself. He'd been diagnosed with kidney cancer when their daughters were five and eight.

Alice reached for her phone. "It'll be like a slumber party. Here, let's take a picture of the two of us." She knew how much I relied on my pictures.

We took a "selfie" of ourselves, a picture I would cherish during future chemo and the dark days to come. We're both sitting on the bed in our pajamas, looking ruffled and unkempt, but smiling and grateful to be together.

"Tell me about Chuck," I whimpered as I crawled under the covers. "Tell me how it was dark and scary and then everything was okay."

"You already know the gist of the story," she said, stroking my hair. "But I'm not sure I've ever told you everything. We used to think there was nothing in the world we could want. We were successful and young and healthy. Remember how Chuck used to work for Trammel Crow twenty years ago? When Trammel took the company public, we suddenly had a windfall. It was a lot of money for a very young couple. We thought we were invincible. What could possibly go wrong?

"And then Chuck was diagnosed with kidney cancer. The first surgeon, after seeing the scan, said to my husband, 'Get your affairs in order.' Kidney cancer usually shows up when it's too late."

I shuddered, imagining how scary that must have been.

"It no longer mattered how much money we had," Alice said. "Because when someone tells you you have cancer, you're on your knees. We started praying like crazy. I remember being down on my knees, saying, 'Take it all, God. Take every penny we own. But don't take my husband. I need him. I can't do this without him. I have two little girls.' All of a sudden, our priorities changed. What we'd thought was so important wasn't important at all anymore.

"And so the surgeon performed the surgery. He took Chuck's lymph nodes and his kidney. I'll never forget what he said to me once Chuck was safe in the recovery room, cancer-free. The doctor was holding the new scan in his hands, and he was overjoyed. "This hospital is going to make a fortune off this scan," he cried, "because your husband's life has been saved."

Oh, Alice. I couldn't tell her how much it meant to me, hearing this. I felt like she had just given me a warm, comforting sip of something sweet—like the tea she'd made for me.

God saved Chuck's life, I thought. *Maybe he'll save mine, too.*

Chapter 55

MARCH MADNESS

MONDAY MARCH 4

"HI LOVELY LADIES.

I WAS ABLE TO HAVE CHEMO TODAY. I WILL SEND UPDATE MANANA. OFF TO BED TONIGHT.

IN HONOR OF HOW I FEEL ABOUT EVERY SINGLE ONE OF YOU, I WANT TO SEND YOU THIS QUOTE TO KEEP YOU WARM AND COZY AS YOU SLEEP TONIGHT. THIS QUOTE EXEMPLIFIES HOW I FEEL IN THE DEPTH OF MY HEART AND SOUL ABOUT EACH AND EVERY ONE OF OUR TEAM.

'Respect people who find time for you in their busy schedule. But love people who never look at their schedule when you need them.'

I LOVE YOU ALL SO MUCH.

WHO KNEW CANCER COULD CREATE SUCH A REMARKABLE GROUP OF ANGELS WHO FIGHT LIKE HELL FOR ME AND EACH OTHER?

xoxoxoxo WILLOW."

I sighed as I sank back into the pillows. Chemo had been a very close call—too close for comfort. My doctor almost wouldn't let me have chemo, and I about screamed in his face in utter frustration and despair. *I'm this close. THIS CLOSE!*

It was disappointing, to say the least. *My sweet body is fighting its tail off, and just when I think I am so strong, my body lets me down.* I was doing my best to have as little stress as possible—I was eating and drinking tons of water—but it was emotionally hard when they told me chemo was doubtful. I was just in shock.

I found myself asking *Why?* a lot. I knew I shouldn't compare myself to others, but it was hard not to. I had spoken to so many cancer patients, and each of them had said that, by this point in their treatment, their levels were so much better and chemo was "a breeze." I doubted chemo was ever a complete breeze, but I knew what they meant.

Meanwhile, my levels were not getting better. It was hard for me to understand and difficult to cope. That day at chemo, when my doctor told me my counts, I couldn't hold back tears. I usually tried not to cry in front of him but this had just rattled me.

My doctor was sympathetic. "Let me see what I can do," he said. "I'm going to call down to the chemo room and explain that, even though your counts are low, I want to overrule them."

The minute he left, I broke down and sobbed in Amelia's arms. Amelia had been my rock—she had come over to my house countless times, and not just on Wednesdays. She had gotten down on her hands and knees and cleaned up my vomit more times than I cared to remember. She had sat by my side in the chemo ward, reading me everything from Scripture to magazine articles, trying to keep my spirits up. And now here she was, in what was supposed to be my third to last chemo, stroking my back as I wept in her arms.

"Shhh, sweetie," she said. "It's okay. It's all going to be okay. Whatever happens, whether you get chemo today or not, you're going to be okay. God is in control."

I thought of that Bible verse about how "God knows the number of hairs on your head." *What hairs?* I thought bitterly. *I have none.*

Oh please, God, I prayed. *Please let me get chemo today. I don't want to go home and be on house arrest and feel so afraid and have to go through this whole ordeal again in a few days.*

The Lord was listening. It took ten minutes, but when my doctor came back, he nodded briskly.

"You're on the edge, Willow, but I overruled it. You can get chemo today."

What a relief. Amelia smiled back at me—it was a joy for both of us to hear.

"See?" she said. "God is in complete control."

Only two more of this round, I thought to myself. *Monday March 11th and Monday March 18th.*

"You can do this," Amelia said.

I can do this, I repeated to myself. For once I actually believed it.

***

Monday March 11th, I was turned away.

My ANC was .5 and my white blood count was 1.4. I was so frightened when they told me.

"I can't let you get chemo today," my doctor said sternly. "Those levels are just too low." *Shockingly low.*

At home I crawled into my closet and cried, my chest heaving like it would crack open. My mom had come down from Chicago for a few days and I didn't want her to see me this distraught. I was just so sick and weak, and I needed someone to take care of me. She was downstairs making something for Wiles and Oliver to eat, and when I heard her coming upstairs, I crawled out of the closet and lay down in bed.

"Are you sleeping, sweetie?" she said, peeking through the crack in the door.

"No," I said. "I can't sleep."

"I can't tell you how many visitors you've had come by the house this afternoon," my mom said. "Once all your girlfriends heard you couldn't get chemo today, they've been lining up at the door to see you. I've turned them all away!"

"But I want to see them," I murmured.

"No," she said, shaking her head. "Not when you're this sick. I'm putting my foot down."

I would find out later that she had literally barred the door when Emily tried to barge in. My Angels were used to letting themselves in and running to my bedside, but now that my mom was here, she was resolute on making sure I was resting and didn't get too riled up from a bunch of visitors. She knew I always wanted to make my guests comfortable, and that I could be easily overwhelmed.

"Besides, Willow," my mom said. "You don't know who might be sick. The last thing we need is for a mom with a runny-nosed kid to come in here and make you even sicker."

That night I heard a knock on the door. *One of my Angels,* I thought hopefully, but it was just after nine p.m. and I knew there was no way my Mom was going to let them in. I heard a woman's voice saying, "I promise I'm not sick. All my kids are really healthy. I'll wash my hands."

Who is that? I wondered. *Don't get your hopes up, Willow—Mom's not going to let her in.*

Imagine my surprise when, a few minutes later, I heard *two* sets of footsteps on the stairs.

"Willow?"

I saw Morgan's face at the door. "Morgan!" She was wearing baggie clothes, a coat, and a beanie on her head, but she looked as adorable as ever.

"Shh, don't get up. Don't you dare get up! I promised your mom I would not get you out of bed." She set her phone down on my dresser and started fiddling with it. "I just came to give you a little show."

Whaaaat? I thought, but before I knew what was happening, music was coming out of Morgan's phone, and she was dancing.

Morgan had always loved to dance. I had forgotten about that from our young modeling days. *Chemo brain.* Anyone who knew her knew she didn't need much of an excuse to dance.

My mom was standing in the corner of my bedroom, and to my surprise, she wasn't mad or annoyed at all. She'd had a long day of telling people NO, they couldn't come in, but she was smiling. I could tell she thought Morgan was the cutest thing, dancing away, no fear of embarrassment, just happy to be here dancing for me. And, more importantly: it was having the most wonderful effect on my mood. Morgan's moves *were* cheering me up.

"Look at you go!" I said, grinning as Morgan shimmied and shook her hips. She was turning my bedroom into a nightclub. The same bedroom that had been a place of misery and sickness and pain for far too long. She was making it *fun*.

"I wish I could get up and dance with you!" I cried.

Morgan told me later that, when she walked into my house, she saw all the gifts my Angels had given me—the beautiful flower arrangements, the various bags from Neiman Marcus and Hermès—and she thought, "What can I possibly give Willow that her Angels haven't already given her?" And then the answer came to her. *I can dance.*

And dance she did. It was a gift like no other—and I loved it.

***

THURSDAY MARCH 14

"HI LADIES,

I WAS ABLE TO HAVE CHEMO TODAY. BLOOD LEVELS PUT ME ON ROOM ARREST. THAT WAS FUN. NOPE! JUST KIDDING! NO FUN. BUT BETTER THAN HOSPITAL IN A BUBBLE. . . YIKES. I WAS SUPPOSED TO GET CHEMO ON MONDAY BUT MY LEVELS WERE TOO LOW. . . THANK YOU GRACE FOR TAKING ME TO CHEMO, AND FOR ENDURING MY TEARS WHEN WE WERE SENT HOME."

I took a deep breath and sipped my cup of tea. I repositioned myself on the sofa. My eyes were raw from crying; it had been a particularly hard week.

I took a deep breath. *Time for raw, unfiltered honesty.* I was working on that, and I was getting a whole lot better at it than I'd ever been before.

"I RESOLVED MANY MONTHS AGO THAT IT WAS MY MISSION TO APPEAR STRONG AND SHOW U ALL I WAS STRONG AND WE

COULD DO THIS. WELL. . . THIS WEEK THAT WAS NOT THE CASE. I LOCKED MY BATHROOM DOOR AND SOBBED FOR HOURS INTO MY PILLOW. MONDAY WAS A REALLY BAD DAY. I FELT LIKE THIS WOULD NEVER END.

BUT I MANAGED TO SELF-SOOTHE AND PRAY MY WAY TO TODAY. YOU ALL PRAYED MY WAY TO TODAY. THANK UUUUUUUUUUU.

THANK YOU TO MY COUSIN ELLA WHO HAD ME ON THE FLOOR LAUGHING. THANKS TO MORGAN FOR DANCING FOR ME. I WAS SO SCARED FOR SPRING BREAK—I WAS AFRAID FOR THE TEAM TO LEAVE TOWN, BUT U ALL WERE HERE AND CAME.

ALL SADNESS ASIDE, TODAY WAS A BEAUTIFUL DAY IN OUR CHEMO HISTORY, LADIES. WE HAVE ONE MORE. **ONE MORE.**

STILL HARD TO WRAP MY BRAIN AROUND IT."

So many of my friends had asked, "Why do you have to have sixteen chemos?? Isn't fifteen enough?!?!?"

I didn't know the answer. But I trusted my doctor and had faith he knew what he was doing. I hoped and prayed that sixteen chemo treatments would grant me a long lifetime to raise my kids, spend time with my family, watch my nieces and nephews grow up . . . and drink wine with my friends while talking about real stuff. *What a joy that will be. I can't wait.*

"Mom! Mom, where are you? I want to show you something!"

Wiles burst through the door, a ball of energy and excitement. It always made me happy to see him. Caroline's mom had given us tickets to a Mavericks game, and I was so grateful they'd taken Wiles. It was March Madness, the best possible time to see the Mavs play. I knew he would have the time of his life.

"Mom, it was so cool!" Wiles waved his phone in my face. "I chased down the cheerleaders to grab a photo with them!"

I looked at the picture and smiled. There was my cherubic son, surrounded by beautiful, sexy cheerleaders who obviously thought he was the cutest thing they'd ever seen.

"I love it. You're such a ladies' man," I teased.

I made a mental note to thank Caroline's mom for the Mavs tickets when I finished my update email.

As Wiles went upstairs, I thought of all the many gifts my Angels had given me. The gifts were countless, innumerable. I felt my eyes well up with tears. Instead of the voices of fear and unworthiness that had been whispering noxious lies in my head for so many years, my inner monologue was now drenched in kindness, generosity, and love. I knew exactly what I wanted to say in my email.

"YOU WOMEN HAVE SAVED ME FROM MYSELF AND MY FEARS.

YOU WOMEN TAUGHT ME I WAS WORTHY.

YOU WOMEN TOLD ME WHAT I NEEDED TO HEAR.

YOU WOMEN TAUGHT ME WHAT I WAS HERE TO BE AND TO SHOW OTHERS.

YOU ARE THE ONES WHO SHOULD AND WILL BE CELEBRATED FOR YOUR DETERMINATION AND YOUR LOVE, YOUR STANCE TO NEVER LEAVE ME, AND THE IMMEASURABLE GIFTS YOU'VE ALL TAUGHT ME.

YOU STAYED. YOU CAN'T IMAGINE HOW THAT FEELS TO ME. IT'S SIMPLY AWESOME. YOU STAYED."

I was getting all weepy now, so I tried to steady myself by getting back to logistics.

"NEXT WEEK WE FINISH CHEMO. I WILL FIND OUT TOMORROW IF IT IS TUESDAY OR WEDNESDAY. THEN:

MASECTOMY APRIL 9TH

RECONSTRUCTION SURGERY ON BREAST IN AUGUST

FINAL ARM SURGERY IN SEPTEMBER IN NYC

AND FINAL BREAST CANCER TREATMENT DECEMBER 21ST.

THAT'S THE PLAN.

WE CARRY ON. WE ARE THE GREATEST TEAM EVER.

THERE ARE NO WORDS.

THANK YOU FOR CARRYING ME. I LOVE YOU ALL.

ENOUGH SAID."

Enough said indeed. With love in my heart and a smile on my lips, I pressed "Send."

Chapter 56

WALK THROUGH THE VALLEY

The next few months unfolded in a blur of surgeries and Herceptin treatments. My hair began to grow back—a hideous mousy brown, but I was still grateful to have it. My friends assured me it was growing back fast. Liam, my hair dresser, said I looked like an eighteen-year-old Mia Farrow. He came by one afternoon to take me out to lunch, and I put on a beautiful dress, heels, and makeup for the occasion. I hadn't put my wig on yet—I would put it on before we went out into the world, but since Liam was my hairdresser, he obviously knew the truth.

When I came down the stairs to meet him, Liam's eyes immediately filled with tears. "I've never seen you look so beautiful," he said, and he actually meant it.

Of course, I was pissed at the way I looked. I certainly wasn't comfortable having ugly brown hair half an inch long. But when I looked in the mirror, I was starting to see something different, someone beneath that close-cropped mousy brown fuzz. I was starting to see a woman who was strong. *A fighter. A superhero. A woman who won't let cancer take her down.*

I sent out my updates to my Angels when I could, keeping them abreast of what was going on with me. But the time between each email grew longer. My own world was full of changes and subtle shifts.

"APRIL 8, 2013

Mastectomy tomorrow. I can't begin to tell you how ridiculously frightened I am. I am in a total state of shock and feel paralyzed. I really want to run and hide. BUT if I run and hide, I won't have you all to pick me up and save me from my self.

Thank you, Poppy, for coming in from Chicago to be here with me.

Thank you for the PRAYERS, emails, texts, calls, cards, pictures u sent me. . .

I live thru the pictures of you all LIVING. I love it, keep sending them.

. .

I AM GOING NOWHERE WITHOUT OUR TEAM. Hang on tight!"

"JUNE 10, 2013

Reconstructive surgery this Thursday at 11 a.m. Thank you, Mom, for coming to Columbus to walk with me through this. I would be lying if I said I was looking forward to this week, but I am also grateful. I am grateful to get the final breast surgery behind me. I will be without much use of either arm for about a week so I will type out an update about a week after surgery."

"JULY 1, 2013

Surgery was two weeks ago and went well. I am still unable to drive for two more weeks, and typing is hard because of 'the arm' and stitches on both breasts. Reconstruction is tricky. . . The plastic surgeon had to go into the original wall that had been stitched up during mastectomy. No infections. . . (THANK GOD) I feel a smidge better each day!

One hiccup, ladies. . . the mastectomy implant is collapsing. It is unfortunate and doesn't happen that often but again, it could be MUCH worse. SOOOOOOOO that said, we have ANOTHER surgery. September for that. I know, I know. It's ok. . . WE can do IT!!!!!!!!

If I could stop this breast cancer stuff for a moment, I would really like to go to NYC and FIX "the arm". . .

For the moment, my last treatment will be December 3rd.

Those are the facts. Not great but they could be worse. Emotionally, I have the power of prayer. . . Our Team, my family. . . And we are taking back my health. What else do we need??????

There is never a day I don't thank God for every single one of you. We are all the hands and feet of the Lord and what a TEAM we are and have become! I am the luckiest girl in the world. We are showing others what it means to love those faced with cancer. We are a group to be reckoned with. We NEVER give up. We are winning.

I LOVE YOU.

Willow."

"**AUGUST 12, 2013**

Hi Ladies,

I am in so much trouble from so many of you for not sending an update. I am sorry. The shell I call my physical body has been battered a lot and it is tired. I have Herceptin, doc, labs all day this Friday, then leave for New York City Sunday for my FINAL (God willing) arm surgery!!!!!!!!!!!

Can you imagine me in ANOTHER cast?? It's kinda so ridiculous it's funny. . . It will be number 17 since October 2011, I know. . . hard to imagine. . . And no driving again. I just got my driving privileges back from the mastectomy and reconstruction! It was fun having a little freedom.

When you get cancer. . . EVERYTHING changes. . .

Your emotional self.

Your physical self.

Your spiritual self.

Your friendships.

All your relationships change, really.

People treat you differently, some better, some worse. . .

And you notice the whispers. . . SO sad. . .

And the port, OMG. . . that freaking port. . . It sticks out like a sore thumb and the seat belts in cars hurt the port so badly it makes you want to stay home.

When you have cancer and all those changes happen literally overnight, it's hard looking in the mirror and seeing THE CANCER. Does that make sense?????? I want to look in the mirror and see ME.

I am pasting a pic of me as a small child below. I don't ever remember not having, loving, *needing* long hair. I sometimes reach for my hair in the middle of the night still. You see, I used it like a pacifier—yes, even as an adult. I would wrap my long hair over my ears at night when I went to sleep as a way to comfort myself. I miss that. I miss so many things.

This is a long-ass road and I miss ME (I liked ME!). I miss my freedom, I miss feeling like I had no fear of dying, I miss KNOWING I would be able to watch my kids get married and live happily ever after with my husband until we are old and gray. I miss that so badly.

Next week is a huge week for me. The surgery is big and having Herceptin days before will make it harder. Prayers are always welcome. And thank you for them. I certainly believe they are sustaining me. Nothing else could."

"AUGUST 23, 2013
Hi ladies,

W o w e e e e e e e e !
Wehaveaccomplished SOmuch thesepastsevendays, notsurewheretostart.

We have been given the blessing of having one treatment taken away. We have done Herceptin and we have completed the FINAL arm surgery, that's a LOT. We are well on our way to a long, beautiful, cancer-free, pain-free life. Happiness happiness!

I am on a plane back from NYC with the doctor's blessing to travel home. Surgery went well. I am in a fair amount of pain but that's par for the course. I am just so relieved it's over.

We only have two more treatments. Last one is December 3rd!!!!

I am so exhausted. But interestingly enough, the doc said that when I am tired, do not rest. He said, "GET UP and walk!"

The movement will help with the joint and bone aches, and with overall exhaustion. He said it doesn't make sense but it's actually fact: The more I move, he says the better I will feel. So ladies. . . let's keep walking. . . !!!!!!!!!!!!!"

I leaned my head against the cool glass window on the plane, a smile playing at my lips. Even amid the darkest parts of this experience, there were moments of sweetness and laughter—and they almost always came from my friends. Whether they literally walked with me through the streets of Bullitt Park or down the beaches of Miami, my Angels had all walked with me physically, emotionally, and spiritually through my ordeal.

I hadn't been alone for the arm surgery in New York. My cousin Ella had come from California and taken care of me. When Ella and I were toddlers, our moms used to put us in two cribs that were side by side. I would flip myself out of my crib, and Ella would stare at me like I was crazy. My mom would put me back in, and I'd flip myself right out again, while Ella calmly watched it all go down. *Lather, rinse, repeat.*

I turned my computer back on and typed out this story to my Angels. *They'll enjoy it. It's a lighter side to this whole sad and scary experience.* I tapped it out with my left pointer finger, which I'd gotten so good at doing.

"I guess I've always been super spastic," I wrote. "Thankfully, Ella still has her eyes on me—and she is still taking care of me as I flip out of my crib."

***

Later that week I sent my team a picture of my arm now that the surgical cast had been taken off. It was the first time I'd seen my own flesh in ages. All the metal and pins were gone—you could see where the pins *had been*, so there were holes. It was both fascinating and gruesome.

"If you have a weak stomach, do not look below," I told my Angels. My arm was impossibly white and sickly, the long scar coiling up it like a nefarious snake. It was horrible looking, the stitches violent against my pale skin.

All this suffering, I thought, as I tenderly touched my own arm, the first time I'd been able to do so in months. It was hard to imagine that my suffering would ever end, but I could see it on the horizon now, like a golden sun just beginning to rise. *Praise the Lord.*

I lifted my Bible off my bedside table as I settled back into my pillows. I had taken to carrying my Bible just about everywhere—something I never would have done before cancer. These days it was never more than an arm's reach away.

I flipped open to the Book of Job, which had offered me great comfort and solace. Job 30:30: "My skin is black upon me, and my bones are burned with heat. My harp also is turned to mourning, and my organ into the voice of them that weep." Again, I traced the scar tissue snaking down my arm. I thought of the months of indescribable pain I had suffered when there was an infection eating away at my bone and no one believed me. *My bones are burned with heat.* I felt like I could understand Job.

The thing I loved most about the Book of Job was that although everything was taken away from this man—*everything*—he didn't lose his faith. The world around him was falling apart, literally crumbling down around him. He lost his flocks, his wealth, his home, his wife, his children. The pain of loss was unreal—but Job persevered.

He questioned God, absolutely. He begged God to put an end to his suffering. But he never turned his back on the Lord.

I thought of something Gigi had told me when we were reading Job together. "You can let pain paralyze you, or you can let it propel you into your future. Some people run away from pain, but we always have the choice to carry it. What's it going to be for you, Willow?"

I closed my eyes and saw Amelia's beautiful face smiling down at me. "God has designed you to walk through the pain, Willow. Face it. Keep moving. You may have to crawl, but you have to keep going. And I know you. You will." Amelia had certainly seen me crawling at many points over my journey, and she'd never shied away from it or left me alone.

Another piece of Scripture materialized before my eyes. Psalm 23:4. "Though I walk through the valley of the shadow of death. . ."

I thought I was going to die. I was ready to take my own life. I was in that valley. The darkness was closing in around me.

I flashed back to what Amelia had told me so long ago. "By killing yourself, Willow, you would rob us of the memories that *we* get to make with you. Walking through your suffering alongside you, supporting each other: that's a gift. This is the love we can share together—don't rob us of that."

I got a chill just thinking about it. I didn't get it at the time. I thought, "She's crazy! Why would she want to be at my house every Wednesday? Why would any of my friends want this burden?" Now, as I looked back at the chemo and everything we'd been through, I realized Amelia had been right all along. I just couldn't see it.

Oh my God. I would have robbed myself of that. I would have robbed all of us of this love and this change. We've all been transformed. Before I had cancer, nobody in my group of friends would have carpooled together or gone out to lunch, but now we were all in the habit of driving together, talking about things we never would have talked about before. We were talking about things that really mattered! It was no longer, "Hey, I got this new Valentino dress." All of that had crumbled down—the ego, the superficiality, the focus on appearances. We were talking about what truly mattered in our lives.

Through it all, I had kept walking. *Keep on walking!* said the voices in my head. *Keep on walking!* said my Angels. I didn't know when all the pain and suffering was going to stop, but I knew it *would* stop, eventually. I just had to push forward.

I let other comforting Scriptures swim around my head. I knew so much more Scripture now than I ever had before. The verses Emily had taped up around my house had carried me through some of the darkest, hardest times.

The rest of the verse came to me. "Though I walk through the valley of the shadow of death, I will fear no evil: for You are with me; Your rod and Your staff, they comfort me."

I felt suddenly overwhelmed by emotion. *God's been with me all along. Right here by my side. And everyone he sent me, my friends, my family—they really were his Angels.*

I felt a lump forming in my throat. *I was walking with Angels.*

I always had been. I just never knew.

Chapter 57

THE LAST CHEMO

*D*ecember 3, 2013.

It's ending. It really is all coming to an end.

I sat in the chemo chair, waiting for the nurse to come and hook me up. My port had been removed on November 7th—I no longer needed it. Having that thing out of my body felt like having a thousand-pound millstone removed from around my neck. *I feel free. I am free. Or at least I'm about to be.*

My mom knelt beside me, tinkering with my blouse. She helped roll up my sleeve while we waited for the nurse to insert the IV.

"How's that, Willow? Too tight?"

"Well, I can't really feel my arm," I said dryly. "But anything is better than the port!"

I was in fairly high spirits. It was the final chemo—the final final chemo—the day I had been counting down toward for as long as I could remember. *December 3rd.* It was a day of salvation, relief, and joyous celebration.

Of course, I wasn't celebrating. Not yet. I'd spent most of that morning holding my breath. Holding my breath that everything was going to go according to plan, holding my breath that my doctor wouldn't have a last-minute change of heart and tell me I'd had it wrong all along. The scenario played out like a nightmare in my head: "Oh, did you think I said twenty-eight infusions, Willow? Actually I said *thirty*-eight . . ." It was too horrible to even consider.

Dare to hope, said a voice inside my head. *Have faith, Willow. Have faith in a God who loves you. Have faith in yourself. This pain and suffering you've been through—it's made you stronger, not weaker. You're almost done. Walk on.*

I blinked, surprised that those voices were coming from my own head. It sounded like my Angels talking. Was I actually learning to believe in myself? To be kind to myself *without* the nurturing presence of my Angels?

"It's almost over, Willow," my mom said gently. "You're so close. So very close."

She and my dad were both in town for the occasion. They were going to take me out afterward to celebrate. I didn't care where we went—I just wanted to leave that oncology center behind me and never look back.

I heard a ruckus at the far end of the chemo ward. There were women's voices, and a nurse saying something, and then she was drowned out.

"What's all that commotion?" my mom said, craning to see.

I couldn't answer. My jaw had dropped.

Amelia and Gigi were storming the chemo room and charging toward me. Amelia's arms were full of flowers. Gigi held my favorite iced tea.

"Willow!" Amelia cried. "Are we in time?"

I couldn't believe it. "What are you doing here?"

"It's your last treatment," Gigi said. "You really thought we were going to let that one slide by unnoticed?"

"But they only let . . ."

"Two people at a time, right?" Amelia set down the flowers and folded her arms over her chest. "I'd like to see them try and stop me."

I looked to my left where the nurses had gathered. They were speaking in low voices and I knew they were talking about us. I recognized Amelia's old nemesis: the nurse who always insisted on having the Food Network on in the chemo room until Amelia read her the riot act.

Melia chuckled. "I know what she's thinking. She's thinking, 'That crazy woman is back! I'm not gonna mess with her!'"

I was about to ask Amelia and Gigi how long they'd been planning to come to my last chemo when I looked up and, to my genuine surprise, saw Grace and Emily bustling toward me.

"Good Lord," said Emily. "Did I miss the party? Hope not . . . because I brought the party poppers!"

I watched in amazement as Emily pulled a package of tiny firecrackers out of her purse, the plastic kind where you pull on a little string and the gunpowder makes a loud POP.

"I'm not sure we can have those in here," I whispered.

"I won't tell if you won't," she whispered conspiratorially, and flashed me a huge grin. "We can always do them outside once you're all through."

"Hello, beautiful," Grace said, sweeping elegantly across the floor to kiss me on the forehead. "I don't know how someone can look so gorgeous in the midst of chemo, but somehow, you've managed." She pressed a small makeup bag into my hand. "Just a few treats I thought you might enjoy."

How had Grace not told me she was coming? She had come over to my house that very morning to do my makeup before I left for the hospital. I never wore makeup to chemo, but since it was a special day, Grace had come over that morning to do a whole, beautiful face. And now she was here, too. I couldn't believe she'd been able to keep the secret!

"What is with the mood in here?" cried a voice from across the room. "Everyone's so dour! We need to spruce things up a little."

I looked up to see Millie, looking fabulous, a perfect pink bag swinging from her arm. "Your favorite fashionista, here to save the day," she said with a wink, and pulled out a brand new clutch.

I hardly had time to thank Millie for the bag when Nicole came striding through the doors with Alice. Nicole was wearing one of her ponytails—the kind that you attach in the back—and she'd brought a whole bag of hair.

"Your hair's growing back so quickly, Willow," she said, "that soon you'll put us all to shame again with that long blond mane. So I brought the rest of us some hair to level the playing field!"

My Angels laughed, and a few of them reached into the bag of hair, helping each other pin and primp.

Alice pressed another gift into my hand: a gorgeous engraved Bible with delicate gold-lined pages.

"Oh, Alice," I said. "It's beautiful."

"It has all our names in it," she said, beaming. "All of your Angels!"

"I can't believe this," I said. "You are all so amazing. I can't believe you're here!"

My mom smiled at me as she gave Alice a big long hug. "I knew your girls were cooking something up. I didn't know the full extent of it, but I had my suspicions."

"Hold on, now," said Emily. "Who is *that* gorgeous creature? It looks like the Dancing Queen has arrived!"

I looked up with surprise to see Morgan walking in the doors of the chemo ward. But she wasn't *walking* exactly—she was dancing! Music was playing from her phone, and I realized that Emily hadn't been kidding: the song was Abba's "Dancing Queen." The nurses clustered together, trying to block her way, but she danced right past them. Nothing could stop her.

Morgan cranked up the music on her iPhone and sang. My Angels started to sing along, much to the nurses' dismay. But one fierce look from Amelia and they stayed right where they were. No one was going to cross Amelia King.

"I don't even know what to say," I stammered, as my Angels crowded in around me, each with their own personality, their own unique flair.

"Hey, girls!"

I looked up to see Caroline filing in, wearing her surgical mask—just like when she'd taken me out to Lindey's on Valentine's Day—with her big sunglasses pulled down low. She looked like a movie star.

Caroline came right over and gave me a big hug. Then she pulled out a second pair of sunglasses and handed them over. She pulled her own shades down over her nose and gave me a wink. "Thelma and Louise forever," she said. "Rebels *with* a cause. Because you won, Willow. You beat it. You beat cancer."

A strange new feeling was coursing through me. I couldn't even identify it. *Gratitude? Hope? Love?* It was all of the above—but more, too. I felt love pouring out of me toward these women who had carried me through so much . . . but I also felt love for *myself*. And that was an entirely new feeling. It was tremendous and sweet and heady and amazing.

I *loved* it.

Frenny shuffled in the door next, always shy and quiet around my friends, but still so happy to see me. She started crying the minute she hugged me, and we stayed like that for a long time.

"I'm just so overwhelmed," I said. "I can't believe you're all here!"

"You better believe it, sister," Amelia said.

No sooner had she said "sister" than I heard a familiar voice and saw Chloe, my sister, running toward me. We were such an emotional family: as soon as she scooped me up in her arms, Chloe, my mom, and I all started crying.

"But your kids!" I burbled. "Your husband! Your whole life is in Lake Forest . . ."

"You really think I'd miss this?" she said, brushing the tears off her face, then off my face, and then off my mom's face, too. We all started laughing through our tears.

"Poppy's here, too," Chloe said. "I brought her with me from Chicago!"

Poppy joined our hug fest, stroking my hair and telling me how fast it was growing, how I looked like "the Willow we all know and love."

"And look who we found at the airport!" Poppy exclaimed.

She stepped away to reveal Jules, lovely Jules. My Miami friend was always so *present* wherever she was, and even in that moment of happy chaos and hubbub, she radiated calm. "Look what I brought you," she whispered in my ear, placing a small vial in my hand. "It's sand. So now you've got a little sand and sunshine with you, wherever you go. I know how much you miss Miami."

"You have no idea," I murmured.

"Well, now you don't have to miss it. You just paint your toes and put your flip-flops on, because I brought the beach to you."

"Thank you, Jules. Thank you so much."

"Is there room for one more?"

I caught a blur of motion and energy, and then as the sea of my friends parted, I saw one final Angel barreling toward me: my dear cousin.

"Ella!" I cried.

"Willow!" she shouted. "You've flipped out of that crib for the last time, girl—and I am here to put you back inside it! For GOOD!"

All my Angels erupted into cheers.

"So," Ella said, once we'd all calmed down. "Are you actually going to get chemo today, Willow? Or are we all going to stand around yapping?"

"Yoo hoo!" Emily waved her arms over head. "Where is everyone? Is no one working today?"

The nurses, who had been staying away in awe but maybe also a little bit of terror, slowly began to tiptoe toward us. I couldn't really blame them: we were a formidable force to be reckoned with. My Angels were fierce and fiery and determined to love me the way they saw fit. I wouldn't want to cross them, either!

My girls began to chat and whisper and laugh, the noise rising once again, until the head nurse pushed her way through the tittering crowd. "Mrs. Adair," she barked at me. But there were so many people talking, I could only see her mouth moving.

"MRS. ADAIR," the nurse tried again.

Gigi signaled the roomful of women and suddenly everyone went silent.

"Are you ready, Mrs. Adair?" said the nurse.

I looked at all the smiling faces all around me and didn't see a dry eye among them. I felt a new kind of strength and calm, even as the tears rolled down my cheeks.

I nodded at the nurse. "I'm ready," I said.

"Okay then."

My body felt as if it were floating high above the room, looking down on all my Angels, looking down on my own ravaged body that had been through so much. I felt as if I was lifting up off the ground, as if a warm current flowed through my veins, as if I were a hot air balloon suspended above the chemo ward, above the James Cancer Hospital, above my own glorious life. And no, it wasn't the last bout of chemo drugs flowing through my system that made me feel this way. *It's so much more than that.*

What I felt flowing through me now was different. It was something I had never truly understood, something I had never thought I deserved. I felt it, this thing I'd spent my whole life in pursuit of. I felt it in every fiber of my being. I had it all around me, and through me, and inside me, too. At long last, I had it.

It was love.

Chapter 58

MY LIFE NOW

I woke up in Miami and looked out the window at the blue-black sea curling into the sand. *This is my life now. I get to live it however I want.*

I stretched luxuriously—with both arms high overhead—and got out of bed. I slipped into my bathing suit and wandered down for a morning swim.

I was alone, but I wasn't lonely. As I swam out into the ocean, I let myself float in the salty water and felt a new and different kind of peace.

For years I had listened to the voices in my head telling me I was unworthy. *Not good enough, never good enough, not worthy of people's time or attention or love.* I had allowed myself to be neglected and abused. Over the course of my cancer and my arm, the voices came disguised in many different costumes, but they were all variations on the same theme. *You're imagining the pain. You've seen more doctors than anybody. You're making a big deal out of nothing. You're a hypochondriac. You're too needy. You're a grown woman— you don't need all these people taking care of you.*

I felt the warm water rush over my limbs as I floated on my back, suspended in the water. At the heart of each of those lies was the same message: *You're not worth all this trouble. You're just not worth it.*

I stared up at the purple Miami sky. It was majestic, glorious, and I was here to see it. I was alive. I had survived. And I would never, ever be the same.

Now I saw those voices for exactly what they were: lies. Insidious, hateful lies—not just the ones that were told to me, time and again, but the ones that lived and breathed inside my own heart.

I began to gently backstroke, swimming farther and farther from the shore, the water moving like silk across my skin. The voices in my head were now singing a very different tune. An *angelic* tune.

For many months and years, my Angels' love and encouragement had become a heavenly host of voices, and the song they sang was not about guilt or shame or unworthiness. *You are beautiful,* they said. *You are good. You are deserving.* They hadn't just taught me this through their faith in God: they had taught me by the consistency of their showing up. *You are worthy, Willow. Not just in God's eyes, but in our eyes. In your family's eyes.*

As I swam out even deeper into the ocean, I knew there were no Angels nearby to save me if I drowned. I flashed back to the day of my cancer diagnosis almost eighteen months before. I had actually wanted to kill myself. It seemed like a lifetime ago, back when I thought my life wasn't worth all the love and attention my friends were giving me.

Now I let the voices swirl around me as my ears dipped beneath the surface of the water. *I AM worth all this attention. My life IS worth all these people. Not only do I deserve it—I'm going to ask for it. Because now I have a choice. I have recovered my voice.*

In October of 2012, I had wanted to kill myself. I felt that worthless. Now, in the sunny spring of 2014, I felt like I was worth my weight in gold.

I have a voice. I'm worth it. My decisions are different now. I'm not putting up with the same tripe. I deserve so much more than what I've been settling for. I am loved. I am loving. I am free.

I swam for a bit longer, until my limbs grew deliciously tired. Marveling at the wonder of God's creation all around me, I swam back to shore. As I stepped out of the ocean, the beads of saltwater dripping off me onto the warm sand, I saw a boy sitting on a rock and strumming his guitar.

I stood for a moment, my towel wrapped loosely around me, just listening to him play. His guitar was pale, white wood, with chips and dents and deep grooves in the surface—proof that it had been well played and well loved. The boy's hands flowed easily over the strings. He had the most beautiful smile, and the music moved through him like a school of fish through the sea.

And then I realized, as I watched him, what a perfect analogy this was for everything I had been through.

I see myself as a beautiful guitar. I am "white," pure, made perfect in God's eyes. Even though my shell is cracked and broken, I am whole.

I stared down at my right arm, touching the tender skin around my scar. I could feel my breasts in my swimsuit—not the ones God gave me, but who cared? *I may not have all the knobs and original strings anymore, and, like that guitar, I don't sound like I did before. But it's better. I'm more refined and even more beautiful than ever.*

As the boy played his soulful tune, I realized how true this was. A new, shiny guitar fresh from the rack at Guitar Center did not have a story to tell. It hadn't been through the war; didn't bear a living history in every nick and scratch. But this boy's guitar: it could make beautiful music because it had been *through* something.

You can let your battle scars paralyze you, or you can grow even stronger from them. It wasn't my Angels speaking now: it was me.

I fought back the tide of tears rising behind my eyes. Wasn't this true for all of us? Your being, your love, your gratitude—*that's* your music. It takes place inside of you, and you are the machine that can play. There's no other instrument like you, nowhere in this world. That's what makes you unique. And you can play the most beautiful music, even without the right strings. Even with deep gashes and scars. Even if the shell of your body has been broken, and at times you feel your spirit might break too.

None of that matters, I realized, with stunning clarity. *The outside doesn't matter one bit. The peace comes from within.*

I took one last look at the boy and his guitar, and then I turned and walked up the beach. The sand squelched between my toes, and I let my towel float out behind me, no longer worried who saw me. My body was wonderfully imperfect—hence perfect. It was proof I had survived the war.

I didn't know where I was walking. I still don't, in some ways. But I know I'm walking away from the life I was "supposed" to live—and toward a life that fits me. A life on my terms, defined by my sense of self-worth. With boundaries to keep me safe and healthy and whole. I'll never let those boundaries be compromised again.

I can't walk away from everything. There are commitments I've made, people who are dependent on me. But I know I am worth fighting for. It took nearly dying to realize how much I want to live.

I live in Miami now. I walk every day, sometimes for miles on end. I walk down the beach, toward the future I fought for, the tomorrow I deserve. I'm walking, and I will keep walking, and I will never stop.

My Angels are never far behind.

Morgan James
Speakers Group

www.TheMorganJamesSpeakersGroup.com

We connect Morgan James published
authors with live and online events
and audiences whom will benefit
from their expertise.

CPSIA information can be obtained
at www.ICGtesting.com
Printed in the USA
BVOW04s1225170317
478657BV00003B/3/P